## *BROWN-EYED GIRL*

"In the tradition of such bestselling suspense authors as Sandra Brown and Tami Hoag, Mariah Stewart crafts a mesmerizing tale. . . . The world of romantic suspense has a new rising star and her name is Mariah Stewart!"

—*Under the Covers Reviews*

"Deftly combines the tingling excitement of a thriller with the passion of a true romance."

—*Romantic Times*

"Mariah Stewart proves she can deliver first-class, pulse-pounding suspense while still retaining the type of romantic characters she is renowned for."

—*The Belles and Beaux of Romance*

"Another great book by Mariah Stewart. . . . A story that will appeal to readers who enjoy the psychological thrillers of Tami Hoag and Linda Howard."

—*America Online Writers Club Romance Group*

"Mariah Stewart is sure to become the new Goddess of Romantic Suspense. *Brown-Eyed Girl* is a hardcover quality read at a mass-market paperback price readers will love."

—*CompuServe Romance Reviews*

"The romantic suspense book of the year."

—*Midwest Fiction Reviews*

## PRICELESS

"The very talented Ms. Stewart is rapidly building an enviable reputation for providing readers with outstanding stories and characters that are exciting, distinctive, and highly entertaining. Four and a half stars."

—*Romantic Times*

"The best of romance and suspense. Flowing dialogue, wonderfully well-rounded and realistic characters, and beautifully descriptive passages fill the pages of *Priceless*. . . . Not to be missed."

—RomCom.com

"Ms. Stewart's story lines flow like melted chocolate."
—America Online Writers Club Romance Group

"In the style of Nora Roberts, Stewart weaves a powerful romance with suspense for a very compelling read."

—*Under the Covers Reviews*

"An exceptionally gifted storyteller with a unique ability. . . . [Stewart has] a rare talent that places her in the company of today's bestselling romantic suspense authors."

—CompuServe Reviews

## MOON DANCE

"Enchanting . . . a story filled with surprises."
— *The Philadelphia Inquirer*

"Stewart's books, like Nora Roberts' sibling sagas . . . are about relationships. I can't think of many writers who can do this better."
— *Under the Cover Reviews*

"Filled with excitement, suspense, and a passionate love story, told by a master storyteller. A book to cherish."
— *The Belles and Beaux of Romance*

"[Stewart] hits a home run out of the ballpark . . . a delightful contemporary romance."
— *The Romance Reader*

## WONDERFUL YOU

"You can't help but be caught up with all the sorrows, joys, and passion of this unforgettable family. Four and a half stars."
— *Romantic Times*

"*Wonderful You* is delightful—romance, laughter, suspense! Totally charming and enchanting."
— *The Philadelphia Inquirer*

"Mariah Stewart exceeds her own high standards of excellence with a work that compares favorably with the best of Barbara Delinsky and Belva Plain."
— Harriet Klausner, Amazon.com

# MARIAH STEWART

# VOICES CARRY

**POCKET BOOKS**

New York   London   Toronto   Sydney   Singapore

An *Original* Publication of POCKET BOOKS

POCKET BOOKS, a division of Simon & Schuster, Inc.
1230 Avenue of the Americas, New York, NY 10020

Copyright © 2001 by Marti Robb

ISBN: 0-671-78591-5

First Pocket Books printing February 2001

10  9   8  7   6  5  4  3  2  1

POCKET and colophon are registered trademarks of
Simon & Schuster, Inc.

Front cover illustration by Ben Perini

Printed in the U.S.A.

For our much-loved cousin,
Bonnie Bricker Almquist,
who took me to a place where
this story *could* have happened.

# VOICES CARRY

# 1

The nightmare always began the same way.

Outside, the monotonous drone of cicadas would drift through the sultry midnight air. There would be faint light from the single bare yellow bulb that hung outside, over the front door, and cast a small pale spot of illumination within. Cheap handmade curtains, pulled back tightly to one side to permit the maximum amount of still air, hung on windows screened against mosquitoes and all those other things that flew about at night.

She lay upon her cot, her light brown hair tousled around her child's face, curled in sleep that had been long coming. She'd been willful that day, sneaking off during morning meditation to pick flowers to take to her older sister who'd been confined in the camp's infirmary with another of the recurring headaches that had plagued her that summer. One of the counselors had reported the girl's transgression to Brother Michael, and he'd chastised her—though not by name—before the entire camp at the end of evening prayers, rambling on and on about how some little camper's spirit needed purification. She'd been standing near the back of the group that gathered in the prayer circle, and hadn't been able to see him—she'd gone just about all summer without seeing his face—but she knew he'd been talking about her. Just about everyone knew that she'd been the one who'd made a forbidden raid on the flower garden that afternoon.

She'd been surprised at having been let off with nothing more than a public berating. It had been well worth a few moments embarrassment to see her sister smile at the offer of a few daisies and the handful of pretty stones, stones that could be rubbed for luck and hidden under the pillow while she waited for her headache to wane.

Only the sympathetic glances from some of the older girls as she'd passed them on her way to her cabin had disturbed her. She'd lain awake that night for a long time after lights out, trying to decipher what exactly it was that she'd read in their faces. After several hours of trying to define what she did not understand, she'd finally fallen into a sleep so deep that she hadn't heard the cabin door open.

Hadn't felt the thin blanket being drawn down, nor the hands that had, with practiced deliberation, lifted her from her bed and carried her with measured steps out of the cabin and into the night.

It wasn't until he stumbled on the path, jolting her, that she'd awakened, disoriented and confused.

"What . . . ?" she muttered.

"Hush," he'd whispered gruffly.

"But where are you . . ." She attempted to twist away from him, but his arms only tightened around her.

"Hush, I said."

"But I don't want . . ."

Damp grass tickled her bare feet as she was lowered to the ground in one quick motion. One strong arm tightened around her neck, the hand clasped over her mouth.

He dragged her along, the light of the moon dimly illuminating the path into the dense woods before them and playing off the gauzy white robe that hid all but his hands.

She struggled, fear surging through her thin limbs with every step that he forced her to take.

"I've been watching you, Genevieve. You are headstrong and disobedient and in need of purification," he said in a low voice, not quite a whisper, now that they were on the path leading down through the woods toward the playing fields below, far away from the cabins. "It is my duty to consecrate your body and drive away the impiety that infects your spirit."

"Let me go." She kicked blindly backward, catching his right knee with the sole of her foot.

He grunted as her small foot hit its mark, then punished her with a blow to the back of her head with his fist.

"I can see that you will require more than the usual hallowing." He spoke softly, calmly, directly into her right ear.

"Help! Hel—"

The hand clasped over her mouth again, and he dragged her farther into the woods, her heart racing frantically as she struggled against his strong arms.

Everyone knew that something bad lived deep in the forest, back beyond the pines. It was whispered among the younger girls that the woods were haunted, and sometimes late at night, she had thought she'd heard hushed cries carried on the sultry night wind. She, like the others, had sworn to never go past the dense wall of pines that bordered the end of the soccer field. She squeezed her eyes tightly closed. If one of the dreaded specters lurked about, she was pretty sure she didn't want to see it.

Finally, they reached a clearing where white candles set upon the ground glowed in the shape of an arc and where, with one swift movement of a foot, he took her legs out from under her and dropped her, flat on her back, onto the ground.

Falling on top of her, he closed his eyes—those dark eyes that burned with an unnatural fire from within the frame of the hooded garment—and began to pray, even as he ripped her nightgown from the neckline to the hem.

The last thing he'd expected was a well-aimed foot, powered as much by fury as by fear, to land squarely in his scrotum.

Howling with pain, he fell back and to one side, just long enough for her to scramble onto her knees, onto her feet, and to disappear into the night.

Clutching the halves of the torn nightgown, she ran along the dark path, swallowing back her cries as jagged stones and thorns, burrs and sticks, tormented the soles of her feet. But she never stopped running, and she never looked back. She simply ran and ran and ran, through the deepest part of the woods, her heart beating like the wings of a tiny bird within her chest, her breath coming in anxious puffs from her tired, tortured lungs in spite of her best efforts to make no sound, lest he hear and find her. Beneath her feet, unseen things crackled, and overhead, something called to the night. And still she ran, with no thought but to escape from Brother Michael while at the same time avoiding whatever other demons inhabited the dark places.

At the edge of the woods, just a stone's throw from the shoulder of the road, she paused. Crouching behind a large oak and straining her ears to listen, she gathered her tattered nightgown around her so that it would not flutter in the slight breeze that had picked up. As the pounding in her chest and in her head began to subside, she realized that no footsteps followed behind her on the path. Was it possible that he'd given up trying to find her? Afraid to believe that he or something else equally evil wasn't just beyond the last bend in the path, she did her best to blend into the shadows, alternately watching the road and watching the path.

Headlights from an approaching car lit up the night suddenly, then just as suddenly disappeared.

Somewhere nearby, she knew, was a lake. And around the lake, there were cottages. That would surely be her best bet to find a safe place to hide. But which way was the lake?

She leaned back against the tree, trying to get her bearings, trying to remember what Mrs. Allen, her teacher, had told the class to do when you are lost. This was the same Mrs. Allen who had taught them that when someone tried to touch you in places where you knew they shouldn't, that you needed to get away by any means possible and get help. Mrs. Allen's advice had already come in handy once that night.

*When you're lost, retrace your steps.*

Well, she couldn't very well do *that*. Not with Brother Michael—and who knows what else—back there someplace.

She concentrated really hard, forcing herself to think, trying to take that journey again in her mind.

Brother Michael had taken her down past the tennis courts. Across the soccer field. She remembered seeing the goalposts in the moonlight. Then down a path slightly to the right, far into the woods, to the clearing where the candles had flickered and glowed. From there, it seemed she'd run downhill a lot.

She remembered that once she had stood on the top bleacher at the soccer field, and she had seen the lake straight ahead. There was a narrow stretch of beach there, but nothing else, a cyclone fence closing it off to the rest of the world. Somewhere off to the right, however, beyond the fences, there had been small houses. And, she reasoned, since she'd run to the right through the woods, the lake and its cabins should be just ahead, on the other side of the road.

She rose quietly, cautiously, then as quickly as she could, ran from the shelter of the trees to cross the road. Slipping furtively as a wraith into the small grove of wild roses, she waited, still listening for the sounds of a pursuit that did not come. When she was convinced, finally, that she had not been followed, she picked her way through the thorny bushes, and keeping to the shadows, walked toward the lake and the small community of summer cottages she knew awaited just around that curve in the narrow road.

All she wanted was a place to hide, a place to rest for a few hours. What she would do after the sun rose the next day . . . well, she'd have to figure that out in the morning.

Exhausted, she leaned against the mailbox at the end of the short driveway of the first house. The dog barking from the screened porch frightened her, and she skittered away in the dark, on feet too painful to think about, to the next house.

A dim light over the front steps cast just enough of a glow that she could find her way to the back of the small cottage, which had a deck overlooking a long expanse of grass that led down to the lake. Hugging the shadows, she crept up the three wooden steps and settled into the farthest corner, her back to the wall, her knees drawn up to her chest. She was cold all of a sudden, despite the night's heat and humidity, and she began to shiver. Pulling the torn nightgown tightly around her small form, she tried to keep sleep at bay by singing, in the tiniest of whispers.

"Jesus loves me, this I know . . ."

Over and over, until finally, even this comforting assurance could no longer keep her awake.

She was barely nine years old.

Genna Snow awoke in a sweat, shaking and disoriented, her fingers twisted tautly in the sheets. She slammed herself upright, her back against the wooden headboard, and drew the soft, lightweight blanket up to her neck. And there she sat, shivering with the deep chill that invaded her entire body, her heart racing, while she tried to will her erratic breathing under control.

Eventually, her heart slowed to its regular beat, the sweating stopped, and her hands loosened their grip on the blanket. She stretched her legs out in front of her, the muscles aching from having been clenched so tightly in the same position for . . . how long?

From the next street, church bells chimed one, the only sound in her oh-so-quiet apartment.

One o'clock in the morning. The dream had come just past midnight.

*No great mystery there,* she thought as she swung her legs over the side of the bed where she sat for another moment or two, taking deep breaths. The dream had always come around the same time, though it had been so long since she'd had it that she had almost convinced herself that her demons might be gone forever. Disconcerted to discover she'd been wrong, Genna lowered her feet to the soft carpeting and trudged into the bathroom where she snapped on the light and without confronting her image in the mirror, turned on the faucet and splashed water on her face, over and over again, as if to wash away any last remnants of the dream. It wasn't until she lifted her head to dry herself with a soft blue towel that she caught her reflection.

Damp hair the color of rich, dense honey, more brown than gold and mussed from sleep, curled around a face that watched the world from a wary vantage. Pallid skin, devoid of its usual natural blush, set off by dark hazel eyes that were wide-set and haunted.

"Hardly the face of a self-assured FBI agent," Genna muttered, dispassionately assessing the woman before her.

Turning off the bathroom light, she returned to her bed, where she straightened the summer weight blanket before getting beneath it. Punching the pillow to slightly elevate her head, she stared at the ceiling, trying to figure out why the dream had come back now. She'd done her best to keep certain old memories where she believed they belonged—in the past—and wasn't pleased that through the dream, they had surfaced to disturb her now, when she had more than enough on her mind.

*That must be it*, she assured herself as she turned over in the dark. *It must be just that there's so much going on at work right now—so many cases to deal with.* And that situation being compounded by the fact that Steven Decker, the Special Agent in Charge, or SAC, of the field office to which she'd been reassigned earlier in the year, had called her late in the previous afternoon to tell her that she needed to be in his office at ten the next morning. It wouldn't have done any good to have asked why. Decker liked his little moments of suspense, liked to keep his people guessing. It was just one of the little games he liked to play with the agents under his command.

*Maybe he's come up with a new report form he wants us to start using*, she almost smiled, relaxing—finally—for the first time in hours. Decker loved his forms. . . .

Genna reached one arm out from under the covers and smacked the alarm clock into submission when it taunted her at six the next morning. She smacked it again at six fifteen, then once more at six thirty. At six forty-five, she rose reluctantly and headed for the shower, annoyed with herself for having overslept.

Her disposition hadn't improved much by the time she arrived at her office just before eight A.M. and clicked on the harsh overhead light. Stepping over the piles of files that littered her floor, she dropped her briefcase onto her chair, turned on her computer, and sought coffee. Next she checked her e-mail and found responses from two law enforcement agencies in upstate New York that she'd queried about the arrests of alleged child pornographers suspected of being part of a larger network along the eastern seaboard. As a member of the Violent Crimes and Major Offenders Program, Genna's assignments were mainly kidnapping cases or cases involving the sexual exploitation of children.

The case she was working on at that moment was giving her major headaches. One step forward and three steps back. She shook her head, wondering when she'd get the break she needed. So far, she'd received nothing but shadows where she needed substance. She printed out the information—sketchy though it was—before forwarding the notes via e-mail to several other agents in her office, then read the hard copy again as she sipped at her coffee and wondered if the respective police departments would be able to keep the suspects under lock and key until someone from her unit—preferably her—was able to get there and have a chat with all involved parties.

Three follow-up phone calls to the sending agencies later, she had memos of her own to share internally before refilling her coffee cup and rising to straighten her gray linen skirt and head for Decker's office, five minutes early, as was her style. She'd been taught that punctuality was a virtue, and that early was infinitely better than late.

Sharon, Decker's secretary, was on the phone when Genna reached the end of the hallway that dead-ended where the SAC's office began.

"He said you'd be early and that you should just go on in," Sharon covered the mouthpiece with one hand and waved Genna onward.

Genna knocked lightly on the half-opened door,

then stepped in without waiting to be acknowledged.

"Good morning, Genna." Steven Decker stood at the windows, looking out, greeting her without turning around.

" 'Morning, sir." Genna took a seat in the chair at the right corner of her superior's walnut desk and slid an unused coaster over to place under her coffee mug, waiting for him to begin with his usual line. *I guess you wondered why I called you in this morning. . . .*

"I guess you wondered why I called you in this morning," he said, turning now and walking toward her across a well-worn carpet.

Genna suppressed a smile and nodded. "Yes, sir."

"Do I recall correctly that you spent considerable time out in the western part of Pennsylvania while you were growing up? Near Erie, was it?"

"Yes." Genna's smile began to fade, and she wondered where this would lead.

"And your foster mother still lives in that area?"

"Patsy lives outside of Pittsburgh, though she does still own a summer cottage on Bricker's Lake, maybe twenty miles southeast of Erie."

"Would you say you know the area well, Agent Snow?"

Whenever Decker switched from first name to title, something official was in the air. Genna's heart sank. The last thing she wanted now was to be taken off her current case.

"Yes. I know the area well."

"Growing Amish population in the area, I understand."

"The Amish have been in that area for decades. Certainly for as long as I can remember."

Decker walked around from behind his desk and sat on the left corner, opposite from where Genna sat. It was the most casual gesture she'd ever seen him make, and a sign that he was getting to the point.

"Have much contact with them—the Amish—when you were growing up?" He asked.

"Very little. Most of the Amish kept to themselves. I did get to know a few kids very slightly when I was thirteen or fourteen. Patsy knew their grandmother. She bought eggs and produce from Mrs. Frick—Granny Frick, they call her—every week. Still does. I usually went with her, but I always felt pretty awkward there, you know. I was the odd one, the outsider."

Genna leaned against the hard chair back and watched Decker pace a few steps in either direction, his hands shoved into the pockets of his trimly fit jacket, his face showing no small amount of concern. Finally his lanky frame found its way around the desk and lowered itself into his chair.

"We have a situation there . . ." he began, causing Genna to lean forward and ask, "At Bricker's Lake?"

"Close enough. Wick's Grove. You know the town, of course."

"Of course. It's the only town for several miles from the lake. I always think of it as the town that never changes. It still has the same grocery store, the same gas station with the same little newsstand, run by the same families as when I was a kid." Genna smiled. "Wick's Grove is the only place I've ever been where there's no dry cleaner, no pizza place, and no place to rent a video."

"The Amish influence, I take it?"

"They own the greater part of the land in the area

by far, have, for generations." Genna nodded.
"Wick's Grove is little more than a crossroads on the
way from Erie. It's one of those places that time
hasn't seemed to touch."

"Well, time's catching up to it, I'm afraid."

"What do you mean?"

"It appears that three young Amish men—
cousins, we think—are suspected of being involved
in laundering some of the money that's coming in
from Canada."

"WHAT?" Genna almost fell forward from her
chair. "That's too preposterous . . ."

"Preposterous, maybe, but the information we're
getting indicates that there's a connection within the
Amish community and a local bikers' club that calls
itself JYD. Junk Yard Dogs."

Decker tossed an envelope across the desk to a
mute and stunned Genna, who caught it with both
hands and opened it. A stack of black-and-white
photos slid out. Decker watched her face as she
thumbed through the pictures, occasionally raising
an eyebrow in surprise.

"Who exactly are these bikers?" She waved several of the photos.

"A few Canadians, a few Americans. All ex cons—
mostly drugs, weapons offenses, assaults. Nothing
surprising there. And the fact that they're involved in
drug trafficking isn't anything new. What is new is
the fact that they've managed to tangle a few of these
Amish kids in their net."

Genna shook her head. "It defies belief. You're
talking about people who don't have electricity or
modern farm equipment. To visit one of their farms
is like going back in time a hundred years or so."

"That's pretty much what I'd like you to do. I'd like you to visit a farm. This farm." He picked up a second, larger envelope, and held up a photograph. "I believe you've been there before."

Genna turned sharply in her seat, swiveling around to look up at her boss.

"The Frick farm?" Her eyes widened with disbelief. "You can't be serious."

"I'm afraid I am."

"But . . . the Fricks . . . they're the backbone of the Amish community out there. My foster mother has known Granny Frick for, oh, Lord, since Patsy was a child . . ." Genna's voice trailed off.

"That's why I'd like to send you out there for a few days to check into it."

"But, sir," she tucked a loose strand of hair behind one ear and tried to figure out how to remind her boss that she was not a member of OCDP—Organized Crime/Drug Program—"right now I'm working on the child pornography . . ."

He held up a hand to stop her in midsentence. "We have reason to believe it's all run by the same organization."

"But the Amish have never been involved in such things. They rarely associate with the English, even on a legitimate basis. I simply can't conceive of anyone coming from that background—particularly a member of the Frick family—being involved in such things."

"Every chain has its weak link, Genna, even the Amish community." Decker sat back down on the edge of the desk and said, "I doubt greatly that the three young men we've been watching have any idea of just what they're involved with. I suspect that one of them got suckered in by the organization and drew in the other two."

"With what?"

"Drugs. Crack."

"You think these kids are selling?"

He shook his head. "Using."

Genna sat silent, digesting this, before asking skeptically, "You know this for a fact?"

"It's the most likely scenario."

Genna laughed out loud, shaking her head. "It's the most unlikely scenario. I'm sorry, but I just can't imagine it."

"The photos speak for themselves."

She picked up the photographs and went through them again. "With all due respect, sir, these photos of a couple of bikers making purchases from a roadside produce stand aren't very conclusive."

"Three times a week, same days, same times, same guys on the same bikes. Notice the large leather bags on the backs of each of the bikes."

"Which they appear to be packing with tomatoes and peppers." She tossed the photo onto the desk. "Maybe they're making salsa."

"Maybe they're making change. We think they're dropping off cash and the boys are moving it for them and getting paid in drugs. We thought maybe we'd send you out there for a few weeks just to nose around and maybe see what you could do to help out the state police."

"Did they ask for our help?"

"I got a call a few days ago from Lt. Mallon, who's been in charge of the ongoing operation. They know that there's something going on but at the moment, they have no probable cause for a warrant. The locals just can't get close enough to see what's going on back there."

"The Frick place is huge, and set back from the road by at least a quarter of a mile. The biggest farm in the area, by far. There are at least four, maybe five, generations of the same family living there. They've built onto the original house over the years, and the last time I was there, they were building a new place for one of the sons—one of Granny Frick's great-grandsons, that is—who'd just gotten married. Their land covers a lot of acreage."

"You think you can get back there without raising any suspicion?"

"I can probably get back to the farmhouse," Genna nodded, "but I can't very well start poking through their barns. What would I be looking for, anyway?"

"I don't know," he answered honestly. "But being the good investigator that you are, and having known these people over the years, I guess I'm just hoping that if there's something obviously amiss, that you'll pick up on it and at least help the locals obtain their warrant."

Genna tapped her fingers on the desk, trying to decide just how much a waste of her time this venture would be.

"How long has it been since you've had a vacation?" Decker asked.

"A while," she conceded. Since the trip she'd taken to Mexico two years earlier with the man she'd been in love with at the time. Genna snapped off the memory before she had time to think about how wonderful those ten days had been.

"And your mother—that is, your foster mother—still spends her summers up there at the lake?"

"Patsy's been summering on Bricker's Lake for more than half a century. She always says she'll die on that lake, and she wants her ashes flung from the back of a powerboat so that she never has to leave."

"I imagine she'd be happy to have you there with her for a week or so."

"She'd be ecstatic," Genna admitted with a nod. "So when do I leave?"

Decker held his hands up, a gesture of finality. "You can leave as soon as you can get packed."

"But what about the case I've been working on? We just got our first really decent leads."

"Liddy will take over while you're gone. Fill him in before you leave."

"Fine," she said, though it wasn't really. "I'll just finish up the paperwork I started this morning for the file, then I'll go over everything with Liddy." Genna stood and smiled halfheartedly. "Thanks for the unexpected vacation."

"You're welcome." Decker stood as well. "I'll let Lt. Mallon know that you'll be there by tomorrow afternoon."

"I seriously doubt that these Amish kids have any idea of what or who they're involved with," Decker said as he walked Genna to the door. "And no one's been able to get close enough to them to figure out just what their role is in all this."

"I don't know that I'll be able to find anything that will be helpful."

"All we're asking is that you scope it out." Decker opened the door. "You never know where it will lead."

Genna chewed on her bottom lip as she walked back to her office. On the one hand, she hated putting her ongoing case on ice, even for a week or so. On the other, thinking about how pleased Patsy would be to hear that Genna would be joining her at Bricker's Lake for a surprise visit put a smile on her face. Of course, Patsy wouldn't need to know any of the details or the reason for the trip. After all, what she didn't know couldn't hurt her.

Genna buzzed Paul Liddy and let him know he'd been tapped to fill in for her for a week. After briefing him and kicking a few ideas around for the better part of an hour, she packed up a few files she'd been needing to find time to read, and tried her best to ignore the calendar that insisted upon reminding her that today was her sister's thirtieth birthday. They hadn't seen or spoken to each other in eighteen years.

Pushing aside the images that threatened to crowd her, Genna snapped the lid of her briefcase and flicked off the light in her office, and headed out into the heat of a summer day.

# 2

At the precise moment that the oven timer went off and the phone rang, someone leaned hard on Genna's doorbell.

Without missing a beat, she turned the timer off with her left hand, lifted the cordless phone from the wall with her right, and reached the front door before the bell could ring a second time.

"No, thanks," she told the salesperson on the other end of the phone line, juggling the potato she had been about to pop into the preheated oven. "I don't need my basement waterproofed. I don't have a basement, and I . . ."

She'd leaned close enough to the peephole to see that the man waiting in the hallway had dark brown hair, cropped short, and was wearing the requisite dark suit and white shirt. In one hand, he carried a large bag from Genna's favorite restaurant, and in the other, a large bouquet of coral-colored roses. She opened the door and leaned against the jamb, blocking the entrance, and, not being able to think of one word to say to him, merely stared. She disconnected the phone call and stopped playing with the potato.

"And it's wonderful to see you again, too,

Genna," he said in that deep voice she knew so well. "And yes, I think I'd love to have dinner with you, thank you."

"I don't recall having invited you to dinner," she replied with as little emotion as she could manage.

"But you were just about to." He grinned and held up the bag from Gagliardi's. "Tomatoes in basil vinaigrette. Grilled swordfish for you, veal scaloppine for me. New potatoes in dill and garlic butter for both of us. And a fabulous assortment of appetizers."

She smiled in spite of her best efforts not to, and shaking her head in resignation, accepted the coral roses, her all-time favorite. No one knew her better than John Mancini. Former FBI Academy instructor. Special agent. Former love of Genna's life.

"Tiramisù," he leaned forward and whispered, waving the smaller bag slightly in front of her.

Genna laughed out loud and stepped aside to let him enter her apartment.

"You know, they always say that the way to a man's heart is through his stomach. But I think we both know the truth about that, don't we?" John winked and walked past her and into her kitchen as if it was something he did every day and lifted the bag onto the counter. "Me, I can eat just about anything, but nothing seems to get your attention like a really great meal."

He opened a cabinet and took down two plates, then paused to ask, "The deck or the dining room?"

"Since you brought it and are obviously preparing to serve it, why don't you decide?" Genna turned off the oven and the timer, and dismissing the lone potato she'd planned to bake, opened another cabinet and reached for a blue glass vase, which she filled with water.

"Now, why aren't you always this agreeable?" he grinned at her from over one shoulder, the warmth of his smile nearly stopping her heart in her chest.

Ignoring him, not ready to accept the fact that she really wanted him there in her apartment, and needing an excuse to put a little distance between them, she plunked the roses into the vase and placed it on the counter before unlocking the door that led to the small balcony off the dining room. Not quite a deck, as John had called it, there was room for little more than a table, two chairs, and a large planter which she had, for the third summer in a row, neglected to fill with plants. On the railing sat a bird feeder, which she had forgotten to fill with birdseed, and a window box that held only some dried dirt and the debris of last year's petunias and geraniums— planted by Patsy—that hung under the sole window.

The table would need to be washed off before they could put plates on it, and the chairs would need to be cleared of dead leaves before they could sit down. It would give her something to do, and prolong the conversation she knew they would have. Genna went back into the kitchen and reached around John for the roll of paper towels that fit snugly into a white plastic holder fastened to the wall behind him.

"Excuse me," she said, avoiding his eyes. She grabbed the roll of paper towels at the same time he grabbed her arm and encircled her wrist with one hand. She waited for him to speak, a current passing through him to her, causing her pulse to race, the way it always did when John got a little too close.

"Are you all right?" He asked, finally, his voice softer, his eyes holding hers. "Things okay for you?"

"Things are okay." She nodded. "You?"

"They're okay. Good, even, you could say. For the most part."

"I'm glad to hear that."

Genna backed away, unable to stand one more minute looking into his face, and to her surprise, he let her go. She opened the door beneath the kitchen sink and began to look for a plastic bottle of some sort of cleaner.

"The table and the chairs on the balcony need to be cleaned off." She found what she was looking for and started back outside.

"You know, we could eat inside," he suggested, almost as if he was the host and she the guest.

Genna paused to consider this, then decided that outside with John felt infinitely safer—meaning much less intimate—than inside with John. She forced a smile and said, "It will only take me a minute."

"Fine. I'll fix our plates."

"Fine." She nodded, and went back through the small door into the warm June night.

"Fine," she muttered to herself as she sprayed first the table, then the chairs and wiped them down.

"Just peachy," she whispered as she dried off all with the paper towels.

"What was that?" John asked as he stepped through the doorway, a fat yellow candle in one hand, a pack of matches in the other.

"I said, the chairs won't take any time at all to dry." Genna stood up, her hands on her hips.

John laughed out loud and, setting the candle on

the table, reached for her, his arms twining around her waist and drawing her in as gently and smoothly as one might hold a child.

"Ah, Genna, I've missed you," he told her. "Just let me hold you for one minute, okay?"

"Not okay." She put her hands on his chest and pushed him back from her.

"You know, you hold a grudge longer than anyone I've ever known," he pronounced solemnly.

"John, I do not feel like going there right now," she told him, the last vestige of her smile fading. "Do you want to eat, or do you want to talk about the same old things again?"

"I guess eat." He sighed. "Go ahead and sit down. I'll bring dinner out."

*But sooner or later, before the evening ends, we'll talk about those same old things again. However many times it takes . . .*

"So what's the latest?" John asked as he placed a tray laden with two plates filled with their entrees and another of appetizers wrapped in phyllo, on the tabletop. "What's the latest big case?"

As if he didn't know. As if he hadn't spent nearly an hour in Decker's office that afternoon.

"The dregs. Kiddie porn." She grimaced involuntarily. "There's a network that seems to be getting bolder and more prolific with every passing month. Really nasty stuff."

Her face clouded. "I hate getting that close to it, but I love the thought of putting it out of business."

She got up and went into the kitchen and returned with two goblets filled with ice water. She handed one to John and sipped at the other as she sat down.

"Decker tells me you're taking a little unscheduled trip to see Patsy." John lit a match and touched it to the candle's wick, holding it until the flame caught and burned.

"Then I suppose he told you about the Amish boys and the bikers?"

"He did. Sounds pretty bizarre to me."

"Doesn't it? The Amish have such a closed community, it's hard to imagine anyone penetrating that and drawing them into something that's not only illegal but immoral."

"Decker said they only want you to nose around a bit."

"What else did Decker say?" She looked mildly annoyed to find that her latest assignment had been the topic of conversation between her boss and her former lover.

"That you've been working seven days a week for the past nine months and that he was happy to have a legitimate excuse to send you off to visit with Patsy so you could get a little rest."

"He obviously doesn't know Patsy," she muttered and John laughed.

"That's what I told him. Patsy still taking life on two wheels?"

"Every chance she gets." Genna managed a smile. "That woman is sheer kinetic energy. I've never known anyone like her. She simply cannot sit still and is not capable of doing one thing at a time. If she's on the phone, she's cooking, she's dusting, she's emptying the dishwasher. She accomplishes more in one week than most people do in a month."

"She taught you well."

"Yes. Yes, she did, John."

*And she gave me a home when I was no longer welcome*

*in my own. She took me in when I had no place to go, and sheltered me when my world fell apart. She restored my faith when I had none. And she loved me when I had come to believe I was no longer lovable. Yes, Patsy taught me well. . . .*

"What are you working on these days?" Genna asked politely, no longer comfortable with the conversation.

Their knees touched briefly under the table. Genna deftly recrossed her legs.

"Same game, different players." John shrugged. "You should try one of these appetizers, cold though they are at this point, and somewhat out of sequence with the meal. These are shrimp, scallops . . ."

"I'm allergic to shellfish," she reminded him.

"I haven't forgotten. I'm merely pointing them out to you so that you know which ones to avoid," he said softly.

*I haven't forgotten a damned thing.*

Aloud, he said, "These are chicken and those little triangles are mushroom."

"Thank you." Genna cleared her throat and stabbed one of the pastry-wrapped goodies that John had identified as mushroom. "What brought you to Woodside Heights?"

*You did, dammit,* would have been the honest answer. But knowing how she'd react to such a declaration, he said, "I'm on my way back to Virginia. Thought I'd stop in since I was in the neighborhood."

No need to mention that her neighborhood was almost forty minutes out of Manhattan on a good day, and that a plane from Boston would have had him back at his own apartment outside of DC hours ago.

"Then you're on your way back home from someplace else."

"I've been in Boston for the past two weeks," he nodded.

"The university?"

"Yes."

No need to ask which university, since the murder of five young women over the same number of weeks had gripped the attention of the nation. As a special investigator with an unparalleled track record and uncanny instincts, John had been called to Boston after the third coed had vanished without a trace. A sigh of relief could be heard from one end of the city to the other when a suspect—an assistant track coach—was apprehended two days ago.

"I heard about the arrest on Tuesday," Genna said. "I thought it might be your work, quick and clean. No fuss, no muss."

"Thank you," John said, feeling enormously pleased at her praise. Professional admiration wasn't exactly passion, but it would have to do for now. "I appreciate the compliment."

"So. What comes next?" Genna moved past the moment before he could turn it into something else.

"Back to the office and the twenty-five or so cases that were pushed to the side while I went to Massachusetts."

It was on the tip of her tongue to ask if that was wise, for him to jump back into the same frying pan that he'd jumped out of a year earlier when he'd taken a leave of absence from everything. Including Genna.

She was still fighting the urge to do so when he said, "You're wondering if I should be dealing with this stuff again, after what happened before."

"It crossed my mind." She put her fork down.

"Those were very different circumstances. That case—the Woods case—was unlike anything I've ever been involved with. Every depravity, every evil that man is capable of, that was all embodied in Sheldon Woods. And I stayed on the case too long, I admit it, though it hadn't seemed as clear to me then. I should have backed away when I felt it getting to me the way it did. I saw too much of his work, over far too long a time. I allowed it to get inside me. I let him control the case, the investigation. And in the end, he was controlling me."

She picked up her fork and sliced a piece of potato in two, then moved the halves around on her plate. She'd heard the story before. She knew how it ended. The retelling of it wouldn't change a damned thing.

"We don't have to talk about it, John."

"Of course we don't. Talking about Woods might lead to talking about other things that could conceivably lead to talking about us." John quietly put his own fork down on the side of his plate.

"How many times do I have to say I'm sorry, Gen?" He asked. "What do I have to do to make it up to you?"

"It isn't a matter of making it up to me. It's done, John. When something is done, it's over." Genna spoke softly, hoping to conceal the tremor in her voice.

"Genna, everyone makes mistakes," he said, as softly.

"Your leaving me was not a mistake. It was a conscious action. You chose to walk away."

"It wasn't quite that simple."

"It was only as complicated as you chose to make it."

"Not to make excuses for my behavior, but you of all people had to know that I was in way over my head. I was drinking way too much and falling way too far down that deep hole. By the time I realized what was happening to me, it was too late. I had to let it all go for a while, Gen. I had to get my life under control again. I was too close to destroying myself, and more than anything, I was afraid of taking you with me."

"I could have helped you. You should have let me be there for you." Her voice rose in spite of her resolve to keep it from doing so.

"But you were with me. Every hour of every day . . ."

"Well, that was just fine for you. Unfortunately, I wasn't aware of where you were or what was wrong or what I'd done . . ."

"It was never *you*. If it hadn't been for you, I might not have had the strength to fight it. God knows where or what I'd be now, if it hadn't been for you . . ."

"I went through hell, John." Genna's voice finally cracked.

"If I could change that, I would. There was just so much going on inside my head, those first few months after we brought Woods in. If I hadn't walked away when I did, I think I would have ended up . . . well, ending it all."

"Every time we try to talk, it always comes back to this, doesn't it?" She tried not to sound bitter.

"And it always will, until you forgive me and we straighten this out."

Genna sighed. "I've forgiven you, John. Do I trust you not to do it again? Frankly, I don't know. It hurt too much the first time. We can be friends—I'll always be your friend. And I will always have total respect for you on a professional level. So that's it, as far as I'm concerned. Buddies. Colleagues. But that's all."

"If that's all I can have, then that's what I'll have to take. For now. But you should know that I'll never give up on you." John stood and dug his hands into the pockets of his jacket. "I loved you enough then to walk away when I was afraid I'd destroy you. I love you enough now to do whatever it will take to win you back. I'll wait for however long I have to."

"John . . ."

"Those few months I spent by myself were the worst of my life. As much as I'd dealt with over the years, Woods was different. It affected me in ways, on levels, that I'd never suspected a case could. I'd been so close to the monster . . . I was becoming afraid that I could become him. It was all starting to creep into my soul and under my skin. I'd learned how he thought and what he wanted and how he went about getting it."

"It's always been like that. For all of us."

"You're absolutely right. It is. But the difference with the Woods case was that I couldn't get away from it. He wouldn't let up on me and there was no place to go to get away from him. Not until we caught him." John stood and walked to the edge of the small balcony, turning his back on her to look down at the grassy area below. "Just my luck to have a homicidal pedophile pick me as his main man."

"I sympathize with everything you went through.

God knows I couldn't have handled the situation as well as you did. But I wouldn't have walked out of your life without telling you why."

"If I'd been thinking more clearly at the time, it wouldn't have happened that way. I was just so afraid of what might happen, so afraid that I'd hurt you somehow."

"You did hurt me. In the one way that hurt the most."

It hung between them, the way it always did every time they got to this point in this same discussion, and her words stung, just as they always did. For Genna, John's leaving her the way he had was the worst thing he could have done. It resurrected her deepest heartache and raised memories of a painful past. Abandonment. Betrayal. As a child, she'd been there. As an adult, she'd tried to put it behind her and just move forward.

To John's mind, he'd done the right thing, leaving when and as he did. Going toe to toe with the murderous Woods for three solid months had nearly broken John Mancini. The man who mutilated and murdered fourteen young children had contacted John—and only John—several times every day during his bloody reign of terror. Before he had been caught, Woods had become so brazen that he'd even called John while in the act of torturing his victim, forcing the frantic agent to listen, helplessly, as a child was brutally murdered.

By the time it was over and Woods was captured, there was little left of John Mancini that hadn't been badly mangled by the experience. Fight or flight, he'd thought at the time. Having no one to fight, he'd fled, hoping to cleanse himself of all the demons that had crept under his skin, hoping to emerge a stronger man for it. And eventually, he had, thanks to time off alone followed by months working with a psychiatrist handpicked by the Bureau. He'd regained the sense of himself that he'd barely hung onto during those twelve weeks he'd been inside the mind of the most despicable killer he'd ever run across. He'd washed himself as clean as one could of it all, and somehow had survived the process. He hadn't realized that the price to regain his sanity and his soul would be the loss of the only woman he had ever loved.

John understood that to continue on with this line of conversation was a lose-lose situation. To permit the silence to keep on filling the space around them was just as deadly. He slapped his hands on the railing of the deck and returned to his seat at the table.

"My sister Tess sends her best and wants to know when you want that week at her beach house that she'd promised you." John cleared his throat, admitting defeat, and sliced into his veal. It was cold and somewhat chewy, and seemed little more than a prop at this point.

"Did she? That's sweet of her. I'm looking forward to seeing her at Angie's baby's christening. It was nice of your sister and brother-in-law to think to invite me."

"Everyone's happy for the opportunity to see you again, too."

"Is Tess still dating Nate?"

"She's been dating Nate since she was fifteen. Took a hiatus only long enough to marry Adam, which we all know was the biggest mistake she ever made." John relaxed a little, relieved to have entered gentler waters.

"But she has her son . . ."

"The only thing Adam Conti ever did right in his entire life was to father that child. He's a good kid, Jeff is." John nodded.

"How is he?" Genna asked, equally happy to talk about something else—anything else—other than what had happened between them.

"Jeff is fine. He's doing really well in school and he's doing even better on the ball field. He's going to several football camps over the summer." John grinned. "He thinks he's going to be the next Dan Marino. That kid has an arm you wouldn't believe. He thinks he's got a shot at being the starting quarterback when he goes to high school this fall, but I keep telling him not to get his heart set on it. He can't assume that they'll let a freshman take that starting spot away from last year's man, you know?"

"Oh, sure." She waved her fork in the air. "I know all about that stuff."

"Sorry," John smiled, pleased that the Genna he'd known and loved was starting to resurface. "I get carried away sometimes when it comes to my nephew."

"I don't mind. He sounds like a great kid. I think it's wonderful that you're so proud of him."

"It would be hard not to be. He's been through a lot. The divorce was very difficult for him, and with his father remarrying last year, he had to let go of his dream that someday his family would all be back together again. I guess all kids go through that, when their parents split up, and you never know how it will affect them in the long run. So far, though, he seems to be keeping his feet on the ground."

"That's good. I'm glad to hear it." Genna stood up. "Coffee?"

"Sure. Want some help?" He offered.

"I can do it."

She picked up her plate and reached over to take his as well, and John fought the urge to grab her hand. But they'd had their go-round for the night, and he wasn't eager to start it up again. It had been too long since he'd been able to sit and watch a candle's light flicker across that much loved face, to hear her voice not in memory but in real time, to bask in that smile that turned up at both sides of her mouth like a pixie's. These things would stay with him when he left her that night, and would have to do until he found the key to making it work for them again.

He handed her his plate and watched her disappear into the apartment.

She returned with two cups of coffee, then went back inside for the flat Styrofoam container of tiramisù and two small plates.

"Yum, this looks wonderful. This was really very, very thoughtful, John. Thank you."

"You're welcome," was all he said.

They finished dessert and sipped their coffee, making small talk while the sun set behind them and the dots of light from the first of the season's fireflies flickered across the expanse of grass below. They could have been any two old friends, catching up after an absence from each other's lives. But they both knew better, and they both were saddened by the knowledge.

When the last of the coffee had been drunk and the last bit of small talk made, John stood to leave and Genna made no effort to talk him into staying. She walked behind him through the dining room, and paused, when he did, at the doorway to her living room.

Glancing at the many photographs that lined one wall, John said softly, "It would have been nice if you had framed one picture of us from the good times, Genna. If only to prove that you thought there was at least one memory worth keeping."

Without looking back at her, he opened the apartment door and disappeared into the hallway.

Genna had no idea of how long she stood leaning against the door, as if frozen in the moment he'd walked through it. Finally, like a survivor of a battle she hadn't wanted to fight, she moved on wooden legs. To the balcony where she blew out the candle and gathered the cups and saucers and dessert plates. To the kitchen where she rinsed the dishes under hot water before placing them absently into the dishwasher. To the front door where she slid the dead bolt. To her bedroom, where she sat on the edge of the bed and lifted the polished wood picture frame from the small table that sat under the window.

There was just enough light from the hall for her to make out the image of John standing at the top of a Mayan pyramid that was overgrown with vines, one arm around a laughing Genna, the other lifted in salute to the French tourist who had snapped the picture for them.

Hard to believe that little more than two years had passed since they'd been so happy together.

John had planned that trip and made all the arrangements for them after Genna had made a casual remark one day that she'd always wanted to see the Mayan ruins on the Yucatán peninsula. They'd spent a week in the jungle, then a long weekend on the beaches in Cancun. It had been the first time that they'd gone away together, and, as fate would have it, the last. They'd come back home just as Sheldon Woods had abducted his third victim, and the next few months had passed in a blur.

Genna knew she'd never been happier, before or since, than she had been for those ten days. She wondered if life would hold any more such perfect moments for her.

Unaware of the tears that rolled down her face, Genna gently returned the photograph to its place of honor on her bedside table, turned on the light, and began to pack for the next morning's trip.

# 3

A low, dense gray cloud greeted Patsy Wheeler when she raised the wooden blind and looked out through her bedroom window to take her first look at this new day. Undaunted by the fog, she went into the small bathroom and turned on the shower, whistling while she stripped off her short-sleeved cotton nightgown, humming as she stepped beneath the hot spears of water and lathered her arms with her favorite lavender-scented soap. Singing as she dried her hair—"Don't Cry for Me, Argentina"—and later as she made the day's first pot of coffee—"Just You Wait, Henry Higgins," it being a show tune kind of morning—Patsy's natural exuberance could not be dampened by a little thing like early morning fog.

Dressed in white cotton shorts and a green pullover shirt, Patsy unlocked the screen door and stood just inside, peering out at the lake. The first of the bass fishermen were already out on their boats, silently gliding fifteen feet out from Patsy's dock, drifting through the pale gray remnants of the fog that had begun to lift as the sun rose. Content with the knowledge that all was right with her world, Patsy returned to her small kitchen and poured herself a cup of coffee, relaxed and happy on a peaceful Wednesday morning in midsummer.

A single woman in her sixty-third year, Patsy had never married. "Married to my career," she had often replied when inquiring relatives would comment on her state, and it was largely true. That coming fall, for example, Patsy would celebrate exactly forty years in the same school where she'd started her teaching career the September following her college graduation. It was, in fact, the same elementary school she and her two sisters had attended.

If Patsy's life seemed to reflect a certain sameness, a lack of apparent excitement, it did not want for fulfillment. She had chosen to stay in the house she'd grown up in after her parents had passed on, buying out both of her sisters' interests, because she loved the house and couldn't imagine living anyplace else. She'd had the same feeling about the cottage on Bricker's Lake. Her parents had built it years before, shortly after their marriage, and the entire family spent every summer thereafter swimming, boating, and fishing off the dock that jutted into the lake like a stubby finger. Every year without fail, just as her parents before her had done, Patsy opened the cottage for the season on Memorial Day weekend, and closed it up for the winter on the first weekend in October. Oh, she'd taken the occasional trip, visited Europe several times and enjoyed every minute she'd spent touring the French countryside and drinking Guinness in Irish pubs and exploring solid German castles. But she never tired of the cottage that faced the lake, never tired of her neighbors, though so many of the original folks were gone now, their little summer homes having changed hands.

And over the past few summers, she'd seen more and more of the cottages rented out, an entirely new phenomena. But that was okay too. Patsy brightened. Always fun to meet new people, to make new friends.

*Like that woman who is renting the Palmer place next door.* Patsy unconsciously peered through the curtains at the well-kept cottage to the right of her own. *Seems like a nice enough soul, though it would be easier to get to know her if she was here during the week instead of just on the weekends. Said her job kept her traveling so much, but she was looking forward to spending as much time as she could here.*

Patsy tried to recall exactly what the new neighbor—Nancy, her name was—did for a living. Something about computers . . .

She hummed a few bars of "Camelot" and sipped her coffee, thinking how nice it would be to have a friend here at the lake this summer. Not that she was lonely, or that she lacked for friends. She had good neighbors here and back home in Tanner, a little town just north of Pittsburgh, and there were colleagues and students she'd known over the years. She never felt that her life wanted for much. On the contrary. Patsy Wheeler would tell anyone who asked that she felt blessed and fulfilled, especially since that hot, humid August morning almost nineteen years ago when she opened the back door and found a child huddled, sound asleep, in the farthest corner of her deck.

One of the Cotters' kids, Patsy had thought at first, thinking that perhaps one of a neighbor's seven children had slipped out during the night and had wandered a little too far down the road.

Patsy had put her coffee down on the deck railing and squatted next to the sleeping form, stretching one hand out to gently touch the girl's shoulder. The second that contact was made, the child's eyes flew open in terror and one word—"NO!"—split the serenity of the morning.

"Shhh, it's all right, honey," Patsy had cooed. "It's all right. There's nothing to be afraid of."

The girl's large hazel eyes had filled with tears and she began to sob.

"Oh, now, baby, it's okay." Patsy attempted to ease the child into her arms for comfort, and it was then that she noticed the girl's nightgown was ripped straight down the front, and that even in her sleep, she had clutched both sides, wrapping the gown around her slender body like a robe.

And her feet—dear God, the child's feet were caked with dirt and dried blood, as if she'd walked barefoot for miles through glass.

Patsy gently turned the girl's face to hers, and her heart just about broke. There were scratches on her neck and one cheek, while the other bore an ugly bruise that started just below her eye and ended just above her chin.

"Oh, sweetheart, who did this to you?" Patsy whispered and drew the little girl to her.

The girl began to tremble, her small hands clenched in dirty fists, the tears now silent as they flowed in irregular paths down her cheeks and dropped onto the jagged neckline of her nightgown.

"It's all right now, honey. No one will hurt you here. I promise." Patsy bit her bottom lip and rocked the weeping girl until the tears finally stopped.

"What's your name, sweetie?" Patsy asked when

she sensed that the girl's breathing was returning to normal.

"Genevieve Snow," the girl replied in a small voice.

"Genevieve is a lovely name," Patsy said, still rocking the girl in her arms.

"My friends call me Genna," she offered.

"I like that, too. Which do you like better?"

The girl paused, as if trying to choose.

"Genna."

"Then that's what I'll call you," Patsy said, then cautiously asked—though almost afraid of the answer—"Can you tell me what happened to you, Genna?"

"Brother Michael. Ripped my nightgown." Genna had raised her small, battered face to Patsy's, whose heart, already broken, had shattered right then and there.

"Brother Michael?" It had been an effort for Patsy to reply calmly, afraid to react lest she frighten the girl into silence. "Your brother, Michael?"

"No." Genna shook her head. "Brother Michael. At camp."

She pointed past Patsy, in the direction of the road and the woods beyond.

"Do you mean the church camp up on the hill?" Patsy asked. "Do you mean Shepherd's Way?"

Genna had nodded.

"Is Brother Michael one of the other campers? Or a counselor?"

"He's the Shepherd," Genna told her.

"He's the Shepherd," Patsy repeated flatly, having heard all too many times over the years how adults in positions of authority used that authority to abuse those in their trust.

How much, Patsy wondered, should she ask, and how best to phrase it?

"Did he hurt you?"

Genna nodded. "He hurt me when he hit my head and when he held me down and got on top of me. My head hit the ground and it hurt then, too." She rubbed the back of her head. "So I pushed him"—she shoved her hands out in front of her as if shoving someone away—"and he fell back and I pushed him in the stomach with my feet and he fell away. And I got up and I ran and ran and ran through the woods. I thought he was following me, but he didn't find me, did he?"

A flicker of triumph crossed her face and her swollen mouth turned up slightly on one side.

"No, Genna." Patsy forced back the rage that was welling inside her. "No. He didn't find you."

"Am I going to be in trouble for running away?" The smile was short-lived as this possibility occurred to her.

"No. You won't be in trouble." Patsy stood and held out her hand. "Let's go inside and we'll see about those feet and have a little breakfast while we think about what we're going to do."

Once inside, Patsy locked the door behind them—just in case—and helped Genna up onto one of the stools at the counter in the kitchen. The child needed cleaning up—she'd hobbled on those bloody feet all the way from the deck—but there was the question of evidence and what might be destroyed.

She poured small glasses of milk and orange juice and sat them before Genna.

"Are you hungry, Genna?" Patsy asked, debating whom to call first. What to do first.

On the one hand, Patsy knew the authorities had

to be called immediately. On the other, Genna was a scared and injured child, and years of caring for wounded children, in her classroom and in her home as an occasional foster mother, had taught her that, above all else, a child needed to feel safe.

"Yes, ma'am, I am."

"Is cereal all right?" Patsy opened the cupboard where several boxes of cereal lined up like soldiers awaiting her command.

Who do you call first when you find an abused child outside your back door?

"Yes, ma'am. Thank you."

"What kind do you like best?" Patsy stood aside to let Genna choose.

Perhaps the state police?

"This kind," Genna pointed to a box of flakes, then added, "thank you."

"You are welcome." Patsy poured the flakes into a blue plastic bowl.

Calling the police first seemed a bit, well, harsh. Would that not frighten the child all over again?

"Peaches?" Patsy asked, trying to maintain an outward calm.

"What?"

"Would you like peaches cut up in your cereal?" Maybe Brian, her nephew, who was a county assistant district attorney?

"I never had that."

"Would you like to try?" Or her niece, Pamela, who was a social worker?

"Yes, ma'am. Thank you."

*The child is too damned polite,* Patsy thought as she sliced a ripe peach atop the cereal. *After what she's been through, should she be this calm?*

"How old are you, Genna?" Patsy asked without turning around.

"I was just nine on my birthday."

"You look younger than nine."

"That's because I'm small." Genna nodded.

Patsy served Genna's breakfast, and having no stomach for food herself, sat down on the stool next to Genna's and watched as one spoonful after another made its way neatly from the bowl to the girl's mouth.

"Honey, I think we need to tell someone that you're here," Patsy said. "And I think we need to call your parents."

"Why?" The spoon hung suspended midway between the bowl and Genna's mouth.

"What Brother Michael did to you was wrong, Genna. It was very wrong. Your parents need to know. And they'll be worried when someone from the camp calls and tells them that you're missing."

"But I'm not missing. I'm right here."

"But here is not where you're supposed to be," Patsy said gently. "Do you know the phone number where I can reach your parents?"

Genna looked at Patsy with eyes that spoke of her infinite patience.

"Of course, I know the phone number. But I'm not going to call them." Genna took a sip of her orange juice and placed the glass gently on the counter.

"Why don't you want to call them?"

"My daddy and momma will be real mad at me and I'll get a beating," she announced matter-of-factly.

"Genna, you haven't done anything wrong."

"I did." Genna shook her head, and tears like tiny

pearls welled up in the corners of her eyes. "I did not obey Brother Michael."

"If Brother Michael was trying to hurt you—trying to do something to you that was wrong . . ."

"Jesus said, 'Obey the counselors.'" What little color Genna had was beginning to drain from her face, confusion and doubt playing off each other in her eyes.

"Genna, I don't think that what Brother Michael did was exactly what Jesus had in mind. I think you were right to do just as your teacher told you to do. Running away was the right thing."

Patsy paused. She didn't know exactly what Brother Michael had done, though the child's terror had been genuine enough and the torn nightgown sufficient proof that whatever the counselor had done, it was a safe guess that it probably wasn't anything that Jesus would have sanctioned.

"Genna, I'm going to call someone who can help us straighten this out. . . ."

Thirty minutes later, a dark blue Mustang pulled into the narrow dirt and gravel driveway that ran parallel to Patsy's house. A tall young man got out and, after a cursory knock at the front door, walked right in.

"Aunt Patsy?" he called.

"In the kitchen, Brian."

Brian Henderson walked into the kitchen to find his favorite aunt sipping coffee and feeding breakfast to a small girl with pale honey-colored hair and the biggest hazel eyes he'd ever seen.

"Genna, this is my nephew, Brian. He is a lawyer. This is Genna, Brian," Patsy had said with exaggerated calm, "and she has a story to tell you. . . ."

And tell her story, Genna had. Though reluctant at first, once she realized that the story was going to have to be told, Genna gave it her all, not missing a beat from the second that she woke up in Brother Michael's arms to that very minute that Brian walked into Patsy's house. Brian, looking shaken, had called the state police and within less than ten minutes, two state troopers pulled into the drive behind Brian.

By noon that day, all hell had broken loose at the Way of the Shepherd Summer Camp.

And Patsy's life had never been the same since.

She couldn't help but smile, though Lord knew that she'd have done anything—anything—to have spared Genna from all that had happened. The attempted rape should have been the worst that could have happened to the child, but in the long run, what came after had perhaps caused even deeper damage to the girl's soul. Over the years, Patsy did all she could to make it up to Genna, but even she knew that she could never completely undo the past. Patsy had stood by Genna through it all, and in the end, with the court's blessing, had taken the child home and raised her as her own.

"And never regretted one minute of it," Patsy said aloud as she stepped out onto the deck and headed toward the lake. "Not one minute."

She walked across the flat expanse of grass, thinking back to Genna's phone call the night before. She had decided to take a little time off and thought she might join Patsy at the lake for a week, if, of course, that was all right with Patsy.

Patsy chuckled. There was nothing that pleased her more than having Genna there for whatever time she could spare out of her busy schedule. A day, a weekend, a week—Patsy looked forward to whatever time they had together. That Genna was not of Patsy's flesh and blood was only a technicality, as far as Patsy was concerned. Genna was her girl. One of Patsy's proudest days had come one year on Mother's Day when Genna, away at college, had sent Patsy a card in which she had written that the best part of her life began the day that the fates had led her, literally, to Patsy's door. Every once in a while, when Patsy was missing Genna too much, she'd take that card out and read it again. It never failed to fill her eyes with tears and her heart with pride.

*And by dinnertime tonight, she'll be here.*

Patsy walked along the old wooden dock and stood at the very end, and gazed out across the lake.

*By dinnertime tonight, my precious girl will be home.*

Coming back to Wick's Grove always filled Genna with conflicting emotions. For years after she learned to drive, she would take an out-of-the-way road that would wind through back roads for almost ten minutes in the opposite direction just to avoid driving by the old campgrounds. At the beginning of every summer she promised herself that this year she would take the most direct route and drive past the deserted camp, but every year, she found herself making the detour that would permit her to circumvent the area. And at the end of every summer, she'd promise herself that next year, she'd do it. She never had.

Some ghosts were more difficult to exorcise than others, Genna rationalized, as she paused at the stop sign marking the point where Freedom Road intersected with Tolliver, the very point where she would decide whether to go straight, or to once again make that turn that would take her out of her way.

Straight or turn? Straight or turn?

An impatient driver behind her issued four short blasts of his horn. Her concentration broken, Genna made the turn, just as she always ended up doing for one reason or another.

*Next time, I will go straight,* she told herself. *I will.*

A half mile down Tolliver Road it occurred to Genna that this route would take her past the Frick farm, and she relaxed. No need to berate herself for her lack of courage this time. She did, after all, have a job to do.

Up ahead just a little farther was the stand from which the Fricks sold their fresh farm produce. Genna slowed, noticing the cars parked on either side of the road just before the small grove of ancient oaks under which the wooden tables stood laden with that morning's harvest. Genna pulled to the shoulder and parked her aging Taurus behind a station wagon that had two car seats in the back.

Tucking her pocketbook under her arm, she strolled leisurely over the clumps of grass at the edge of the field that had been turned over by the spring plowing and from which dandelions and thorny thistle grew. There were six or seven customers picking over tomatoes that had been arranged in neat rows, mounds of dark green squash piled high, and deep purple beets, their stems tied together to form bunches, all with patches of pale dried dirt still clinging to them. Genna took her time, looking over the vegetables, as if she had all the time in the world, selecting a cantaloupe here, a few tomatoes there, not approaching the young woman who served as the cashier until the other customers had started back to their cars.

Placing her selections on the overturned wooden box that served as a counter of sorts, Genna smiled and said, "I think this will do it for today."

"The cantaloupe are really sweet this week." The young girl, whose dark brown hair was pinned tightly to her head and held in place by a pale netting, never looked up from the small slip of paper upon which she tallied up Genna's purchases. "The squash is good, too. And the string beans."

"I didn't see string beans," Genna turned back to the table.

The young woman walked past Genna to check, then frowned.

"My brother was supposed to bring some down." She shielded her eyes from the sun and looked up the long dirt lane to the sprawling farmhouse and the barns beyond. "He's coming, but he's taking his time about it."

"It's all right." Genna assured her. "I'm not in any hurry. And besides, you have other customers."

Genna gestured to the woman and her teenage daughter who were assembling a bouquet from the stems of cut summer flowers that stood in tall tin buckets at the end of the table.

*And it will give me an opportunity to linger for a few minutes and to observe.*

Not that she expected a host of bikers to come roaring up on their Harleys in a cloud of dust. But it had been a long time since she'd been to the Frick farm, and a few minutes to orient herself could be helpful.

Genna strolled with apparent aimlessness toward

the grove of trees. Three young girls between the ages of ten and twelve were trying to keep a half-dozen toddlers occupied and away from the road. Tall stalks of corn lined the long drive on either side, and somewhere up beyond the barn to the far left, Genna recalled, was a pond.

Her arms folded across her chest, Genna leaned against the side of one of the wooden tables and tried to pretend that she was not watching the two boys who were walking toward her, each carrying a basket. Both boys looked to be in their late teens, both were dressed in the traditional black pants and blue short-sleeved shirt, both were beardless, as would denote their single status. But the boy on the left walked with a purposeful stride, while the boy on the right appeared to trip over nearly every stone and clump of grass he passed, causing his companion to pause and wait for him, and causing Genna to wonder at the nature of his infirmity.

It wasn't until he reached the table that she saw his eyes, saucered and bloodshot, the lids at half-mast. He was sniffing with every third breath he took through a nose that one, familiar with the symptoms of cocaine abuse, could detect the faintest trace of white powder.

Without speaking, he dumped the contents of his basket onto the wooden table. Watching him out of the corner of one eye, Genna sorted through the string beans and put her selections into a brown paper bag from a stack left there for that purpose. She handed the bag to the young woman and waited for her to weigh the contents.

"That'll be no charge," the girl told her, "since you had to wait for them."

"Oh, but I didn't mind—"

"Your mother is waiting for you," the boy with the bloodshot eyes interrupted sullenly as if Genna wasn't there.

"And it's your fault if she is," the girl hissed.

"Well, we're here now, Lydia." The other boy stepped in front of her to take the two zucchini, almost as long as baseball bats and nearly as thick, from the hands of the woman who stood next to Genna. "Your sister said to bring the little ones back now and get them cleaned up for supper."

"As if I'd leave them here with you and him," Lydia grumbled, her eyes narrowing as she leaned closer as if to inspect the face of the boy with the bloodshot eyes. "What's wrong with you, Eli?" she asked.

"Nothin'," he mumbled.

"Go on, now," the second young man told her. "I'll take care of things here. You're needed up at the house."

"But Eli—"

"Your brother will be fine," he assured her. "All of the dust from the hay in the barn is just making his nose run."

*That, and what he's been stuffing it with*, Genna was tempted to add.

Having spent as much time as she could seeming to arrange her bags, Genna lifted all and walked to her car where she opened the rear driver's-side door to put her purchases inside. Not having expected to get lucky so early in the game, Genna watched in her rearview mirror as she pulled away. The boy with the "dust allergy" was stretching out beneath one of the trees, while his companion waited on the customers.

As she drove the rest of the way to the lake, Genna tried to recall the photographs that she'd seen in Decker's office. There had been three Amish boys around the same age as the boys she had just seen, though in the photos, their faces had not been clear. The young woman had not been in the pictures, and the toddlers had not been under the trees. But the shadows had been shorter, indicating an earlier hour in the day. Perhaps late morning, she speculated, when the smallest members of the family might be napping, and the women would be preparing the noon meal.

Genna turned onto the road leading down to the lake, wondering how long young Eli's supply would last, when his friends would be bringing him more, and just what he was doing in return for the favor.

# 4

The long way to the lake took Genna down Coldstream Road, past the general store and the area's one fine restaurant, Sally's Lakeside, where *all you can eat* meant exactly that. Genna drove slowly, as one was forced to do here on the thin asphalt ribbon that circled Bricker's Lake in a narrow arc that barely permitted two SUV's to pass each other. There were other sections of roadway that had never been paved, but over here, in the more highly populated section of the community, macadam had been put down a few years back. On Patsy's side, the road was still hard-packed dirt that could be a real problem during times of heavy rain, but many of Patsy's neighbors were elderly and could not afford to pitch in for the paving.

Slowing to watch three teenage girls slip their catamaran into the water, Genna smiled, recalling many a summer day when she'd done that. Though not with friends. Genna hadn't had many of them. When she wanted to sail, it had been Patsy who had accompanied her.

As soon as she rounded the last gentle curve in the road, Genna could see Patsy, there at the end of the

pebbled drive, clipping long stems of Queen Anne's
lace from a clump that grew wild near the mailbox.
At the sight of Genna's Taurus, Patsy straightened
up, tucked her clippers into a pocket of her apron
and pulled off her headset, letting it rest around her
neck, and placed her flowers on the ground. With her
hands on her hips and a smile on her face, she
watched Genna park.

"Pull up a little farther, honey," Patsy called to her.
"Your tail end is hanging out onto the road."

Genna did as she was told, Patsy chattering the
entire time.

". . . and even though I've told him a hundred
times, 'Wayne, don't drive so close to the side of the
road . . .'"

"You still picking on that poor mailman?" Genna
grinned as she got out of the car.

"Well, that poor mailman knocked over old Mr.
Parker's mailbox two weeks ago." Patsy paused long
enough to wrap Genna in a close hug. "I've told him,
Nancy's told him . . ."

"Who's Nancy?" Genna returned Patsy's squeeze
before letting go and leaning into the car to pop the
trunk latch.

"Mrs. Palmer's summer renter, next door. I told
you about her." Patsy reached through the open passenger side window and lifted out Genna's purse.
"You weren't going to leave this in there, were you?"
Patsy frowned. "Things aren't the way they used to
be around here, you know."

"Or anyplace else, I venture," Genna said, adding,
"I'd have come back for it."

Genna sat her suitcase on the grass, Patsy eyeing it
as if she thought she could judge how long Genna

would be staying by the size of her suitcase. However long it might be, it was never long enough.

"I stopped at Frick's on the way by," Genna told Patsy as she retrieved a cantaloupe from the backseat and held it aloft for Patsy's inspection.

Patsy nodded her approval and grabbed for Genna's suitcase.

"I'll take that," Genna told her.

"I have it."

"You take these." Genna passed her the basket from Frick's. "And don't forget your flowers."

"You think I can't handle that?" Patsy gestured to the suitcase with a bob of her head, then turned to pick up the Queen Anne's lace. "Ha! I'm as healthy as a horse. I'm going to be around to take your babies on their first spin across the lake in the kayak."

"I don't know that I'd want to be holding my breath, waiting for babies," Genna smiled, "but I'm hoping to get a few spins around the lake myself while I'm here."

"Tomorrow, maybe," Patsy told her as they walked up the front step of the cottage. "Tonight you relax. I can tell by your eyes that you haven't been getting enough sleep lately. You work too hard, Genna."

"Probably," Genna agreed, stepping inside and unconsciously breathing in just a little more deeply, inhaling the welcoming scent of the place. She never entered through that door without experiencing a sense of welcome, of relief. That feeling that she'd reached her sanctuary.

"You bought new carpets and didn't tell me?" Genna asked, standing in the center of the living room and taking it all in.

"They were installed last week. I thought the new decor would be a nice surprise for you. I thought it was time." Patsy nodded. "The last time I bought carpets, you were fifteen, remember?"

"I do. You let me help pick out the color."

"Which explained the red, white, and blue tweed carpet in the bathroom all these years."

"I thought it was patriotic." Genna grinned.

"It was. Though I always had to fight the urge to salute before using the facilities."

Genna laughed, then admired the new carpet, telling Patsy, "This beigy color is very nice."

"Taupe," Patsy said as she disappeared into the kitchen. "The salesman called it taupe."

"Whatever. It's great with the sofa."

"I'm glad you like it."

"I do."

"Honey, why don't you take your things into your room and get settled?" Patsy reappeared with a green vase into which she had loosely arranged the Queen Anne's lace and placed it in the center of the table.

"I was just going to do that."

Genna hoisted her suitcase and followed the short hallway past the living room to the first door on the left. Patsy had earlier opened the curtains to let in light and whatever breeze might blow in off the lake, and Genna stood, just for a moment, in the doorway to take it all in.

The old maple double bed was draped with the same old blue and white quilt that it had worn the first time Genna had slept in this room. Something about that quilt had given her great comfort that night, and she had never been able to give it up, no matter how worn from use and from washings it had become. The antique oak dresser still stood at an angle in one corner, its tall, attached mirror tilted to get the best light. The walls were still palest yellow—painted several times since Genna had come, but always in the same shade—and the same framed print—daisies in a mason jar, set upon a small square table—hung over the bed. Many a night Genna had fallen asleep on a pillow propped at the bottom of the bed so that she could count the number of petals on the flowers.

*They love me. They love me not. . . .*

And last was the small chair covered in flowered chintz that had once graced the bedroom of Patsy's younger sister back in Tanner. Nothing had changed much over the years, save for the new carpet, the same as that which now covered the floor in the living room and most likely, Genna surmised, Patsy's room as well.

Here, in this room, more than anyplace in the world, Genna felt at home.

"I thought we'd have dinner around six," Patsy announced from the living room, as if they ever had dinner at any other time. You could set your watch by Patsy's sitting down for her evening meal every night at six P.M.

Genna glanced at the small clock on the dresser.

"Think we have time for a sail?"

"Time, perhaps, though there's not enough of a breeze. But if you're up to paddling, we can take the canoe out. Or the kayaks."

"The canoe would be fine. Give me two minutes to change."

"I'll meet you down at the lake."

Two minutes had been two minutes too few, but soon enough, Genna had traded her trim denim skirt and neat cotton shirt for an old pair of khaki shorts and an oversized tee, her leather sandals for bare feet. The fragrance from the lilies she and Patsy had planted years ago along the side of the house greeted her as she stepped onto the deck, and along the way to the lake she passed the ancient hydrangeas that Patsy claimed her parents had planted the year they built the place. It was all so achingly familiar, so wonderfully precious to Genna that she all but hugged herself with the pleasure of seeing it all again.

Patsy turned and waved from the edge of the water where the canoe was tied from one of the pilings on the dock, and Genna joined her.

"You ready?" Patsy asked.

"Definitely."

"Go on and get in, then, while I untie 'er."

Genna walked through the warm, shallow water to the canoe and stepped in, pushed off a bit with her paddle into deeper waters. Patsy joined her and together, they paddled along, falling into their old, practiced rhythm, traveling the lake's perimeter. Occasionally Patsy would stop the action momentarily to point out "the MacDonalds' new deck" or "the Clausens' new catamaran. They bought it from the Taylors over on the other side of the lake, so it's not exactly new. . . ."

And so on, until they'd come full circle and returned to their own dock.

"It's time to start dinner," Patsy announced as they lifted the canoe from the water.

"I'll help."

"Sit down on the dock and just relax, honey. I'll call you when it's ready."

"Tomorrow I'll sit on the dock and watch the dragonflies and listen for the fish to jump." Genna draped an arm around Patsy's shoulders and fell in step. "Tonight I want to help get dinner ready."

*And sit at the counter, there in that tiny kitchen, and get in your way from time to time. I want to listen to the sound of your voice and even the occasional silence. I want to set the table with the dishes I bought for your birthday that year I had my first job, and I want for just a little while to bask in your warmth. That same warmth that saved me so many years ago still soothes me. And Lord knows I could use a little of that warmth now. . . .*

Genna was relieved when she awoke the next morning and realized that she had not had the nightmare. She always feared that her proximity to the camp would bring it all back in shrieking detail, and there were times, over the years, when she'd lain awake for hours, here in her small room that faced the back of the cottage, afraid to fall asleep. Afraid that the night demons could find her so much more easily here than anywhere else. But last night she'd slept like the proverbial log, and awakened refreshed.

She padded on bare feet into the living area and found Patsy gazing out the back window.

"Morning, Pats."

"Morning, Gen." Patsy turned from the window, grinning, and added, "I do believe you just set a new record."

"For . . . ?"

"Most hours slept under this roof."

"What time is it?" Genna frowned.

"Almost nine."

"Nine o'clock? I slept until nine o'clock?"

"Imagine that! Why, what is this world coming to?" Patsy laughed, and patted Genna on the back. "You must have needed the sleep, honey."

"I can't remember the last time I slept until nine." Genna scratched at a mosquito bite on her upper arm. "And I was dead to the world, too. The last thing I remember is listening to the crickets and every once in a while, a splash from the lake."

Genna stretched her arms over her head and yawned.

"You go on and get your shower," Patsy told her, "and I'll fix you something good for breakfast."

"Oh, yum," Genna grinned. "Surprise me?"

"Sure thing." Patsy folded her arms over her chest and watched Genna amble off to the bathroom at the end of the hall.

"She's too thin," Patsy mumbled as she went into the kitchen and took out the last of the eggs and a carton of milk. "She's not eating right, I just know it. No time to cook, no time to eat, no time to sleep."

Patsy searched a cupboard for a frying pan.

"Well, not while she's under my roof," Patsy continued her dialogue. "When my girl is home, she'll be well fed and well rested. Sunshine and good food and sleep. We'll fix her right up, won't we, Kermit?"

Patsy addressed the cat that had appeared at the back door and announced himself with a practiced yowl.

"You come on in, now." Patsy opened the door and the large orange cat sauntered in. "I suppose you're hungry, too."

Patsy leaned down and rubbed the cat under the

chin, and he thanked her by batting at her hand with a large, flat paw. She batted back at him playfully with a spatula, and he reached for it with both of his front paws.

"Ah, no time to play right now," Patsy told him. "You go see what I left in your bowl. I have breakfast to make for Genna."

Kermit sniffed at his bowl, then walked imperiously into the living room.

"Might I suppose you already ate?" Patsy called after him. "I hope it wasn't one of the birds, though. I hate it when you do that. And besides, if you don't eat your kitty food, how am I to know if you've eaten at all? I can't give you your insulin unless you have something in that old stomach of yours. . . ."

"Who are you talking to?" Genna, wrapped in a large white towel, stepped out of the bathroom and into the short hallway that led into the kitchen.

"That diabetic old tom of yours," Patsy waved the spatula. "He's been out catting around and I don't know if he's found something to snack on or not. He hasn't had his insulin since last night, and you know what happens when he doesn't get his shots on a regular basis."

Patsy shivered, recalling the last time that Kermie had had a seizure. They'd almost lost him that time.

Genna walked into the living room and spied the cat who'd found a spot of sunlight and was now curled in its warmth.

"There you are." Genna knelt down next to the cat she had named after the famous frog, because even as a kitten, Kermit's back feet had been enormous. "Thought you'd sneak in and try to make me think you'd been here all night, did you?"

Genna heard the sound of a camera's shutter behind her.

"Patsy, would you put that damned thing away?"

"No." Patsy replied. "It's a nice shot, you there on the floor with Kermie."

"Wearing nothing but a towel and some extraneous body hair that I was planning on shaving off," Genna stretched one leg out in front of her and inspected it.

"Not to worry, I didn't have it on zoom."

Genna laughed.

"Now, get dressed and come sit down and eat some of this delicious French toast I'm about to make."

"I'll gain ten pounds here," Genna pretended to complain. "I always do."

"You could stand to gain a little." Patsy told her as she returned to the kitchen. "And you haven't stayed here long enough to gain ten pounds since you were in high school."

"Touché." Genna stood up. "Give me five minutes. I'll take a cup of coffee now, though."

"No, you won't. It'll slow you down. You can have your coffee with your breakfast."

"Tyrant," Genna muttered just loud enough for Patsy to hear, smiling as she did so, and went to her room to dress.

"Think we can get in a sail today?" Genna asked when she arrived in the kitchen and sat down at the small counter where plates had been set for two.

"Maybe. The clouds look a little iffy, but they could pass over." Patsy handed her a plate upon which she'd piled fat slices of French toast, golden from the frying pan and wearing a sprinkling of white powdered sugar.

"Heaven. Sheer heaven." Genna smiled. "And worth every blessed calorie, and every bit of cholesterol, fat . . ."

Patsy smiled and poured orange juice and coffee for them both, then sat down next to Genna.

"I used the last of the eggs for the French toast," she commented. "I don't usually go through a dozen so quickly, but between the cake I made for last night and the toast this morning, I went through that carton in less than a week."

"If I'd known, I could have picked some up yesterday."

"No matter. I can make a quick run this morning." Patsy shrugged. "I was thinking about making a lemon soufflé for dessert, so I will need the extra eggs."

"How is Mrs. Frick doing?"

"Well, she's old as the hills, as you know. Must be in her nineties. Spry little devil, though. Still raises her hens and sells her eggs and works on those quilts of hers, though she doesn't make as many as she used to, and they seem to take her longer these days."

"Maybe I'll go with you," Genna said, pleased that she wouldn't have to wait too long for an opportunity to visit the farm. "It's been years since I've seen her."

"Oh, most days I don't go up to the house anymore." Patsy sipped at her juice. "I just buy from the stand. Unless I'm having something made—a baby quilt or something—that I have to talk to her about."

"Actually, I was thinking about just that. A baby quilt, that is." Genna hadn't been, but she was now that the opportunity presented itself.

"Oh? Who's having a baby?"

"John Mancini's sister. Angela. And she already had it." Genna concentrated on cutting off a piece of toast with her fork, not wanting to look at Patsy's face and having to see that spark of hope she knew she'd find there. Patsy had adored John and had been very vocal about where she hoped that relationship would eventually lead.

"She had a boy, by the way," Genna added. "Carmen Anthony DelVecchio the second."

"Oh. How nice. And nice of you to think of having a quilt made for her son. You'll be seeing her, then?"

"The baby will be christened next Sunday, so I doubt there's much time to have a quilt made. With luck, Mrs. Frick will have a few already made up for me to choose from. And yes, I've been invited to attend the christening." Genna's mouth twitched at Patsy's attempt at craftiness.

"By Angela or by John?"

"Anyone ever tell you that you're very nosy?" Genna fought a grin. "And not very subtle?"

"I'm sure I don't know what you mean," Patsy sniffed with mock indignation. "I'm always interested in everything you do."

"Especially when it concerns what might loosely be referred to as my love life. Or lack of it."

"Didn't Angela just get married last summer?" Patsy chose to ignore Genna's comment and forged ahead. "Have you seen her since the wedding?"

"June before last. And it's been a while since I've seen her. Now, what time would you like to go to the farm?" Genna changed the subject.

"We can go after breakfast, if you like."

"Great. And when we get back, maybe we can take a swim, if the clouds lift."

"I should make a list," Patsy muttered to herself and took a small notepad out of a nearby drawer. With the attached pencil, she began to jot down several items she wished to purchase at the farm, humming "She's Got You," being in the mood for a little Patsy Cline at the moment.

An hour later, Genna was slowly driving up the long lane that led from Tolliver Road to the Frick farmhouse and trying to remember just how long it had been since she'd made that drive. Years, she thought as she slowed even more, anticipating the appearance of the rambling old house with its many additions that lay just beyond the walnut trees, and tried to recall the layout of the farm. With the windows rolled down and the air conditioning turned off, the interior of Genna's car was beginning to fill with dust kicked up from the dry road.

"I always forget how quiet it is back here," Genna noted.

"Even though there's so much activity going on right now, there's always that element of deep quietude. The men are working in the fields and tending to the animals and the women are either doing laundry or putting up some of the crops, but you hardly hear any of it. No machines, that's why."

"It's so hard to believe that people still live like this." Genna stopped the car under a tree and sat with the engine at idle for a moment. "No real modern conveniences. I guess that's why they hold such a fascination for so many of us 'English.' "

The front door opened, and a small girl poked her head out and disappeared. Seconds later, the door opened again and this time an elderly woman, who actually looked years younger than she really was, stepped out and waved.

"Miss Wheeler, you're welcome, as always!" The woman was drying her hands on a once-white apron as she walked toward her two visitors. "And who is this you've brought with you?"

"Now, Mrs. Frick." Patsy smiled broadly. "You know my Genna."

"Genna?" The woman crossed her arms over her chest and appeared to inspect Genna carefully. "So old you look."

"So old, I am," Genna laughed. "How are you, Mrs. Frick?"

"Good," the old woman nodded pleasantly. "I'd be doing good."

"We're glad for that," Patsy told her. "And we'll be gladder still if you have some eggs left today."

"Well, now, the boys left for the market in Erie early, but there may be a few eggs still in the henhouse." Mrs. Frick turned toward the house and called, "Rebecca, take a basket down to the henhouse and see if there are any eggs that were missed this morning."

A young girl of about seven appeared in the doorway.

"Get a basket, girl, and go along."

The girl closed the door behind her, presumably to return once the basket was located.

"What else might I do for you this morning?" Mrs. Frick asked.

"Well, one of Genna's friends recently had a baby, and she thought perhaps one of your quilts might do nicely for a gift," Patsy told her.

"A boy or a girl, is it?"

"A boy," Genna told her, wishing she could think of some pretext that would give her access to another part of the farm so she could take a look around.

"I do have some made, you'd be welcome to look. I'll bring them out for you to see. The light's better out here, if you can wait."

Genna nodded.

"We're in no hurry."

The child—Rebecca—emerged from the house with a small basket over her arm.

"Rebecca, could I give you a hand?" Genna asked on impulse.

Rebecca looked from Genna to Granny Frick—most likely the girl's great-grandmother—as if she did not understand the question.

"I mean, could I go with you to the henhouse?" Genna turned and asked, "If that would be all right, Mrs. Frick?"

"I don't see harm."

"Come on, then, Rebecca, and show me how you get eggs from the chickens." Genna fell into step with the girl.

Making idle chatter with the girl, who without doubt thought Genna strange for thinking a trip to the henhouse was one worth taking, Genna missed nothing on their way to the large fenced in pen where the chickens were kept. There appeared nothing out of order on this late summer morning, nothing to indicate that anything might be amiss.

*What did you expect to find, anyway?* Genna chided herself. *Boys in black, dusty from the fields, clustered behind the barn, drawing straws to see who gets to smoke the last of the crack?*

"You have to be smart opening the gate," Rebecca

told Genna shyly as she slid back the wooden latch, "so the hens don't get out."

The hens ignored the intrusion into their enclave, even when Rebecca lifted the nesting birds to take their brown eggs and place them carefully in her basket. When she had gathered twelve eggs, she looked up at Genna and said, "And that's what you do."

"Thank you for showing me." Genna smiled from the doorway.

While Rebecca had been gathering eggs, Genna had been scoping out the lay of the land. The old barn stood to their right, a silo attached to the far end. Beyond the barn were separate fenced areas for the cows, pigs, and goats. The horses were kept in a smaller stable, to the rear of the property, and another outbuilding housed farm equipment and the family's several buggies. Off to the left was a pond surrounded by endless fields of corn that had another month or so of growth to go. Plowed areas closer to the house provided gardens for the vegetables they grew to sell in their stands and to the markets, and for the use of the large extended family that called the farm home. Several long, straight rows dazzled the eye with their variety of summer flowers.

But it was the depression near the center of the tall stalks of the hollyhocks that caught and held Genna's attention on their way back to the farmhouse.

"Rebecca was a good teacher," Genna announced as they approached the porch, the railing of which was draped with a half-dozen colorful quilts.

"You found eggs for Miss Wheeler, then, Rebecca?" Granny Frick asked, and Rebecca handed her the basket. "This should do fine. Now take them

into the house and put them in one of those cardboard egg holders."

"Yes, Granny." Rebecca went into the house to
complete her assigned task.

"Mrs. Frick has several quilts completed," Patsy
stated the obvious.

"So I see."

Genna smiled and stepped onto the porch to take
a closer look at the array lined up for her inspection.
Though all were lovely, the log cabin design in
shades of blue with green and light yellow on a
white background caught her eye. She held it up to
take a closer look. It was just right for a baby boy.

"They're all lovely, but I do like this one. What do
you think, Patsy?"

"I like that one, too."

"That one it is, then." Mrs. Frick nodded.

"Mrs. Frick," Genna asked as the elderly woman
folded the quilt and set it aside, "do you still sell the
cut flowers?"

"You mean from the field there?" she asked as she
neatly folded the remaining quilts.

"Yes."

"Were you wanting a bunch?"

"Well, those zinnias are tempting." Genna smiled.

"You go on out and pick yourself what you might
like," Granny Frick nodded, "while I get Miss
Wheeler some of that strawberry-rhubarb jam she's
so partial to."

"Thank you. I'll just be a minute, Patsy." Genna
searched her leather bag for the Swiss Army knife
she usually carried, and tucked it into her pocket,
and leaving Patsy and her old friend chatting on the
back steps, headed off alone to the flower beds.

"Pick some of those red zinnias, Genna," Patsy called to her, and Genna waved to indicate that she'd heard.

With her small knife, Genna cut a few stems here, a few stems there, all the while working her way closer to the depression where something clearly had flattened out a good part of several rows of flowers. Finally close enough to peer through a stand of leafy cosmos, Genna was not at all surprised to see a boy passed out atop the blooms, the front of his dark blue shirt bearing a dusting of white. Leaving her cut flowers on the ground, she reached through the dense stems to check his pulse. That his heart rate had already returned to normal was evidence that it had been some time since he'd last fed his nose with cocaine. It was the same young man she'd seen the day before—the boy they'd called Eli—and judging by the fact that he was out cold today and had been using the day before gave her an indication of just how much of a habit he'd developed.

The scene was a study in contrasts, Genna sighed with disgust. How totally incongruous that Eli Frick would be sleeping off his cocaine high in the middle of a field of summer flowers, with bees and butterflies drifting around him.

How, she wondered, had he been lured? What had been the bait? Had none of his family members noticed anything unusual about his behavior? And if they had, could they even begin to imagine what was causing it?

And what exactly was this young Amish boy doing in return for the temptation that took him from his simple farm background into the world of illegal drugs and who knew what else?

It was time to call the locals and let them know that their suspicions were right on target. After she called Decker, of course.

Patsy was still chatting away when Genna finally returned with an armful of zinnias in every shade and a few long, graceful stems of cosmos.

"What do I owe you for the quilt and the flowers?" Genna asked.

"The quilt is forty dollars," Granny Frick told her, "the flowers are free. You and Miss Wheeler will enjoy them."

"We will, thank you." Genna took two twenty-dollar bills out of her wallet and exchanged them for the baby quilt. "Where's my friend Rebecca? I'd like to thank her for the quick lesson in egg-gathering."

"Oh, she went on down to the stand to help her brother." Granny Frick pointed to the roadside stand at the end of the lane.

"Well, tell her I said thank you, if you would."

Genna placed the folded quilt on the backseat and her flowers on the floor, then got in behind the wheel and waited for Patsy to finish saying her good-byes to her old friend. As they waved good-bye and drove slowly down the lane, she thought how like paradise this peaceful farm was. And how, like paradise, a serpent had managed to find its way in.

Well, it's just going to have to be driven out, she thought as she approached the end of the lane, fighting a pang of guilt. How terrible for the Fricks to have such a thing going on in their family, and how sad that she would be the one responsible for bringing it to light. Knowing the shame that would be brought upon this fine family sickened Genna.

A roar like thunder shattered the silence just as

Genna reached the end of the lane. Four motorcycles had stopped along the shoulder of the road, their drivers now turning off their machines and heading toward the stand.

Genna slowed to a stop, and sat for a long minute, watching.

"Genna?" Patsy touched her arm to get her attention.

"I was just thinking that we should have picked up another cantaloupe. And a few more tomatoes," Genna said to Patsy without turning toward her. "Didn't you say that you might invite your friend, the woman who is renting the house next door . . ."

"Nancy," Patsy supplied the name.

" . . . that you might invite Nancy to join us for dinner one night over the weekend?"

"Yes, but I think we have plenty left over from . . ."

Patsy paused as Genna turned off the car and got out, watched as she sauntered up to the nearest table and began to sort through the tomatoes.

*What in the world . . . ?* Patsy shook her head.

Genna picked over produce and surreptitiously memorized the tattoos that she would later compare to those on the biceps of the men in the photos that Decker had given her.

Large snarling blue dogs with angry, open mouths.

Genna approached the cash register with three tomatoes and an absently selected cantaloupe in her arms, searching her purse for her wallet. All the while, her eyes behind dark glasses continued to watch the men dressed in denim and T-shirts with the sleeves ripped off, one of whom was attempting to juggle a few green peppers. Several of the other customers exchanged nervous glances, but the men sporting the snarling blue dog tattoos appeared not to notice.

As Genna placed the tomatoes on the scale, she noticed Rebecca leaning on the end of the table.

"Thank you again, Rebecca, for showing me how to collect eggs," Genna said to the small girl.

"Welcome," Rebecca replied softly.

Genna smiled and opened her wallet and pulled out a bill that she thought would cover her purchases, was just about to hand it over to the young man at the register when Rebecca asked, "What's an F-B-I?"

Everyone froze where they stood, from the boy whose hand had just accepted her money, to the dark-haired juggler.

No one spoke for a long minute.

"Where'd you hear *FBI*, Becky?" her brother asked.

"Granny Frick said that she," the girl pointed to Genna, "Miss Wheeler's girl, was an *FBI*."

"FBI means Federal Bureau of Investigation, Rebecca," Genna answered with forced nonchalance. "People who work for the FBI investigate crimes."

"Like the police?" Becky stated.

"Sometimes we work with the police," Genna nodded.

The pale blue eyes of the boy holding Genna's money darted anxiously from one of the bikers to the other. Genna pretended not to notice. She lifted her cantaloupe and held out her hand and asked, "Do I get change?"

The boy mumbled something and handed her a few bills, which she pretended to count as she walked back to the car, knowing that all eyes were on her.

Inside she was shaking with the effort it took to keep from yelling in frustration.

*Damn. Damn. Damn. Damn. Damn. Damn. Damn. Damn.*

"Is something wrong, Genna?" Patsy asked as Genna slid behind the wheel.

"What could be wrong?"

"I don't know," Patsy replied. "You look distracted."

"Everything's fine."

"Did you get everything you wanted?"

"Yes." Genna smiled tersely and put the car in gear, driving away slowly as if nothing was amiss.

*Damn.*

She'd have to call Decker and give him the good news as well as the bad.

Two miles up the road, a half mile before the turn for the lake, Genna saw the two bikes in her rearview mirror. They approached quickly, then slowed down, staying with her, one on her right rear bumper, the other on her left.

Patsy turned nervously to look over her left shoulder.

"What are they doing?" she asked.

"Just trying to act cool," Genna told her. "Ignore them."

"Are they following us?"

"Of course not. Why would they follow us?"

"Genna, are you hiding something from me?"

"No."

Why bring Patsy into this? Genna thought. Especially since her own part in the investigation had just been brought to a screeching halt. Genna flicked on her left turn signal and slowed down. Both bikes cut around the Taurus and passed it with a deafening roar.

Genna couldn't help but feel that she'd just been given a message. With Patsy so often alone at the lake, she hoped that she was wrong.

# 5

John Mancini leaned back against the fake rattan headboard of the king-sized bed in his room at the Cozy Nook Motel off Route 13 in Delaware, just a breath from the Maryland border, and crossed his arms behind his head. He was tired and irritable and wished to God that he hadn't answered the phone on Tuesday morning. If he'd let Connie, the receptionist, pick up he wouldn't have had to speak with Calvin Sharpe. If he hadn't spoken with Sharpe, he wouldn't be here, right outside of Nowhere, Delaware, a stack of photographs of a headless woman resting on his lap, a warm beer on the nightstand, and an attitude brought on by indigestion and lack of sleep.

But he had picked up the phone, and when your boss asks you to drop everything and hold the hand of his son-in-law who happens at that moment to be on the verge of screwing up a major investigation, chances are he isn't really asking at all. To ask implies that there is a choice of responses. When you're dealing with Calvin Sharpe, there really was only one choice.

One headless woman found in a county park is a sign that there's a nasty killer on the loose.

Three headless women in as many weeks is a sign that he's enjoying it. And since Sharpe's son-in-law, Kurt Fraser, was the chief of police in the sleepy town where the bodies were piling up, and since Sharpe feared that Fraser might have already bungled the investigation of the first victim completely, the second one marginally, Sharpe couldn't move quickly enough to send in one of his own to help out.

Helping out meant, among other things, to help Fraser—and therefore Sharpe—to save face.

John had met with the young police chief earlier that morning, and quickly recognized that while Fraser was not totally inept, he was inexperienced and intimidated by his father-in-law's high standing within the Bureau. The first of the three crime scenes had been totally corrupted when the troop of Cub Scouts, who had stumbled upon the body, had gone running off in all directions, covering any and all footprints and disturbing any trace evidence that might otherwise have been recovered. And it hadn't been Fraser's fault that a torrential rain had flooded the creek near where the second body had been left, not only washing away almost everything that could have been left behind but moving the body as well. To his credit, Fraser had been smart enough to figure out where the body might have been dumped a quarter mile upstream, by calculating where the creek had crested the night before. Working as a one-man forensic unit, because the small town lacked the funds for full-time specialists, Fraser had personally compiled the detailed notes, over which John Mancini now pored.

The discovery of the last body had been made late the previous morning by an elderly woman who was

walking her dog. John had read her statement of the
morning's events at least three times.

"Jelly and I walk here twice each week," the
woman had related. "Always in the same part of the
park. I've been bringing Jelly here since she was a
pup—she's eight now, so she knows the area. She
goes off on her own, just so far ahead of me, then she
comes back. Then she goes off again, then she comes
back. We were halfway back to the parking lot when
she took off, but didn't come back. I called and
called, but she wouldn't come. Finally, I heard her
barking and followed the sound. I thought perhaps
she'd cornered something, a deer maybe—that's
happened before—or maybe that cougar that people
around here keep saying they've seen. Well, there
was Jelly, standing over that woman. Of course, at
first I wasn't sure it was a woman. It was there on the
ground. . . ."

"What do you think?" Fraser had asked when
John arrived on the scene. "You seen anything like
this before?"

"Close enough," John had replied as he knelt
down carefully beside the body.

"Where do you suppose the head is?" asked the
young police chief.

"That's anybody's guess at this point," John muttered.

"It never fails to amaze me that anyone could do
something like this." Fraser shook his head. "This is
really the *worst*."

John could have told him that this, this headless
woman left in a park to be found by an elderly
woman in the middle of a summer morning, while
gruesome, obscene, was by no stretch of the imagina-

tion the *worst*. And compared to some of the cases John had handled in his career, the headless woman had met a relatively benign end. The body showed no sign of abuse, no wounds, no mutilation below the line of decapitation. There were several cases on John's desk at that very moment where the victim had met a much more horrific end.

John looked over the photos of the site where the body had been found, on its back, arms crossed over the chest, legs crossed demurely at the ankles. Fully dressed. The body had not yet begun to decompose. Poor Mrs. Turner could well have passed the killer as he had made his way out of the park.

The phone on the table next to the bed began to ring.

"Mancini here."

" 'Mancini here.' What the hell kind of way is that to answer the phone?"

John grinned at the sound of his sister's voice.

"Hey, Ang. How's it going?"

"I'll tell you how it's going. Ma's on the warpath. She wants to know why she has to depend on the noontime news to find out that her son is close enough to home to come to dinner."

"I was going to call as soon as I got back to the motel but it was late by the time I got here and . . ."

"And that's another thing she was not happy about. 'A little more than an hour and a half from his mother's house and he's sleeping in a motel? What will people think?' "

John laughed out loud.

"I guess I'd better give her a call first thing in the morning."

"If you were smart, you'd make a beeline in the

direction of Passyunk Avenue first thing in the morning and forget the phone."

"Can't do it, Ang. I'm going to be tied up for at least another day here. But I promise I'll give her a call."

"Don't wait too long, pal. The rest of us still have to live with her, you know."

"How is everyone?"

"Show up at the baby's christening on Sunday and find out for yourself."

"I have all intentions of doing that. How is my little nephew, by the way?"

"Cutest thing on God's green earth, I swear to God." Angela gave a motherly sigh.

"I can't wait to see him again."

"You remembered that Genna is coming? She is still coming, right?"

"When I spoke with her a few days ago, she said she was planning on it."

"Good. I liked her. We all did."

"I know, Angie."

"So what should I tell Mom?"

"About what?"

"Dinner tomorrow night."

"Doesn't look good."

"I'll tell her you're still with the body. That's about the only excuse she's going to buy."

"Thanks for the warning."

"You're welcome. We'll talk on Sunday. Call your mother. I gotta go. Carmen's home."

"Tell him I said hi and that . . ." John smiled even as his sister hung up the phone, ". . . I'll see him on Sunday."

Angela was their mother all over again. Tiny, small boned, dark-haired, smart mouthed. One hundred percent South Philadelphia Italian and proud to be. Such a contrast to Tess, the youngest of the three Mancini children, who was soft-spoken, mild tempered, and gentle of spirit. And John, the only son, fell somewhere between the two.

Their mother, Rita Theresa Esposito Mancini, was a force to be reckoned with, every bit as formidable as Calvin Sharpe. And first thing in the morning, her only son would call her.

John sat on the end of the bed and grinned. He knew exactly how the conversation with his mother would start.

"So you're only one state away and you can't come for dinner?"

And how it would end.

"So you won't forget to not wear your gun to the christening, right? You know how nervous the DelVecchio boys get when you're around. You being the FBI and everything."

The DelVecchio brothers all reportedly had some nebulous ties to the Philadelphia Mafia, except, of course, for Carmen, who had married the sister of an FBI agent whose reputation had achieved legendary status in the neighborhood. It never failed to amuse John that certain members of the DelVecchio clan always seemed to be just on their way out when John arrived at family functions.

John closed his briefcase and placed it on the dresser that stood along the opposite wall, then turned the covers down, snapped off the light, and got into bed. He wondered if Genna was still awake. In the dark, he could see the face of the clock on the table. It was almost midnight. Too late to call the cottage. Patsy was an early-to-bed, early-to-rise type.

John turned over in the dark, wishing he'd called her earlier. He should have called before he picked up that stack of reports and photographs. He should have known how involved he'd get. If Angie hadn't called when she did, he'd probably still be lost in the details of this stranger's death. It was only when he'd stopped for a moment that he realized how tired he was. They'd been at the crime scene from late afternoon the day before until the sun had come up this morning, then at the police station where he'd met with various members of local and state agencies and the press until well after the dinner hour.

He hoped that Genna was enjoying her week with Patsy. Hoped the weather was good so that they'd have lots of opportunity to sail and swim and fish, all those things that they so enjoyed. All those things, he half-smiled in the dark, that city boys like him had to be taught. He thought back to two summers ago, when he'd spent several long weekends at the lake with Genna and Patsy, who seemed to keep up a nonstop pace of activity.

When told they were going to go bass fishing, John had smiled at Patsy and said, "I'll pass. I think I'll just grab a lounge and sit in the shade and read a book."

"John, there is no lounge," Patsy had told him.

"No lounge?"

Patsy had shaken her head. Behind her, on the deck, Genna had appeared vastly amused.

"Just a folding chair, then . . . ?"

"Sorry."

"What do you sit on when you come outside to read?" he asked.

"I don't," she told him. "I read inside, at night, or

if it's raining. But when the sun is up and the bass are biting, or the water is right for swimming or the wind right for sailing, or it's a good day to hike, then that's what I do. And right now, the sun is up and the bass are frisky. Put the book down and take your shoes off. We're taking the boat out. You'll like it."

John hadn't exactly liked it, but he hadn't really minded it much, either, which more or less had satisfied Patsy. But later that day, when she'd suggested a hike around the lake, he'd driven the twenty minutes into Wick's Grove and headed for the nearest shopping center, where he found a store that sold outdoor furniture. He purchased a lounge and a couple of folding chairs, and when he arrived back at the cottage, he planted himself solidly on the deck in the shade and with no small ceremony opened his book. Patsy had good-naturedly brought him a glass of iced tea before she and Genna set off on their trek.

John lay on his back in the dark and stared at the ceiling of his motel room. He had really loved those days at the cottage with Genna, had loved seeing the interaction between Genna and Patsy. Loved watching Genna's face when she and Patsy bantered, loved the tenderness she showed the older woman, loved the woman that Genna was when she was there in that place where she felt so secure. There was something about Bricker's Lake that brought out Genna's most vulnerable side, and John had found that aspect of her personality sweetly appealing.

Other images played through his sleep-deprived brain. Genna in short shorts, standing at the end of the dock, watching an early morning fog so dense that he could barely see her from the lake's edge.

Genna in the sun, her head thrown back, laughing at something he'd said. Genna in the moonlight, the night the two of them took out a canoe and paddled down to a quiet stretch of man-made beach at the far end of the lake, where they'd rowed to shore and spent an hour wrestling in the sand . . .

"Genna." He whispered her name aloud in the dark room, and closed his eyes, trying to imagine what the rest of his life would be without her in it.

The picture wasn't pretty.

Right now, they shared friendship, professional respect, memories. There had to be more. Damn it, there *would* be more. Having once had Genna's love, John would not be content until they were together again.

Somehow, someway, he'd have to find a way back into her life, back into her heart. He *would* find a way. He couldn't see where he had a choice.

He just had to figure out the right way to go about doing that.

Tomorrow, he'd call her, if for no other reason than simply to hear her voice.

And then he'd call his mother.

Genna stood in the doorway that opened onto Patsy's deck, her hands on her hips, watching Patsy instruct her new friend and next-door neighbor, Nancy, on the finer points of tying a fly onto the shank of a fishhook. An avid fisher all her life, Patsy simply could not resist seeking a convert to her favorite pastime. When Nancy commented that she'd never gone fishing, Patsy proceeded to plan their day around when the bass might be striking in the lake.

". . . and of course we practice catch and release," Genna overheard Patsy tell Nancy.

"What exactly does that mean?" Nancy raised a well-penciled brow that arched over very blue eyes.

"It means that after we catch the fish, we take great pains not to injure it while we remove the hook so that we can let it go."

"And why might we do that?"

"It's a way of protecting the species, a way of ensuring that there will be lots of big fish, not just small immature ones, in the lake or stream."

"So why bother?" Nancy shook her flawless blond page boy.

"For the sport of it."

"Hmmph. If it's sport I want, I'll go to the track and bet on the ponies. If I spend all day chasing after a fish, I expect to eat it."

Genna smiled and stepped back into the cool of the cottage. Outside the debate continued, and Genna was glad for it. How wonderful that Patsy had someone closer to her own age to do things with. Although Genna wasn't altogether certain that Nancy and Patsy were totally on the same wavelength.

For one thing, Genna observed through the window as she rummaged in her purse looking for her cell phone, in their two brief meetings, in spite of her more athletic bearing, Nancy had impressed Genna as being more, well, *girly* than Patsy ever was, with her carefully manicured nails, and carefully made up face. Two, Nancy seemed to favor long, gentle summer skirts over the shorts and slacks that Patsy lived in. Where Patsy was barely five-feet-five and slightly rounded, Nancy was tall, at least five ten, and slender, muscular almost. And while Patsy could keep up a full day's worth of activities, Nancy seemed to pace herself, preferring to work on her laptop computer while seated on the deck of her rented cabin.

*But they do seem to get along just fine, and that's all that really matters,* Genna thought as she finished dialing the number, wondering absently if perhaps she hadn't met Nancy somewhere before. Was there something about her that stirred something far in the back of Genna's memory? Her walk perhaps? Genna couldn't put her finger on it.

*But at least she's good company for Pats and I'm grateful for that. Too bad she's only here on weekends . . .*

"Decker." The ringing phone had been answered.

"Hi. It's Genna Snow."

"Just got off the phone with Lt. Banks up there at the state police barracks."

"And he told you I was busted by a seven-year-old Amish girl named Rebecca."

"Yes. Tough break. Though Banks seems to think that the information you gave him will be sufficient for a warrant."

"I hope they get on with it, then." Genna bit her bottom lip. "Sir, I have to tell you that I'm not comfortable knowing that the bikers could probably find Patsy if they wanted to. It's all too easy to put two and two together and come up with Patsy Wheeler."

"I'll mention that to Banks and get his word that he'll keep an eye on her and her cottage even after he makes his arrest."

"I'd appreciate that. If someone wanted to hurt me . . . well, she's my most vulnerable spot. And she is pretty much alone here except on weekends when there's a neighbor next door."

"I understand. I'll call him right back." There was a slight pause, then Decker told her, "I think you should go ahead and take the week off as planned. You're due. Then come back next Monday and kick ass on this kiddie porn ring. Liddy has come up with a few good leads. I think he's already e-mailed them to you."

"I have my laptop with me. I'll take a look."

"Do. Ah, it appears my nine-thirty appointment is here. Rest up, Genna Snow. I'll see you next week."

Genna turned off the phone and slipped it back into her bag, then plugged her laptop into the phone jack and proceeded to read and send e-mail for almost forty minutes. When she had finished and closed up her computer, she looked out the window, her attention drawn by the sound of shared laughter, Patsy's like a bell choir, Nancy's throatier but no less merry as they inspected a bed of brightly colored daylilies that grew along the side of Nancy's cabin. Genna opened the back door and went out to join them.

"I take it you gave up on fly fishing," Genna said as she walked the narrow space between the two small houses.

"Not at all." Patsy shook her head. "We just got off on a tangent about daylilies. Nancy knows a lot about plant propagation and hybridizing and cultivating, so much more than I."

"Now, Patsy, you look at how much you've already taught me about making those little May fly things."

"Nancy's a natural at tying flies, Gen. Her fingers are ever so much longer." Patsy held her hands up for inspection. "Short and stubby doesn't tie quite as well."

"Those short stubby fingers have tied thousands of flies over the years, don't let her fool you, Nancy."

"I'm not fooled in the least. Anyone could tell that Patsy knows her way around a tackle box."

"Is that my phone?" Patsy frowned.

Genna turned to the house and listened.

"It is," she said, taking long strides to the steps, which she took two at a time. "I'll get it."

"Thank you, honey. You know," she turned to Nancy as they followed Genna at a slower pace, "I keep meaning to get an answering machine, but every time I go into town, I forget to pick one up. . . ."

Genna was pacing the length and width of the small kitchen, then into the living room as far as the wall-mounted phone would reach, when the two women came into the cottage. She was speaking in a soft voice, and the slightest hint of a smile played about her lips.

When Patsy pointed to the phone and made an inquiring gesture, Genna put one hand over the receiver and whispered, "It's John."

"Oh." Patsy brightened, then turned to Nancy and asked, "Iced tea?"

"That would be nice. Thank you."

Humming as she filled three glasses partly with ice, then with tea from a pitcher in the kitchen, Patsy tried her best to pretend that she wasn't at all interested in Genna's conversation, though of course, she was. She handed Genna a glass of tea and took the others into the living room where she and Nancy sat and talked in hushed voices so as not to disturb Genna. When the phone had been returned to its cradle, however, Patsy called to her and asked, "How is John?"

"He's fine."

"Was he calling from the office?"

"He's in Delaware."

"Oh. Is he working on the headless women case?" Patsy called into the kitchen. "I saw on the national news the other day that they found another headless body and that they had called in the FBI."

"Yes, John is there." Genna leaned against the doorway.

"Patsy told me that your boyfriend is some kind of special investigator for the FBI. I'm so impressed . . ."

"He's not my boyfriend," Genna made a point to tell Nancy, who sped right past her.

". . . to know someone who knows someone like that. I saw a show on cable not two weeks ago about how the FBI can create these profiles on serial killers." Nancy turned to Patsy. "It's uncanny, how they can tell so much about a person with so little to go on. And so often, they're right on the money! Why, they went over all the details on this one case, and they had this man pegged to a T."

"It's true, it seems uncanny, but it's really not at all random. There's very little guesswork involved."

"Now, what does your boyfriend work on when there are no serial killer cases?" Nancy asked.

"There's always another serial killer," Genna told her. "Most serial killers are never caught. They travel, they move around. They get lucky or they are very careful. They die of natural causes and are never found out for what they really are. But most of them are never caught until they do something stupid or predictable."

"Well, then, tell me . . ." Nancy leaned forward slightly, her eyes narrowing.

"Nope. No more." Patsy shook her head vehemently. "I refuse to waste any more of my day talking about serial killers and crazies."

Patsy stood up and waved all the ugly thoughts away with one sweep of her hand.

"Now. Who's ready to do a little fishing?"

# 6

The evening lights in the parking lot had just come on when the shadow appeared at the top of the steps. The concrete stairs led down to a path that served as a shortcut through a small park to the housing development beyond. Off to the right was a stream, and beyond the stream, a golf course. The man standing at the top of the steps knew every blade of grass and stone between the parking lot and the houses, between the park and the stream and the golf course.

Who was it who had once said that the man who would meet with the most success was the man who had the best information?

He smiled, knowing he had done all he could, was as well prepared as he could ever hope to be. For the past several days, he'd followed her—from a safe enough distance, of course—to learn her routine. Once he knew her daily route, he made certain that she encountered him several times under the most benign circumstances, catching her eye and smiling somewhat absently. And the route, well, it couldn't be more perfect. There was hardly ever foot traffic here at this time of the day. Those who habitually chose to park not in the lot but along the street at the edge of the woods were long gone. Of those souls who lived in the development and worked for the university—a mere six people—well, five of them had already gone home, as he'd known they would. For the past three days, he'd been watching them, too. And other than his nondescript dark blue van, there were no other cars parked along the woods.

And by now, she was so accustomed to seeing him, that she'd barely notice him at all.

All so that when he came to take her, she would not be alarmed at his approach.

He'd rehearsed this night so often in his mind, there was surely no way he could fail. The key to success, he'd once heard, was to be able to imagine oneself actually doing whatever it was one wanted to do.

God knew that he'd imagined the scene over and over and over again.

In his mind's eye, he'd walked toward her—past her—making brief but casual eye contact, as he had done over the past several days. Looking just like everyone else did, his hands in the pockets of his jeans (where he could caress the switchblade, but she, of course, wouldn't know that). Walking not too quickly, not too slowly—purposeful, but distracted so she would have no sense of dread. Then, after he'd passed her, he'd spin around and grab her from behind, and before she could scream, he'd have her unconscious.

He closed his eyes and took a deep, slow breath, letting it all play out in his head. He could see himself carrying her the short distance to the shallow stream, then across it and up the bank to the golf course. Where they'd play and play and play until he didn't feel like playing anymore.

And Darlene Myers would pay him back, minute by agonizing minute, for her part in what he'd gone through for all those years. And even then, he wouldn't be quite finished with her.

# 7

___

Genna couldn't help but have mixed feelings about the part she had played in the arrest of the Frick boys on drug trafficking and possession charges. The case marked the first time since the Amish had migrated to that part of the state years before that any member of that community had been charged with a major crime. There was virtually no juvenile delinquency, unless you counted the buggy races on Saturday evenings, or the stealing of a kiss behind a barn.

And Patsy, of course, had known right away, the minute the story broke on Thursday afternoon, that Genna's hand had been in it. She looked at Genna from across the living room after turning on the five o'clock news that had led with film of the police van driving down the dirt road on their way to the farmhouse, and said, "I doubt I'll ever be able to face Mrs. Frick again."

"I'm sorry, Patsy. The boys were in way over their heads. Now they'll have to pay the consequences. It's unfortunate, yes, but it was their choice."

"How do you suppose those bike people got to them? How did they get those boys to even experiment with drugs?"

"I guess it will all come out, sooner or later. I don't know the details, Pats. My only involvement was as an observer."

"When we went to buy eggs." Patsy shifted uncomfortably in her seat. "The day you bought the baby quilt . . ."

Genna nodded.

"Well, I guess someone had to put a stop to it. It's so sad, though." Patsy sighed. "Mrs. Frick told me once that when she moved out here with her husband, she was a young wife with two small children. One of the reasons they came here was to escape the encroachment of the modern world into their lives. To protect their children. I wonder what she thinks now. . . ."

Genna reached over and took Patsy's hand.

"I'm sorry that your friend was hurt, Pats. But it had to be done."

"Oh, honey, I don't blame you. I just know that Mrs. Frick will be so bewildered by everything that will come next. The trial. If they're convicted, they'll go to prison. And that's just no place for a young Amish boy." Patsy shuddered slightly, then turned to Genna and said without emotion, "But this was why you came this week. It wasn't just a vacation. And now that the arrest has been made, you'll leave."

"Decker knows that I come here as often as I can. He did ask me to take a few days and just take a look around the farm and see what I could see. Unofficially, of course. I did that." She paused for a second before adding, "I think you should consider going back to Tanner for a while, at least until the locals are certain that they have taken everyone into custody who's been involved in this."

Patsy looked at Genna as if she'd spoken in a foreign tongue.

"Whatever are you talking about?"

"The bikers saw me at the farm. It wouldn't be difficult to find this cottage, or to find me if anyone took it into their head to look."

"Why would anyone make a connection between you and this?" She pointed to the television.

"Because sweet little Rebecca Frick identified me as an FBI agent right in front of them."

"Oh." Patsy's face folded into a frown. "That is unfortunate. She may have been standing on the porch when Mrs. Frick asked me what you were up to these days, and I told her. But what does that have to do with me?"

"We're pretty isolated over on this end of the lake. Except for old Mr. Corbin, who is deaf as a stone, and the MacKenzie's across the road, you're all alone here during the week."

"So?"

"Don't play dumb, Pats."

"You think someone is going to come after you and mistake me for you? Ha. Not on my best day."

"Don't make light of this, please."

"I'm not making light of it. But if everyone's in jail, then there's no one to come looking for you, now, is there?"

"Just for a few weeks, Pats. Till we find out if they make bail—"

"They won't make bail." Patsy pointed to the television again. "They just said that the judge was expected to set bail at a big number."

"I'd still be happier if you weren't here alone."

"I'll call my sister Connie and see if she can take

some time off, maybe spend a week or so, if it makes you feel better. And you'll be here, at least until Nancy arrives tomorrow. But I'm not worried, honey. Don't you be."

"I can't help it, Patsy. I love you."

Patsy squeezed Genna's hand again, holding it longer this time.

"I love you, too, Genna. You're the child of my heart."

There was more Patsy could have said, but the lump rising in her throat blocked out any other words that might have been spoken. But Genna knew. It was all there in Patsy's eyes.

"And you're my fairy godmother." Genna smiled gently and reached out to touch the older woman's face. "I couldn't bear it if something happened to you."

"Nothing will," Patsy assured her. "Now. No more glum talk. Let's go out for dinner. The Methodist church over in Parsons is having their annual fish fry tonight, and I'd hate to miss it. I'll give you fifteen minutes to get ready, no more."

Patsy absently straightened the kitchen while she waited for Genna to duck into the shower and wash off that lake water she'd spent the afternoon swimming in. Patsy wasn't about to be scared into running back to Tanner. She'd spent every summer of her life right here, at Bricker's Lake, and she'd be damned if some little biker-boy with an attitude was going to change that. Besides, Genna worried too much.

Of course, she would call Connie, as she'd promised Genna she'd do, but Patsy was more concerned about Genna's safety than she was about her own. After all, it had been Genna, not Patsy, who'd given information that led to this morning's arrests. Genna, not Patsy, who was known to be an FBI agent. Genna, not Patsy, who'd be the most likely target for retaliation.

Patsy tapped her fingers on the counter, debating, then picked up the phone. Genna was just starting to dry her hair. Plenty of time for Patsy to put a call to her nephew, Brian, who was now with the state attorney general's office and still had connections within the state police. It wouldn't hurt to let him know what was going on. And if Brian felt she—or Genna—needed someone watching out for them, he'd be sure to let them know. He'd arrange it himself. Patsy didn't know why she hadn't thought of him sooner.

Disappointed at having to leave voice mail, rather than speak with her nephew directly, Patsy still hung up the phone with a sense of satisfaction. That takes care of that, she reasoned. Nothing at all to worry about. Brian will take care of it.

Patsy wiped off the breakfast counter for the fifth time, trying to convince herself that today's developments explained that creeping sense of foreboding she'd had since the beginning of summer. It had hung over her spirits in exactly the way that the early morning fog hung over the lake, dense and nebulous. There had been absolutely nothing she could put her finger on, no moment when she'd first noticed it. It had simply been there, that shapeless precognition, that impression that something was about to strike.

And yet it had been a peaceful enough summer, a pleasant summer. The fishing had been good, if not great, and she'd had lots more company than she'd had in the past. Certainly, she'd spent more time this

summer with Genna than she'd had through all the
past winter and spring.

*Or maybe I'm just getting old.* Patsy shook her head
and wiped down the top of the stove. Again.

"Ready, Pats?" Genna emerged from the bathroom, fully dressed except for her feet. "I just need to
get my sandals," she said as she breezed through the
kitchen.

*Or maybe all the years worrying about my Gen are
finally catching up with me.*

Patsy sighed.

Bikers and drug dealers, child pornographers and
white slavers. No wonder she was feeling uneasy, all
that talk about killers and deviants last weekend.
Nancy had been fascinated, and it had all seemed
harmless enough at the time. Now, in light of the
day's developments, Patsy wished the conversation
hadn't gone on for as long as it had.

She also wished she'd made more of an effort to
talk Genna into a career in teaching when she'd had
the chance.

It almost hurt to breathe.

For the third night since the weekend, Genna awoke
in a sweat, her hands fisted in the sheet, her jaws
clenched, her heart racing. She sat up slowly, pushing
herself quietly into the headboard, bringing her knees
up to her chest, orienting herself to her surroundings.
Realizing where she was, she was grateful that she
hadn't cried out. She wouldn't want to awaken Patsy,
wouldn't want her to know that she still had the
dreams, that the old devils still taunted her.

It's just that I'm so close to the camp, she rationalized. I've had the dream here before.

But not night after night, she reminded herself. She'd never had the dream this many times in succession. And each time, she'd awakened feeling those piercing dark eyes focused on her.

It's the stress from this whole drug thing with the Frick boys. Worrying about Mrs. Frick, worrying about the entire Frick family, how they'll cope. Worrying about the boys going to prison.

Worrying about Patsy in the aftermath.

That was the big one, she acknowledged. Worrying about Patsy. Though it had eased Genna's mind to know that Patsy had called Brian. Surely he will see to it that she is watched carefully until this is over. Brian would move in here himself if he thought there might be a problem. Hell, he'd move the National Guard in if he thought he had to. She wished she'd thought of calling Brian herself.

On tiptoe, she walked through quiet rooms into the kitchen, where she poured herself a glass of water. Taking small sips, she calmed herself before unlocking the back door and stepping out onto the deck. A three-quarter moon shimmered behind the trees on the far side of the lake and clouds drifted in ragged shreds across its face. A mosquito made itself at home on her bare arm, and she slapped at it with a vengeance. Somewhere, up on the road above the lake, teenage boys revved their car engines and prepared to race that long, flat stretch of asphalt. The familiarity of it all calmed her.

*It's just that I'm so close to the camp*, she repeated. *The dreams will stop as soon as I get back to my apartment tomorrow night.*

\* \* \*

But the dreams had persisted, even after she had arrived home.

The first thing that Genna did upon entering her apartment on Friday evening was to throw open all the windows in the hopes of banishing the stale hot air that lay stagnant in the quiet rooms. She listened to the messages on her answering machine and made notes of the numbers she needed to return calls. She opened her suitcase and put away her clothes. She searched a closet for a box suitable to wrap the baby quilt in. She went into the kitchen and searched the freezer for something she could make for dinner. Finding nothing that fit her mood, she went back into the bedroom and grabbed her purse from the bed where she'd earlier dropped it.

She'd gone to the mall and picked up a cute gift bag and a card for the baby quilt. She'd checked her favorite boutique for a summer sale and picked up a few great selections for dinner in the food court. On her way home, she'd stopped to grab a movie at the video store.

And then she'd called a tow truck when the Taurus died in the parking lot outside the video store.

An hour later, she was back in her apartment, wondering if the car would be fixed in time for her to drive to Philadelphia on Sunday for Baby Carmen's christening. Wondering if perhaps the car's demise might not be a sign that she should not be mingling with the Mancini clan. That maybe she should use the convenient excuse to skip the entire thing and spare herself an entire day in John's company and in the always-gracious hospitality of his family.

Maybe this was fate's way of letting her know that

maybe it hadn't been such a good idea to have accepted Angie's invitation.

Or maybe it was just another reminder that the Taurus was in fact on its last legs.

She crossed her arms over her chest and walked to the front window, pondering her options. Maybe there was a train.

*If there's a train on Sunday morning, maybe it means I should go.*

She reached for the phone and dialed information, called the train station and jotted down the Sunday schedule. There was an early train into Philadelphia that would arrive with plenty of time to take a cab to the church. If she chose to take it.

On the other hand, maybe she should just skip it. What was the point, anyway? She wasn't even dating John anymore. And what would be more awkward, for her to show up and be with him, or to show up and *not* be with him? What was Angie thinking of anyway, inviting her? And what had she been thinking of, accepting?

Better to skip it, she reasoned. Better for everyone to avoid the situation altogether.

She could mail the gift.

But she should call Angie and make her excuses.

Genna rustled in her handbag for the old scrap of paper on which she had long ago jotted down Angie DelVecchio's phone number. She could have sworn it was in her wallet. . . .

Perhaps in her briefcase.

Or a desk drawer.

Twenty minutes later, Genna decided it would be easier to just call John and leave her regrets on his answering machine.

That decision made—for the moment—Genna found herself looking for something to keep her mind off the dreams that had plagued her all week, leaving her weak with fatigue and edgy with anticipation of . . . what?

Brian had stopped at Patsy's cottage yesterday morning and while he'd agreed that he'd be happier if Patsy went back to Tanner for a while, he'd promised to make certain that his mother—Patsy's sister Connie—moved up to the cottage for a few weeks. He also made arrangements for a private security guard to move into a cottage across the road after he contacted its absent owner and asked if he could rent the place for a few weeks. Remembering Brian as a child and happy to make a few unexpected dollars, the elderly gentleman was pleased with the arrangement.

So Patsy should be fine.

*And I'll be fine, too,* Genna assured herself as she settled in to watch the romantic comedy she'd picked up. *All I need is a good night's sleep and a return to my normal routine. Both of which I hope to get soon.*

She stopped the tape and went into the kitchen and lopped off a piece of the chocolate cake that Patsy had made the night before and forced Genna to take home with her. She poured a glass of cold milk and carried her snack back into the living room. She licked the frosting off the fork and idly studied the train schedule she'd scribbled on the back of an envelope, looking for the Sunday morning trains to Philadelphia. It still wasn't too late to change her mind.

She called John's apartment in Virginia and left a message on his answering machine asking him to call her. She wondered if he was still in Delaware, or if his case had concluded and he'd driven straight to his mother's house. Either way, he'd check his answering machine for messages.

On the other hand, she thought, it would be good to see John's family again. They were a raucous crew, but good-natured and fun to be with. The christening would be in the same church where Angela and Carmen had been married just shy of two years ago. On that occasion, John's mother had taken the opportunity to tell Genna that every major event in their family history had taken place beneath the roof of that church. Both she and John's father—rest his soul—had received all the sacraments of the Church there, baptism through marriage. John's father had been buried from that church. And all of their children had done likewise, except for Tess eloping and everyone knew how *that* had ended up, as if breaking with family tradition had alone been responsible for her unsuccessful marriage. Genna couldn't help but think that Mrs. Mancini was letting Genna know what the consequences might be for bucking the system, just in case Genna might be thinking of marrying into the family and harbored thoughts of having the wedding elsewhere.

And everyone, it seemed, had engaged in heavy speculation over Genna's involvement in John's life. She'd just about gotten used to that when John had disappeared last year.

Maybe he was out to dinner tonight.

Maybe he had a date.

She chopped off a piece of cake with a little more force than the confection deserved.

She leaned forward and slid the cake plate onto

the coffee table and picked up the remote control and began to channel surf.

Maybe he'd finally given up on her and was looking for—or found—someone else.

The thought of John falling in love with someone else rippled through her like a shot. She tried, unsuccessfully, to ignore it.

Well, maybe it would be better for him if he did. After all, we both give so much to our jobs, what do we really have left to give to each other?

Genna squirmed in her seat. Rationalization had never been her strong suit.

She knew exactly what she and John had given to each other. Knew she'd never experienced that depth of emotion with anyone else, and suspected that she might never again do so. Just as she knew she had never stopped missing him. Maybe never stopped loving him.

Genna had never known a man like John Mancini. From the first time she saw him, standing in the front of the classroom at Quantico and her heart had gone thump, there had been no one else in Genna's thoughts or in her heart or in her bed. John was tall and broad shouldered with dark hair and equally dark eyes, an irreverent sense of humor, and a twinkle in his eye. And up until that moment, Genna had scoffed at the idea of love at first sight. John was smart and his classes were among the most popular, not only for their content—psychological profiling—but for his mesmerizing personality and easy smile. She'd barely opened her mouth in his class, so afraid she'd say something totally stupid or that the words would come out in a chirp and she'd sound more like a high-school girl than a future agent for the Federal

Bureau of Investigation. Somehow Genna had managed to complete John's course with barely a conversation having passed between them.

Not that John hadn't made an attempt. At least in the beginning. But she'd given him no encouragement whatsoever and he'd backed off. At least that's what she had assumed when he'd stopped trying to catch her eye every chance he got. Once the course had been completed, however, he made up for lost time.

On the evening after the last class, John had shown up at the local bar where the future agents had gathered to celebrate the successful completion of yet another round of classes. He'd approached the table where Genna sat between Claire, her roommate, and Dennis, another recruit, and pulled a chair from a nearby table to place himself at Genna's left elbow. He'd bought a round of beers for the group, and while they were being served, leaned over and quietly asked Genna to have dinner with him the following night. When she recovered from her surprise, she'd said yes. They were together from the night of their first date until the morning of Sheldon Woods's arrest and John's breakdown in the aftermath.

There were times when Genna missed John's presence in her life so badly she'd awaken with tears running down her face, other times when the pain of his abandonment was so fierce she'd wished she'd never met him. But she'd never been able to deny that she had loved him deeply.

And maybe still did, even now.

She wished she could get past it, get on with her life, but that seemed impossible, with John popping back in and out of it every chance he got.

With a quick click of the remote, Genna turned off the TV, then carried her plate and glass into the kitchen.

*Maybe I should just go on Sunday. Maybe it won't be so bad. Maybe John and I can really learn to be friends,* she told herself.

*Yes, of course,* her little inner voice taunted her. *And maybe between now and then, you'll learn to ignore the way your heart flips over when you look at him.*

*Maybe you'll learn a way to forget what it was like to kiss him, the feel of his mouth and the strength of his hands. And what it was like to make love with him. To . . .*

"Oh, shut up," she growled aloud as she snapped off the living room light.

There were, she later acknowledged as she climbed into bed and settled onto the pillow, some things she'd never forget, despite her best efforts to do so. The thought came to her, as her eyes closed in sleep, that maybe if she allowed herself to remember, she might find a way to forgive. That maybe in forgiving, they'd find a way to start over.

And maybe that was exactly what she was afraid of.

# 8

When Genna's train pulled into Philadelphia's Thirtieth Street Station at twelve-ten on Sunday afternoon, John was there on the platform, waiting for her. Even had his height not made him the tallest man in the sparse crowd, the joy in his smile when he saw her would have caught her eye.

"Hi," he said as he leaned down to kiss the side of her face. "You're right on time."

"Yes." Genna cleared her throat, not for the first time this morning questioning the wisdom of having let him talk her into coming. "The train was running right on schedule. It was nice of you to offer to pick me up. I appreciate it."

He glanced over his shoulder, looking somewhat amused. "I'd never have heard the end of it from the family. No one arrives for an official Mancini event in a taxi. A limo, maybe, but never a taxi."

She followed his lead through the crowd that had emerged from the train and headed up the steps to the concourse, her heels clicking on the marble floor. Overhead, the painted ceiling loomed. She had never walked through this station without admiring it.

"You look wonderful, by the way," he told her. "I

like that color on you. It brings out that greenish tint to your eyes. What are they calling that shade these days?"

"Hazel."

John laughed.

"I didn't mean your eyes. I meant the color of your dress."

"Oh. Turquoise, I guess."

"Well, whatever, I like it. It looks good with that tan you're getting." John held the door open for her.

Genna looked down at her arms. She'd spent a goodly portion of her time at Patsy's out on the lake in the sun and was secretly pleased that for the first time in the past few years, she'd been outside in the sun long enough to get that bit of summer color. That John had noticed, pleased her even more.

"Of course, next to my sister Tess, we'd have to call that more of a *pale* than a *tan*," he teased.

"No fair comparing. Tess spends every weekend on a beach in New Jersey."

"Hey, you're welcome to join the family down the shore anytime. You'd love it. Can't you just picture yourself, sitting on the sand, watching the waves crash onto the beach. Ocean breezes in your hair. The smell of the salt air . . ."

"The scent of burning flesh as the summer sun fries all that exposed and oiled skin," Genna continued wryly. "The grit of sand in your face, kicked up by the tiny feet of the four-year-old on the blanket next to yours."

"You've been spoiled by so many years on that lake of yours, where there's no one to infringe upon your space. Hell, on the Jersey beaches, infringement is a sacred right and duty."

They stepped outside into the shadow of the portico where John had left the car double-parked, but even the relative cool there, shielded from the sun, could not belie the fact that they were already well into one hot summer day and that the humidity swirled around them in a near-tangible mass. Genna's legs stuck to the front seat of John's older model Mercedes sedan as she eased onto the well-heated leather. John opened the windows just long enough to let out the steamy air and turned on the air conditioning as he pulled from the parking lot, then headed across the bridge that spanned the Schuylkill River and led into the heart of the city.

"How's the new case progressing?" Genna asked, smoothing her skirt, deliberately chosen as not too short for a church yet not so unfashionably long as to appear dowdy.

"It's done," he told her without looking over at her. "We got a lead on Wednesday afternoon that turned out to be right on the money."

"Wow. That doesn't happen very often."

"Not that quickly, anyway. Cases like this can drag on for years, but sometimes all you really need is that one witness who is willing to come forward. You just don't usually get it as fast as you need it. This time, we did."

"Congratulations on the early wrap-up."

John shook his head.

"I had nothing to do with this one. The kid—that would be Kurt Fraser, old man Sharpe's son-in-law—is not quite the dolt Sharpe seems to think he is. Once he got things organized, he really did a fine job. He personally screened the leads that came in. Picked up on something that one of the callers had said. Found our man. Led us, literally, right to the front door. Fraser has good instincts and he knows his community. Sharpe can be proud of him."

"Did you tell Sharpe that?"

"Of course. Now, whether he thinks I was just telling him what I thought he might want to hear . . ." John gave a quick wave of his hand.

They were on Market Street now, the massive City Hall building straight ahead, its statue of William Penn at the very top presiding over all. A surprising number of people filled the streets of center city on this Sunday morning, a few on bicycles, a few on roller blades while the older, more professional crowd took their time strolling to their destination. Several young couples pushed strollers, some with toddlers lagging behind. Genna had always liked Philadelphia, had always felt surprisingly at home here.

"We'll be going directly to the church," John was saying as he made his way around a yellow taxi that had stopped, for no apparent reason, in the middle of the street. "Did you remember to eat anything today? It'll be a while before we'll be getting back to the house."

"Yes, I had breakfast, but I ate light. I haven't forgotten the last Mancini family event I attended. I couldn't zip my jeans for a week."

"Ah, yes. Tess's birthday party." He chuckled at the memory. "My mother went to Mass every morning for two weeks before that party, lighting candles and praying that Tess would announce her engagement to Nate."

"I don't recall that that happened."

"It didn't. But my mother is not one to give up

easily. Every family gathering is a stage set for a big announcement, as far as she's concerned. I heard her telling my Aunt Rose last night that maybe today would be the day." John grinned. "You know, in some ways, all the women in my family are exactly alike. My mother, my aunts, my grandmothers, they even sound alike. I think it's something in the water in South Philly. Even my sister Angie sounds like them."

"But not Tess."

"Tess has always been different. A divorced mother with no interest in remarrying, who owns her own business and does her own thing? Definitely out of the mold."

"Funny then, that she stayed here," Genna observed.

"She did have an apartment in Queens Village for a while, after she separated from her husband, but right around that time, our dad got sick and Tess started filling in for him at work. You know, my dad started that insurance agency almost forty years ago, built it up himself. Serviced all his clients himself. After he started his treatments for the cancer, he had less and less energy to give to the business. Tess started coming down at night after she finished work to handle the day-to-day paperwork that Dad couldn't get to. When it became apparent that the business would go under without someone at the helm full-time, Tess quit her job and started working with Dad those few hours each day that he could get himself into the office. He taught her everything he could in the time that he had left. The week before he died he had his lawyer draw up papers turning the business over to her. Tess moved herself and Jeff back to the old neighborhood. That was three years ago, and she's given no sign of leaving anytime soon."

"Well, it's not such a bad thing to walk into a business that's already established, especially since there must be such strong emotional ties there. And I'd guess that many of your dad's clients stayed on after he passed away."

"Most of them didn't have a choice." John's mouth eased into a grin.

"What do you mean?"

"My dad sold insurance to a lot of people who were . . . how do I put this delicately? . . . bad risks."

"What kind of bad risks?"

"Guys whose cars have a high probability of being shot up. Guys whose life expectancies might be considerably lower than the national average."

"Guys who . . . oh. You mean, like . . . like, *GoodFellas?*" Genna turned to face him. "I thought all that Philly mob stuff was just in the movies."

"Things have quieted down a lot over the past few years, but when my dad first started that agency back in the early sixties, there was a lot of stuff still going on."

"So people's cars would get shot up and they'd call your father and he'd have to call the insurance company and report that as an accident claim?"

"Most times they didn't bother to report that sort of 'accident.' "

"Then why did they buy the insurance in the first place?"

"Because that was the respectable thing to do. Besides, they bought auto insurance more for the liability coverage, in case they hit someone else. And because they bought their homeowners insurance and their life insurance and their business insurance from him as well."

"Their business insurance?"

"Sure. Most of his clients owned legitimate businesses."

"How did your dad get to be the insurance agent for all of these . . . clients?"

"Some came over with his father."

John slowed down as he turned the corner, then slowed even more as he scanned the line of cars parked along the street in front of the church.

"Do you see anything that even barely resembles a parking place?"

"There's a car leaving." Genna touched his arm as the black Buick emerged from a spot about five cars up the street. John pulled in as the Buick pulled out.

"This is a beautiful church," Genna said as she got out of the car and stared up at the magnificent stained glass window that arched over the wide front doors.

"My mother's family's church since the turn of the century. And surprise, surprise, there's my Aunt Josephine waiting at the top of the steps. I'll bet you five bucks that my mother sent her out here to watch for us, and the first words out of her mouth will be, 'Johnny, you're late . . .' "

John took Genna's elbow as they walked up the steps.

"Johnny, you're late," his aunt scolded as a way of greeting. "Your mother is having heart failure in there; she sent me out here to keep watch."

John winked at Genna even as he leaned down to kiss the woman who, in her early sixties and dressed in yellow and purple, reminded Genna of a large Easter egg.

"My mother started having heart failure last week, just thinking about the possibility that I might be late. Aunt Josie, you remember my friend Genna, don't you?"

"Of course, of course. The lady FBI agent that you work with." Aunt Josie's eyes narrowed. "Such a strange job for such a pretty girl . . ."

John laughed and led both women into the cool, dim interior of the church.

To one side, a gathering of familiar faces turned at his arrival.

"Thank God." John's mother Rita fanned herself with a folded sheet of paper and all but sprinted toward them. "You're giving me a seizure, Johnny. You should have been here thirty minutes ago."

"Is Father Dellisi here?" John bent to kiss his mother.

"No, but if he had been, they couldn't have started till you got here." She folded the one-page church bulletin and smacked him with it. "I told you not to be late."

"And I'm not, Mom. We have another fifteen minutes yet." A smile played at the corner of his mouth. "Now, say hello to Genna."

"Hello, Genna." Rita Mancini offered a hand bejeweled on several fingers. "Forgive my bad manners. My son is always late and always holds up the family."

"Mom, I feel compelled to point out that Angie's not even here with the baby and that the priest hasn't arrived yet."

His mother dismissed the facts with a wave of her hand.

"Technicalities. There could'a been traffic, you could'a been stuck on Broad Street for an hour. You should'a been early." Movement near the door drew her attention. "There's your sister. Thank God. We can get started."

Grabbing John's arm, she steered him toward the doorway, where Angie stood proudly, gently holding a white bundle in her arms.

"Angie, your brother's here. We can start."

"Hi, John," Angie DelVecchio smiled and blew a kiss. "And Genna! I'm glad you came. We'll talk later. Where's Mary Anne? Carmen, where's your sister? She's the godmother. There's Father Dellisi. Carmen, is your mother here? How can we have the christening without the baby's grandmother here? Is she late? Who has a cell phone to call Carmen's mother?"

"I'll just sit here and watch," an amused Genna whispered to John as she slid into a pew at the rear of the church. "You go ahead and do whatever it is the godfather is supposed to do."

John touched her shoulder. "This doesn't usually take too long."

"Whatever," she smiled. "I'm in no hurry."

The immediate families and the prospective godparents, all present and accounted for, grouped together near the baptismal font, and Genna sat back in the pew surveying the interior of the church that was rich in well-polished woods, cool marble, and colorful stained glass. The priest's voice became a distant murmur as Genna studied the main altar. Fresh flowers were everywhere. The members of the parish obviously took great pride in their church.

John's sister, Tess, arrived quietly with her son,

Jeff, a tall lanky boy who had yet to grow into his hands and feet. Genna watched as they slipped into their seats, Tess turning once and glancing over her shoulder to wink at Genna before settling in to the ceremony at hand.

The last time Genna had been in this church had marked the only other time she'd ever been in a Catholic church. As the child of a country preacher who had railed against graven images and idolatry, she'd never been permitted to set foot inside such a place. Even today, she'd chosen a seat in the far back of the church, as if hiding from watchful eyes.

She sat very still, as if waiting for a bolt of lightning to pierce the domed ceiling and strike her dead, as her father had promised one might do should she ever venture into a church such as this. When none did, she leaned forward in her pew, just a bit, to focus on the baptism.

Then, from the corner of one eye, Genna caught a small dark figure quietly shuffle up the side aisle and kneel before one of the cool, ethereal marble statues at the front of the church. The woman was tiny and wore a black kerchief over her head and a long dark coat, even though it was midday on a hot summer Sunday. After a few minutes, she rose slowly and lit two small white candles, then knelt again, unaware that from the back of the church, Genna watched, wondering what it was that the old woman prayed for.

Without warning, a whispered plea, fervent and frantic, uttered so long ago in a faraway courtroom, rang inside Genna's head, shattering her with all the fury of that bolt of lightning she had begun to think she need not fear.

*Please, God, make my momma and daddy come back for me. Please don't let them leave me here. Please, God, I'll be so good forever. I'll never be willful or stubborn again, I promise. I'll never make Momma unhappy and I'll never make Daddy mad. Please make them come back for me. Please, God. Please let me go home. I just want to go home. . . .*

The voice—her voice—had been so clear, so impassioned, that Genna sat up with a jolt and looked around, mortified by the certainty that she'd cried aloud. But no one had turned to give her side-long looks or to hush her. Her face flushed, her heart pounding wildly, she tilted her head down, biting her lip to keep from screaming out at the pain that ripped through her as the words, so long forgotten, echoed inside her head in a frenzied rush.

*Momma, please, come back. Please take me with you. Momma, please. Please don't leave me. I'll never be bad again, I promise. Please, Momma . . .*

Sweat beaded on her lip and her hands began to shake. She closed her eyes and could see it so clearly . . .

The courtroom, crowded and chaotic once the trial had ended and the verdict had been announced. Genna sat between two social workers in the first row, behind the long wooden table where the prosecuting attorney and two of his associates sat. The one sitting closest to her, a young woman with long stringy dark hair and long thin fingers, had held Genna's hand as the judge had pounded his gavel, demanding that order be restored. Turning in her seat, Genna had seen her parents rise, their silence wrapped around them like dark cloaks. She stood up and called to her mother, who, at the sound of

Genna's voice, had turned away. Her father had met Genna's gaze with turbulent eyes and an air of finality as he firmly took his wife's arm and led her to the door, and through it. Bewildered, Genna scrambled to stand on her chair and called above the crowd to her mother, who gave no sign of having heard her child's cries.

And just like that, Genna had been dismissed with the same detachment with which some might tie a dog to a fence and walk away, leaving it to its fate.

Even now, so many years later, waves of nausea spread through her, stunning her, and she fought it back, praying that it would not overcome her completely. Oblivious to what was going on around her, Genna rose on trembling legs and all but ran from the church. Once outside, she leaned against the cool stone of the building and willed her legs to hold her up, her hands from shaking, and her lip from trembling. As she took in deep gulps of hot city air, the old woman who had been kneeling at the altar emerged from the church and stood on the top step, adjusting her kerchief. Grasping the railing, she took the steps with studied caution, then tottered about halfway down and seemed about to fall. Without thinking, Genna rushed to her and took her right arm gently to steady her.

"*Grazie.*" The woman looked up at Genna without smiling.

At the foot of the steps, Genna released her, and started back to the cool shadows outside the doorway, but surprisingly strong fingers gripped her forearm. The old woman held her with one hand, while the other searched a pocket of the old coat. A near smile on her lips, she withdrew something from her pocket and pressed it into the palm of Genna's hand, nodded to Genna, then turned and walked away.

It wasn't until Genna returned to the shade that she opened her hand and looked at the offering. It was a small medal of some sort, engraved with a face that had been partially worn off over the years. She wasn't sure whose face it was, but she figured since the unexpected gift had been intended as a thank you, the person on the medal must have been important to the giver. Genna slipped her hand into her pocket, the tiny medal still between her thumb and index finger, and returned to the cool of the church.

The ceremony had ended, and the guests had just begun to gather in the aisles. Walking toward Genna with a purposeful stride and a worried look on his face, John took her hands in his and asked, "Are you all right?"

"I'm fine." Genna tried to smile convincingly.

Declining to comment, John took her arm and walked with her to the back of the church, where they greeted his cousins and neighbors and old family friends and waited their turn to congratulate the beaming parents and admire the now sleeping child. It wasn't until they were back in the Mercedes that John said, "So, are you going to tell me why you ran out of the church?"

"I just needed a little air."

"It's ninety-two muggy degrees outside and the air is so dense with truck exhaust from I-95, you can slice it."

"I just needed some space."

"Who was crowding you?"

"Memories," she replied softly, unaware that in her pocket, her fingers fiddled with the medal.

Without further comment, John drove slowly through narrow streets where cars parked on either side made the passage narrower still. Through neighborhoods where sagging awnings sheltered the front windows of the red or yellow brick row houses from the afternoon sun, where old men sat in clusters on folding chairs and old women swept imagined dust from their front steps.

John had parked the car without her realizing it, and it was another long minute before Genna was aware that he was staring at her.

"What?" she asked, clearing her throat.

He took her hands into his and pressed back the fingers that shielded the medal in her palm.

"Where did you get this?" he asked, lifting it to get a better look.

"While I was outside, there was an elderly woman. She'd been in the church. I had watched her praying up near the altar."

"Mrs. Romanelli." John told her.

"She seemed to be having trouble getting down the steps outside the church, so I gave her a hand. She gave me the medal."

John turned the medal over once or twice.

"Do you know whose face that is, on the medal?" Genna asked.

"No. But someone in there," he motioned toward the house with his head, "will probably know." He handed the medal back to her. "If you're all right, we'll go in. And maybe later you'll feel up to telling me what spooked you back there."

*The child that I once was spooked me,* she ached to tell him. Over the years she'd shared bits and pieces, but never the whole picture. The thought that she might be able to share it all with someone, with him, both frightened and comforted her.

The small row home of Angela and Carmen DelVecchio was marked from the outside by an enormous bouquet of blue and silver balloons that were tied to the wrought iron railing that separated their front steps from those of their next-door neighbor. Already the crowd had begun to spill from the living room onto the open porch in the front and down the steps onto the sidewalk. Rooms never intended to hold so many seemed to visibly expand as more and more guests joined the festivities. The men had shed their jackets and ties, the women their high heels, and all at some point converged into the dining room where an impressive buffet was already being assembled. The rooms were at once noisy with chatter and laughter and music from the CD player one of Carmen's brothers had placed on an open window ledge.

"Are you hungry?" John asked over the chorus of Jim Croce's "Bad, Bad Leroy Brown."

"A little," Genna admitted. "Do you see either of your sisters? I was hoping to get a chance to chat with both of them."

"Tess and Angie are just going up the stairs with the guest of honor. Poor little guy must be pretty tuckered out right now. But I guarantee that my mother and my aunts are all in the kitchen." John took her hand, saying, "Here, let me help you get through this crowd."

John led her toward the back of the house, through an endless sea of cousins and aunts and uncles who conversed with him in both English and Italian. Small children squeezed around the adults, some balancing plastic plates holding all manner of delicacies. It took ten minutes to make their way into the kitchen, where Rita Mancini was arguing with her sister Anna about which fabric shop on Fourth Street had the best inventory.

"Goldberg's. No question." John's mother's firm pronouncement, met with a nodding of heads and a chorus of affirmatives, appeared to be accepted as the last word on the subject. Turning toward the doorway, she called over the heads of her nieces, "Genna, did you have something to eat? John, did you feed her yet? She's a rail. Here, Genna . . ."

Reaching behind her, Rita grabbed a dark blue plastic plate and in one motion, served lasagne from a pan on the stove, sausage and peppers from a still-bubbling pot, and scooped salad from a wooden bowl that had been set on the counter.

"Johnny, you serve yourself . . . no, not from the dining room, from my pots, here in the kitchen." She handed Genna the plate, piled now with food and said in a low voice, "Mary Giordani made the lasagne that's in the dining room. Two words, Genna. *Canned tomatoes.* You want mine. I make my own, everything from scratch. It's much better. Johnny, grab a fork for Genna—she doesn't need a knife to cut my sausage. And put down that salt shaker. I put salt in. Now, go on outside and eat."

She held the back door open and Genna followed John down the back steps.

"Mary Giordani uses canned tomatoes in her sauce?" She whispered out of the side of her mouth.

"It's the talk of the neighborhood." John shook his head solemnly.

Genna nibbled on a slice of sausage seasoned with

fennel. "Oh, God, this is good. Someday, when I have time to really learn how to cook, I'm going to learn how to make tomato sauce just like this."

"Shhhhh." John held a finger up to his lips. "Do not let my mother hear you say that. She'll be at your apartment first thing in the morning, bunches of basil and parsley in one hand and a basket of plum tomatoes under her arm."

"There are worse ways to start your day," Genna told him as she sampled the lasagne.

Neighbors wandered in and out of the back gate, and soon the small yard had filled up as tightly as the inside of the house had, with nearly as many guests.

"Can I get you something else?" John asked, noticing that Genna had stopped eating.

"Are you kidding? I started out with a full plate. Do you see anything left?" She grinned. "I was just thinking that I should walk back to North Jersey, and I should probably start now."

"That might be a bit of a hike." John took her plate and stacked it atop his own. "But as soon as I get rid of these plates, we can go for a walk around the neighborhood. That way, you'll be ready for dessert. No one leaves a Mancini party without a slice of my Aunt Concetta's Italian rum cake."

Genna groaned and leaned back against the cyclone fence that surrounded the small backyard.

Laughing, John headed up the back steps and opened the door, just as his sister Tess stepped out. They chatted quietly for a moment before John disappeared into the kitchen.

"Genna, it's good to see you." Tess joined her at the back of the yard. "I was hoping we'd have a few minutes to talk. It's been a long time."

"Yes." Genna cleared her throat. "How's Nate?"

"He's fine. He's out on the front porch talking antique cars with Uncle Vinnie."

Tess sliced a meatball in half with her fork, choosing to toy with it rather than eat it.

"I was so glad to hear that you were coming today. I owe you a big apology," Tess said at last.

"Apology? Why?" Genna raised an eyebrow in surprise.

"For blaming you for the problems that John had last year," Tess said bluntly. "I'm so sorry, Genna. There was just so much I didn't understand. You know, you and John and people like you have to deal with things that the rest of us thankfully never have to see, don't even really have to know about. I don't know how you can face such terrible things and still function in the real world with the rest of us. It's a wonder you aren't all crazy."

Genna crossed her arms over her chest, still not certain where Tess was headed.

"It was so hard for John to put everything back together after all that murderer put him through last year. None of us could reach him," Tess said without looking at Genna. "None of us had ever seen him like that. It's just not in John's nature to shut out the people he loves, the people who love him. It must have been so terrible for you."

"Then he told you . . ."

"Pretty much everything." Tess nodded. "I only wish he had told me sooner. Unfortunately, he wasn't speaking to anyone. Certainly not to me, and apparently, he wasn't speaking to you, either. I just wish I'd known."

"I didn't hear from him for months," Genna said,

feeling oddly comforted to learn that she had not been singled out by John to be kept in the dark.

"If I'd been aware of what he was putting you through . . . well, as it was, we all thought that you . . ." She paused, as if searching for words. "Well, that you'd broken up with him and that was the reason he was so . . . distant. It was the only explanation we could come up with. The only reason why we could imagine him wanting to be alone for all that time."

"Alone?" Genna frowned. "For some reason, I thought that you and Jeff were down there with him."

Tess shook her head.

"John stayed in our house, but he wouldn't let any of us stay with him. He just told us that he had things he needed to think about and that he needed to be alone. It wasn't until later that I found out that he was so afraid of self-destructing, so afraid of having anyone near him when he did. So afraid of tainting anyone who he loved with what he was afraid he was becoming. Please understand that in our experience, only a fatal disease or a broken heart makes a person behave like that. And since John swore he wasn't sick—"

"You thought I'd broken off our relationship," Genna said softly.

"I found out all too late that it was much more complicated than that. And so I apologize. For not being there to help you through it, as a friend. And for thinking the worst of you. I hope someday I'll find a way to make it up to you. In the meantime, it's important to me to know that you forgive me."

"Of course." Warmed by the offer of friendship, Genna held out her hand, and Tess took it and gave it a squeeze. "You know, there were times last year when I did think to call you. But since I'd thought that John had dumped me, I just figured it really wouldn't be fair to put you in the middle—"

"Well, I'm glad to see that you're back together—" Tess said, then seeing the look on Genna's face, stopped and said, "Oh. I'm sorry. I guess I shouldn't assume. I don't mean to pry."

"It's okay. I'm here because Angie invited me as a friend. I'm with John because he offered to pick me up at the train station after my car died . . ." Genna's voice trailed away.

"Don't feel that you have to offer an explanation. It's none of my business. But you know how our family is. Everyone looks out for everyone else. And we all love John." Tess hesitated only momentarily before adding, "And he loves you so much . . ."

"Hey, Gen," John appeared in the open doorway. "You ready for that walk now?"

Genna turned to look at the man who stood on the top step. In spite of her best efforts to deny it, a rush of longing washed over her.

"Sure. A walk sounds great," she nodded.

"Tess, you up for a walk around the market?" he asked.

"I was there yesterday," she told him dryly. "When everything was open."

Tess turned to Genna and hugged her with her free hand. "I'm glad you're back in John's life, in whatever capacity. It's been a long time since I've seen him so relaxed. So happy."

"Thank you, Tess." Genna returned the hug.

"We're not leaving the party, Gen, we're only going for a ten-minute walk," John told her.

"One second," Genna called back to him. Searching her pocket for the medal, she held it out to Tess and asked, "Would you know who this is?"

"On the medal?" Tess turned it over in her hand. "I think it's Saint Anthony. My grandmother had one like this. She called him the Saint of Lost and Found. She even had this prayer she used to say. 'Dear Saint Anthony, please come around. Something's lost and can't be found.' Something like that. Where'd you get it?"

"A woman gave it to me outside of church earlier," Genna told her.

"Maybe she thought you looked like someone who was searching for something," Tess told her as she returned the medal. "I hope you find it, whatever it is."

"Thank you," Genna whispered and tucked the object back into her pocket.

John held out his hand to Genna as she climbed the steps, telling her, "We'll go out through the front. But stay close. It's a jungle in there . . ."

"Where are we going?" Genna asked as they emerged into the crowd that milled about on the front porch.

"I thought we'd walk down to the Italian Market," he told her, lacing her fingers with his own and setting an easy pace as they crossed onto the shaded side of the quiet street. "Just a few blocks. It's a Philadelphia landmark. Oldest outdoor market in the country and it's hardly changed over the past one hundred years. You haven't been to Philly till you've been to Ninth Street."

The fabled street was nearly deserted, late on this Sunday afternoon. John paused and pointed to a storefront midway down on the opposite side and said, "My grandfather Mancini worked there after he arrived here from Italy in 1932. One of his cousins owned it, imported olive oil and cheeses from the Old Country. When the cousin, who had never married, died, he left it all to my grandfather, who promptly moved his wife and young children into the apartment up there on the second floor. I used to stop here every day on my way home from school. My grandmother made a pizzelle that could knock your socks off. She kept a tin filled with them on top of her refrigerator."

They continued past a few more storefronts.

"My cousin Millie owns the spice shop across the street." John led Genna across the street and stood in front, peering through the window. "My great-aunt Magda works here a couple of mornings each week. She has a table there in the back corner."

"Magda? Your mother's Aunt Magdalena? Isn't she eighty-something?"

"Yes." John said, looking amused.

"What does she do?"

John seemed to consider the question before answering.

"She's sort of a consultant."

"What kind of consultant?" Genna glanced at the sign above the doorway.

"I guess you can best describe her as a curse consultant." John rubbed his chin thoughtfully. "Aunt Magda has the gift. For a fee, she can put a curse on someone. For another fee, she can remove it."

"You mean, you can go to her and pay her to place a curse on someone? And then, if you are the person who's been cursed, you can pay her to take the curse away?"

"That sums it up quite neatly."

"That's silly. No one believes that."

"You ever notice the jewelry the woman wears? The gold bracelets? The diamond rings?"

"It's hard not to."

"People *believe.*" John said meaningfully, and they both laughed.

"What costs more, having a curse put on or having one taken off?" Genna asked.

"Having it removed, definitely."

"Did you ever have her curse someone for you?"

"Nah. When I was growing up down here, the most effective curse one guy could put on another was with his fists. Same for having a curse taken away. You did for yourself."

They walked along in silence for a few minutes before John asked, "Are you going to tell me what spooked you today?"

Genna debated for a long moment before replying, "I was watching the old woman pray, wondering what she was praying for. And then, the next thing I knew, I heard my own voice, inside my head, praying just like I had in the courtroom and I was back there—"

"You mean, you had a flashback, to Brother Michael's trial?"

"Yes." She nodded. "It was like watching a movie. I remember how the courtroom exploded when the jury foreman read the verdict. Guilty on all counts. It was chaos. I turned in my seat to look for my parents, but I couldn't see them and I stood on the chair. They were about ten rows back. I called to them to let them know I was ready to leave. I knew they had been angry with me for testifying against Brother Michael, but I couldn't lie, you know? I'd put my hand on the Bible and said I would say only what was really true. After the verdict, I thought that it was *over*, all of it, that it wouldn't matter anymore, that it was done and we'd just go home . . ." Genna bit her bottom lip in the hopes of making it stop trembling.

"What did you pray for that day?"

She looked up at him, the sorrow of the child reflected in the eyes of the woman.

"I prayed that they would come back for me."

# 9

"You really didn't have to drive me all the way back home, John," Genna said for maybe the sixth time since they'd crossed the Walt Whitman Bridge. "I really did have a train ticket."

"I'm scheduled to fly out of Newark Airport tonight anyway," he repeated, hoping that this time she wouldn't ask why he hadn't flown out of Philly, the airport being less than twenty minutes from his mother's home. He had an answer all prepared, but he wasn't sure how credible it would sound. The truth being that he just wasn't ready to say good-bye to her yet. Hadn't looked at her enough today. Wasn't ready to relinquish the sense of completion that filled him when she was with him.

"So what's so pressing that you have to take the red eye to DC tonight to make a nine o'clock meeting tomorrow morning?" Genna asked.

The Mercedes had just glided past Exit Eight on the New Jersey Turnpike. The lights that lined the sides of the highway flashed across the front seat like a strobe, casting John's face alternately in shadow and in light that highlighted the angle of his jaw. Genna watched from the passenger seat, trying to ignore the fact that no one had ever affected her, on every level of her being, the way he did, and wondered just what, if anything, she was going to do about it.

Perhaps some rethinking was in order here.

"It's a really odd case," he was saying. "I've never seen anything quite like it. We've gotten reports of missing women from six different law enforcement agencies in different parts of the country over the past three weeks."

"Runaways?" she asked as she searched for the lever that would move the seat into the recline position and allow her to settle in comfortably.

"No. Definitely not runaways," he shook his head. "My gut's saying abductions."

"Based on what?" Now he had her full attention. Kidnappings were her specialty.

"Just a feeling that I have."

"Who are the victims?"

"All of the women are in their late twenties, early thirties. All but one married, all happily, by all accounts. Several of them have small children, almost all have solid jobs and full, active lives."

"Ransom notes?"

"None."

"No phone calls? No bodies?"

"*Nada.*"

"But you think they're related somehow." It wasn't a question.

"They feel exactly the same."

"But women go missing every day. They walk out on bad marriages, they leave for another man . . ." she rationalized.

"None of these women fit that pattern. There is

nothing in any of their backgrounds that suggests that any one of them would simply walk away from their homes, from their husbands or their young children."

"A rash of abductions, though, in different parts of the country . . ." She couldn't help but play devil's advocate. "What do they have in common?"

"I'd say they've all been very carefully planned. In each case, no one saw anything and no one reported anything unusual. Each time, the woman has gone out on a routine errand or to work, and has not been seen again. It's as if she's been plucked from the face of the earth."

"By someone who has apparently been watching them closely enough to know their routine," she said softly. "You think it's the same someone?"

"I do."

"Have any of these abductions been witnessed?"

"No. The closest we came was in the Omaha case, where a neighbor reported having seen an unfamiliar dark blue van in the neighborhood, but she didn't know the make, model, or year. Know how many dark blue vans of indeterminable age and make there are in Omaha?"

"What's the connection between the victims?"

"This is the most intriguing thing. On the surface, there doesn't seem to be a connection," he told her, "other than the fact that they were all within a certain age range and the fact that they all disappeared so mysteriously. Rex Egan has been brought in also, and he is, as you know, very good at finding common threads. He hasn't been able to find a thing. We've had agents in each of the cities—Wilmington, North Carolina. Kansas City, Omaha, Chicago. Wheeling,

West Virginia and Mystic, Connecticut—talking with the locals. Haven't found a thing that would connect these women."

"To jump around geographically like that could imply that he or they or whomever is following some sort of blueprint. Otherwise, it wouldn't make any sense."

"I agree, but I can't for the life of me figure out what the reason might be. We're going to go over all the info that's been gathered from the field in the morning. Egan has sent it all through the computer, but so far, there just hasn't been anything obvious enough that the bells have gone off."

"I guess they've already investigated their backgrounds to see if the women went to the same school. Or belonged to the same sorority or the same church?"

"That's exactly the type of information they were looking for. It would have been great if something had popped up, but so far, nothing has."

"Funny I haven't heard a thing about this."

"And with any luck, you won't for a while," John told her. "They are keeping a lid on this big time, hoping the press doesn't pick up on it just yet and muddy the waters. So far, we've no motive, no suspects, absolutely nothing but six victims and six terrified families."

"When was it determined that they could be related?"

"About four days ago."

"Then there really hasn't been enough time to sort through it all and see if there is a connection."

"There could have been something that was simply overlooked as inconsequential at the time of the initial investigation. Or maybe there was something that didn't make it into the reports because it just didn't seem relevant. But the pattern—the preparation—seems so similar. . . ."

"For example?" she asked.

"The first victim was last seen leaving her office building at five o'clock on a Thursday afternoon and heading for the subway. She had to have been taken from some point between the building and her home, but no one saw a thing." John slowed the car as he approached the toll plaza. "The second victim left her office on a small university campus and set out to walk home the same way she always did. Out the back door of the building in which she worked and across the parking lot. Stopped and chatted with a coworker. Now, at one end of the parking lot, there are steps leading down to a walk across a sort of commons, and through a lightly wooded area that separates a residential area from the university. This woman lived in that development on the other side of the woods. She never made it home."

"And the coworker?"

"Saw nothing or no one out of the ordinary."

"And there are no bodies and no phone calls and no ransom notes. And no reason to believe that any of these women would have left home on their own accord."

"That's right."

"So we have someone watching his victims to learn their patterns. I wonder how long he watches before he feels he knows them well enough to move in. Assuming that it's a he. Would have to be someone strong, I would think, to overpower these women. And then he takes them someplace.

Where?" Genna closed her eyes. "What does he want from them? What does he do to them? Is he killing them? If so, how is he disposing of the bodies? Or is he keeping them, like trophies . . ."

"Those are some of the questions we'll be addressing tomorrow morning," John said as he made a right turn into the parking lot behind Genna's apartment building.

"It's an interesting case," she said as she brought her seat back to an upright position.

"They're all interesting cases." John turned off the engine and reached for her in the dark. "None, however, more interesting than you."

Without protest, she moved into his arms and felt them close around her, and in a heartbeat, his mouth was on hers, needy and eager. She kissed him back, surprised to find herself doing so, surprised that she was every bit as needy. He traced the inside of her mouth with his tongue, and every muscle in her body turned to water. For Genna, it had always been like this with John. She had tried for months to forget what it felt like to kiss John Mancini, to have his lips and his hands on her, but she never had. All it had taken to bring it all back was for his mouth to find hers.

He kissed her slowly now, surely and deliberately, then left the hot well of her mouth to trace the outline of her jaw with his lips, so so slowly that she reached for his face and brought his mouth back to hers.

Finally, he drew back, and resting her head on his chest, stroked her hair with his hand. There were so many things he wanted to tell her, so much to say. He struggled with the words. Where to start? What would be too much? What would be not enough?

"I should be back by the end of the week," he said

at length. "Maybe we could take a few days and try to sort things out."

"John . . ."

"I've missed you, Gen. I've missed you every day and every night. Can you honestly say you haven't missed me, even a little?"

"I have missed you." She admitted as much to herself as to him. "Maybe more than a little."

"That's a start." He nuzzled the side of her neck, then glanced at the clock on the dashboard. Time was running short. He'd have less than forty minutes to make it to Newark Airport. He sighed and said, "I'll walk you inside. Do you have the goody bag my mother gave you?"

"You mean the four pounds of lasagne, the freezer bags stuffed with meatballs and sausage, the box of cookies and the wedge of rum cake that could feed forty people? I could cater lunch at my office for the next week with all the food she sent me home with. Not that I'd think of sharing, mind you."

"She thinks you're too skinny." John grinned. "She and my grandmother and the aunts were discussing that very thing in the kitchen."

"Ha! So that's what they were talking about in Italian when we came in to say good-bye."

Genna reached for the door handle and he stopped her. Turning her back to face him, he said, "I think that you need to know that I've never stopped loving you, Gen. I never will. Whatever else happened, I never stopped loving you."

He put one finger to her lips when it appeared she was about to speak. "It's something you need to think about."

He reached across her and opened her car door for

her, then said, "I remember, one time when I was in my teens, I saw a movie where the guy says to the girl, 'You're my heart. You're the other half of me.' I never forgot the line because at the time I thought it was a really stupid and incredibly wimpy thing for a guy to say. How could anyone be the other half of someone else?"

He raised her fingertips to his mouth and told her, "Now I know."

Later, Genna lay alone in the dark, her eyes closed, the tiny medal slipped under her pillow, and wondered if perhaps Saint Anthony could help her and John find what they'd lost.

She fell asleep trying to remember the words to John's grandmother's special prayer.

Three days later, Genna stood at her desk and stretched to get the kinks out. She'd been at her desk almost solidly since one that afternoon, and it was now almost eight-thirty. The only break she'd taken had been around five-thirty, when the secretary she shared with three other agents poked her head into Genna's cubicle to announce that she was leaving and that John Mancini was holding on line three.

"How's it going?" Genna had asked.

"Maddening. We can't find one single thing to connect these women." He paused, then said, "And there's been another one."

"Another missing woman? Where? When?"

"This morning, in Kentucky. A twenty-nine year old woman named Shelly Fielding dropped her four-year-old son off at nursery school and never came back to pick him up. Her car was in her driveway, so we know she made it home."

"Witnesses?"

"None. Her house backed up to a creek."

"What's on the other side of the creek?"

"A parking lot."

"This guy is good."

"Well, I'm hoping that sooner or later, we'll be better. But not knowing exactly where the other women disappeared from makes it impossible to locate evidence that we could compare."

"So much easier to investigate the crime scene when you know where it is," she sympathized.

"Damn," John muttered, "I'm running late. I'm going to have to be leaving for the airport in about twenty minutes."

"You're going to Kentucky?"

"Assuming I make the plane."

"Stay safe," she told him, meaning it.

As she tucked one last file into her briefcase, the rumble from her stomach reminded her that she hadn't eaten since noon, and then it had only been a container of blueberry yogurt and a banana. The sun had already dipped low behind the trees and was probably but a few more minutes from disappearing completely. Genna grabbed her handbag from the back of her chair where she'd hung it at eight that morning, and snapping off the light, walked into the outer office to find that she was the last person in the office.

She'd known that, she reminded herself. Decker had poked in at seven-thirty to let her know he was leaving and to remind her about a conference call they'd be making at eight the next morning.

Her heels clicked sharply on the highly polished wood floor of the hallway. At the front desk, she signed out and gave an absent smile to the night guard. Strolling into the late July dusk, she paused to adjust her bag onto her shoulder, then walked to her car that she'd parked near the middle of the lot's second row. The sun had already settled in for the night, casting a placid lavender over the early evening sky.

Setting the briefcase on the ground, she searched her pockets for the keys to her old Taurus, wondering for the third time in as many weeks if it would start. The new starter she'd just had installed aside, perhaps the time had come to trade it in, maybe for something smaller, sleeker, and faster. She wondered if the mundane errands of her life—grocery shopping, the dry cleaner, the mall—would seem less like drudgery if she got to zip there in a great little car. Maybe with the top down . . .

Something . . . *something* . . . caused the hair on the back of her head to stand up.

Glancing around, Genna scanned the parking lot. There was nothing. No one.

And yet she felt unseen eyes following her.

Spooked, Genna felt her bag for her gun even as she slid behind the wheel and locked the doors, hoping that this would not be one of those times when the Taurus decided to play with her and refuse to start.

It was not. The engine turned over, and she backed out of her parking place a little more quickly than she normally did. Forcing herself to drive at a snail's crawl, she toured the parking lot, taking care to look between cars and behind them. There was nothing moving. There was not even enough of a breeze to stir the bamboo that grew along the grassy stretch between the road and the building.

Genna forced a sigh of relief and headed home, feeling silly.

*It's only the power of suggestion. All that talk about women being stalked and abducted. I should know better,* she berated herself.

And yet unable to shake the feeling she'd had in the parking lot, she locked her bathroom door later that night when she went in to take her shower, and tucked her Glock into the deep pocket of her bathrobe.

Before going to bed, Genna checked the dead bolts on her front door and the door to the balcony. Pulled the drapes shut on the living room windows, and turned off all the lights. She stood in the bedroom, peering out the window to the woods beyond. There was nothing.

She had similar experiences the following day, and was beginning to wonder if perhaps she wasn't the victim of her own overactive imagination. She hadn't mentioned it to anyone until John called later that night.

"Any movement on your case?" she had asked.

"Just that a second round of questioning two of the victims' coworkers revealed that just days before they disappeared they'd felt like they were being watched."

"*What?*" Genna sat bolt upright.

"Followed or watched. The type of thing where you're walking down the steps and feel like someone's behind you, or that someone's watching you, but when you turn around, there's no one there."

Genna's breath caught in her throat.

"Gen? You there?" John asked.

"Yes."

"Something wrong?"

"You just described the exact sensation I've had for the past two days."

"What do you mean?"

"I mean, that for the past two days, I've been feeling like someone's watching me. It's unsettling, to say the least."

"Did you talk to Decker?"

"Haven't had a chance. But to be honest, I've tried to dismiss it. I'm still not sure that it isn't my imagination playing with me."

"I don't like it," he stated bluntly. Genna could almost hear the frown in his voice. "Talk to Decker and make sure that someone watches you leave at night. Maybe get someone to follow you home."

"That may be a bit drastic. I think I've been thinking too much about your case and not enough about my own."

"Maybe you shouldn't stay alone this weekend. Any chance I could talk you into going up to the lake and staying with Patsy?"

"I'll think about it," Genna told him.

"Stay in touch, Gen," he said, suddenly sounding weary, "and be careful, okay? Watch out for yourself."

"I will."

Genna stopped at Decker's office on the way out, but his lights were off and she recalled that he'd left for a meeting in New York right after lunch. She asked the night guard to watch her walk to her car, though she felt foolish doing it. Even so, she felt a prick along her spine as she crossed the parking lot.

Silliness, she tried to tell herself. Who would want to follow me?

No one, she answered her own question as she got

into her car and turned on the lights. Except maybe a couple of hundred people—and their immediate families, friends and loved ones—that she'd helped to convict over the years. Or the porn king whose neck she was currently breathing down. Or the bikers who'd led the Frick boys astray . . .

The first thing Genna did upon arriving home was to pick up the phone and call Patsy.

There was no answer.

Genna ate standing up in the kitchen because she was suddenly too antsy to sit still. She tried to watch television but couldn't concentrate. She dialed Patsy's number twice, unsuccessfully, before getting ready for bed. Sitting on the edge of the bed, she splashed clear polish on her nails and called Patsy's cabin again.

"Hi, sweetie!" Patsy said before Genna could so much as say hi.

"How did you know it was me?"

"Caller ID. Connie and I went to the grand opening of the new shopping center in Wick's Corner yesterday and I broke down and bought an answering machine. It has caller ID on it."

"Why didn't the answering machine pick up when I called?"

"Oh, I haven't figured out what message I want to leave yet. But I do feel very high tech."

Genna laughed.

"How's Aunt Connie?"

"She's already turned in for the night. Said she wants to get an early start in the morning."

"Where's she going?"

"Oh, she'll be going back home. She—"

"Does Brian know you're going to be alone?"

"Sweetie, I won't be alone. Nancy will be here most likely by noon tomorrow. And Brian still has that security guard coming and going at the Miller house just across the road . . . you remember old Mr. Miller? Had that blind collie dog that you used to take for walks? Remember that dog, honey?"

"Yes, I do. Pats . . ."

"Connie and I drove each other crazy this week trying to remember the name of that collie."

"It was Buster." Genna sighed.

"Buster. Of course. I knew you'd remember. Wait till I tell Connie."

Genna could hear a pot rattling in the background, and the sound of running water. Patsy was making herself a cup of tea.

"Now, let me tell you about this new shopping center that just opened up . . ." Patsy launched into a store by store description.

Genna leaned back against her pillow, and turned off the light, nearly falling asleep as Patsy chattered on and on about the new shops and what she bought.

It wasn't until later, after they'd hung up and sleep was just about to claim Genna for the night, that it occurred to her that she never did ask Pats why Connie was leaving, or when she'd be coming back.

# 10

He leaned closer to the computer screen to read the address and smiled with satisfaction. Yes, he thought perhaps this would be the right one.

Shaking his head slightly, he marveled at the wonders of all this new technology. Why, with just the slightest bit of information, one could locate just about anyone one wanted to find. So far, he was batting 1.000 in his search. There was no one he hadn't been able to locate.

And here, he'd thought the task would be so difficult. As it was, he'd be finished in no time. No time at all.

He looked out the window and pondered his future. What might he do, after all these loose threads had been tied off?

He giggled at his choice of words. How clever he was, even when he wasn't trying to be.

His fingers glided swiftly over the keyboard. He loved the computer, loved the power of the information it gave him. Loved knowing it was taking him just where he'd been dreaming he'd go, all these years. He loved the speed of it, the ease.

"Bingo," he whispered. "There you are, Mary

Alice Tunney, nee Bancroft. I think it's time for a little reunion."

He laughed again, out loud this time, there being no one to hear him.

Oh, and a grand reunion, indeed, these past few weeks had turned out to be. How perfect it all was. In every detail.

There had been no one—*no one*—who'd suspected, though there had been a tense moment or two along the way. But no one had known him. Naturally, he'd left nothing—absolutely nothing—to chance. The phone calls he'd made using a disguised voice, of course, were made weeks in advance of his coming to call, long enough before his visits that no one would ever make a connection between the call and what came later. And he'd learned long ago how best to become anonymous in any situation. Dress like the locals. Blend in.

*When in Rome . . .*

He giggled again. Mary Alice Tunney hung her hat in a house on Egan's Lane in Rome, New York.

It was just all too perfect.

It was all, obviously, God's will.

With the click of the mouse, he brought up the file containing the entire list. He typed the address and phone number next to the name of the unsuspecting Mary Alice, then scanned the list to see how many more he needed to find.

The list was amazingly complete.

Of course, the last name on the list already had the address filled in, there'd been no problem finding her.

Oh, no. He'd known right where to look, even after all these years.

But he had to wait, though there were times when the waiting nearly drove him crazy. He had to take them in order. That was very important. After all, if you're going to do something, for heaven's sake, do it right. Isn't that what Mother always said?

Sticking to the plan was important. It was the right way to do it.

It was just so hard sometimes to look at her and to let the game play out.

Five more.

There were only five more before he could finally have her.

He'd simply have to wait.

And remind himself once again of the pleasures to be found in saving the best for last.

# 11

*He is one ugly son of a gun,* Genna thought as she flipped through the stack of surveillance pictures of Allen LeVane that she'd received via e-mail and printed out just minutes earlier. Just looking at his face made her skin crawl. The closely set dark eyes. The fleshy nose. The thin lips stretched over too-perfect-to-be-real teeth in a genial smile, a chilling touch considering the loathsome business in which he was engaged.

He'd been picked up at ten that morning as he left a town house in a fairly upscale neighborhood outside of Trenton. He'd arrived with a child of perhaps six or seven. He'd left alone. Only the patience and tenacity of the local police combined with the skills and the resources of the Bureau had prevented the child from being subjected to the unspeakable. Genna had stood across the street and watched as three adults were led out of the house in handcuffs, the child in the arms of an officer specially trained to work with juvenile victims. It had taken five police officers all day to load up the photographic equipment and the boxes of video tapes from the three floors of the house.

Good riddance to bad rubbish, Patsy would have said. Yet Genna knew that unless the judge set the bail at an unusually high number, by the next morning LeVane would be back at home in his luxurious penthouse in one of New York's finest hotels.

But he was on the hot seat now, and the little boy who'd been lured from his mother's side in a mall in Cleveland the previous week had been returned to his anxious family, not, unfortunately, before LeVane had taken a personal interest in the child. It would take years for the boy to recover from less than two weeks in LeVane's company.

Genna closed out the computer file after sending the photos via e-mail to the Cleveland police. She'd had enough for one day. Hell, she'd had enough for the month. She snapped off her computer and stood up to stretch. A few hours at the gym would be greatly appreciated right about now. She gathered her belongings and left the office, cautious, as she'd become over the past week, and more attentive to her surroundings. But her "spidey sense," as John called it, was quiet as she walked to her car, and she drove directly to the gym she'd joined months before but rarely had time to attend. Tonight she'd run a few miles on the track. Ride a stationary bicycle. Maybe lift a few weights. Then finish up with a swim followed by a hot shower. She'd been working like a demon on this case, and she was due a little downtime.

As she methodically followed the indoor course around the elliptical-shaped track, Genna wondered what she'd be working on this time next week. There was no break between one case and the next. There was only the next squeaky wheel. There were a number of them already sitting on her desk. Between now and Monday morning, any one of them could blow up.

Best to get in a good workout while one could.

The disappearance of the wife of the president of a West Virginia college dominated the news on the television that hung over the juice bar where Genna stopped on her way out of the gym.

Hadn't she seen a phone message that John called Decker that morning from Beckley, West Virginia?

Damn.

It would only be a matter of time before someone started to add up the number of missing women. How many had there been? Eight? Nine? How much longer did the Bureau think they could keep this under wraps? And of course, the certain notoriety would only make John's job that much more complicated.

The exercise and the swim should have relaxed her, but it seemed it would take more than a workout to relieve the tension of the past few days. Maybe, she told herself wryly, she should try aromatherapy. Or yoga. She'd had a roommate back at the Academy who swore that yoga was the only thing that kept her inner self balanced.

Genna suspected that it would take more than yoga to balance out her inner self right now, and was thinking about signing up for an aerobics class as she made the turn into the parking lot at her apartment building. *Someone must be having a party,* she thought, as up one row and down the next, she searched for an available spot.

*Must be one hell of a party.* She frowned as she spotted a vacant place near the end of the third row.

Music drifted from one of the end apartments and floated over the parking lot.

*Wonder how long before someone calls the manager,* she mused as the volume was turned up on a particularly spirited song dating from the seventies.

*Don't let 'em tell you disco's dead.* Genna smiled to herself, walking in time to the music across the dimly lit lot toward her building.

She was almost to the walkway when the prickling sensation began to creep along her spine.

Whether a snap of a twig or the rustling of last fall's forgotten leaves, something drew her attention to the darkened area off to her left. Slipping her hand into her bag, she sought the reassuring cold metal of the Glock. She slowed her pace as her fingers closed around the handle, and her eyes searched the shadows for a shape that shouldn't be there.

And there, close up to the side of the building, she found it. Someone crouched between the shrubs.

Dropping her gym bag to the ground, Genna drew the gun and called, "Come out with your hands up. Now."

For a long moment, the figure remained motionless.

"You've got to five." Genna took several steps toward the landscaped area. "One . . . two . . ."

The figure stood slowly, and arms raised, began to pick its way through the shrubbery.

"Keep your arms up. Out here, into the light where I can see you." Genna motioned with the Glock in her right hand.

"I didn't expect you to welcome me with open arms, but really, Genna, pulling a gun might be a wee bit extreme. Even under the circumstances."

Genna froze, every muscle in her body tensing. Even after all the years that had passed, she knew the voice that drifted out of the darkness.

The figure moved into the light, arms no longer held overhead, but out in front as if to show they were empty.

"Crystal?" Genna's eyes grew wide with disbelief. "*Chrissie?*"

"Hello, Genevieve."

The young woman stopped almost ten feet away from where Genna stood, and while Genna's eyes and ears told her that Crystal Jean Snow, her older sister, was the woman who stood before her, her brain was having a hard time believing it.

"A 'hello, Crystal' might be a nice start." The woman's arms dropped to her sides.

"Chrissie..." Genna appeared stunned. "How...?"

"How did I find you?" She laughed softly. "You have to be kidding. You're famous. Genna Snow, intrepid FBI agent. I saw you on television last year, there was a news special about that magazine heiress who was being stalked up in New England by some crazy who had killed her sister. It took me a while to get up the courage to come looking for you, but it wasn't hard to find you, once I made up my mind."

Genna wished there was a place to sit down. Her knees had begun to knock together.

"I can't believe this. After all this time . . ."

"Eighteen years, Genna."

"I should invite you in." Genna said as if to herself.

"It's okay if you don't want to. I wouldn't blame you. I only wanted to see you, Gen. I just wanted to see if you were as pretty in person as you were on television. I wanted to see just how tall you'd grown over the years—just look at how much taller than me!—and what color brown your hair had finally settled on." The woman dug her hands into the pockets of her light jacket. "And I wanted you to know that they're gone."

"Gone?" It didn't occur to Genna to ask who. She knew. "When?"

"About three months ago."

"How did it happen?" Genna asked.

"Car accident. They were run off the road, so the witness says. But who knows? All we know for sure is that the car went down an embankment and flipped over once or twice."

"Why'd you wait so long to let me know?"

"For one thing, I wasn't sure you'd care. And for another, I've been . . . *away* . . . for a while." Her voice dropped.

"Away?"

"I had a breakdown a few years ago—that's what they called it, a breakdown. It's taken me a good while to get back on my feet, though God knows I still feel a little broken. Anyway, after I got out, I was in a group home, a halfway house of sorts. Then I found out about them and went back for a time." The touch of the old South crept steadily back into Crystal's speech. "I was cleaning out the house . . . they spent the last few years in that little house out back of Grandma Petersen's, remember? That little three-room place that sat out by the apple orchard?"

"I remember," Genna whispered.

"Well, I was cleaning it out—hoping I'd find something of enough value to sell, to be honest with you. It's been a while since I've worked." A nervous hand found its way to her neck. "Anyway, I was pulling stuff out of there and Dwight—you remember cousin Dwight—he was bringing his truck out to take the furniture down to the secondhand store. He was helping me take the mattress off the bed. I found these, tucked under the mattress." She took something from her pocket, and held them out to Genna. "You can probably put the gun away. I swear I'm not armed."

Surprised to realize she was still holding the Glock, Genna opened the top flap of her bag and, after making sure the safety was on, slipped the gun back in.

"What is it?"

"Take a look."

Genna reached for the envelope, and taking it, walked toward the light that illuminated the very front of the building. One by one, she studied the photographs.

Pictures of Genna and her mother.

Pictures of Genna and Crystal. Of Genna and Crystal and their mother.

Pictures from Easter Sundays, the Snow girls dressed in their best dresses, their hair in tight braids. Chasing the ducks on the pond behind Grandma's house. Sitting with her mother on the porch swing at Aunt Mary Claire's house that summer she and Crystal had gotten poison ivy so badly they could barely open their eyes. Their mother had sung to them, read to them. Rocked them in her arms when the itching had gotten so bad they couldn't sleep.

Genna couldn't bear the memories. They hurt and

confused her and took her breath away. She'd never been able to reconcile the mother who had been so caring with the woman who had walked away from her without a backward glance.

It was too much to deal with at one time. Genna put the photos back into the envelope with shaking hands.

"I could offer you some coffee or something," she said weakly.

"Only if you want to, Genna. I'd understand if you didn't."

"I think I want to." Genna walked back to where she'd dropped her gym bag and fished the keys out of the pocket. "I think there's still some iced tea left from yesterday, if you'd rather have that . . ."

"Whatever is the least trouble for you, Gen. I know you weren't expecting me, and I don't want to put you out."

Crystal followed her up the steps and into the lobby, across the dark green and navy plaid carpet to the elevator. Genna hit the *up* button and stood aside when the doors opened and Crystal stepped in. She hesitated slightly, prompting Crystal to quip, "It's okay, Genna. I won't hurt you. I promise. Besides, you're still the one who has the gun, remember?"

"I'm sorry," Genna told her. "I'm just so stunned. I never thought I'd see you again. I don't know how to react."

She reached out and hit the button for the fourth floor. They rode in silence until the doors slid open and Genna stepped out.

"It's the door at the end." Genna said.

They walked the length of the hallway, and it wasn't until they had stepped into the cool of Genna's apartment and she'd turned on the lights that Genna took a good look at her sister for the first time in eighteen years.

Crystal was shorter than Genna, and her dark hair bore traces of a strand of gray here and there. The lines in her face made her seem older than her thirty years, but all in all, Genna thought she'd probably have recognized her anywhere.

"Are you glad to see me?" Crystal asked.

"I don't know."

"Well, there's something that hasn't changed over the years. You're still painfully honest." Crystal tried to smile. "Honest to the core, our Genna. At whatever the cost."

Genna turned from her and walked into the kitchen and snapped on the light. "Would you like something cold to drink? I have soda, iced tea . . ."

"Whatever. Anything is fine. Ice water is fine." Crystal stood in the doorway. "I think that since I'm here we should get it out of the way early, Genna."

"I don't . . ."

". . . want to talk about it? Any shrink will tell you that's a very unhealthy attitude. There's something that's been standing between us for more than half our lives, Gen. I need to get it off my chest."

"If you're talking about the fact that I didn't hear from you all that time, about the fact that you never made any attempt to contact me all these years . . ." Genna's control was forced, the words shooting out of her mouth beyond her control.

"I was a kid too, remember." Crystal's hands shook as she accepted the glass of iced tea that Genna held out to her. "I didn't have the means or the opportunity to come and find you. And I didn't have the guts, either."

Genna reached past Crystal to grab her own glass from the counter.

"I never had your sense of right, your sense of justice. I never had your strength, Gen." Crystal sipped at her drink. "I wish I had. But I never did, even when I wanted to so badly. Even when I knew I should, knew how important it was for me to . . ."

Genna stepped past her and turned off the light, gesturing for Crystal to follow her into the living room. At that moment, she wasn't sure of just how much she wanted to hear, and she moved like a cornered animal, wary and watchful and suspicious.

Crystal stood in the doorway, watching as Genna hit the message button on her answering machine. There were four messages. Crystal stood patiently waiting for them to end.

Genna sat back on the sofa and put her feet up on the coffee table.

"You can sit down," she said, without her characteristic grace.

"This isn't easy for me." Crystal perched on the edge of the dark green hassock and studied her sister's face.

"Well, it was your idea, Chrissie. You must have thought it out."

"I thought out what I'd say to you. I couldn't think out how I'd feel."

"How do you feel?"

"Worse than I expected to. Maybe this wasn't such a good idea, after all. Maybe I should leave."

Genna withdrew the envelope holding the photos and tossed them on the table. Several escaped and fell onto the floor. "You can take those with you."

"I just thought you'd like to see . . ."

"See what? The best moments of my early child-hood? The smiling, loving face of my mother, who let that wacko, crazy, abusive man who fathered us, control her life, control her emotions, turn her against her own flesh and blood? That loving mother who abandoned her own child for the crime of telling the truth?" Genna grabbed one of the toss pillows that graced the corners of the sofa, and pressed it to her stomach as if to press away the pain that shot through her. "Do you really think I need photographs to remind me of what I lost, Crystal?"

"I'm sorry, Genna. I thought maybe you'd want them." Crystal stood up. "I thought maybe it would be good for both of us. I was very wrong."

Crystal picked up the pictures that had slipped onto the floor and tucked them back into her pocket, her face red with embarrassment.

"This was clearly a disaster," Crystal said as she picked up her bag with trembling fingers. "Just another example of how bad my judgment is. I just wish . . ."

Genna looked up at her with eyes darkened with emotions she'd spent years denying, but did not trust herself to speak.

"Well, I just wish you could have been just a little happy to see me." Crystal crossed the carpet toward the door.

"I'd have been a lot happier if you hadn't waited all these years to show up," Genna said curtly.

"That door swings both ways, Gen. Your resources are much more sophisticated than mine." For the first time since she'd arrived, a touch of anger rose in Crystal's voice and she stopped at the door, her hand on the doorknob. "How much of an effort did you make to find me?"

"I was the chick who was pushed out of the nest, remember?"

"I wasn't the one who was doing the pushing. And for the record, you just don't know how lucky you were." Crystal opened the door and let herself out, closing it quietly behind her.

For several long minutes, Genna sat on the sofa, trying to make sense out of what had just happened.

The last person in the world that she'd expected to show up on her doorstep, just had. The pain that initially had been dulled by shock began to spread through her chest, and she clutched the pillow tighter.

"Crystal. Crystal was here." Genna said the words aloud as if to convince herself that it had really happened.

She rose and carefully replaced the pillow on the sofa, then bent to pick up one of the fallen photos, missed, apparently, when Crystal gathered up the others. Genna, her brown hair in tight, neat pigtails, dressed in a hand-me-down dress of ugly green and gray plaid that someone in the church had given them, posing for her school picture. Crystal had worn it the year before. Genna studied the face of the child she had been. This must have been in second or third grade, she recalled. The side of her jaw bore the faintest tinge of purple, where her father's fist had taken its toll for some infraction the weekend before. Genna searched her memory for what her transgression had been that time . . .

It occurred to Genna then that her mother must have taken great pains to hide the photographs that

Crystal had brought with her. Her father had forbidden them to have their pictures taken.

*Looking at yourself promotes vanity.*

Even in the silence of her apartment, so far from that small house in Kentucky where they'd lived the year the class photo had been taken, Genna could hear his voice. The backwoods church had been without a preacher and when her father had been offered the position, he'd jumped at it. For a while, Genna and Crystal had been almost happy. The house backed up to a woods where they could sneak off and play on those afternoons when their father had been busy counseling members of his congregation. And the busier he was, the less time he had to worry about the many ways in which they were leading themselves into the arms of the devil.

There in the woods, Genna's imagination could run wild, unrestricted by constant quotes of Scripture that reminded her that this world was not her home. The two girls would gather sticks and lay the outline of the grand mansion they pretended to live in. A mansion that had lots of windows that were always open to let in those gentle breezes that would push out the stifling air of their father's dominance that hung over them all.

It was there, in Kentucky, where her father had first come to the attention of Clarence Homer, a wealthy man from the small town of Lindenwood in the southwesternmost point of Pennsylvania, just over the West Virginia border. Homer had been visiting the Blue Grass members of his family when he'd first heard Reverend Snow's fiery rhetoric, and his own fundamentalist leanings had been incited. Returning to Lindenwood, which at the time had a church but no resident preacher, he convinced his brother elders that Reverend Snow was just the man they needed to bring around the wayward in their community. Reverend Snow had a definite gift for reminding transgressors of what awaited them in the hereafter.

The move to Pennsylvania had proven, for a while, to be their salvation. Back in Kentucky, school had been an endless series of religious lectures presented by dour teachers in a small clapboard building over which their father ultimately presided, for the school was run by the church. Mr. Homer, however, had felt Preacher Snow's time far too valuable to be spent in the classroom, and had effectively removed him from the educational process. The children in Lindenwood attended the local public schools, as had Mr. and Mrs. Homer and each of their six children, and *they'd* all turned out just fine.

And so Genna and Crystal had their first exposure to public education, with books to read that told stories that weren't just from the Bible. It had taken the Snow girls a good two weeks to adjust to the changes—none of which, they agreed, they should discuss with their parents—but before the first month had passed, they'd become acclimated to their new school. Happier than they'd ever been, they knew instinctively to keep that joy under wraps at home, lest their father find a way to take it from them in the guise of saving their souls. It seemed the more they enjoyed their life and their new surroundings, the wider their horizons became, the more their father's vision narrowed.

And then came that first summer, and Mr. Homer's pronouncement that the Snow girls should spend the months of July and August at the camp that was owned by his family and run by his brother, Michael, in the woods upstate. Before their father could object, Genna and Crystal had been shuttled off to the Way of the Shepherd where, besides endless hours memorizing yet more Scripture—much of which they interpreted during arts and crafts—they learned to swim and play soccer and baseball. Rarely, if ever, had Genna seen Brother Michael, who roamed the camp like a wayward monk, his white robes flowing around his ankles, its loosely fashioned hood folded around his head and hiding his face. Genna's only contact with him had been at morning and evening prayers, and so he had not been a factor in her life. Not until that second summer, anyway . . . and even then, she'd never seen his face.

Only his dark eyes.

Genna went to the window that overlooked the parking lot, searching for Crystal in the dim light, but there was no movement to be seen. Perhaps she had parked along the street side. She pushed aside the living room drapes and peered out toward the main road. There, halfway to the corner, a woman walked slowly in the shadow of the street lamps.

*She must have taken the bus,* Genna realized. *She came all this way on a bus, just to see me. Just to find me.*

*I can't even begin to count the number of times I've thought of her. Wondered where she was. How she was. What her life was like.*

Genna turned from the window, the sight of the lonely woman growing smaller and smaller in the night more than she could bear.

*We shouldn't have had to wonder about such things.*

*We should have been able to grow up together*, Genna thought as her anger began to swell inside her. Anger at her parents. At the fate that had separated her from that one member of her family who hadn't voluntarily walked away from her.

*Then why such anger toward her*, Genna asked herself. *Because they cared enough about her to keep her?*

*But Chrissie couldn't have prevented what happened*, her conscience reminded her. *It's not fair to be angry with her now because of what others did so long ago.*

*And regardless of anything else that may have happened, we are still sisters. Strangers, yes, but in the end, we are still sisters. . . .*

Grabbing her keys, Genna unlocked the front door and ran down the hallway. Too impatient to wait for the elevator, she raced down the steps and through the lobby. Her long-legged stride carried her quickly to the corner, where she found Crystal seated on the bench, blowing her nose and trying to pretend she wasn't crying.

"I'm not used to all the car fumes," she said without looking at Genna. "I've lived in the country all my life, you know."

Genna sat down on the hard concrete arm of the bench.

"Where was the halfway house?" Genna asked as she struggled to catch her breath.

"Outside of Hazard."

"Kentucky?" Genna's eyebrows raised in the dark.

"Yes."

"Near Gramma's house?"

"Actually, closer to Uncle Neil and Aunt Hazel's."

"Hazel from Hazard," Genna whispered, and in spite of themselves, both women smiled. "Remember when we were little, we always thought that sounded so funny?"

"And a sweeter woman God never did put on this earth." Crystal nodded. "She never did come around to Momma after they . . . after you . . ."

"After the trial?"

"Yes. When she realized what had happened, she lit into Daddy like no one ever had." Crystal shook her head, remembering. "Momma turned white as a ghost, I swear it. She just stood there like a statue. Shocked, I guess, that anyone—least of all her own sister—could stand up to him that way, or talk to him like that. No one had ever defied him, you know." Her voice dropped and she added, "Except, of course, for you."

"And I guess Aunt Hazel fared about as well as I did as a result," Genna said wryly.

"Momma never spoke to her again." Crystal searched her pockets for another tissue.

"Seems she paid an awfully big price for loving him."

"Oh, I don't know that I'd call that love." Crystal shook her head. "Daddy had an iron grip on her will, Genna. Which he did, as you will recall, enforce with his fists, if nothing else was handy. Suffice it to say that Momma had a lot of problems that really started to surface more and more after you . . . after you were gone."

"Like what?"

"Like being afraid to go outside. She wouldn't go anywhere after a time, not even to church, no matter how much he yelled at her. Like crying all the time, though I always figured that was because she missed you. I never thought she wanted to leave you, Gen. I just think she wasn't strong enough to face him down. None of us were. We were always so afraid in that house, remember?"

"Yes," Genna said softly. "I remember."

They sat in silence, watching the headlights of the Greyhound approach.

"There's probably another bus in the morning." Genna took her hand. "Maybe there're still things we need to say to one another."

The bus pulled up to the curb and stopped.

"Maybe you won't want to hear it all," Crystal told her. "And after you do, you might wish you hadn't."

"Maybe I should hear it anyway."

The bus door opened with a *whoosh*. The driver sat staring impatiently at the two women on the bench.

Finally, he called out to them.

"Hey! You two gettin' on, or are you just passing time?"

"Just passing time," Genna told him.

He slammed the door shut and the bus pulled away in a huff of exhaust.

"I thought they were supposed to have some emission thing on them to keep all that crap out of the air."

"They are." Genna stood, pulling Crystal with her. "Come on. Let's go on back to my apartment and we'll start all over."

Crystal shifted her bag onto her shoulder as she rose to her feet.

"Do I have to stand in the bushes again?" Crystal asked as she fell in step with her sister. "Because if I do, I hope you have a lot of calamine lotion. The mosquitoes are really fierce around here."

"Jerseys," Genna nodded. "We grow 'em big and mean."

They were halfway back to the apartment building when Genna asked, "Did you ever miss me, Chrissie?"

"Oh, my God, Genna, every day. I can't even begin to tell you what it was like." Crystal's voice caught in her throat.

"Tell me. Tell me what it was like after I left."

"You sure you want to know?"

"Yes."

"We weren't allowed to mention your name. It was like you had never been. Like I was the only child and there had never been anyone else."

"Jesus," Genna growled, her hands unconsciously closing into fists.

"And Mr. Homer told Daddy right off—right after the trial started—that he thought perhaps it might be better if we left, though I never was sure if it was because he was angry with you for blowing the whistle on his brother, or angry with himself because he knew what his brother was and he hadn't blown the whistle himself. In any event, the people in the church were really divided over the whole thing. Some people believed you and the other girls were telling the truth, and some others—like Daddy— thought that you were lying and that the social workers and the child psychologists had talked the other girls into lying, too."

"Why would he think that I would make up something like that? I've never understood it. I know that he did, because he tried to beat it out of me. I just never understood why."

"I think it was to hold onto his church. He'd never

in his life had a church like that one, and he'd never had a congregation near that big. And you telling on Brother Michael, well, that just brought shame to the entire community. Remember that Michael was the only brother of Daddy's benefactor. Because of you, Daddy lost it all. His church, his congregation, Mr. Homer's favor . . . everything. Going back to Kentucky, goin' from one country church to another again was a big blow to him, Genna. He'd thought he'd never have to see that preachin' circuit again, and there he was, right back on it."

"He'd rather have seen his daughters raped than lose his church?"

"Yes. Apparently, he would. But it wasn't just the church. It was the position. The power. The feeling of importance."

"And after it was done, he pushed me out of his mind as if I'd never been born."

"I'm sorry. But you asked. And it hurt me, too. You were gone out of my life in a blink, but I wasn't ever allowed to grieve."

"Is that what put you in therapy?"

"Part of it. And partly it was because it just got too hard to be perfect. And because of what I . . ." her voice trailed away.

They stopped in front of the apartment building.

"It isn't too late, Genna. We can stop now, and I can go back to the bus stop. Maybe it would be better if I did."

"Better for who?"

"For both of us. Maybe in the long run, there are things you'd be better off not knowing."

"Not at this stage of the game." Genna put an arm around Crystal's shoulder. "After all these years, I don't think I can let you walk away just yet. So, come on, we'll go upstairs and . . ."

"You may not want me in your house after you hear what else I have to say." Crystal took a tentative step backward.

"Then say it now and get it over with," Genna told her.

"When they came back without you, at first, I didn't think a whole lot of it. I mean, you'd stayed up north there for a while before the trial . . ."

"The district attorney had to get a court order to keep me there. He was afraid that if they took me out of the county, that they wouldn't bring me back for the trial and the case would fall apart." Genna swallowed hard and asked, "What did they tell you? What reason did they give you, when they came back without me?"

"A few days after they got back, Daddy announced, 'Genevieve is lost to the devil. We will not speak of her again.' And we never did." Crystal crossed her arms over her chest as if to hug herself. "But then I started to wonder, if I did something that really angered him, wouldn't they send me away, too? There'd never been much margin for error in that house. But if I was very good, then they'd keep me. So I tried and tried to be good as I could be. But as time went on, it became harder and harder. I could never falter, never make a mistake. I was so afraid of him. I was afraid all the time. But I never talked back. I never showed anger. I always did everything I was told to do. I was the good daughter. The one good enough to keep."

Crystal paused, then added, "And then one day I started adding up what it had cost me, and I realized that it hadn't been anywhere near worth it. I'd paid far too much for the privilege. And ending it seemed to be the only way out."

"You tried to kill yourself?"

"Jumped off a bridge. Most people don't survive a jump in excess of one hundred and thirty-five feet into the water, did you know that? The death rate is just about one hundred percent from that height." Crystal nodded her head slowly. "Well, I survived it. Some damned do-gooder fishing off the damned bridge radioed for help on his cell phone, then jumped into the water after me."

"Chrissie, why didn't you come sooner?" Genna whispered. "Why did you wait so long to look for me?"

"Because after all that happened, I couldn't face you. I just felt so damned guilty."

"You were twelve years old that summer. What do you think you could have done that would have made a difference?"

"I could have told the truth." Crystal swallowed the lump in her throat and forced herself to say the words. "I could have told them."

"Told them . . . ?" Genna's eyes narrowed suspiciously.

"About Brother Michael. I knew that you were telling the truth, Gen. I knew exactly what he had done to the others, what he'd tried to do to you." Crystal raised her face to look directly into her sister's eyes. "I knew, because for all that summer and the summer before, he'd been doin' it to me."

# 12

Genna sat down on the front steps to the apartment building, her legs having gone so weak she'd been afraid they'd collapse beneath her. Unable to speak, she sat numbly for a long time.

Finally, Crystal said, "And that's why I didn't come to find you sooner."

"*My God, Chris, why didn't you tell them?*" The words ripped from Genna's throat.

"I just didn't have the nerve. I almost did, back there at the very beginning, but I was so ashamed. I'd let it go on so long without telling. I had no idea he'd been doing it to so many other girls. How many came forward in the end, fourteen? Fifteen? I'd had no idea. I thought I was the only one, and I felt so dirty and helpless. . . ." She shook her head. "And then, later on, I felt like such a worthless coward. Here I'd endured being raped over and over again, never telling, just letting it happen because I was too afraid of him. Of what he'd do if I told. Of what people would think if they knew. And there was my little sister, who not only fought back and got away from him, but who brought it all to an end. I wasn't as brave as you, Gen. I never was as strong. And when

Daddy started saying how the devil had gotten into you and made you tell those lies and 'Praise the blessed Lord, we have one child whose tongue is unsullied by lies. . . .' "

Crystal blew out the breath she'd been holding for too long. "I wanted to tell the truth, Gen, but I just couldn't bring myself to do it. I tried so many times, but I could never make the words come out."

"You let me go through all that alone. You watched them turn against me. Shove me out of their lives . . ."

"Yes," Crystal said simply, tears flowing down her face.

"Do you know how many times over the years I called home, just to hear Mom's voice? To hear yours?"

"You always called late in the afternoon, after school but before supper."

Genna stared at her sister.

"I used to pick up the extension and listen to your voice. I'd stay on the line even after Momma hung up."

"How could she do that, Chris? How could she know that I was there, calling for her, and *still hang up on me?*"

"By that time, she'd pretty much gone around the bend herself, I guess. I wasn't old enough to figure it all out, and back then I didn't know anything about mental illness. But I do know that was just about the time when she started to fall apart for real. She never could stand up to him, and eventually it broke her. Piece by piece. Just like it broke me."

Genna buried her face in her hands and began to cry.

"I'm sorry." Crystal sat down next to her on the concrete step, wanting to put an arm around her, but afraid that her offer of comfort would be rejected, sat with her arms folded over her chest, hugging herself as if to ward off a chill. "I'm so sorry. I shouldn't have come. I should have just let it be. I'm so sorry. I should have known it was a bad idea. I told the psychiatrist that it was a stupid idea, but she thought it would bring closure of sorts. I never stopped to think of what it might do to you. I guess when it comes to you, I never do the right thing. It's terrible, isn't it? I've always loved you so much, and yet I never seem to do the right thing where you are concerned."

"You did the right thing." Genna shook her head. "This time, you did the right thing."

"How can you say that? Look at yourself, you're obviously distressed—"

"It's okay."

"*Okay?*" Crystal's jaw dropped. "You're doubled over in pain, you're sobbing and shaking, but it's *okay?* What's *okay* about that?"

"I've been doubled over in pain for eighteen years." Genna wiped her wet face on the sleeve of her shirt. "You didn't bring the pain with you, Chris. It's been inside me all this time. But telling me was the right thing. I only wish I'd known sooner. It might have helped."

"How would it have helped to know that I'd sold you out?" Crystal asked bitterly.

"Is that how you see this, as you selling me out?"

"Don't you?"

"I don't think so. I mean, it's going to take a while to sort it all out." Genna ran a hand through her hair. "Very honestly, on the one hand, I want to toss your butt back up to the bus stop for letting me go through all that alone back then. I have never been able to express to anyone what that was like for me then."

Genna rose and began to pace.

"You want to talk about feeling worthless? How much more worthless can a child feel than to know that she's been abandoned? That she's done something so unacceptable that she's not worthy of her parents' love. And to know that the unacceptable thing that she's done, was simply to tell the truth about something so terrible . . ." Genna swallowed hard. "If a child can't go to its parents when something so terrible has happened . . ."

Crystal buried her face in her hands, unable to bear her sister's anguish, even now.

"But those were choices that they made, not you, Crystal." Genna fought to compose herself, to remain rational. "You were a victim, too. Their victim and his—Brother Michael's—same as I was."

"If I'd spoken up that first time, none of the rest of it would have happened," Crystal reminded her.

"What makes you think that they'd have treated you any differently than they'd treated me?" Genna asked. "Why would you think for one minute that they'd have been kinder to you? That they wouldn't have turned their backs on you just as they did to me?"

"All that time I let it go on, all those other girls who were hurt by him . . . I could have stopped it. I could have prevented what happened to them."

"Any one of them could have stopped it, Chrissie. None of them did."

"You did," Crystal said softly. "You stopped it."

"And paid a terrible price for it."

"Would you change it? If you had a chance to go back and do it again, would you have told, knowing what was going to happen?"

"Yes," Genna said without hesitation. "Yes, I'd tell."

"I've asked myself that same question over and over a thousand times. What would I do if I could just live that first summer all over again," Crystal told her, her eyes wide and glistening in the overhead light. "I'd like to think that I'd be the one to tell. And then everything that happened to you, to you and to all those others, never would have."

Genna sat down next to her sister and put her arm around her shoulder and drew her close enough that their heads were touching.

"It's so hard when you're little like that and something terrible happens to you and you don't know what to do." Crystal sniffed back another round of tears. "You don't understand that sometimes you only get one chance to do the right thing."

"It's never too late to tell the truth. You did the right thing by telling me now," Genna assured her. "You're helping me to understand things that have haunted me all these years."

"Like what?"

"Like maybe she didn't leave me because she didn't love me."

"Knowing that she was terrified of him makes it better? How could knowing that her fear of him was greater than her love for you make it easier?"

"Maybe her fear of him, the abuse she suffered at his hands, did things to her that we'll never know about. Maybe in time, knowing that will help me to understand her a little. I've never been able to recon-

cile the fact that when we were little, she was such a
good mother."

"Remember how she used to take us to Gramma's
every summer? Back then I used to think it was so
that she could see her family," Crystal said. "Now I
think she just wanted to get us away from him. So
that someday we could look back and remember a
time when we weren't afraid."

"Remember how Gramma used to sneak us pep-
permints because Daddy didn't let us have sweets?"
Genna's mouth twisted, half sob, half smile. "Little
mints wrapped in cellophane."

"And she always wore lily of the valley cologne.
Every spring when I see those little white flowers, I
think of Gramma. If she'd been alive when all that
was going on . . . oh! I almost forgot." Crystal dug
into her jeans pocket. "I brought you this."

She took Genna's hand and placed something in
the palm. Genna turned to the light that hung over
the door to the lobby and exclaimed, "Oh! Gramma's
pansy pin! I always loved this! Where did you find
it?"

"Under the mattress with the photographs."

Genna closed her eyes and remembered the last time
she'd seen the dark blue and yellow enameled pin. Her
grandmother had worn it on her seventieth birthday.
Six months later the beloved woman had died.

And later that summer, Genna had fallen from
grace.

Everything about that year seemed to blur now in
Genna's mind as she sat holding the enameled pansy.
So many images swirled around inside her head that
she thought she'd explode.

"Don't you ever wonder how things might have

been different, if Gramma hadn't died?" Genna whispered.

Crystal nodded. "For a long time after she passed on, I used to think that I dreamed she came back for us. Then I realized that when I saw her, I wasn't asleep, but I wasn't afraid when she came in my room. She would just sit on the end of my bed and rub my foot, remember how she used to do that? I always thought she'd be there in the morning, and we'd take Momma and we'd come find you and we'd all live in Gramma's house together. All of us except for Daddy. Gramma wouldn't have had him under her roof."

"Do you think she knew? About how he used to beat us?"

"She knew when she came to see me, after she passed on." Crystal dug her fists into her jeans pockets and said, "I know that sounds crazy—maybe that's what made them first start thinking I was crazy, that I saw Gramma. Talked to her. But she didn't know when she was alive. She just thought he was a mean son of a bitch. She didn't know just how mean until after she passed on."

Crystal paused, then asked, "Did you ever see her, Genna? Did she ever come to see you, after she passed on?"

"No," Genna shook her head. "She never did."

"I wonder why not."

"Maybe she thought you needed her more than I did."

Genna patted Crystal on the knee. "It's late. Come on back upstairs with me."

"I can't believe you'd invite me back into your home."

"There's so much more we need to say to each other. So much to learn about each other." Genna stood and tugged on her sister's hand. "Now's as good a time as any to start."

Crystal hesitated. "Do you think we can ever learn to be friends again, Gen, like we were when we were little?"

"Let's work on learning to be sisters first"—Genna pulled Crystal to her feet—"then we'll worry about being friends."

Genna lay in her bed, trying to make sense of the fact that her sister had shown up out of the blue and told her a story that brought back every feeling of worthlessness and fear she'd fought for her entire adult life. And yet for reasons she could not explain, she felt as if an enormous weight had been lifted from her heart.

Was it easier to accept her mother was psychologically unbalanced, or that she simply hadn't loved her enough to fight for her? Was the fact that her father had been a dictatorial, abusive tyrant reason enough to forgive her mother for abandoning Genna when he had insisted that she walk out of that courtroom and not look back? Or had the forced abandonment of her child caused the mental breakdown of a woman whose will had already been beaten down? Genna would probably never know for sure.

She did know, however, that right at that moment, she felt no remorse at learning of her parents' death. They had died to her so many years ago, as she had to them, that she had mourned them all she could. In truth, the hollow place that had once held her love for her parents was still there, still hollow. How to reconcile that empty place with what she now knew of her mother's sad life? Was she to be pitied? Despised?

Genna blew out a steady stream of air and tucked her arms behind her head. And what of Crystal, who now slept on Genna's sofa, having refused the offer of the apartment's only bed. What of her part in Genna's disgrace? What would have happened had she come forward with her own truth all those years ago? Would it have made a difference? Or would her mother have left both of her daughters behind?

She'd have done whatever he'd demanded she do, Genna knew.

In her mind's eye she could see him, small round eyes, humorless and cold. A long thin face and nose, long slightly peaked ears, and straight black hair.

It occurred to her now, all these years later, that she had never seen her father smile. It was the last thought she'd had before falling asleep, and it was still in her head when she awoke the next morning.

"Did you ever see him smile?" Genna asked, as she watched Crystal putter in the kitchen, insisting that Genna let her make scrambled eggs and toast for both of them.

"No." Crystal shook her head, knowing exactly who *he* was. "I never did. What made you think of that?"

"I guess I was wondering what she saw in him. Or why she stayed with him."

"She stayed with him out of fear, but before that? I don't know why she married him. I've wondered about that for years. Had she loved him once? Had he ever loved her?" Crystal broke the first of four eggs into a yellow-ware bowl and added, "But I can tell you this, Genna. If that's what love does to you, I'm not having any of it."

"That wasn't love. That was two weak people sucking the best out of each other, leaving only the worst behind. That isn't love," Genna repeated as she plugged in the coffeemaker.

"Have you ever been married?" Crystal asked.

"No. Have you?"

"Nope. Ever come close?"

Genna thought of her relationship with John, of how close they had been, how much they had shared.

"Maybe. Once," she replied before turning her back to take the toast from the toaster.

"Didn't work out?"

"Not that time."

"What happened to him?"

"Nothing happened to him. I still see him, if that's what you mean. Though not so much lately."

"Why not?"

"We have . . . issues," Genna said succinctly.

"So resolve them."

"Maybe we will."

"If you care about him enough you will."

"Sometimes caring isn't enough."

"What else is there?"

Genna sighed. "For starters, there's the fact that he disappeared from my life for almost six months."

"Must have been one hell of an argument."

"There was no argument. Everything was fine. Perfect. At least, I had thought it was. Then, bingo. Gone. Out of my life. No good-bye, not a word that he was leaving. He was just gone."

"Wow. That's terrible. What happened, he met someone else?"

"No, no, nothing like that. John had this case—he's an agent, too—it was really intense. He got a little too caught up with what was going on."

"What do you mean?"

"A few years ago, there was a series of child abductions and murders in Baltimore. The press had nicknamed the killer the Pied Piper, because he lured kids away and they were never seen again."

"I remember that. It was on all the news." Crystal visibly shivered. *"Terrible* stuff."

"Well, that was John's case. He was just another agent on the investigation until Woods—that was the Piper's name, Sheldon Woods—took a fancy to him. He started calling John just to talk. Then he called him with details of what he'd done. Soon, he was calling to tell him what he was *going* to do. As if to taunt John to catch him. Finally, he was calling John while he was in the process of . . . doing what he was doing."

"I saw the story on CNN. I remember thinking at the time that having to listen to . . . well, all that agent had been forced to listen to, would have been hell on earth."

"It broke John. After Woods was arrested and the paperwork was done, John just took off by himself."

"Well, who could blame him?"

"No, you don't understand. He just left without telling anyone he was going."

"Including you?"

Genna nodded.

"That's pretty terrible, I can see. You must have been frantic, not knowing where he was."

"I did find out where he was. He was at his sister's place at the Jersey shore. Trying to put his head back together, he said."

"Did it work?"

"Did what work?"

"Was he able to get his head back together okay?"

"Yes. Eventually."

"Good for him. I sure wish it had been that easy for me. Not that I think it was *easy*, mind you. Facing those broken parts of yourself, well, it never is. I'm sure you were very proud of him."

"I was proud of him. His capture of Woods saved the lives of unknown numbers of children."

"I meant because he faced his problems straight on and worked them out."

"I would have been happier if he'd let me know what was going on. If he'd let me help."

"What exactly do you think you could have done?"

"Well, I could have been there for him . . ." Genna frowned.

"To do what, watch him suffer?" Crystal shook her head. "Sometimes you just have to leave it be and let a body go through what they have to go through. Alone. Trust me, when you're wrestling with what's inside you, the last thing you want is for someone else to be looking on."

"Whose side are you on?"

"It's not a matter of sides. It's just the way it is. There are just some places you have to go to on your own, like it or not. Your John was apparently in one of those places." Crystal lifted her chin slightly. "Just be glad he came back. I'm sure he had a really rough time of it."

"He did, but so did I."

"It wasn't about you," Crystal said softly.

Genna said nothing, busy fighting back her indignation over the fact that Crystal seemed only to see John's side in the matter.

"So what's he doing now? Is he back at work?" Crystal asked.

"Oh, yes. He's been back. Took six months off, disappeared, came back, spent some time in therapy and then went back to work again. That's the short version, of course."

"I'm impressed that he could do that. He must be quite a guy."

"He is quite a guy. If you like them tall, dark, and handsome."

"What's not to like?" Crystal sighed. "And you'd let a little thing like disappearing from your life for six months come between you and a guy like that?"

"It was a long six months," Genna grumbled. "He broke my heart."

"Well, broken hearts can mend more easily than broken spirits or broken minds. He healed. You can too."

"It's been hard without him," Genna acknowledged. "He is one pretty terrific guy. Everyone likes him. Even Pats. She *loves* John."

"Pats?"

"Patsy Wheeler. My foster mother." Genna let the eggs slide from the frying pan onto a serving plate.

Crystal followed Genna into the dining room.

With one hand, Genna placed two plates on the table, with the other, poured coffee into the cups that Crystal had brought in.

"What was it like? Living in someone else's home?"

"Compared to the home I had come from, living with Patsy was paradise."

"Was she rich?"

"No. She was just . . . normal. A well-adjusted, happy, hardworking woman who had—has—an extraordinarily loving and generous heart."

"How could the judge just have handed you over to her? I never understood that."

"Well, there had been a social worker with me both before and during the trial. When it became apparent that I'd been abandoned, just left there in the courtroom, it seemed that they had a decision to make. Force my parents, who clearly didn't want me, and who everyone suspected of abusing me, to come back and get me and take me home, or let them go, have the court suspend their parental rights until such time as they petitioned to have me returned to them, and place me with someone I already knew and had learned to trust. Someone the court and social services department knew and trusted. Looking back, it doesn't seem like much of a choice. Though I didn't really know much about the legal steps that were taken at the time."

"You said the court already knew her?"

"Patsy had taken in a number of foster children over the years. Her niece worked for the county children and youth agency, and they had called upon Pats on a number of occasions to take in a child or two. So there they had me, and after all I had gone through, they didn't want to force my parents to take me back. I think it must have been pretty clear what had been happening. No one believed for a minute that my arm was in a cast because I'd fallen down the steps. I think by the end of the trial, everyone, from the social workers to the judge to the reporters who covered the trial, was afraid of what would happen to me if I had to go back."

Crystal motioned for Genna to sit, then went into the kitchen, returning with the plate of eggs that she set between them.

"So after the lawyers did whatever it was they had to do, I went home with Patsy, which was probably the best thing that ever happened to me. Patsy encouraged me to do everything. Everything that he had frowned upon, from reading books to going to the movies to roller skating and riding a bike. All those frivolous, unnecessary things that kids love to do. Every Sunday afternoon, Pats took me to the movies. The matinee. And we'd have dinner on the way home, always someplace interesting. Different types of cuisine, different kinds of restaurants. Some nights we'd sit in front of the television with a bowl of popcorn or bowls of ice cream and we'd watch movies. If it was sad, we'd cry together, passing the box of tissues back and forth. A comedy, we'd laugh until our sides hurt. And there was always music in the house. Patsy loves music! She has the worst singing voice you'd ever want to hear, but that has never stopped her from belting out whatever tune strikes her fancy at any given moment."

"She sounds wonderful," Crystal said quietly.

"She is wonderful. She loves life and shared that love with me. She took me to plays—Patsy *loves* the theater! We used to go into Pittsburgh a lot, but sometimes for a special treat, we'd take the train to New York and go to Broadway."

Genna pushed her eggs around on the plate with her fork.

"I had the time of my life, and at the same time, I was rubbed raw inside, every day. Patsy taught me to laugh and to sing, made me feel like a whole person for the first time in my life. And yet, at the same time, I knew I must be terribly wicked. So terribly wicked that my own parents didn't want me." Genna ripped off a piece of toast, but did not raise it to her mouth. "So on the one hand, I had a wonderful home. A treasure of a foster mother, who loved me and who opened up the entire world to me. And on the other hand, well, I just knew that I didn't deserve any of it."

"How did you ever resolve all that?" Crystal whispered.

"With the help of a very, very good child psychologist. And a lot of work on Patsy's part. I never could have survived it all without her. She was an angel."

"You were in therapy, too?"

"From the time Patsy took me in, until I was a sophomore in high school. Pats knew right away I was going to need a lot of help, and she saw that I got it. She let me decide when I didn't need help anymore."

The two women sat and stared at each other.

Finally, Genna said, "It's amazing, isn't it, what they did to us? And yet here we are. We both survived. In spite of it all, they didn't destroy either one of us."

"I wish I'd known your Patsy," Crystal said.

"So do I. I wish she could have been there for you, too, back then. Things might have been different for you. But you can meet her and know her now. I don't know anyone whose life hasn't been better just for knowing her."

Genna sipped at her coffee, thinking of the years that Crystal had spent growing up under their parents' roof, and what it had done to her.

For the first time in her life, Genna began to think that abandoning her had been the best thing her parents had ever done for her.

John had expressed that very sentiment when he called the next evening, and Genna told him of her surprise visitor.

"Your sister?!" he'd exclaimed. "Genna, that's wonderful! I'm so happy for you! What's she like?"

"I don't know for sure yet."

Taking the portable phone from the kitchen, where Crystal was doing the dishes, to the small balcony overlooking the woods, Genna told John about Crystal's abuse at the hands of Brother Michael, and her decision to hide the fact.

"She was how old at the time, Gen?" John asked softly.

"Eleven or twelve, I guess."

"Can you imagine what she went through?"

"I've been trying to. It's all so complicated. I think about what I went through, then I think about what she went through . . . and I know that my road was ever so much easier than hers."

"Ironic, isn't it?"

"What's that?"

"That in the long run, leaving you behind might not have been the worst thing that they did to you."

"I was thinking that very thing last night. Crystal's had a terrible life, a terrible time growing up, nothing like what I had with Pats. All those years of abuse, then being committed to a hospital for a while—"

"What?"

"Crystal. She said she'd had a breakdown, that she'd attempted suicide. . . ."

"I'm so sorry. She must have really been suffering."

*That's what she said about you.* Genna bit her lip to keep the words in. How might John feel, if he knew that his own problems had been the topic of conversation only the night before?

"Why did she come to see you, Gen?" John asked. "Why now?"

"I think she needed to do this, to face me with the truth, regardless of what my reaction might have been, in order to get on with her life," Genna told him. "I think it's been torturing her all these years, and she couldn't get past it."

"I hate to play amateur psychologist, but it sounds to me that maybe she just needs for you to forgive her," he said, "so that she can begin to forgive herself."

"That would be my guess, too."

"And have you? Can you?"

"I think so. She was just a child then. She was only twelve years old."

"But you were a child, too," John reminded her. "Why should she be held to a different standard?"

"Crystal said last night that she'd never been as strong as I was, and she's right." Genna sighed deeply. "She was older, but she was never able to stand up to anyone. Not to our parents, not to the other kids in school. Not even to me. Crystal was the one who always ran from the fight. She never rose to the challenge. She always took the easy way."

"Except for this time," John pointed out.

"Yes. Except for this time." Genna agreed.

"Well, I guess it's never too late to try to make things right."

"That's pretty much what I told her. I know it wasn't easy for her to come here and say the things she had to say. I admire her for that."

"Well, then, that's a good start. Where do you go from there?"

"I'd like her to stay with me for a while. I wanted to take her up to the lake to meet Pats."

"How does Pats feel about that?"

"As you might expect. She can't wait to meet Crystal and take her under her wing. You know how Patsy is, John. If she suspects you have a wound, she has to try to heal it. I was going to drive out there this weekend. . . ."

"That's a long drive, Gen. Why not fly out and have Patsy meet you at the airport?"

"Because I was thinking that we needed the time together, Crystal and me, but—"

"A sort of sisterly bonding road trip?"

"Yes, that's what I had in mind. But as it turns out, Patsy is coming here, since she just couldn't wait until the weekend. And besides, Crystal just doesn't feel that she's ready to be that close to the camp."

"I'd forgotten that Patsy's cottage is so close. Does Crystal know how flattered she should be, that Pats thinks that meeting her is important enough to leave the lake during bass season?"

Genna laughed. "I told her. She's nervous about meeting Patsy, but I think she'll be fine."

"I'm looking forward to meeting her, too."

"I want you to meet her. Other than Patsy, I have no other immediate family."

"Well, it sounds as if the two of you are off to a pretty good start. I'm happy for you, Gen. I really am."

"Thank you. I can't say that this hasn't been difficult emotionally, but all in all, I'm really happy that she's here. I never thought I'd see her again." Genna blew out a long breath, then added, "Actually, if the truth were to be told, for a long time, I tried not to think about her at all. It just hurt too much."

"Well, maybe that's one more hurt you can put behind you now."

"I'd like to think so."

"How long will she be staying?"

"I don't know for sure. She doesn't have a job, and she doesn't have a home, other than the halfway house she's been staying in. I don't know that she has a timetable, and frankly, I didn't want to ask her. I didn't want her to think that I was trying to figure out when she was going to leave."

"So she might be around for a while."

"I would say so, yes."

"Well, then, I'll let you know as soon as we wrap up here. Maybe we can all get together then."

"You're on. Now, tell me your news. What's the latest with your mystery man?"

"Nothing. Not a damned thing. I'm so damned frustrated. This guy has left nothing behind. No evidence at the crime scenes. Hell, we don't even know for sure where the crime scenes are, because we still don't know where these women disappeared from."

"But you still feel they're all related, that it's the same person . . . ?"

"More than ever."

"Where is he taking these women? Is he killing them? Is he burying them someplace? What is he doing with them?" Genna thought aloud.

"Those are the same questions we've been asking

all along. And there still have been no ransom demands, no contact whatsoever with the families of his victims. Frankly, I'm beginning to think that these women are no longer alive. Where could you keep this many women captive, alive, for weeks at a time, without anyone knowing about it?"

"You sound as if you're not sure, though."

"I'm not sure about anything. I have the over-whelming feeling that he's collecting these women in a systematic way, but we don't know why. As if he has a list, or a game plan, and he's following it. His actions just haven't fit any pattern that I've dealt with before. Usually, this high degree of success would cause the perpetrator to get careless. But he hasn't dropped a stitch. It's just got us totally baffled. And we're no closer to this guy than we were when he took his first victim."

"Sooner or later something has to break."

"Better sooner," John told her. "We don't know how many more women are on his list, or what will happen when he gets to the end of it."

# 13

"Jennifer Duncan."

Just to say her name aloud brought a smile to his lips, so he said it again as he held her photo aloft, as if to pay her tribute. Which in a way, he was doing.

"Jennifer Duncan."

Hadn't she been his first, his first *ever*? He sighed, recalling that first time.

The terror in her eyes had inspired him, causing the desire to swell within him to such heights that he'd barely made it to the appointed place.

Oh, and even now, if he closed his eyes, he could see it all, in sharpest detail. He'd been to the woods earlier in the day, had set the stage for the drama that would play out there when the moon rose high that night. He'd been so excited that he wasn't certain he'd be able to go through with it, but the images he had fought all summer had become so strong, the urges so demanding, that they could no longer be denied.

Sometimes, in his darkest times, just the thought of that first one, that first time, restored his spirit. After all, through them, had he not fulfilled his purpose?

Had they not been brought to that place to tempt him? Was it not his job to purify them, to consecrate their bodies with his own? Once it became apparent to him that purification was the only way of saving them, well, what could he do? It was clear to him that he'd been chosen for that very purpose, the shepherd who would lead the children out of sin. Wasn't that why he'd been sent there in the first place?

And Jennifer Duncan, at age eleven, had been the first of the wayward to be taken under his wing, the first to be purified by the spilling of his seed.

She'd also been one of the first to break the covenant. And one of the first to be taken.

He stared at her photo, trying to decide which of his times with her had been the most memorable. The first, so many years past, or the last, just a few short weeks ago?

Sadly, she'd been the first to be lost.

He shook his head. He had simply miscalculated how long she could go without water.

The others could thank her for forcing him to take greater pains with their care. It just hadn't occurred to him that the extreme heat that first week would have increased her need for liquids. He should have thought of it, but he hadn't at the time. He'd had so much on his mind. He had things under better control now, though, which was a good thing, considering his absences.

He studied the photograph for one more long moment before slipping it back into the envelope. Someday, he'd take the time to put them into an album. He smiled at the thought of having so perfect a record of his finest hours, then laughed as he mentally titled the book which would surely be a thick one.

How I Spent My Summer Vacation.

# 14

"... and this was Genna's graduation," Patsy was saying as Genna unlocked the door of her apartment to find Patsy and Crystal curled up on the sofa with a box of photographs between them.

"For heaven's sake, Patsy," Genna exclaimed, "what are you doing?"

"I'm giving Crystal the opportunity to share in her little sister's growing up," Patsy replied without looking up. "Now, as I was saying, this was graduation..."

"From high school?" Crystal leaned over slightly to peer at the picture, still in the cardboard frame it came in.

"From college. Genna graduated Magna Cum Laude," Patsy told her proudly. "Of course, I have a larger version of this framed and hanging in the living room back home."

"College?" Crystal looked across the room at Genna. "You went to college?"

Genna nodded.

"Where?" Crystal asked.

"Bloomsburg University," Genna replied. "It's just about in the middle of the state. Of Pennsylvania, that is."

Genna dropped her briefcase and walked toward the sofa.

"What did you study?"

"I majored in biology. Secondary education. I thought I wanted to teach high school."

"Did you?" Crystal asked. "Teach high school?"

"For two years."

"Not nearly long enough," Patsy muttered.

Genna sat down on the end of the wooden chest that served as her coffee table.

"No one in our family ever went to college, before you," Crystal noted, then added, as if embarrassed by the admission, "I didn't even finish high school."

"Why not?" Genna asked.

"Because Daddy lost his church after . . . well, right after that whole business with Brother Michael. Mr. Homer was so upset about his brother—" Crystal turned to Patsy to explain, "Brother Michael was Mr. Homer's real blood brother, I'm guessin' you knew that. And Mr. Homer was a very important man in the church where Daddy preached. He just didn't think it was fittin' for Daddy to stay there after, well, after what had happened."

"So where did you go?" Genna toed off her high heels.

"First we went back to Kentucky. Daddy preached some down there, then we went to West Virginia for a while, then back to Kentucky again. We didn't stay anyplace too long. That's why I didn't get to finish school. We just never stayed long enough in one place." Her face clouded over and the drawl crept back into her voice. "And Momma was just getting worse and worse as time went on. Cryin' all the time and refusin' to go outside. Got so bad she barely even went to church anymore, and of course, that just infuriated Daddy no end."

"Your mother had a breakdown?" Patsy asked softly.

"Yes. She wasn't diagnosed by a psychiatrist, you understand. Daddy wouldn't have stood for that—he was heavy into faith healing and didn't put much stock in doctors in general." Crystal added somewhat wryly, "But over the years I did come to recognize the signs."

"Genna said you'd been hospitalized yourself," Patsy said with the same ease with which she'd comment on someone's choice of clothing.

"Yes. On and off for many years."

"And are you still under treatment?"

"Patsy!" Genna turned to face her, surprised by her uncommon bluntness.

"It's okay, Genna. Patsy's just trying to establish the rules. I appreciate that. Everything out in the open, right, Patsy?"

"Right," Patsy nodded, impressed by Crystal's insight.

"Yes, I am still under treatment. I've been living in a halfway house, but under supervision."

"Why? What do they suppose you might do if you're not supervised?"

"They're not sure if I might try to kill myself again."

"I see." Patsy bit the inside of her bottom lip. "Will you?"

"I don't think so. A few weeks ago," Crystal shrugged, "I'm not so sure. But things are different now." She cleared her throat. "I've dropped a lot of old baggage over the past few days."

"Does your counselor or whomever know where you are?" Patsy asked.

"I called yesterday. They wanted me to come right back. They wanted to send someone for me, to bring me back. But I'm not ready to go back just yet. And Genna said I didn't have to."

"Of course, you don't have to. I'm just concerned that if you're supposed to be getting something— therapy or medication or whatever—that you're doing without, well, we'd need to be thinking about that." Patsy patted Crystal on the knee.

"I have enough medication to take me through another few weeks, but I am supposed to be continuing with my therapy twice a week," Crystal admitted. "I already skipped last week, and my doctor wasn't too happy."

"Well, now, what shall we do about that?" Patsy asked.

"I . . . I don't know."

"Maybe we could call your counselor and see what she can suggest."

"She'll suggest that you send me back to Kentucky, since the state pays her for my treatment."

"Then we'll just have to ask what her second choice might be," Patsy said thoughtfully, "and maybe I can help you come up with something suitable for while you're here. For however long that might be."

*I'd bet on it*, Genna smiled to herself and went into the kitchen to start dinner. When had Patsy ever not succeeded in coming up with something suitable when it was necessary?

Genna wasn't at all surprised to discover that Patsy had already started dinner. One sniff from the kitchen door told her that Patsy's favorite chicken casserole was baking in the oven, and unless her nose was playing tricks on her, that was one of Patsy's fresh peach pies cooling on top of the stove.

"Dinner will be ready in about twenty minutes," Patsy called to Genna from the living room. "We weren't certain when you'd be home, so I put it on a little later than usual. It should be ready by seven."

"Patsy Wheeler, I could just fall over and faint," Genna stood in the doorway, fighting the smile that threatened to play at both corners of her mouth. "You're off schedule by an entire hour."

Patsy laughed and nodded, saying, "I know it's a shocker. But there are times when we must make allowances for other more important things than precedent. Tonight seemed to be one of those times. I wanted the three of us to have dinner together."

"Thank you, Pats." Genna locked eyes with her foster mother from across the room.

"Think nothing of it. Now you go on and change your clothes and Crystal and I will get dinner on the table."

"I won't be but a minute."

"Take your time, honey." Patsy turned to Crystal and said, "Chrissie, honey, I think it's time you started on that salad dressing you were talking about making. Does it have garlic in it? Good. Come along. I'll chop for you . . ."

Over the next few days, Genna watched as Patsy worked her magic on Crystal, drawing her out more and more, earning her trust in little ways. When Patsy finally proposed that Crystal might want to see Dr. Berger, a psychiatrist friend of hers who just happened to have a cottage across the lake, Crystal agreed with little hesitation. Dr. Berger could call Crystal's counselor in Kentucky, Patsy had suggested, and get copies of her records and her prescriptions. Only if Crystal wanted her to, that is, just in case Crystal thought she might want to stay around for a little longer.

Crystal thought she might.

"I'll just give Nancy a call, if you don't mind, dear," Patsy said on Friday evening. "I don't want her to worry. Not that there's reason to, of course. Brian still has his watchdog set up in the house across the road. Frankly, it gives me the willies, knowing that someone is watching my house all the time."

"Who is watching the house all the time?" Genna asked.

"Oh, that security guard that Brian hired. I know it's not right to judge someone else on such pettiness, but this Kenny Harris just flat out gives me the creeps sometimes."

"Patsy, that's so unlike you." Genna mused. For Patsy, who was the only person Genna had ever met who always looked for the best in everyone she met, the comment was downright uncharitable. "What is it about him that bothers you?"

"I can't put my finger on it. He just doesn't say much, you know? He'll sit in that little screened porch out front for hours looking across the road, but when you walk over and try to talk to him, he just sort of brushes you off."

"Maybe he's just shy," Crystal offered.

"Maybe so."

"Well, a little shyness never stopped you before, Pats," Genna teased. "I'll bet you'll have him eating out of the palm of your hand before the summer's over."

"We'll see."

"I can't see anyone bein' immune to you, Patsy." Crystal shook her head. "You could charm the warts off a toad if you wanted to."

"I'll take that as a compliment, honey. Thank you." Patsy grinned and reached for the phone.

"Come on out to the deck," Crystal said, enthusiastically waving Genna toward the dining room. "Wait till you see . . ."

Crystal unlocked the door and pushed it open, then stood back while Genna stepped out onto the small deck.

"Doesn't it look beautiful?" Crystal pointed to the window boxes that overflowed with purple and pink petunias and some sort of viney thing that trailed down a foot or so past the window.

"Oh, that is *so* beautiful!" Genna exclaimed. "Did Patsy do this?"

"Patsy and I both worked on it while you were at work today. We picked out the flowers together, and she showed me what to put in the box before the plants went in. Honestly, Genna, the dirt that was in there was hard as a rock."

"I'm afraid I don't have much of a green thumb. Every year, Pats plants that window box up for me, and I get all involved with what I'm doing, and I forget all about it."

"Well, I'll make sure it's kept watered," Crystal said, then hastened to add, "For as long as I'm here, that is."

"I'd appreciate that." Genna squeezed her sister's hand. "For as long as you're here."

"Actually, Patsy said we'd only be around for another day or so. Dr. Berger can't see me until Tuesday, so we'll go on up to the lake on Sunday, Patsy said. And then . . . well, who knows what then?"

"You're welcome to stay here, but I know that Patsy would be delighted to have you stay with her for a while."

"She did offer. I can't believe how wonderful she is." Crystal shook her head. "She's every bit the angel you said she was. I've never met anyone like her."

"I'm sorry you couldn't have met her sooner, Chris."

"So am I," Crystal said. "Maybe I wouldn't be as screwed up as I am. Although . . ."

She stopped and looked out toward the woods at the far end of the parking lot.

"Although what?"

"I was just thinking that I've actually felt so much better these past few days, that maybe I don't need my medication anymore."

"Don't mess with it, Crystal. Let the doctors decide that. Maybe in time you'll be able to cut it back, maybe eliminate it, but I don't think that's something you should arbitrarily play with."

"I guess you're right. In any event, I can understand now, after spending a few days with your Patsy, how you turned out the way you did." Crystal turned her back and leaned her arms on the deck railing. "I'd be lying if I said I wasn't jealous."

"I'm sorry, Chrissie. If I could reach back through time and change things, I would."

"I know. And I appreciate that you're willing to

share her with me now. That you're willing to let me be a part of your life after everything—"

"Move past it, Chrissie." Genna cut her off. "We can't change what was."

"I'm just feeling a little humbled by all this. By the way you treat me, even after . . ." She paused, then smiled a tiny smile when Genna raised her eyebrows in warning. "Okay. I won't say anymore."

"Good." Genna pulled out a chair and sat in it, then motioned toward the other one, saying, "Now, why not sit for a few minutes and tell me where you learned to make a lemon soufflé like the one you made for dinner tonight . . ."

By Sunday morning, the axiom "Three's a crowd" had taken on a whole new meaning for Genna. After several years of living alone and sharing only occasional living space with Patsy at the lake, the tight quarters in the apartment had begun to wear on her nerves. So she was surprised to feel a little bit of a letdown when she arrived home on Monday after work to the quiet space she'd been longing for just forty-eight hours earlier.

"Be careful what you ask for," she reminded herself as she sifted through the leftovers Patsy had stored in plastic containers in the refrigerator.

The roast beef left from Saturday's dinner caught her eye, and she sliced some thinly to top a bowl of mixed greens and bright wedges of tomato that Patsy had brought with her.

"They're not from Frick's, you understand," Patsy had told her with a touch of apology. It wasn't necessary for her to explain why she'd gone someplace else for her produce.

"I'm so sorry, Pats." Genna touched her shoulder. Patsy shrugged and turned away.

"You miss seeing Mrs. Frick." It wasn't a question.

"I do. She's a dear, dear lady."

"Surely you don't think she blames you . . . ?"

"Of course not. Their stand's not been open these past few weeks. I heard they were trucking everything down to the market in Wick's Grove." Patsy grabbed a paper towel and cleaned an imaginary spot from the counter. "But on the bright side, I did get to meet the people who bought the Dreshers' farm, over on the other side of the lake. Their produce is quite nice. And they've been busy as all get-out since the competition closed." Patsy folded the towel and smoothed it out as if it was made of linen instead of paper. "It's just a shame, that's all."

"Have the bikers been around?" Genna asked.

"Sometimes one or two of 'em might go by," Patsy shrugged, "but I haven't noticed that they so much as slow down when they do. They just drive by, minding their own business. I figure they've just found themselves a nice little shortcut around the lake."

"Does Kenny Harris know about that?"

"Sure does. He's sitting on his duff out there on the front porch every time they go past, but they really don't bother anyone."

"Does Brian know?"

"I suspect so, since after they leave, Kenny picks up the phone and makes a call. I imagine he's following Brian's orders to call him every time someone who doesn't belong on the lake shows up."

Genna had said nothing further on the subject, but had made a mental note to call Brian as soon as she got into the office the following morning.

"I hear Aunt Patsy has taken in another little bird." Brian picked up as soon as he heard it was Genna on the line.

"Then I guess you've heard who that little bird might be."

"Gen, I'm delighted for you. I know you've had to have been missing her all these years."

"I have. And she's missed out on so much—I'm assuming that Patsy told you all about Crystal's illness?"

"Yes. But I'm betting that a few weeks with Aunt Pats will work wonders."

"There's no doubt in my mind that by the end of the summer, Chrissie will be an entirely different person."

"Now, let me guess what's behind this call." Brian pretended to ponder for a moment. "Let's see, could you be calling for a rundown on what my security guard has come up with over the past few weeks?"

"You know me all too well, Brian."

"I've been expecting the call. It's not like you to take no interest in such things."

Genna could hear the rustling of some papers.

"Here we go," Brian was saying. "I've been keeping a log. We've had daily runs past the house by several of your biker buddies. The guard has film of this activity, by the way, so we've been able to identify most of them."

"Were any of them arrested in the Frick case?"

"No. So far as we can tell, that group is maintaining a pretty low profile. Which of course means nothing when you're dealing with criminals."

"So they made bail?"

"Oh, yes. The Amish fellows didn't, but the bikers were out as soon as they could get the cash counted."

"I thought bail was set steep."

"It was. But these guys are part of a larger organization. Money is usually no object for this sort of thing." Brian paused, as if reading. "Yes, it looks like daily runs past the house, but they've never stopped. I think it's more an intimidation tactic than anything else at this point."

"They obviously don't know Patsy," Genna murmured.

Brian laughed out loud. "You're right. If they did, they'd realize they're wasting their time. It would take a hell of a lot more than a few scruffy looking guys on motorcycles going past her house to intimidate her."

"But you're certain they've never stopped . . ."

"Positive. Not once. If they did, Aunt Pats would probably have invited them to join her for iced tea and homemade pound cake on the deck."

"I'm hoping she's taking this more seriously than that."

"You know Pats. She truly believes there's good in everyone, and if you dig deep enough you'll find it."

"What if they came at night, from the back of the house. From the lake side . . ."

"We'd know before it would happen."

"How? Does Kenny Harris have night vision? Doesn't he ever sleep?"

"The D.A.'s office has someone on the inside." Brian said softly.

"You mean one of the bikers—"

"—is C.I.D., yes."

"So you're not worried?"

"I'm concerned, but not worried," Brian replied after a moment's hesitation. "Between our undercover man and Harris watching the cottage, I feel we're about as secure as we can be. We're also keeping an eye on all of the new people at the lake, particularly the renters."

"A little off the record background check?"

"A very little. I'm justifying it under the classification of 'forewarned.' Nothing heavy. No wire tapping or surveillance cameras on the unsuspecting." Brian chuckled. "We leave that sort of thing to you guys."

"I'll have you know I've never engaged in such activity." Genna pretended to be offended.

"Right. And I'm Howdy Doody."

"So did you learn anything relevant about Patsy's neighbors?"

"Not really. There really weren't any surprises, actually."

"That's no surprise," Genna said. "Most people who go to places like Bricker's Lake aren't looking for much more than peace and quiet."

"So it would seem. Though there is that next door neighbor of Patsy's . . ."

"Nancy?" Genna asked. "What about her?"

"We really couldn't find much on her. Of course, we didn't ask for more than the preliminary. We just didn't turn up anything on her. She could be recently divorced and returning to her maiden name, who knows? My mother would say she told us so."

"What are you talking about?"

"My mother doesn't much care for this woman."

"Why not? Nancy's pleasant enough, the little I've seen of her, and she's been wonderful company for Pats this summer."

"I'm sure she has been. And frankly, I'm thinking

that might be the biggest part of it. Maybe Mom's afraid that Nancy's better company for Aunt Pats than she is. Mom doesn't think much of the security guard either, by the way."

"Patsy doesn't seem to care for him, either. Thinks he's odd."

"He's a bit of an oddball," Brian agreed, "but he's apparently quite good at what he does."

"May I ask how you found him?"

"He came on a reference from a friend who had used him earlier in the summer. I'm not at all concerned about whether or not either Mom or Aunt Pats likes him, as long as he's doing his job. Which, so far, he's been doing."

"I admit I feel a little better knowing that he's there. And better still knowing someone's keeping an eye on our bikers from the inside."

"If anything comes up, of course, I'll let you know. In the meantime, I think you can just go about your business of rounding up the bad guys and let me worry about Pats."

"And Crystal," Genna added.

"Yes, of course. And Crystal."

After inquiring after Brian's wife, Allison, and their three sons, Genna hung up the phone, feeling infinitely better than she had when she'd placed the call. Knowing that others were keeping their eyes on Patsy had removed a heavy load from Genna's shoulders. Now, especially that her sister had joined Patsy at the lake, it was good to know that they weren't quite so vulnerable.

That bit of her life tidied up, Genna turned to the business at hand, that being her review of an interview with the mother of a recent kidnapping victim.

She had read through to the second to the last page when Decker's voice jumped at her through the intercom.

"Genna, you there?"

"Yes, I'm here."

"Get in here. Now." Though not raised above conversational level, there was a tenseness to his voice that brought Genna out of her seat without a second thought.

Assuming that "here" was Decker's office, Genna practically ran down the hallway. Sharon pointed to the open door as Genna reached the secretary's desk, and without a word, Genna hurried in to the cool office.

Decker was standing in the middle of the room, his hands on his hips, staring at the television that sat upon the credenza opposite the desk. Genna took the chair he motioned her toward, and sat down, leaning toward the screen to see what crisis had developed while she was typing up her report that morning.

"What's going on?" Genna asked. "What's happened?"

Ignoring her questions as if he hadn't heard her, Decker reached for the remote control and increased the volume.

"Sir?" She repeated. "What's going on?"

"The shit, as they say, Agent Snow, is about to hit the fan."

A trim man in his forties—obviously a law enforcement type, with his close cropped hair and the requisite dark suit—stood at a podium, adjusting the microphone even as he spoke.

". . . in touch with the other police departments and will be sharing what little information we have with each other and with the FBI. Yes . . . the gentleman in the red tie in the second row . . ."

The man at the podium pointed with his index finger, and the camera followed, resting on the man who stood in the center of the row of folding chairs, each of which was occupied. The man's lips moved, and he gestured several times with his arms, but the microphone failed to pick up his words.

"The question is," the man at the podium repeated for the sake of those not close enough to have heard, "why has it taken the FBI so long to figure out that there is a serial killer running loose at will all around the country. I think I'll let the FBI answer that."

He stepped aside and was replaced at the podium with a tall, thin man with a faint dusting of light brown hair on the crown of his head.

"That's Rex Egan," Decker told her.

"Yes, I know. What is he—"

"Shhhh," Decker hushed her. "Listen."

"First of all, no one . . . let me repeat that emphatically, *no one* has said that any of the missing women have been killed, so your use of the term 'serial killer' is irresponsible and inaccurate. We believe what we have here is a series of abductions which may or may not turn out to be related. But no one has come forward with any evidence to suggest that any of these women are dead. There are, however, striking similarities common to all of the disappearances that have led us to believe they are related, and we are proceeding on that theory."

"What are those similarities?" a reporter close to the podium asked. "What evidence do you have to indicate that there is in fact a . . . let's use the term serial abductor, for lack of something better."

"Actually, the most striking bit of evidence is that there is no evidence at all." Egan cleared his throat as the murmur from the crowd began to rise. "Each of the victims has disappeared into thin air, literally, while in the course of their own daily, well-established routines."

"But I thought Chief Halloran said earlier that these abductions have taken place all over the country, in no particular order," a woman near the back of the seating area rose to ask. "How can a random series of kidnappings—"

Egan interrupted her.

"No one used the word *random*. On the contrary, we believe that the abductor is following a very highly organized plan in a very specific order."

"And that plan is . . . ?" a man in a brown sports jacket and casual khaki pants asked.

"Known only to the abductor."

"But if he's not killing them, what's he doing with them?"

"That's an excellent question. Unfortunately, we don't know."

"Have you been able to develop a profile?"

"Only a very sketchy one. We believe that he's white—all of his victims are white, and as you all know from all the law enforcement TV you watch, crimes such as these are usually perpetrated within the same race. He's male, between the ages of thirty and fifty. Physically strong enough to overcome the victims with no apparent struggle. He's very smart, and very adaptable. A chameleon of sorts. He's been able to fit in every place he's been without being seen. On not one occasion has a witness come forward with a description. Which means he's stud-

ied his victims well, well enough to know exactly
how to blend in completely enough as to become
invisible. He's patient enough to plan things
through and choose his moment. We believe that
he's researched the routines of his victims over a
period of time so that he knows where they go and
what they do and when they will be most vulnerable. That would imply that he has mobility, time on
his hands, and a source of income or enough cash
that he can travel around the country at will. He's
probably a loner—lives alone, there'd be too much
explaining to do. There's been no gap between
abductions longer than a week, and that only in the
beginning."

A long, dull silence spread throughout the room
as Egan's words sunk in.

A question was asked off camera.

"The question is, How many victims have there
been?" Egan repeated. "Seven, that we know of. But
there could have been more. One of the reasons why
we're here talking about this today is so that other
police departments across the country who may be
investigating similar disappearances will get in
touch with us and share what information they
have."

"But with the number of people who go missing
on any given day . . ." someone said.

"This is different," Egan shook his head. "These
have been very specific, deliberate acts. These are not
runaway teenagers or women who have run off with
the pool boy. Many are solid, professional women,
most of them happily married with young children
to whom they are devoted, with absolutely no apparent reason to leave home. So you can eliminate many

of the other unfortunate missing persons reports because they don't fit the pattern."

"Couldn't it be a coincidence? I mean, don't you always look to the spouse first? Maybe the husbands of these women—"

Egan held up a hand to stop him.

"Have all been carefully investigated. All were at work or elsewhere, clearly documented and witnessed, when their wives disappeared. Believe me, the local law enforcement agencies that investigated the disappearances were very thorough. They are to be commended, each and every one of them, for the manner in which these investigations were conducted."

"Do you think there will be more? More abductions?"

"I think there will be as many as it takes for him to accomplish his goal," Egan said carefully.

"And what would that be?"

"I wish we knew."

Egan motioned off camera, and two men rolled a large map close to the podium. Egan walked to it, one hand in his pocket.

"Wilmington, North Carolina. Kansas City, Missouri. Omaha, Nebraska. Chicago, Illinois. Mystic, Connecticut. Wheeling, West Virginia. Dawson Springs, Kentucky. Rome, New York." With each name that he called, he placed a yellow flag, affixed to a large pushpin, onto the map to mark the place.

When he concluded, he stood aside, looking out across the small sea of reporters who had leaned forward to watch.

Finally, someone broke the silence.

"Why did he skip around like that? Wouldn't it have been easier to, say, start in Chicago, go to Omaha, then Kansas City, maybe Kentucky, West Virginia, North Carolina, then New York and Connecticut? Doesn't sound to me that he's all that organized, if he jumps around like that. That doesn't make sense."

"It does if he's following a specific agenda," Egan said quietly.

"You mean, like maybe a list?"

Egan nodded.

"You think maybe there's a list of names and he's taking them in some kind of order?" A woman asked.

"It's starting to look that way."

"How do you know he's not a traveling salesman who just happens to be in these places?"

"We are looking into that possibility, but we believe that the information that we have gathered points in another direction."

"Supposing there is a list . . . you think there are other names on it?"

"That's one of the things we hope to learn by going public with the information we have. We're hoping that someone will know of some connection between one or more of these women. We've been unable to determine what these women have in common. We're hoping someone out there," Egan looked directly into the camera, "will know what that link might be."

He walked slowly back to the podium, both hands in his pocket.

"We've called together the investigating officers from each of the departments that has been handling one of these disappearances. We'll be meeting together over the next few days to pool our information. Hopefully, something someone says will spark a memory or an image in someone else, perhaps something that had heretofore appeared unimportant."

"What's the FBI's role in this?" someone asked.

"We've appointed some of our best, most experienced agents to a special field team to investigate the matter. Our people will participate in the discussions this week. Hopefully, between the information shared by the investigating officers, and the information that we hope to gather from the public, we'll have enough to track this person . . . this chameleon . . . before he gets any farther down the list."

"And this special team is in place?"

"Yes," Egan nodded, then motioned off to the side for someone to join him.

Genna was not the least surprised to see John join Egan at the podium.

"Some of you may know Special Agent John Mancini. He's been selected to lead this team, and he's been given free range to choose his people. You've got, what, John, three, four men lined up?"

"It's a team of four," John nodded. "Three men—Adam Stark from Phoenix, Dale Hunter from Birmingham, and me—and one woman. Genna Snow, from our northern New Jersey office. All well experienced with missing persons and cases involving abductions."

Genna sat back in her seat and looked up at Decker. "You knew?"

"Yes, but I thought I'd let John tell you," Decker

said as he clicked a button on the remote to turn off the television. "And now that he has, I suggest you go home and pack."

Decker reached into his inside jacket pocket and pulled out an envelope.

"Your plane leaves at three." He handed the envelope to Genna even as he walked to the door and opened it for her. "Keep in touch, hear?"

# 15

The jaunty tune—the theme song for a favorite game show—began to play, and he turned up the volume, filling every corner and crevice of the small motel room with the catchy little ditty. Humming along, he snapped off his laptop and settled himself on the bed, leaning back against the cushions, the remote control held between both hands much the way a child might hold a popsicle. The camera scanned the audience, and as always, he made his own game out of guessing who would be that day's contestants. When the host—he just loved that they called the emcee the host, as if they were all his guests—called down the first lucky player, he grinned broadly and laughed out loud. He'd picked her, that plump little middle-aged redhead, the first time the camera had made its way across the left side of the studio.

It was just another sign that everything was right in his world.

Okay, he conceded as the host promised he'd be right back after this brief commercial break, maybe *everything* wasn't quite right. He was having a little bit of a problem on account of this blasted heat. He'd tried to make allowances for it, tried his best to figure

out how much water and when it would be needed.
So he'd miscalculated a little. It wasn't as if he'd set
out to let them die. Goodness, no. Didn't the Bible
say *Thou shalt not kill?*

And hadn't he compensated by giving the others
extra water, even bringing them oranges, as had been
requested?

Bold piece of business that was, *her* telling him to
bring them fruit. But he'd felt weak that day, after
discovering that he'd lost yet another one, and he'd
given in. Of course, the lost ones were of no use to
him, and he'd had to find a way to dispose of them.
After all, he couldn't very well take them *back*.

Though the thought of it did amuse him greatly, of
returning them to the same places where he'd found
them. In the case of the unfortunate Carin Whitten,
that would have meant driving back to West Virginia
and dumping her at a precise point behind the track
at the high school where she'd been running so very
early on that summer morning. She had been one of
the easier ones, Carin had. He'd watched her for
days, enough days to determine that on Tuesdays
and Thursdays, she left the track by the back gate,
rather than the front, as she did on the others, and
headed to the backyard of a house that edged up to
the tennis courts. To do this, she had to walk along a
very narrow path between the fence on the court
side, and a row of arborvitae on the other. Once at
her destination, she would slip through the hedge
and spend a half hour to forty-five minutes visiting
before leaving by the front door to return home.
Several times he'd seen her in the doorway leisurely
chatting to her friend, as if she had all the time in the
world.

She hadn't.

But she'd been a pretty thing, that's for certain. Mother would have said that Carin had grown up nicely.

He'd felt badly that he'd had to dispose of her the way he had, but, well, she'd live on, in a sense. He had to think of it as recycling in its truest form. He found himself smiling at the thought of it, in spite of his very real sorrow at having lost her and the few others who had succumbed.

The commercials having ended, he focused again on the screen, readying himself for the first round of play. But instead of the familiar face of his favorite game show host, he saw, instead, the face of a well-known news commentator.

". . . interrupt our programming to bring you the following breaking news. We're joining our local affiliate station . . ."

He barely heard the rest.

"What?!" He screamed at the TV, then growled.

He *hated* when they did this. *Hated* it.

". . . press conference is underway. Let's listen . . ."

A man in a dark suit—with *that* hair, he was obviously some type of politician or in law enforcement—was standing at a podium, a look of deep concern on his face. Someone from the audience was asking a question, but with the air conditioner on there in the motel room, he hadn't heard it. The whole thing just made him even more annoyed. It was bad enough that they broke into his favorite show, but to not know *why*, why, that just . . .

What was that, what did the cop-type say . . . ?

*Why, he's talking about . . . he's talking about . . .*
*ME!!*

He moved to the end of the bed, the better to hear.

A press conference, about him! On national TV!

He'd expected some media coverage, eventually, but a full press conference! Important enough to pre-empt the morning game shows!

And so soon!

Could it really be?

His heart began to beat with the excitement of the moment. He increased the volume yet again, lest he miss a single word.

". . . *no one* has said that any of the missing women have been killed, so your use of the term 'serial killer' is irresponsible and inaccurate. . . ." The blue suit was saying with great emphasis and sincerity.

*Hmmmm.* He pondered this. He *had* lost several of them so far, but he hadn't really thought of himself as having *killed* them. Did this make him a serial killer? The thought disturbed him.

*Thou shalt not kill.*

". . . most striking bit of evidence is that there is no evidence at all . . ."

"Yes, of course there's no evidence," he muttered. "How can you find evidence when you don't know where the crime scene is?"

"How can a random series of kidnappings—" a woman was asking.

"Random?" He laughed out loud. "My dear, my dear, nothing has been random."

". . . a very highly organized plan in a very specific order."

"Well, you got that much right." He nodded appreciatively.

"But if he's not killing them, what's he doing with them?" Another question from the audience.

"Ha!" He whooped when the police-type at the podium responded to the question with an admission that he hadn't a clue. "And you're dying to know, aren't you? You're all just dying to know!"

He leaned forward again when the profile was read off, nodding his head in agreement. "Right there . . . and there . . . right again."

"Oh, please, no! UGH!" He cried aloud when he was referred to as a chameleon. Chameleons were slimy little, what, amphibians? Reptiles?

*Disgusting.* He shivered just to think of it.

He couldn't help but swell with a kind of pride when the FBI began to pin up the little flags marking off the sites of his accomplishments.

It truly was his finest hour.

And it was taking place right there, on network television.

That the FBI was going to such trouble for him . . . well, it humbled him, to be sure. To know that he had them so baffled was a tribute to his cleverness, an affirmation that his actions were righteous. He grinned as the FBI asked for help from the public. As if there was anyone smart enough to put it together.

And then, there, on the screen, was the legendary John Mancini.

Legendary because his name was well known throughout the nation's prison system after he'd taken such a beating—mentally, that is—from Sheldon Woods. Anyone who'd been in a federal prison at any time over the past few years had heard about it. And in his own last home, hadn't he been two cells away from someone who knew someone who had once had a cell on the same block as Woods and who'd heard the talk. About how tough Mancini was, but how Woods's persistence broke him down. And here he was, back again, like that little pink bunny on the battery commercials. Woods had said that Mancini had been really hard to break, but the fact that he had been able to get to him would have assured him a certain status in prison had it not been for the fact that he was, among other things, a child murderer.

And what was this Mancini saying? Something about a special unit being formed to track him down?

A team of four. Three men, and one woman.

He sat stunned, even after the press conference had ended. Could anything be more perfect?

He wished he had someone to share the moment with, but then again, if anyone knew what he was doing—kidnapping being a capital offense—he'd probably have to break his own promise to himself and kill them.

*Genna Snow.* Genna would be on the special team that was hunting him.

"*Genna.*" He spoke her name aloud reverently.

He exhaled sharply and pressed a pillow to his chest to keep his beating heart from bursting through.

*Genna was coming after him.*

The beauty of it all but overwhelmed him, almost to tears. The sheer perfection—the *irony*—of it all.

That he—the hunter—was now the hunted.

And she, so soon to be the hunted, was now the hunter.

# 16

Genna leaned forward, her right elbow resting on the conference table, listening intently as Stephen West, the investigating officer from Zanesville, Ohio, carefully reviewed the sequence of events that led to the realization that Terrie Lee Akins, wife of Edward and new mother of Edward, Jr., had vanished the very day after the press conference had aired. The special significance of Mrs. Akins's disappearance was not lost on the group gathered before Detective West. Hers was the only one of the disappearances for which the point of abduction may have been identified.

The detective played back the 911 tape of Ed Akins's frantic phone call when it had become apparent to him that something dire had happened to his wife.

"Sir," the 911 operator said patiently, "if you'll just calm down—"

"I can't calm down. My wife isn't here. She should be here. And the baby . . . she'd never go off and leave the baby in the crib like that."

"Maybe she's at a neighbor's . . . have you called—"

"I've called everyone. You don't understand. She isn't anywhere. . . ."

The officer clicked off the tape.

"And he was right. She wasn't anywhere. Of course, in a case like this, with no sign of a break-in, no evidence of foul play, the first person you look to is the husband. But he'd been in his classroom since at least seven-thirty that morning—he's a high-school history teacher—and had been seen by almost every one of his colleagues and a goodly portion of the student body. Every minute of his day was well documented. And it was clear that the baby had been tended to. The diaper wasn't overly soiled. The baby appeared well fed, though he was red-faced and wailing when his father arrived home just around four. Mr. Akins had spoken with his wife around one-fifteen. She'd been having a normal day. A little laundry in the morning. A leisurely chat with her sister while she ate her lunch and fed the baby a bottle before putting him down for his afternoon nap. The sister says she called back a little before two and left a message on the answering machine when Terrie Lee didn't pick up. It appears that she never did hear that last message. So something happened in the middle of that routine day that turned the blissful life of this young family into a nightmare."

While he paused to take a sip of water from the tumbler in front of him, Genna studied his eyes and found them weary. It was obvious to her that this case weighed heavily on his mind, that even a seasoned officer such as this one, gray-haired and round-shouldered and wise from years on the street, was frustrated by his inability to capture that one thread that could lead to a resolution. His point was well made. There were no apparent threads to be caught.

"The best we've been able to determine is that sometime after one-thirty in the afternoon, Mrs. Akins walked out her front door, down the path that led to the road to pick up the mail from the mailbox. The mailman says that he'd placed the mail in the box at approximately twelve forty-five. But she was on the phone with her sister at that time, then later, with her husband. So the only time she'd had to walk down for the mail was after she'd put the baby down for his nap. She would have most likely waited a few minutes before leaving the house—just to make sure he had in fact fallen asleep. Outside the front door, on the top step, were a pair of gardening gloves and clippers. She'd told her sister that she was going to clip some roses for the dining room table, that this was their first year in their new house and she was amazed at the variety of flowers she'd found there. How she'd kept the house filled with fresh flowers all summer and how it had delighted her." West cleared his throat, then added, "Apparently she decided to bring the mail up first. She never did get around to cutting that bouquet."

He walked to the far end of the room and turned on the wide-screen TV, then slipped a tape into the VCR. Unconsciously, the entire group that had been gathered—law enforcement officers from twelve states and a handful of FBI agents—leaned forward in anticipation. The camera focused on the front of a white clapboard farmhouse that boasted a large grapevine wreath on the front door and a profusion of cheery yellow roses that climbed over both the doorway and one of the front windows in sweeping arches. The person holding the camera then climbed the steps and stood in front of the door, the lens facing out toward the road. Behind him, wind chimes tinkled softly, a delicate soundtrack for a bitter soliloquy. He began to walk along the path, narrating his journey in a voice engraved with hoarseness from years of too many cigarettes and too little sleep.

". . . from the front of the house, down the path here toward the road, which is approximately one hundred feet from the front door." His words popped out between shallow breaths.

He walked slowly, panning the camera from one side of the worn dirt path to the other, until he reached the mailbox. It, too, was cheery, covered with dogwood blossoms that Ed Akins said Terrie Lee had painted herself.

"The shoulder of the road cuts in here, giving more than enough space for a car or small truck to pull in and park. The mailman says he put a packet of mail—several letter-sized envelopes, a few catalogs, a couple of magazines, and a large brown envelope—in the mailbox."

The camera was again focused on the ground, where white envelopes littered the ground and the pages of a catalog rustled in the breeze.

"The roadway is paved as is the shoulder," he noted.

The detective stopped the VCR, freezing the last frame on the screen.

"So she was taken when she went to get the mail . . ." someone in the room commented aloud, unnecessarily, since everyone was thinking the same thing.

"That's the way it looks."

"She took the mail out of the box and was probably focused on looking through it." Genna heard herself say. "Was the brown envelope found?"

"No. Only the mail you see here scattered on the grass."

"Any idea of what was in the brown envelope?" Someone asked.

"A short-sleeved sweater—light blue, with dragonflies embroidered on the front," he recalled without consulting his notes, "that she'd ordered from a catalog the week before."

"So she probably opened the mailbox, saw the big envelope and pulled it out. She was pleased that it had come so soon, and was thinking about trying it on." Genna sat with her hands in her lap, trying to see it all as it might have happened. "She wouldn't have heard the car pull up behind her. Might not have even noticed that someone had gotten out until it was too late. She might have just been thinking about the sweater . . ."

Twenty-two pairs of eyes shifted curiously in Genna's direction from every side of the table. John merely leaned back in his chair and listened. He had seen her do this before, pick up the small pieces and weave them into a scene from a story that more often than not turned out to be accurate. John had never questioned her ability, believing that her insights came from somewhere deep inside, and were part intuition, part empathy. He'd long since come to respect her talent to seemingly slide into the victim's shoes.

"We're certain he knew what time she'd be there, timed his drive-by perfectly. We figure he came up behind her on the road, swung over quickly, hopped

out and grabbed her, hopped back in just as quickly."
The detective who stood with the remote control continued. "From talking to the other officers whose communities had similar abductions, it appears that this was pretty much his MO. He watches his victims carefully, knows their schedules, knows when their most vulnerable time will coincide with his most opportune."

Genna sat staring into space. She could almost see it, as if in a dream, the woman moving in slow motion, turning from the mailbox with her arms filled with white envelopes and colorful catalogs, stashing them under her arm while she sought to rip open the brown mailing packet. She did not hear the van approach, did not hear the cautious footsteps behind her. Was aware of nothing until the hand closed over her mouth and she felt herself being lifted off her feet . . .

"Did someone say that near the suspected scene of one of the abductions a dark blue van had been spotted?" Genna asked.

"Yes. That was ours. In Omaha," replied a dapper looking man in his fifties who sat across the table from Genna.

"When our victim disappeared," commented a voice from the end of the table, "there had been mention that there may have been a dark van sighted. But the witness couldn't remember what the make was, though she thought it looked new. Never saw the license plate. And since we don't know for sure just where she had been abducted from, it's tough to tell whether or not the van had any significance at all."

"It's damned hard to investigate a crime scene

that you can't find." The voice of the detective from the small Kentucky town was heavy with frustration.

"Has the FBI's ERT been there?" A young woman—the lead investigator from Kansas City—asked, pointing to the television screen.

"Yes. They were there when this film was made." The detective switched off the VCR. "When we realized that there could be a tie to the cases that were discussed at the press conference, we called the closest FBI office and asked if they could send in their Evidence Response Team. We knew that this investigation could be crucial. If anything at all was left behind that could lead to tracking this guy, we didn't want to be the ones to blow the evidence."

"They wanted us to blow the evidence," Adam Stark quipped to break the tension.

"However, by the time we realized there could be a connection," Detective West chose to ignore the agent's weak attempt at humor, slipping the video tape back into his briefcase, and snapping the lock briskly, "it had already rained. There was nothing there. No footprints. No tire tracks. Nothing."

The others seated around the table packed their notes up as well, silently reflecting on the unfortunate circumstances but refusing to judge—even to themselves—the actions of the local police. There but for the grace of God . . .

Finally, Rex Egan stood and thanked the members of the various law enforcement agencies for agreeing to meet as they had for the past two days.

"Keep in touch, ladies and gentlemen. We'll certainly let you know how things are going on our end," he promised them as they filed out through the open door. Pausing for a brief moment to lean down and whisper something into John's ear, Egan followed the others into the hallway, leaving only John's chosen few seated at the table.

As the door closed, John rose without ceremony and began to pass out large manila envelopes to each of the other three agents who had remained seated.

"Each one of these envelopes contains a complete copy of the entire investigative file on each of the disappearances. Eight victims, including Mrs. Akins. Four of us. Two files apiece. Read them through. However many times it takes until questions begin to form."

"Questions?" Adam asked.

"The ones that weren't asked the first time. I think it's clear, after all we've heard over the past forty-eight hours, that no one has a clue about this guy, so there's no point, in my mind, to spend any time discussing anything that we've heard. While I think the meeting was a good forum for the locals to share their information with each other, nothing that I've heard here has given me any clearer picture of who or what or why than I had when I arrived. It was a good PR move, but as far as I'm concerned, it's a waste of time to rehash it, so we won't, unless one of you caught something that I missed and wants to throw it onto the table." He paused and looked at the three agents sitting before him. No one seemed to have anything to say, so John continued.

"When you've completely reviewed your files and made notes, we'll get back together and then we'll compare notes. We're looking for that common thread. Something that strikes a familiar chord. Maybe it's in a witness statement or in the comments made by a family member." John sat down in his chair and opened the file in front of him. "Then, when we're done, we'll be calling on the family members, the witnesses and potential witnesses until we find out *why* these women were taken. And hopefully, that knowledge will help us to figure out where they've been taken." John paused, then added, "And if any of them are still alive."

"And if, after we've all gone through the files, there's still nothing?"

"Then I'd have to admit that everything I feel about this case—everything my instincts tell me—is wrong. But I don't see it happening. I don't think it's random. We just haven't stumbled on that one thing that will lead us to the truth."

"We will," Adam Stark said softly. "Sooner or later, we'll get lucky."

"Hopefully, before our chameleon strikes again . . ." Genna murmured.

"Well, I for one am not going to give up until I personally lay eyes on . . ." Dale leaned over his files to read the names off the fronts, "Lani Gilbert and Joanne Landers."

"I used to know someone named Lani," Genna said. "Her given name was Atalanta. Isn't that some name for a kid?"

"That's a mouthful, all right." Adam nodded as he opened the file and began to sort through the papers within.

John looked across the table as Genna opened the first of her files. Their eyes met briefly as she slid the contents out, and she gave him a half-smile. John fully expected their break to come through her. Sooner or later, the more she focused on the victims, the greater the likelihood that they'd get lucky. While he understood that whatever force controlled those little windows in Genna's psyche didn't always open them, he knew from past experience that once Genna's instincts kicked in, they often pointed her in the right direction. John opened the first of his files and began to read.

It was two hours later before Adam Stark, the tall, dark-haired former NFL linebacker, broke the silence by asking, "Is there a reason why I can't take this material back to my hotel room?"

"None at all," John told him. "You're certainly free to work wherever you feel most comfortable."

"Good." Adam stood and stretched. "I think I need a change of venue. We've been in this conference room on and off for too long. I've got cabin fever."

"Let's plan on meeting back here at eight tomorrow morning," John suggested. "Of course, it goes without saying that you'll call if any bells go off."

"That's more than enough time to read through and make notes." Dale nodded. "I think I'll head back to my room, too."

John watched as half his team bunched their files under their arms and left the conference room.

"Genna?" John asked.

"What?"

"Do you want to go back to your hotel room to work?"

"I'm fine here." She looked up from her reading. "How 'bout you?"

"I'm fine here, too." He nodded.

"Good." She turned her attention back to the documents before her.

"Want to take a break?"

"No. I don't want to lose my momentum."

"I think I'll see if I can scout up some coffee." He stood and stretched, much as the others had done. "Want some?"

"Sure," Genna murmured, and he could tell she was totally immersed in the story that was unfolding in front of her.

John left the room quietly. When he returned twenty minutes later with two cups of coffee, she was still sitting in the same position. Hunched over the table, her head resting on her right elbow, the fingers of her left hand tapping slowly, but oh so impatiently, on the file.

He sat the coffee next to her and went back to his place across the table from her without speaking. He'd chosen the seat deliberately, where he could look directly at her without making it obvious that even in the midst of something as important as the investigation at hand, he still could barely keep his eyes off her.

She was always beautiful to him, and John loved to watch her at work. When she concentrated, her brows raised just the tiniest bit and knit together just ever so slightly, giving her the look of an endlessly curious child. It softened her and made her appear so much younger, so much more vulnerable than the cool and efficient mantle she so often wore.

Warmed just to be near her for so long, near enough to catch the light scent of her perfume, John picked up his pencil and went back to taking notes, reflecting, just for a moment, on the fact that Genna never had to write anything down. The times when she did take notes, she did so merely to preserve the information for others. She simply never forgot what she read, or what she heard, and it never failed to amaze him that she could cull from memory the most obscure facts from cases long forgotten by everyone else. Just one more thing that he had always admired about her.

She stirred slightly as she pushed the papers before her into a neat pile and returned them to their envelope.

"Anything?" He asked, even while knowing that had there been anything, she'd have told him so.

She shook her head and reached for the coffee.

"Thank you," she said after taking a few sips and opening the second of her two folders.

Later, after having read through the preliminary reports, she refiled them, and sighed.

"What?" John asked without looking up.

"These two women seemed to be so much alike as to almost be interchangeable. They both come from nice families, nice backgrounds. Went to college. Married nice, stable men. Had children whom they love and close circles of friends, go to church, contribute to their communities. Everyone says how happy they were."

"So?"

"So, I guess I just can't help but wonder if they were always this happy. If their lives were always this perfect. So far, all I've read about both of these women leads me to think that their little boats were never rocked. And frankly, I find that hard to believe."

"Well, you'll have a chance to find out when you start interviewing those same family and friends. I figure we'd take the rest of the day to read through, then we'd spend Friday morning going over what we've found. On Friday afternoon we'll go our separate ways and see if we can learn something that the locals may have missed."

"Sounds like a plan." Genna smiled and pushed herself back from the table.

"Is your hotel all right?" John asked casually. "I'm sorry I couldn't get us all in the same place, but there are a few conventions in town."

"Oh, it's fine. Thank you. The room is lovely," she replied.

He watched as she packed up her files and her briefcase and swung the strap of her purse over her shoulder.

"I guess I'll see you in the morning," she said softly, pausing in the doorway as if wanting to add something, then thinking better of it, left the room without looking back.

John sat quietly for a few long moments, swiveling his chair seat from side to side, deep in thought, wondering how he had managed to spend the last few days in her company without grabbing her by the arms and kissing her until she either collapsed or begged for mercy.

Of course, it pleased John to be working with her once more. No stone would be unturned, he knew, in piecing together whatever tiny splintered fragments of evidence they would be able to uncover at this late date. If it was possible to find a trail, Genna, ever so detail-oriented, would help to locate it. It could be the smallest bit of information that could trigger something in her mind, and that small something could lead to the break they were looking for.

But her presence there meant something more to John. It allowed him to look at her, maybe even to touch her. To be close to her, and he longed for that closeness, had missed it terribly. She drew him like a magnet, and he'd never for a moment considered it a weakness. And he'd never been able to give up the hope that someday he'd win her back.

*Maybe today.* John smiled wistfully to himself as he, too, packed up his files and prepared to leave.

The thought lingered even as he left the building. As he walked to his car. As he drove back to his town house and parked out front.

*Maybe today.*

He sat behind the wheel, the engine still running, remembering how it had been, several years back, when they'd first started dating. How he'd wined and dined her, how they'd taken long, romantic walks in the moonlight, holding hands and talking about their goals, their reasons for seeking out careers in law enforcement, their hopes for the future. Looking back, it seemed to him that they had fallen in love step by step, day by day.

And here they were, just a few short years later, together again in DC, where they'd once spent so much time together.

A smile began to spread slowly across his face and his fingers tapped thoughtfully on the steering wheel. He turned off the car, gathered up his files, and whistling as headed across the parking lot with a spring in his step, planned his evening.

It was close to seven-thirty when Genna heard the knock on her door. Thinking it was way too soon for the tray of fruit and club soda she'd just called for, she opened the door to find a casually dressed John Mancini standing before her.

"I thought maybe you could use a break about now," he said, making no attempt to enter her room.

"Actually, I had just called room service for a snack," she told him, looking over his shoulder in hopes of seeing a cart being wheeled around the bend in the corridor.

"A snack?" he asked. "It's dinner time." He glanced at his watch. "Actually, it's past dinner time. If you're eating on Patsy-time."

Genna laughed and checked the time on her own watch.

"You're right. I didn't realize it was so late. No wonder I'm so hungry."

"Could I interest you in a quick dinner?" he asked nonchalantly, knowing full well that a quick meal was the last thing on his mind.

Genna looked down at the light gray knit shorts and white tank top that she wore. Her feet were bare.

"I'm not really dressed," she stated the obvious.

"I'm sure there's someplace casual close by where we can catch a bite."

She bit her bottom lip, and John knew she was inwardly debating.

Good.

"Just give me a minute to pull on a skirt and to find my sandals." She smiled. "Thanks for thinking of me."

As if he'd thought of much else except her and the case since she'd arrived in the city.

"How about I wait for you in the lobby?" He suggested.

"That'd be fine," she nodded. "I'll just be a minute."

Genna closed the door, and leaned back against it.

What was she thinking? What had happened to her resolve to keep it simple, keep it friendly and professional?

*It's only a casual dinner. I can keep it friendly and professional,* she asserted as she folded up the file she'd been reading. *This is just dinner. No big deal.*

*Of course, it's not,* she told herself cynically, dialing room service to cancel her order. *It's only dinner in the city where they fell in love. Dinner in the city where he broke her heart.*

Hadn't she spent the better part of the past forty-eight hours trying to ignore the fact that every time she looked at him, her heart began to beat just a little bit faster? That she'd had to remind herself on far too many occasions that she wasn't there to stare across the table at him? That there was an important case unfolding before her, that she was an important member of the team intended to investigate it, and that she'd better pay more attention to what was being said and less attention to John's body language?

"I haven't missed a thing," she muttered to herself as she moved hangers around in the closet, looking for a short summer skirt that would be appropriate for a quick meal on a hot summer night in the nation's capital. "I heard every word that was spoken over the past two days. I can recite the names of the missing and where they're from. And before I'm through, I'll know the names of their spouses and the ages of their kids and every move they made on the day they went missing."

She paused in front of the bathroom mirror to run a brush through her hair and pull it up into a tidy ponytail.

*It's just hard, being so close to him. It reminds me of other days when we worked together. Other cases. Other times ...*

"Times long gone," she said aloud, as if to remind herself of that, too. "In the past. Finished. Done. History."

Then why, she asked herself as she closed her door behind her, was her pulse racing and her feet flying to the elevator?

"So, have you gotten any vibes on our case?" John asked after they had been seated in a nearby pub.

"I don't know," she shook her head slowly as she opened the menu and began to read. "I think I'll have the roast beef sandwich."

"Sounds good. Me too." John handed the menus back to the waiter. "Two roast beefs. And a very large order of onion rings."

"I haven't had onion rings in . . . I can't remember when."

"Then you're due to indulge."

She grinned.

"You sound like Patsy. Always prodding me to eat."

"How is Pats?"

"I spoke with her last night. She and Chrissie are having a ball. Patsy's teaching Chris to fish, to sail, to paddle a canoe. All the things she taught me, that first summer I was with her."

"How do you feel about sharing her?"

"You mean, am I worried that Chrissie might take my place with Patsy?" Genna's eyes gleamed. "Not for a second. I know exactly what I mean to Pats. I'm just delighted that Chris is having an opportunity, for once in her life, to feel that special to someone else. You know how Pats is. She makes everyone feel that they are the most important person in the world. Chrissie's never had anyone treat her that way. It's time she did."

Genna poured sugar substitute from a pink packet into her iced tea.

"On the other hand, yeah, sure, I'd rather be sailing, as they say. I'd like to be there to be part of whatever it is they are doing," She sipped at her tea. "Especially since Patsy's birthday is next week."

"Well, maybe you can slip away for a night," John told her. "We'll be doing a lot of traveling around over the next week or so."

"I don't want to take any time from the investigation," she said. "Everyone else will be working sixteen-hour days. I don't want to be the slacker on the team."

"I doubt anyone will ever have cause to call you a slacker. I just meant, maybe you'll get enough of a break to make a little side trip to the lake."

"If I had the time, I'd certainly stop in for a night. I do miss Pats." She sighed. "I'm even missing Chris."

"What's so strange about that? She's your sister."

"All those years we were apart, I tried so hard not to think about her. Not to miss her."

"Any idea of what she's going to do, ultimately?"

"No. I suspect the past few weeks have been overwhelming for her. And Pats probably hasn't given her time to catch her breath." Genna leaned back in her seat as the waiter appeared with their sandwiches and positioned their plates on the narrow wooden plank table. "I think Chrissie came looking for me mostly to ease her conscience, maybe to establish some type of relationship with me, but I'm sure she wasn't prepared for Pats."

John laughed aloud.

"I wonder if anyone is ever prepared for people like Patsy."

"She's one in a million, that's for sure." Genna speared an onion ring from the platter and draped it over the end of her plate. "I'm just hoping that Chrissie is able to adapt. You know, from being without any stable family life for so long, then going into a group home, and from there to Patsy's, well, it might be hard for Chris."

"You adapted." John took another bite out of his sandwich.

"I was younger, and I hadn't seen all that Chrissie's seen. Haven't had to deal with a lot of what she's had. And I had advantages that she's never had."

"Well, she'll have them now," John reminded her.

"If she stays," Genna told him.

"How likely is it that she'd leave?"

"I don't know. We've not talked about the future. I'm not good at looking ahead."

"Not real good at looking back, either," John muttered.

"I heard that," she put her fork down. "I'm working on it."

"Really?" He raised an eyebrow. "That's encouraging. Want to tell me exactly what it is that you're working on? Perhaps I can help refresh your memory."

"Thanks," she said, a soft smile tugging at the corners of her mouth. "I'll let you know."

"I'm counting on it."

"You do that." She grinned, then to change the subject, asked, "Quick, the guy by the door in the seersucker suit. What do you suppose he does for a living?"

"Too easy," John grinned back, pleased that she'd revived the old game they used to play in public places. "Congressional aide."

"You're right. That was a no brainer." Genna bit, then chewed as if contemplating. "Okay, then. The woman in the red blazer sitting alone at the small round table over there."

"Television news," John replied, shaking his head. "I can see you're clearly out of practice."

"Finished, folks?" The waiter appeared out of no where.

"I am," Genna nodded.

"I guess we both are," John told him.

"Can I bring you some dessert? Coffee?"

"Genna?" John asked.

"Nothing for me."

"Just the check, then," John said.

"I'm looking forward to the walk back to the hotel." Genna stood when the waiter returned with the check.

"So am I." John dropped two twenties on the table and took her elbow. "It's a beautiful night."

"So it is." Genna stopped on the sidewalk outside the pub and looked up into the night sky. It was clear, for all it was suspended over a major city, with all its lights and smog, and the moon hung low over the horizon.

They strolled along the narrow sidewalk, their elbows touching, surprisingly content with the shared silence. So Genna was startled to see John step into the street and flag down a taxi. When the cab stopped, John opened the back door and turned to her, saying, "Hop in."

"Where are we going?" she asked as she slid into the backseat.

"Something I want to see." John slid in beside her, telling the driver, "The National Mall, please."

The cab raced through the streets, the driver blissfully unaware that two law enforcement agents were tossed around in his backseat as he cut this corner and sped around that. He arrived at their destination and stopped on a dime.

"Well," Genna said as she stepped out of the cab. "That was an interesting ride."

"I'm guessing we might have been that one last fare for the evening," John said wryly, taking her arm and looping it around his own, then stopped to get his bearings. "It's this way, I believe, to the Korean War Veterans Memorial."

They nodded as they passed an elderly gentleman who stood with his arms folded, looking out at the silent landscape where the statues of poncho-clad soldiers slipped through the night on an eerie patrol.

"Oh." Genna squeezed John's arm. "Oh, look at that. Just *look* at that. Have you ever seen anything so . . . *dramatic* in your life?"

The memorial erected to commemorate the men and women who served in the Korean Conflict caught the eye and held it. Nineteen statues, larger than life, headed up the hill, each man in a different pose, all so lifelike that Genna had gasped. Beautifully conceived, perfectly composed, the stone figures appeared to be more alive in the night than any sculpture she had ever seen.

The couple stood in the dark and watched as the soldiers marched, ever faithfully, against an unseen enemy. The deepening shadows graced the statues with an energy, a force that was almost palpable.

"Amazing piece of work, isn't it?" The elderly gentleman moved close enough to comment, as if needing to share his thoughts on the magnificent sight.

"It truly is," John nodded.

"Your first visit?" the old man asked.

"No. I've been before."

"Did you have someone there, in Korea?" The stranger ventured forward another casual step or two.

"An uncle. My mother's brother," John told him.

"What branch?"

"Army."

"What was his name?"

"Victor Esposito."

"I didn't know him. I'm sorry," the old man shook his head. "Did he come back?"

"No," John said. "He was killed within three weeks of his arrival."

After a moment of silence, the man asked, "Has your mother been here?"

"Yes. She's been a few times, she and her sisters."

The old man nodded and looked off to where the Pool of Remembrance reflected the moon, murmuring, *"Our nation honors her sons and daughters who answered the call to defend a country they never knew and a people they never met."*

He turned to John and Genna and smiled, saying, "That's the inscription over there at the Pool. In Korea 54,269 American lives were lost, and it took till

1993 to break ground on this spot, to honor their memories and to let their families know that their sacrifices have not been forgotten."

The old man drew himself up ramrod straight, saluted John and Genna, and disappeared into the shadows.

"That was a moment." Genna finally broke the silence.

"I'd say the man had memories to deal with tonight. I'm glad we were here, so that he wasn't alone."

"Why did we come here?"

"Today would have been my uncle's sixty-sixth birthday. I promised my mom I'd come by, since I was in the city."

"Thank you for bringing me along."

"I was hoping you wouldn't mind," he said, taking her hand tightly in his own.

"Not at all," she replied, falling into an easy pace as they walked back toward the street. "The memorial is breathtaking, and it's a beautiful evening. If you hadn't stopped by for me, I'd have spent the entire night in my room and I'd have missed it all."

"I'm glad that you're glad." John smiled, feeling pleased with himself. "Now, what do you suppose our chances are of finding a cab at this hour?"

"Not a problem," Genna laughed as she walked into the street with her arm raised as a taxi rounded the corner, looking for a fare.

"Okay, so you got lucky," John muttered good-naturedly as the cab stopped and he opened the door for her. He gave the driver the name of Genna's hotel and settled into the backseat next to her.

He had pretty much decided to take things really

slowly with her this time, being determined to win her back, once and for all, and not wanting to do anything that might scare her away, or give her an excuse not to be alone with him again. But she was so damned close, there in the dark, and she smelled so damned good, that without thinking, he'd drawn her to him, the fingers of his right hand sliding through the soft warmth of her hair and the fingers of the left easing her chin up so that her mouth met his own.

*This wasn't in tonight's game plan,* he silently berated himself even as he kissed her. *I hadn't planned on anything like this tonight. This was supposed to be our get reacquainted/John's really a good guy/no pressure evening,* he reminded himself as his tongue parted her lips and slid into the soft warmth of her mouth.

*Oh, well. The best-laid plans . . .*

He pretended to debate with himself the wisdom of such a close encounter so soon, but she pulled him closer and wrapped her arms around him, offering the sweetness of her mouth. What could he do but give in to the moment?

"That'll be six bucks," the cabbie glanced over his shoulder, oblivious to the fact that the willpower of one of the FBI's best-known special agents had just totally unwound.

"What? Are we here already?" John lifted his head. "Think you could make it once more around the block? Maybe a little slower this time?"

"Sure, buddy," the cabbie shrugged.

"John," Genna whispered, as if having second thoughts. "Do you really think this is a good idea?"

"I think it's the best idea I've had in a long time," he said as he pulled her back to him, and settled in to

kiss her again. "As a matter of fact, I'm surprised I
didn't come up with it sooner."

"Seriously." She kept him at arm's length as she
debated the matter. "We'll be working together."

He digested this as if it hadn't occurred to him
before, then smiled at her through the darkness.

"Only during the daytime," he held her wrists
and guided her arms back around his neck. "The
nights are our own."

# 17

"I need my head examined," Genna muttered to herself as she flicked on the light in the small entry to her hotel room. "I have no self-control, no willpower whatsoever. I lecture myself on how the only way John and I can work together is if we keep it casual, keep it friendly, keep romance out of the picture. And the first time—*the first time*—" she tossed her leather bag across the room and it landed with a thud on the dresser "—he gets that close to me, what happens? We're sucking face in the back of a cab like a couple of sixteen-year-olds, that's what happens."

She stood in the middle of the small room, her hands on her hips, trying to be angry with herself for not reminding John that *that* part of their relationship was supposed to be over. For wanting exactly what she'd been telling herself for months that she didn't want. For needing him as much as she always had.

When she realized that she just couldn't work up a good enough steam, she dropped to the side of the bed and sat down.

"You scare me, John Mancini." She could admit it to him, now that he wasn't here. "I don't think anyone ever scared me as much as you do. There's never been anyone who could hurt me the way you could."

*But he did hurt you once, and you survived,* a small voice inside reminded her. *And there's obviously something still there. For both of you. Maybe you're cheating yourself if you don't look close enough to find out what it is that keeps pulling you back to one another. . . .*

She blew out a long stream of air and slipped out of her sandals, then walked into the tiny bathroom and washed her face. She stripped off her clothes and slid the soft nightshirt over her head, then turned off the light and drew the drapes back to expose a door, which she unlocked. Stepping out onto the small balcony, she looked out over the city she loved. Half a block away, on the opposite side of the side street, stood the hotel where they'd spent their very first night together.

"Mancini, you dog," she muttered, a half-smile on her face. "I'll bet you requested a room with a street view."

She leaned on the railing, permitting the memories of that first night to creep past her defenses. A longing to go back in time to that night, to start over, washed through her. She turned her back on the view and went back into the room and closed the door behind her.

There wasn't much use in wanting to go back. *You can't ever go back,* she told herself as she climbed into bed. *But you can go forward, if that's what you want.*

She closed her eyes and thought back to the cab ride, to the mind-numbing sensation that had engulfed her when John had begun to kiss her.

*Hormones,* she'd told herself at the time.

*More than hormones,* her little inner voice had corrected her. *Ever so much more than hormones.*

What would have happened if John had insisted that he come back upstairs with her to her room, instead of saying goodnight downstairs and kissing her—a bit briefly, she now reflected—at the elevator? Where might they have ended up, had they gone a few more times around the block?

Genna reached her arm out and rested it on the pillow next to hers. She sure enough knew where they would have ended up.

And the thing of it was, she wasn't so sure that she was sorry that they hadn't.

"The thing that struck me about these two women," Adam was saying the next morning when John's team had reconvened, "is how nice their lives were. Besides being married to men who really seem to care for them, they both have nice friends."

Genna nodded. "I felt the same way. I told John yesterday that it seemed like they'd both always had things pretty good."

"Not mine," Dale Hunter drawled, referring to his notes. "One of my ladies definitely had problems."

"What kind of problems?" John asked.

"She'd been in therapy on and off for years."

"Anyone kind enough to say why?"

"Husband told the investigating officer she's had periods of depression. Mother is quoted as having said that her daughter has some 'unresolved issues,' but she declined to elaborate," Dale told them. "The other lady here seemed pretty stable, though."

"Nothing really outstanding about either of mine,

either," John conceded. "Typical suburban lives. One woman worked part-time, the other was a librarian. Nothing exciting."

"Where do we go from here?" Dale asked John.

"To the home of the victim of your choice," John replied. "First one, then the other—Dale, I'm sure you'll be wanting to find out what your victim's 'unresolved issues' might be. Check in as often as you have to. You're all seasoned, I don't have to tell you what to look for, what to ask. I just want to know the minute a red flag goes up. On anything."

"You got it." Adam rose and pushed his chair under the table, as if his mother were standing behind him, reminding him of his manners.

"I hope to see y'all real soon," Dale told them.

"So," John said to Genna when they were alone.

"So." Genna raised an eyebrow.

"So, about last night . . ." He started around the table. Since he'd dropped her off at the hotel, he'd been berating himself for not being able to keep his hands off her. For all but attacking her in the back of the cab. For crying out loud, the plan was slow and easy. And slow and easy did not mean . . . well, it didn't mean going where they'd been headed the night before.

"If you apologize, you're a dead man," Genna said as she rose from her chair.

"Huh?" John stopped at the end of the table.

"I said, if you apologize, you're a dead man." She stood in front of him, her files held in her arms in front of her.

"But . . ." John struggled with words, looking confused.

"We'll talk about it when this is over." She leaned

up and kissed him on the mouth. "We have a lot to
talk about when this is over."

"Give me a hint," he asked as she reached up to
rest the palm of her hand along the side of his face.
He turned his head slightly and kissed her thumb.
"Is this going to be a good talk or a bad talk?"

"It'll be a good talk," she said, then turned to the
door. "I'll call you when I get to Connecticut."

John walked to the door to watch her stride down
the hall, wondering just how encouraged he should
be. For the life of him, he couldn't figure out the way
that woman's mind worked. The only thing he really
knew for certain, he realized as he packed up his
own files, was that the taxi ride the night before had
been the best investment of twenty bucks that he'd
made in a long time.

Genna sat in her rental car in front of the lovely
white clapboard house on the outskirts of Mystic,
Connecticut, and tried to digest what she'd learned
from the despondent husband of Barbie Nelson. That
Barbie had left the house at seven forty-five on the
morning of her disappearance and dropped off their
twin daughters at nursery school. That from there
she went to the video store to return some movies, to
the library for her weekly selection of two books, and
to the pharmacy to have her asthma prescription
refilled. It had been a totally routine Monday. The
movies were dropped off, books were checked out,
but she never did make it to the pharmacy. Wherever
she was, Genna hoped she didn't need her new
inhaler.

Genna checked her watch. It was almost noon.
She'd been at the Nelson home for almost three

hours, looking at photo albums, asking questions, getting to know Barbie Nelson. She probably would have liked her, Genna thought as she started the car, had their paths ever crossed. She seemed to be a decent woman. Her house was warmly furnished and simply decorated, pleasant but without pretension, and Barbie's touch was everywhere, from what Genna could see, from the drapes she'd made for the dining room to the stenciling in the downstairs powder room to the cheery flower beds that overflowed with late summer blooms. Even after having been missing for several weeks, Barbie's presence was still strong. But though Genna had learned about the woman, she'd learned nothing about the crime that had been committed against her.

John's instincts are one hundred percent right on, she told herself as she drove to her next appointment. Barbie Nelson was not a woman to have walked away from the life she had so carefully, so lovingly, made for herself and her family.

At the next stoplight, she pulled the hand-printed note from her purse on the seat next to her and double-checked the directions. Was it left at the next light, or the one after it? Confirming that it was, in fact, the next light, Genna stayed in the far lane in preparation of the turn. It would be interesting to see just what, if anything, Barbie's mother could add to the story. Surely, there had to be something. . . .

Five minutes later, Genna stood on the front steps of the weathered shingled house and rang the doorbell. Seconds later the door opened and a trim, neatly dressed woman in her early sixties invited her in.

"Mrs. Benson, I appreciate your agreeing to meet with me. I know this is a very difficult time for you,"

Genna said as she was led through the house out onto a screened porch that ran across half of the back of the house.

"One of the worst times of my life. But, if there's anything I can do that could help you find my daughter . . ." Sarah Benson held out both hands, palms up, a gesture as much to indicate her willingness to assist as her own helplessness. "Though I have told the police everything I know. Everything they asked."

"I'm sure you have, Mrs. Benson," Genna assured the woman calmly as she seated herself on a white wicker settee and opened her briefcase, preparing to take notes, not for her reference but to preserve what she learned for others. "I'm sure you know that we suspect that Barbie fell victim to the same person who may be responsible for a series of abductions of other women. Right now, what we're concentrating on is what might connect these women to each other, and therefore to their abductor. So we're trying to learn as much about these women as possible."

Genna rummaged around in her handbag for a pen.

"Before we start, could I get you something to drink? I've just made a pitcher of iced tea." Mrs. Benson stood in the doorway, her hands folded in front of her, her bearing somewhat stiff and formal. She wore a dark denim skirt and a white cotton twin set, a haunted look and an air of weariness.

"That would be lovely, thank you," Genna smiled, accepting the offer to give Mrs. Benson one last opportunity to collect herself as well as to give Genna a few moments to observe her surroundings.

The screened porch overlooked a backyard that

sloped down just ever so slightly three hundred or so feet to a wooden dock that overlooked a tiny slice of an inlet. No boats were tied to the dock, however, though the house next door boasted three. The porch itself was comfortably, if not artistically furnished, with a drop-leaf table painted with birdhouses holding a lamp of clear glass filled with colored stones. A painted basket held magazines, and the latest hardback book by a popular woman writer sat on the wicker coffee table next to a bowl of bright summer flowers.

"You have quite a view here," Genna said as her hostess returned with a tray on which sat two glasses of ice and a blue pitcher.

"Yes, don't we?" Mrs. Benson moved the book to the floor and replaced it with the tray, then proceeded to carefully pour tea into the glasses. "I never get tired of it."

"Then you've lived here for a long time?"

"I grew up here. This house has been in my family for generations."

"Did Barbie grow up here, as well?"

"No." Sarah Benson sipped slowly at her tea. "We were living in Allen's Springs—that's in New York State, dear—when Barbie was born. Her father—my first husband, Bob—had grown up there. We met at college, and after we were married, we settled there. Bob went to work for an accounting firm owned by his father and uncle."

"And Barbie is an only child?"

"Yes."

"And you moved back here when?"

Mrs. Benson paused, as if trying to recall. "Seventeen, eighteen years ago. My father had died, and my mother wanted to move to Arizona to live with her sister. As I said, the house has been in the family for years—I couldn't bear the thought of selling it—so Barbie and I moved back."

"And your husband?"

"He . . . wasn't inclined to make the move. He had his business, you see, and, well, it was one of those things." She took another sip of her tea. "We divorced shortly after the move."

"And you remarried?"

"Twelve years ago, yes. Unfortunately, my husband—Joe Benson, my second husband—died three years ago. Oddly enough," she cleared her throat, "he died almost two years to the day after my first husband. Both of heart attacks, by the way."

"I'm sorry." Genna said gently.

"Yes, well, I still consider myself to be a lucky woman. I have my daughter, a wonderful son-in-law, three adorable grandchildren." Mrs. Benson paused, adding quietly. "I hope I still have my daughter. . . ."

"We're all hoping for that, Mrs. Benson." Genna couldn't help but lean over and pat the woman's hand. "Mrs. Benson, can you think of anything—especially something from your daughter's past—that might lead us in another direction? Maybe an old boyfriend who remained in touch perhaps too persistently, someone from school she may have had problems with, a coworker who bothered her . . ."

"No, no," Mrs. Benson shook her head adamantly. "Nothing like that. Barbie didn't date very much in high school, she never really had a steady boyfriend until she met Rich, and they married right out of college. She was a good student, and, really, a very good kid. She never gave me a moment's trouble, really, when she was in school. And if there was something . . . well, she would have told me, I feel certain. Barbie and I are very close, Miss Snow. If there had been anything, I would have known about it."

"And she never mentioned that she felt she was being watched, or that she noticed a strange car or a van?"

"No. Though a month or so ago, she did say that she'd been bothered by someone calling the house and then hanging up. The police know about that, though. They'd never gotten a lead on that."

"Did she say if the caller said anything at all?"

"No. I asked her about that specifically, and she said that he—or she—never said a word."

"Can you think of anything out of the ordinary that Barbie may have mentioned over the past few weeks or months?"

"No, I'm sorry, but no. There's nothing. I've laid awake every night since she's been gone, trying to remember something, anything, that might help, but there's nothing."

"I'm sorry to have made you go through this all again, Mrs. Benson." Genna closed her notebook and slipped it into her briefcase, and taking a card from her pocket, handed it to the woman and said, "If you think of anything—anything, however remote you might think it could be—please call me. You can always reach me at the cell phone number."

"I will. Yes, of course, I will." Mrs. Benson nodded briskly and rose to walk Genna to the front door.

"Oh. One thing I meant to ask you earlier. Did your first husband remarry?"

"Yes. Shortly before I did. Why?"

"Is his second wife still living?"

"I believe so." Mrs. Benson stood in the half-opened doorway. "Why?"

"Because I don't recall seeing a statement from her in the police file, and I would have expected them to have interviewed Barbie's stepmother."

"Barbie barely knew her. She didn't care for her, and Doris—that's the second Mrs. Wright—didn't care for Barbie, either." Sarah Benson stepped aside, a clear indication that she expected Genna to step on out. "So I'm not at all surprised that they didn't call her. I'm sure she'd have had nothing to say."

"I see," Genna said thoughtfully.

"Miss Snow, do you think that she . . . that Barbie is . . . that she's still . . ." The woman could not bring herself to finish the sentence.

"Still alive?" Genna spoke the words the anguished mother could not. "I sincerely hope so, Mrs. Benson. We all sincerely hope so."

Genna walked to her car, feeling the woman's eyes on her back even though the door had been closed behind her before she had reached the street. She sat in her rental car, checking the directions to her next appointment and wondering why there'd been no mention of Barbie's stepmother in the original police reports. Surely the woman would have been contacted, wouldn't she?

Genna was still thinking about it as she pulled up in front of the rambling old colonial style structure that served as the home of the Frog Hollow Day School, where summer camp was in session and Carol Stoddard, Barbie Nelson's best friend, coached tennis. Parking in the narrow lot, Genna made her way to the courts that lay just beyond the swimming pool. As she approached, a woman in her early thirties, dressed in tennis whites, spotted her and waved.

"Agent Snow?" The woman called from the gate that led into the courts.

"Yes." Genna nodded and quickened her step. "I'm sorry I'm late. My last appointment ran a little longer than I'd expected it to."

"Maybe, with any luck, my next student will be a little late as well." Carol Stoddard extended a hand and shook Genna's with a firm grip. "As I told you when we spoke, I have a pretty full schedule today, but if there's anything I can do to help . . ."

The woman's blue eyes filled with tears.

"Damn, it just doesn't seem possible, you know? That anyone would want to hurt Barbie. She's one of the kindest, most gentle people I've ever known."

"That's pretty much been the consensus of everyone who knows her." Genna took a few steps back into the shade. "Everyone who's been interviewed has had nothing but the best to say of her."

"It's all true. She's just an ace, all around. I just can't think of any reason for this to have happened."

"How long have you known Barbie Nelson, Ms. Stoddard?"

"Since she moved here. What's that, sixteen years or something? We were best friends in high school, we stayed close through college. I was her maid of honor. Her oldest is my godchild."

"Then you know her pretty well."

"Better than anyone, except maybe Rich, her husband. And before you ask, no, he couldn't have anything to do with this. He adores her. Surprises her with dinner reservations and flowers at least once a week. He genuinely loves her, very much. There's no way in hell he'd have harmed a hair on her head."

"You say you went to school together . . . perhaps someone . . ."

"Not a chance. Barbie was very well liked—not especially popular, in that sense—but well liked all around. I honestly can't think of anyone who didn't like her."

"Except, apparently, her stepmother," Genna said.

Carol Stoddard's eyebrows raised. "Where did you hear that? Oh. Let me guess. You've been to see Barbie's mom."

Genna nodded.

"And Mrs. Benson told you that Barbie and Doris didn't care for each other?"

"Pretty much."

"That's bull. Barbie loves Doris. And next to me, Mindy is her best friend."

"Who's Mindy?" Genna frowned.

"Barbie's stepsister." The tennis coach grinned. "I take it Sarah didn't bother to mention her."

"That name doesn't appear anywhere in the police file."

"I'm not at all surprised. Barbie's mom would be just as happy if that whole other crew out there just upped and disappeared." Realizing what she had said, Carol Stoddard blushed furiously. "I can't believe I just said that, after Barbie . . . after . . ."

"Do you know how I could get in touch with Mindy?"

"No. But Doris would be easy enough to find. She still lives out in . . . the name of the town will come to me . . ."

"Allen's Springs?"

"Right. New York State, someplace around Lake Erie."

"Really?" Genna raised an interested eyebrow.

"I'm sorry I don't have a phone number."

"I suppose Barbie's husband might, though."

"I'm not so sure about that." Carol hesitated. "For some reason, Barbie never tried to mesh those two parts of her life."

"What do you mean?"

"When she went to visit Doris, she went alone. Never took Rich, never took the kids."

"Why?"

"I haven't the faintest idea. She said once that Rich wasn't really interested, and the kids were too small to cart around on the plane, some silly thing like that. I always just thought that maybe, well, maybe Rich didn't want to go because he'd feel disloyal to Sarah somehow."

Both women turned at the sound of a car door slamming behind them. A man in khaki shorts walked toward them holding the hand of a skipping girl of about seven.

"I'm sorry, my one o'clock lesson is here." The coach waved to the newcomers. "Was there anything else?"

"No. You've been helpful. And if you think of anything at all—regardless of how insignificant you might think it sounds—please call me." Genna pressed a card into her hands.

"I will." Carol smiled at the child and her father, and held the gate open for them to pass into the court area, then turned back to Genna and said, "The thought of anyone hurting Barbie makes me physically ill. Please find her before . . ."

"We're all doing our best," Genna assured her.

Genna stood beneath the broad canopy of the maple tree and watched the tennis lesson for a few minutes, pondering this bit of information she'd gleaned from the victim's friend. Perhaps Mrs. Benson was unaware of just how close her daughter was to her stepmother. Or perhaps she didn't want to know. Maybe she just resented her and chose to believe that Barbie did as well.

When she returned to her car, Genna pulled her states' atlas from her briefcase, and was startled to find that Allen's Springs, New York, was less than a three-hour drive from Patsy's cottage. She tapped her fingers on the steering wheel, debating her next move. When she'd formulated her game plan, she reached for her cell phone, and dialed John's number.

He answered on the third ring.

"Where are you?" He asked.

"I am under an ancient maple tree that shades the parking lot at the Frog Hollow Day School outside of Mystic. I have so far this morning met with Barbie Nelson's distraught husband, her equally distraught mother, and her best friend."

"Learn anything new?"

"Actually, I believe I have. That being Barbie had a stepmother and a stepsister, neither of whose names appeared in the investigative file, neither of whom have been contacted—at least, as far as I can tell, officially—since Barbie disappeared."

"Really?"

"Really. And here's the tricky part. According to the mother, Barbie and the stepfamily had no relationship at all—she never even bothered to mention the stepsister. The best friend, however, says that Barbie was very close to these two women, and has visited them—alone, without husband and kids—on several occasions."

"I'm guessing you're going to check that out."

"You betcha. And you'll never guess where step-mom lives."

"Hit me."

"About three hours from the lake."

"Patsy's lake?"

"The same."

"How convenient."

"That's what I was thinking. I want to talk to Doris Wright, Barbie's stepmother, and if possible, maybe just spend the night with Pats and Chrissie."

"Go for it."

"I think I will. I'll fly into Erie and rent a car, drive to the Wright's, then down to Patsy's. Then the next morning, I can drive back to the airport—"

"Sounds like a plan."

"Have you heard from Adam or Dale?" Genna asked.

"Dale just checked in, I'm still waiting for Adam. Nothing hot just yet, I'm afraid." He paused, then said, "Look, I'm sitting outside the home of Justine Lange's parents and since my plane was delayed, I'm almost an hour late."

"I won't keep you." She hesitated, wanting to say more.

"Call me after you talk to the stepmother, okay?"

"I will."

"Hey, Gen?" John added.

"Yes?"

"I miss you."

"Miss you, too," she replied, meaning it.

"That's nice. I'm glad. Thank you," he said as he disconnected the call.

"Thank you, too, John," she replied, then dialed her office and requested that arrangements be made for her to fly, as soon as possible, to Erie Airport.

Her travel plans in the works, she called information and obtained the phone number for Doris Wright, which she jotted down on the back of the pad in which she'd written her notes from the morning's interview. As she drove from the parking lot, she debated on whether or not to call Doris Wright before her visit, then decided against it. Maybe she'd do better by just showing up.

The ringing of her cell phone jarred her, and she answered it on the second ring.

"Genna?"

"Yes."

"Ok, the best we can do for a flight to Erie is from T.F. Green Airport in Rhode Island later this evening."

"What time?"

"Nine-fifteen."

Genna glanced at her watch. She had plenty of time to make the airport.

"That'll be just fine. Thanks so much."

"Your car will be waiting for you when you get there. I'm assuming you'll need a room for the night?"

Genna thought it through. It would be late when she arrived in Erie, and Allen's Springs was a good hour and a half from the airport. Too late to go knocking on the door of the unsuspecting Mrs. Wright.

"You're right. I will."

"I'll see what I can do. I'll get back to you."

"Thanks again, Sharon."

Genna started the engine and headed back to I-95, north toward Providence, all the while thinking about Barbie Nelson's stepmother, and what she might be able to add to the investigation.

# 18

Genna stood at the end of the driveway and squinted in the bright sunlight, cursing the fact that she'd left her sunglasses on the dresser in the hotel where she'd spent the previous night. Shielding her eyes with her hands, she could see that the number on the Cape Cod style house—18—appeared to be the correct one. A glance at the name on the mailbox confirmed that this was indeed the Wright home. Slamming the car door, she set off up the drive, noting that the lawn, if somewhat dried from the hot August sun, was as neat and well trimmed as the flower beds that outlined the path from the front door to the end of the drive. She rang the doorbell and waited before ringing it once, twice more. When there was no answer, she walked around to the rear of the house, where she found an elderly woman wearing a large straw hat bent over and pulling weeds from around a birdbath that sat in the middle of the yard.

"Excuse me?" Genna called.

When the woman didn't answer, Genna called again, a little louder this time. She was within twenty feet of the woman before she noticed the headphones under the hat and the Disc Man clipped to the woman's waist. She opted to approach from the other side, where her shadow would precede her, rather than from the back where a tap on the shoulder would surely startle.

"Oh!" The woman jumped slightly when Genna was almost upon her. Removing the hat and the earphones in almost one motion, she stepped back and said, "Can I help you?"

"Mrs. Wright?" Genna asked.

"No. Mrs. Wright isn't here. Something I might help you with?"

"You are . . . ?"

"Jeanne Maynard. I live next door. I told Doris I'd keep an eye on the place while she was gone . . ."

"Gone?" Genna repeated. "Do you know when she'll be back?"

"Sometime Monday, I think she said. She's visiting her sister down in Scranton." She paused, then asked again, "Is there something I can help you with?"

"If I leave my card with you, will you ask Mrs. Wright to call me as soon as she gets back? It's very important." Genna searched for a card, then as an afterthought, took a pen from her bag and wrote Patsy's phone number on the back of it. "Tell her she can reach me at any of these numbers."

Jeanne Maynard glanced at the card, her eyebrows raising slightly. "FBI, huh? You'll be wanting to talk to her about Barbie, then, I suppose."

"Do you know Barbie?"

"Certainly. She was born right over in Jamestown, you know. Didn't move to Connecticut till she was, oh, fourteen, maybe. Then, of course, Sarah, her mother, remarried, and Bob, her dad, married Doris, and for a long time, Barbie and her father didn't seem to have much to say to each other. 'Course, I always held that it was Sarah who didn't have much to say to Bob or Doris, frankly, but that's none of my business. Wasn't till Bob got sick that Barbie finally came around. I've always said it was a blessing that she did, there at the end, so's that Bob could go to his grave having said good-bye to his only blood child, you know."

"How long ago was that?"

"Five years ago, maybe."

"And up until that time, Barbie didn't see her father?"

"I don't recall that she did."

"Do you know why?"

Jeanne Maynard considered the question, and in the time it took for her to do so, Genna knew the answer. Of course, she knew.

"Well, I think that's a question for someone else to answer."

"Someone like who? Doris? Sarah?"

"Either one that cares to." Mrs. Maynard crossed her arms over her chest and added, not unkindly, "It just isn't my place to talk about another's family troubles, you understand."

"Any idea why Sarah and Bob divorced in the first place?"

Mrs. Maynard seemed to deliberate this carefully, then replied, "She wanted to move back to Connecticut. He didn't. His business was here."

"Was the business losing money?"

"Makin' it hand over fist, best I could see. Bob always made a good living."

"Then why would she want him to move hundreds of miles away . . ."

"I don't know that she cared if he went with her or not. I think she just wanted away from . . ."

"Away from what?"

"From here," she said uneasily.

"Why? What happened to her here?"

"You'll have to ask Doris." The woman turned her head as if aware she'd possibly said too much.

"I'll do that. Will you be sure to ask her to call me?"

"I will. Certainly." Mrs. Maynard nodded.

"Thank you. I appreciate it." Genna smiled and turned away.

"Miss . . ." Jeanne Maynard took Genna's card from her pocket and glanced at it again, ". . . Snow. Miss Snow."

"Yes?" Genna turned back to her.

"Is Barbie . . . do you think Barbie is . . ." The woman struggled with her words.

"We don't know, Mrs. Maynard. I don't want to even speculate. Right now, we're just trying to find out what might have happened to her."

"I've been prayin' for that girl ever since I heard about it on the news the other night."

"You just keep on doing that, Mrs. Maynard. You just keep on praying for her until we find her," Genna said before turning to walk back down the drive, adding, as she went, "and pray that we find her real soon. . . ."

Patsy dipped the paddle into the water and eased the kayak out onto the lake. Behind her on the dock, Crystal sat, legs dangling inches from the water's surface, her head bent over the book she had selected from a shelf in the living room. Patsy would have liked to have had her along on this little trip around the lake, but there'd been too few books in the girl's life, too few opportunities for Crystal to sit and read by the last light of a summer day, and Patsy didn't have the heart to press her to come along. Besides, she could do with a little solitude tonight. A little time to reflect on all that had happened over the past few weeks.

"It's been a doozy of a summer, that's for sure," she muttered as she passed the Williams's dock and waved to old Mr. Williams, who was, by Patsy's estimation, roughly ninety-two this year, give or take.

First, of course, there was Crystal.

"Poor baby," Patsy sighed.

Patsy shook her head. All those years she'd had Genna in therapy, hoping that someday it wouldn't all hurt her quite so much to look back on the past, and then hadn't the past just popped up out of nowhere, just like that? And while Patsy's first concern had been for Genna—hadn't she made it from the cabin to Genna's apartment in record time, leaving poor Kermie with a few days' supply of cat food and insulin at the McDonoughs' down the road, so that Genna wouldn't have to deal with her sister alone, after all these years. The sight of Crystal sitting on the sofa, her hands folded in her lap as if waiting for disaster to fall from the sky, well, that had just about done Patsy in. She hadn't known for sure what she'd expected to find when she arrived, but Patsy knew she hadn't been prepared for Chrissie's fragility. What could Patsy do, but take her under her wing and try to help out a little? After all, what had that girl had to give her a solid footing in this world? A father who beat her and a mother who stood aside and let him?

And she's such a pretty little thing when she smiles. And she has smiled more lately. A little more each day.

"I'd wish I'd been able to get my hands on Crystal back then, when I'd taken in Genna," Patsy spoke softly as she skimmed the surface of the lake, all deep blue now as the sun dropped a little behind the clouds. "I'm not bragging, Lord, you know that's not my way. But I can't help but think that a loving home and a little stability would have meant the world to this child."

She paddled through a cluster of waxy white water lilies and watched the shadows lengthen across the water. A bat darted overhead, dining on mosquitoes, and off to her right, a fish jumped as the kayak approached. The end of another summer day on Bricker's Lake, with the sky turning shades of pink and lavender and orange. Peaceful. Serene. Patsy rested the paddle across her knees for just a moment, coasting a little before heading back toward her dock, humming a song she'd heard on her favorite Frank Sinatra tape that morning.

She floated as close as she could to the shore before hopping out and walking through the shallow water to haul the kayak onto the shore. It was darker now, and Crystal must have gone inside to start dinner. She was real good about things like that, Patsy reflected. Helpful as could be, with a willingness to join in whatever task needed to be done. She was, in fact, a joy to have around.

Patsy hadn't taken but ten steps up the grassy

slope that led to the cottage before stopping in her tracks. In the quiet dusk, a figure loomed between her place and Nancy's.

"Hey! You! What are you doing over there? Step on out into the light, you hear?" Patsy called into the shadows.

The figure stood stock still, then stepped toward her.

"It's me, Ms. Wheeler. Kenny. Kenny Harris."

"Now, what are you doing, lurking around here like that? Good Lord, Kenny, you're going to give me a heart attack one of these days."

"Sorry, Ms. Wheeler. I didn't mean to scare you. I was just taking a walk around the lake, and you being down there on the lake, and me seeing someone in your cottage, well, I thought I should take a closer look. I didn't realize that Ms. Snow was here this week."

"She's not. Well, it's Miss Snow, but it's not Genna. It's her sister, Crystal."

Kenny stared at her for what seemed to be the longest time.

"What?" Patsy asked, wiping her still wet hands on the front of her shirt.

"I didn't know. I mean, I thought it was Miss Snow. The one we're supposed to be watching after. I didn't know there was another one."

And with that, Kenny mumbled something imperceptible and shuffled off back up the lawn and across the street.

"I swear there's a full moon on the rise tonight," Patsy muttered as she went into the house, where she found Crystal in the kitchen. She was peering down the short hallway that led to the front of the cabin, where the screen door stood open.

"Something wrong?" Patsy asked.

"No. I guess not. Just for a minute, it felt like someone was watching through the door," Crystal told her.

"That was Kenny. I just saw him outside." Patsy gestured toward the side of the house that faced Nancy's cabin.

Crystal continued to stare at the front door, then walked to it, pulled it shut, and locked it.

"Chrissie, are you sure you're all right?"

"Yes. I just figured no one else was here this weekend, with your friend over there, Nancy, not here, and the people in the cottage on the other side having left on Wednesday."

"Well, it is quiet, that's for certain."

"Well, it won't be quiet for long." Crystal turned to Patsy and smiled. "Genna's on her way."

"Genna!" Patsy grinned back. "I thought she was tied up with that kidnapping mess . . ."

"She is. She had to come to New York—someplace just over the state line, she said—to interview someone who won't be back until Monday, and since it's so close to the lake, she decided to come and spend tomorrow with us. She figures to be here early in the morning."

"Well, isn't that a pleasant surprise." Patsy glowed with anticipation of the unexpected visit. "Maybe we should bake something special."

"Like what?"

"Oh, one of Genna's favorite treats, maybe." Patsy seemed to be deep in thought.

"I don't know what Genna's favorites are," Crystal told her.

"Well, then, we'd best get busy." Patsy smiled.

"Now, you just grab that cookbook there, the one with the red paisley cover—yes, that one—and take it into the living room. I'll bring us some tea, and we can look through the list of Genna's favorites. And while we're doing that, you can tell me which are your favorites, and we'll start a list for you, too . . ."

"So, big sister, tell me about the past couple of weeks." Genna lay back on the dock, resting on her elbows.

It was ten o'clock on a steamy August morning. The fog had long since burned off the lake. Overhead, clouds drifted past the sun to darken and gather slowly off to the south. Genna and Crystal had taken an early morning sail and now rested lazily in the sun to dry off.

"Well, it sure is different, being here," Crystal told her.

"In what way?"

"Busy." Crystal shook her head good-naturedly. "Patsy is one busy lady. Goes from one thing right into the next, doesn't she?"

"I guess it could take a little getting used to."

"A little? Ha! I never knew anyone like her. Up at the crack of dawn. 'Let's go for a swim before breakfast.' 'Hey! It's a great morning! Let's just kayak on over to the general store across the lake and get the paper.'" Crystal effectively mimicked Patsy's facial expressions, right down to the raised eyebrows.

"That's our Pats, all right," Genna laughed.

"Oh, look who's coming to join us." Crystal sat up and pointed to the end of the dock, where Kermit strolled as nonchalantly as a British lord out to take the morning air.

The cat rolled over on his back between the two women and accepted the adoration of both.

"Now, where have you been?" Crystal asked the cat, who responded by closing his eyes and purring loudly. "Don't be acting like you don't know what I'm saying. You best not have been after those little goldfinches again, Kermie."

Kermie scooched closer to her, never opening his eyes.

"You're just a big lovey, you are," she told the cat. Looking up at her sister, she said, "You know, I never did have a pet before. Daddy wouldn't hear of letting an animal in the house."

"I remember," Genna told her.

"Did you have pets, growing up?"

"We had a little bit of everything, actually. When I first came to live with Patsy, she had an old dog named Pickle. After he died, she took me to the SPCA to pick out a new pet. That's where we found Kermie."

"Did you know he had diabetes then?"

"No, that was something that developed as he got older. A vet we had once told us that it wasn't uncommon in male orange tabbies, but I don't know if that's true. It's only a problem if he doesn't get his insulin. He's prone to having seizures, and they're terrible to watch. I've never seen Pats get as upset as she does when Kermie has a seizure. And we're always afraid we'll lose him to one, so we move heaven and earth to make sure he gets his shots on time, don't we, old boy?"

"How old is he?"

"He's sixteen, almost seventeen. Old for a cat. Patsy keeps thinking about getting a kitten, but every time she comes close, she decides to wait just a little longer. She thinks Kermie will be upset." Genna grinned. "I think he'd ignore it, frankly."

"It must have been fun," Crystal said wistfully, "growing up. With her."

"It was."

"I wish . . ." Crystal began, then stopped without completing the thought.

"So do I." Genna reached out and took her sister's hand. "But you're here now."

"I'm glad. Thank you for sharing her with me. For sharing . . . this." Crystal gestured around toward the lake, then back to the cottage.

"Well, it's your turn, Chrissie. All those things you didn't get to do before, you can have a chance to do now. So tell me what you've been up to."

"We hiked. We fished. Kayaked, of course. I really liked it, once I got the hang of it. Sailed, something else I've never done. So it's been a lot of firsts. And we spent a lot of time baking and cooking. I don't think I've ever, in my entire life, eaten as much as I have since I've been here. I figured I must have piled on about ten pounds over this past week, but I haven't. I've actually lost a few, if that scale in the bathroom is to be believed. I guess we've just been running so much the fat never had a chance to catch up to my hips."

"Patsy loves to eat, but she hates to eat alone. And she is a good cook, as I've noticed you are, as well." Genna leaned over the side of the dock to watch a young bass swim through the lily pads. "Are you sleeping well?"

"Yes . . ." Crystal replied slowly. "Why?"

"Just wondering," Genna shrugged. "And did I hear a *but* after the *yes?*"

"Well, I fall asleep most nights as soon as my head hits the pillow. From exhaustion, I guess."

"But . . ." Genna urged her to continue.

"But then some nights I wake up . . . I don't know, I guess maybe I'm just a little restless." Crystal rubbed under Kermie's chin and the cat purred louder.

"Nightmares?"

Chrissie sighed. "Sometimes."

"Just sometimes?"

"All right, most nights. Don't tell Patsy, though, okay? I don't want her to think I'm not happy here. I am. Happier than I've ever been, really. I think it's just because we're so close to . . . you know." Chrissie pulled at her hair nervously.

"To camp," Genna said. "It's because we're so close to the old campgrounds."

Crystal nodded.

"Did you ever go up there, Gen? I mean, since . . ."

"No."

"Haven't you ever wanted to?"

"No."

"Why not?"

"Are you kidding? Why would I?"

"Don't you wonder what it looks like now?"

"I couldn't care less."

"Maybe it's all different now. Do you suppose the cabins are still there?"

"I haven't thought about it."

"How could you not have thought about it?"

Silence, and the morning, spread around them, bit by bit. They watched Kermie rise and stalk a dragonfly that posed on the bulkhead.

Finally, Crystal said, "I want to go, Gen."

"No."

"I wasn't asking your permission. And I wasn't asking you to come with me. But it just seems that every nightmare that I've had for close to twenty years now, begins and ends in that place. It has too much power over me. Maybe if I go there, maybe I can take the power back."

Genna shook her head.

"I haven't even been able to bring myself to drive past the entrance, Chris. I just can't face it."

"Well, I'm going up there tomorrow. You're welcome to come with me. I'd like it if you did, but I'll go alone if I have to."

"Why?"

"You face down your fears, you steal their power and you become stronger than them, stronger than you were."

"I can't, Chris. I'm sorry. I just can't." She raised her head, her eyes hollow with regret. "I guess you're the brave one, after all."

But early the next morning, when Crystal crept into the kitchen on tiptoes to avoid waking Patsy or Genna, she found her sister, already up, the coffee made, waiting for her.

"Do you think we should tell Pats?" Crystal asked, and Genna shook her head.

"I think it will just worry her."

"Are you sure you want to do this?"

"I'm sure." Genna nodded. It was a decision that hadn't come easy, and she wasn't about to back down from it now. Besides, if Chrissie could be brave enough, she could, too.

"Do you remember how to get there?" Crystal asked.

"Are you kidding? I've been avoiding it for years. It's right up off the old county road."

They stole quietly from the house, slipping through the early morning fog and out to the car without making a sound. Genna backed out of the drive and drove slowly up to the main road.

"Gen, you don't have to go with me. You can drop me off out by the road and wait in the car."

"Don't be silly." Genna's jaw set tightly. "If you can do it, I can do it."

"Gen, I don't know that that's a good enough reason."

"Oh, hell, Chris, I probably should have done it a long time ago. And you're right. The longer you put something off, the worse it gets. Maybe it's time I got this over with."

Genna followed the narrow, slightly winding road to a sharp right that led uphill before flattening out and stretching straight ahead. They rode in silence for almost a mile before Genna began to slow down and scan the scenery beyond the windshield.

"The road down to the camp should be off to the right up here someplace." Genna slowed a little more and pulled to the shoulder to permit a pickup to pass.

"I don't see a road."

"It was a dirt road, so I would imagine it to be well overgrown after all these years. I know the state police had the place blocked off for a long time."

"Gen, look." Crystal pointed toward a weathered sign nearly covered by tall brush.

Genna stopped the car on the shoulder and read aloud.

*Welcome to the Way of the Shepherd.*
*Enter in peace, and follow my path.*

"Jesus," Genna muttered.

"Jesus had nothing to do with what went on here," Crystal said softly.

"I can't believe that sign is still there." Genna shook her head. "You'd have thought they would have taken it down long ago."

"Well, at least we know we're at the right place."

"You still want to go back there?"

Crystal nodded.

Genna accelerated and made a right turn onto the dirt road.

"Someone's been here," she frowned. "Look at how the brush is packed down, going down the hill to the camp area."

"Probably kids. I'll bet this place gets lots of teenagers out for a thrill."

The road was rutted and bumpy, narrow and steep. At the first quick bend that elbowed sharply to the left, Genna stopped the car and said, "Last chance, Chrissie."

"We're here, Genna. Let's see it through."

The car inched downhill, Genna leaning forward to peer over the steering wheel in an attempt to avoid the worst of the ruts.

"Omigod, what's that?" Crystal gasped, pushing herself as far back into her seat as possible, and pointing out the front window at a low hanging branch.

Genna stopped the car again, her gaze following her sister's.

"Geez, I hope that's not an omen," Genna laughed nervously.

"What the hell is it? I never saw anything so damned ugly in my life."

"It's a vulture," Genna told her. "There are a lot of them up around here."

"Well, don't that beat all. We finally get the nerve to haul our butts up here after all this time, and what do we find waiting for us but a damned *vulture*." Chrissie giggled.

"Still want to go on?" Genna hesitated, not quite as amused as Crystal appeared to be.

"Aw, sure. It's just a big old bird. Ugly as sin, though, don't you think?"

*Must be nervous laughter,* Genna told herself as she once again proceeded down the hill. *Whistling in the dark and that sort of thing.*

At the bottom of the hill was a clearing surrounded by dense woods, solid as a castle wall of stone. Thick vines knit the trees together tightly, and the smell of honeysuckle was staggering.

Genna stopped the car, allowing the engine to idle momentarily as she and Crystal looked around in silence.

"I thought it was bigger than this," Crystal said softly.

"We were just smaller," Genna replied.

"Look down there." Crystal pointed ahead. "That's where the pool was."

"And there's the old changing house," Genna said. "Remember coming down here and putting on our bathing suits to swim in the afternoon?"

Crystal nodded but made no move to leave the safety of the car.

And so the sisters sat, wrapped in the hush of early morning and in memories inside their shelter of steel and fiberglass.

Finally, Crystal asked, "You going to get out?"

"Might as well." Genna turned off the engine and pulled the key from the ignition and pocketed it. The sound of the car doors slamming in unison echoed across the clearing. The air was thick, humid, and heavy with the scent of summer. Crickets chirped and cicadas hummed, and through the trees, wary birds darted.

And overall, in spite of it all, there hung a still-ness, a sense of isolation.

"Want to walk down to the pool?" Genna asked, her voice somber and subdued.

"Sure."

They walked side by side, their hands shoved into the pockets of their jeans, Genna's fingers uncon-sciously toying with the car keys as if to ensure a quick exit if need be.

"Perhaps we should be whistling," Genna said. "You know, to cover up the sound of our knocking knees."

"My knees aren't knocking, but I do admit to a chill running up my spine."

"Looks like you were right about vandals." Genna grabbed Crystal's arm as they approached the old bathhouse, where the door had long ago been pulled from its hinges and tossed onto the ground and now lay rusted and bent. Pieces of an old porcelain toilet lay broken upon the concrete walkway that led down to the enclosed pool.

"Can you believe there's still water in there?" Genna leaned over the cyclone fence to the pool.

"And who knows what else? Talk about your black lagoon! Ugh! That's really disgusting. I'll bet it's filled with snakes and . . ." Crystal shivered and turned away. "I can't even look at it."

"Well, which way then?" Genna asked.

"Maybe back up the other way. Toward the dining hall."

"That would be up to the left, if I recall."

"I think you're right." Crystal fell in step with her sister, and following their memories, the two women went back up the hill.

"There's the old kitchen," Genna said, pointing to an open doorway.

Overhead, clouds drifted past the early morning sun, casting a shadow.

"Looks like we'll get that storm after all," Crystal paused at the threshold.

"Good. It'll give us an excuse not to stay too long."

Together they stepped inside and onto the linoleum floor, long cracked and faded, past the stainless steel counters and the old double sink. Cupboard doors stood open, their contents long since removed. An old stove sat in the middle of the floor, no longer connected, the burners missing. They stepped past it and peered through the doorway into the dining hall beyond.

"It's dark in here," Crystal whispered. "It's so creepy."

"This place would be creepy under any circumstances. The fact that it's dark inside, and it's getting dark outside, only adds to the atmosphere."

"Look, the old piano's still there." Crystal pointed across the room. "I wonder if it still plays."

Genna crossed the bare wooden floor and tapped on a few keys.

"Nothing," she said. "The insides have either rusted out or been eaten out by mice."

"I hate mice," Crystal muttered. "I'll bet there are tons of them in here. Just the thought of what could be lurking around here makes my skin crawl."

"Look down there." Genna pointed to the far end of the long, narrow room.

Piles of mattresses, apparently stripped from the cabins, littered the floor. Some bore charred evidence of having been set on fire. Across one wall, the names Courtney and TJ had been written in huge red letters.

"Wonder if Courtney and TJ's parents know they've been whooping it up in the old camp dining hall," Crystal mused.

"Judging by the mountain of beer cans over there," Genna pointed behind them, "I'd say they weren't alone."

She walked over and peered at the aluminum pyramid that stood against one wall, then said, "Looks like we missed the party by months, if not longer, judging by the amount of dust on the cans. I guess whoever was using this place as a hangout either moved away or outgrew it."

"Maybe they were summer people who didn't come back," Crystal offered.

"Maybe. Frankly, I'm surprised there isn't evidence of more recent intrusion. You'd think a place like this would be a magnet for the local kids." Genna brushed the dust from her hands onto her jeans. "Seen enough in here?"

"Yes." Crystal nodded.

"Where do you want to go next?" Genna asked once they had passed back through the kitchen and out into the what had once been the cook's kitchen garden, now gone to weeds.

"I guess down there," Crystal pointed in the direction of the cabins.

"Are you sure?"

"I'm sure. I came here to exorcise this devil, Genna. Might as well get it all out of my system."

Without speaking, they walked close to one another through overgrown shrubs and entered onto a clearing.

Once white-washed clapboard cabins stood in a semicircle, like long, embracing arms that held a grassy clearing. In the center stood a pile of stone, once a podium of sorts from which the counselors addressed their young charges three times each day: early morning, noon, and evening. The grass, once lush and thick, now grew in sparse patches, as the dense canopy of surrounding trees had meshed quite solidly overhead.

"Dear Lord, it's so damned creepy," Crystal whispered.

Behind them a screen door, nudged by the wind, banged loudly, startling them both.

"SHIT!" Genna exclaimed, then laughed nervously and turned to look back at the cabins that stood in a perfect arc behind them.

It seemed that, over the years, the woods had grown closer, close enough to breathe down the necks of the deserted cabins. Peeling paint left weathered streaks across the front walls, and masses of assorted vines crept up broken steps and across sagging porches to climb toward shingled roofs. Windows were broken out here and there, and doors bore the remains of jagged screens.

And to the right of each door, a large number had been hastily—and sloppily—painted on the wall in watery black that dripped down the wall like after-thoughts.

"Where do you suppose those numbers came from?" Crystal pointed to the number that defaced the cabin closest to them.

"The state police painted them, as a means of identifying the crime scenes by cabin," Genna said without emotion.

"Crime scenes," Crystal repeated softly, as if she'd never thought of what had happened there in those terms before.

"The girls who testified used the numbers when they spoke with the detectives and told them which of the cabins they'd been taken from." Genna pointed straight ahead. "Cabin number five. Mine."

She turned her head briskly and pointed to the small building that was set apart slightly from the others and that bore a 12.

"The infirmary. The girls who testified said that after he'd raped them, he'd taken them to the infirmary and left them for Sister Anna to care for in the morning."

"I lost count of the number of times I . . ." Crystal shook her head and turned back toward the clearing.

Genna put an arm around her sister's shoulder to comfort her. "Do you think Sister Anna knew?" she asked.

"Sure, she knew." Crystal nodded. "She'd give us aspirin for our 'headaches' and something to make us sleep, but she had to have known what had happened to us. She always brought extra desserts when we stayed there. As if an extra slice of cake could make up for having been abused by her wacko brother."

"Was she Michael's real sister?"

"I thought she was, but I don't know for sure," Crystal conceded. "Did it come out at the trial?"

"Sister Anna didn't testify, as I remember," Genna told her.

"How could she not testify?" Chrissie frowned.

"I think they couldn't find her. I don't remember exactly. It was a long time ago, and they didn't let me in the courtroom until it was my turn to take the witness stand."

A sharp breeze pushed through the trees, rustling the leaves noisily and bending the branches slightly with its force. A rumble nearby caused them both to jump, then laugh uneasily.

"I think it's time to leave," Genna said.

"I just want to see the track and maybe the soccer fields."

"We'd better make it fast, then. That storm is moving in pretty quickly."

"I think the path used to be over there somewhere. . . ." Crystal started off to the right, then stopped and pointed, saying, "Well, it looks like it still is. Imagine that."

The shrubs at the edge of the woods were bent and angled, the brush tamped down carelessly, as if, sometime in the not too distant past, someone had tread there.

"Maybe Courtney and TJ ran a few laps before they retired to the dining hall for a couple of cold ones," Genna said dryly.

"I wouldn't be surprised to find that kids were using the sports fields, Gen. I remember the facilities as being pretty nice."

"I never got to play on them too much. Except for

softball. You had to be ten to play on the soccer team," Genna recalled as she followed her sister down the narrow path.

An enormous crack of thunder shattered the silence.

"On second thought, maybe we've seen enough for one day." Crystal did an immediate about-face and grabbed Genna's arm. "We can always come back to see the soccer field another time."

"I take it you're ready to leave."

"More than ready." Crystal tugged on Genna's arm to hurry her along.

"Don't like thunder, eh?" Genna said as they came back up the hill.

"Not when it's that close," Chrissie shook her head. "And look, over there, at the lightning."

Ragged streaks flashed across the ever-darkening sky, and thunder rolled all around them.

"If we hurry, we might make it to the car before the rain. . . ." Genna held up a hand. "Oops, too late, here it comes. Looks like we'll have to make a run for it."

They ran through the clearing, past the cabins, just as the first fat drops began to fall like long-held tears. Crystal reached the passenger side and hopped in, slamming the door behind her. Genna hurried behind the car, then stopped, tilting her head, as if listening for a sound she wasn't sure she'd heard. As a child, she'd believed the woods around the camp were haunted. Night after night, she'd thought she'd heard cries drifting through the dark.

Funny, she thought as she looked back toward the long-neglected buildings, even now, she could swear she heard those anguished voices, little more than whispers, carried on the summer wind.

*Please ... please ...*

Shivering as the rain fell cold and hard against her skin, she opened her car door, slid inside, and started the engine immediately. Suddenly, she could not get back to the sanctuary of Patsy's cottage quickly enough.

And yet later that night, she dreamed that she heard them. Loud enough inside her head to awaken her from her sleep, she had bolted upright, then gone to the window to listen. It was as if the wind had carried the sound of voices that were not quite voices, all the way to the lake.

*Please ...*

*Please ... help ... us ...*

# 19

Genna was less than two miles from Doris Wright's house when her cell phone rang.

"How's it going?" John's voice cut through the static. "Gen, can you hear me?"

"John? Bad connection. Let me call you right back."

Genna pulled over to the side of the road and dialed John's number.

"Better?" he asked.

"Much. What's up?"

"I just heard from Dale. He met with Lani Gilbert's parents yesterday. You'll never guess what Lani's given name was."

"What?"

"Would you believe, Atalanta?"

"You're kidding."

"Nope. So, it does make one wonder. Where'd you know your Lani from?"

"From camp," she replied softly. "She was at camp that summer."

"Gen, by any chance, was she one of the girls who was assaulted by Brother Michael?"

"Yes. Yes, she was."

"Did Lani testify against him at the trial?"

"Yes." Her voice was so low, he could barely hear her.

"Think back. Do you remember the names of the other girls who testified?"

The silence was protracted and fraught with unspoken possibilities.

Genna gave the car enough gas to move back onto the roadway, then accelerated, suddenly in a hurry.

"Gen?"

"I'm on my way to meet with Barbie Nelson's stepmother. I should be there in less than five minutes," she told him.

"Was there a Barbie at camp when you were there?" he asked.

"No," she said. "Not that I remember. But there was a girl named Bobbie."

"What was her last name?"

"I don't know. We didn't know hardly anyone by their last names, only the first. Back then, last names weren't important."

"They are now."

"I'll get back to you." Genna disconnected the call, her hands shaking. Could Lani Gilbert be her Lani, all grown up?

She pulled into Doris Wright's driveway and stopped the car abruptly. As she walked to the front door, she tried to pull up Bobbie's face from her memory bank, but couldn't. Even if she saw a photo of Bobbie as a child, would she recognize her? It had been so long ago. . . .

Doris Wright was at the door even before Genna reached her hand out to ring the bell.

"I'm so glad you could see me on such short

notice," Genna said as she was led into a comfortably furnished living room.

"I've been a wreck, worrying about this girl." Mrs. Wright shook her head. "Just a wreck. I was hoping you were calling to give me some good news."

"I'm afraid right now we have no news." Genna sat on one of the two wing chairs that faced each other across the hearth. "Mrs. Wright, I was wondering if you have a photo of your stepdaughter."

"Certainly," she nodded. "That's her, right there on the mantel." She pointed to a silver frame that sat less than three feet from Genna's head.

Genna rose to look at the beaming young woman on her wedding day. Her arm was looped through that of an older man who was filled with father-of-the-bride pride.

"Your husband?"

"Yes." Mrs. Wright nodded. "I have more recent pictures, though. Actually, I have some from her visit in early July."

"Actually, I was hoping to see some photos of your stepdaughter as a child."

"As a child?" She frowned. "I think her mother took all of them with her when they moved back to Connecticut, but I'll look." She gestured for Genna to follow her into the dining room.

"I keep all my old photos in here." She opened the doors of the sideboard and leaned down, emerging with a lidless cardboard box. "Of course, I keep saying that I'm going to put them into albums, but I never get around to it. Now, let me see what's in here . . . this batch seems to be mostly my daughter, Mindy. . . ."

"She and your stepdaughter are good friends?"

"Oh, yes. It took them a while, but yes, they're quite close now." The woman flipped through loose photos pensively. "Oh, here's one. I guess she was about eight here. She and her dad had gone to some scout picnic and they had some races . . ."

She passed the photo into Genna's outstretched hand.

". . . but I can't see why you'd be interested in an old photo. Bobbie changed so much as she grew up, lost all that little girl pudginess . . ."

"Bobbie?" Genna repeated flatly.

"Her dad always called her Bobbie. She didn't become Barbie until her mother took her back to Connecticut."

Genna held the photo up and took a good look, and her head began to reel.

There was no question in her mind that Barbie Nelson was Bobbie-from-camp, last-name-unknown. Only now Genna was certain that she knew what Bobbie's last name was. It was Wright. Bobbie Wright.

"Excuse me, Mrs. Wright," Genna said, trying to ignore the weight that pressed so heavily against her chest, "but I need to make a phone call . . ."

"Mancini," John said as he picked up.

"Bingo." Genna said softly.

"Shit." John replied.

"Excuse me?"

"I was hoping we were wrong about that."

"Why? This could very well be the thread that we've been looking for." Genna walked to the far end of the living room so that Mrs. Wright would not hear the conversation.

"I just don't like what I see at the end of the thread, Gen."

"What do you mean?"

"I just got off the phone with Brian. I asked him to check to see when Brother Michael comes up for parole."

Genna's mouth went dry.

"It seems his parole date came and went. He's been out since April, Gen." John paused, then repeated, "Brother Michael has been out of prison since April."

When the shock had rippled through her, she cleared her throat.

"Why didn't we know? He's a convicted sex offender—shouldn't someone have been notified?"

"Yes. Someone should have been. Something obviously fell through the cracks."

"What's he been doing all this time? The first of the women disappeared weeks ago."

"He's been watching. Watching and learning."

"Sweet Jesus . . ."

"Exactly. Brian is faxing a list of the thirteen girls who testified against Michael at his trial, into the office. How much do you want to bet that we have a file on every one of them?"

"But there have been twelve victims . . ."

"And thirteen girls who testified." He paused before adding tersely, "Counting you, there were thirteen . . ."

The unspoken hung between them.

"John, his brother used to live outside of Pittsburgh," she said, her mind racing. "We lived there for a time. He—Mr. Homer—was the one who hired my father to come and preach in their church. He owned the campgrounds. Maybe he knows where Michael is."

"Do you remember the name of the town?"

"Of course. We lived there for several years. It was Lindenwood. It's right above the West Virginia state line."

"What's the closest airport?"

"Pittsburgh."

"Call the airport and book yourself on the first available flight. I'll do the same, and I'll meet you there," John told her, adding, "I think it's time someone paid a visit to Mr. Homer."

At seven-ten that evening, Genna and John were standing on the front stoop of the large, aging Tudor-style house and waited for someone to respond to their ringing of the doorbell.

"This house always intimidated me," Genna said in a low voice. "It was the biggest house I'd ever been in, and I thought it was a castle."

"What's it like inside?" John rang the bell again.

"Back then, it was dark, lots of dark wood and dark furniture." She stepped back on the sidewalk and glancing at the heavy drapes that could be seen covering the front windows, noted, "Things don't seem to have changed all that much."

John reached toward the bell to ring it one more time, just as they heard the sound of the lock being unlatched from the inside. The ornate brass doorknob turned, and the door opened only far enough for the person behind it to see out.

"Help you?" A middle-aged woman wearing what appeared to be an old-fashioned housedress peered through the narrow opening.

"We're looking for Mr. Homer." Genna smiled her friendliest smile, in spite of the fact that she had begun to tremble inside as a tide of memories threatened to wash over her. She pushed them back into their place and added unnecessarily, "Mr. Clarence Homer."

The woman looked warily from Genna to John, then back again.

"He isn't feeling well," she announced as she began to close the door. "Not having visitors."

Genna stepped forward and offered her identification. "We're with the FBI. We need to speak with him about his brother."

The woman's eyes narrowed suspiciously.

"He's not here."

"I thought you just said that he wasn't feeling well." John stood behind Genna on the step.

"Mr. Homer isn't feeling well." The woman spoke with exaggerated patience. "His brother isn't here."

"Was he here?" Genna exchanged a quick look with John.

"A few months back. Didn't stay very long. Got what he came for, then left. Upset poor Mr. Homer something terrible. Poor soul hasn't slept a night since . . ."

"What was it that he came for?" John asked.

"You'd have to discuss that with Mr. Homer," the woman sniffed her distaste, "but I'm sure it had something to do with his share of his mother's estate. He took off after less than a week and hasn't bothered to call his brother even once since. And it's not as if he isn't aware of how sick the Mister is."

"Are you a relative, Miss . . . ?" Genna asked.

"Miss Evans. I'm the Mister's housekeeper."

"And you've been here with Mr. Homer for how long now?" John asked.

"Oh, since before the Missus passed on. Why, that must be—"

"Lilly? Lilly!" A voice from the back of the house bellowed.

"I'm sorry, I have to . . ." The housekeeper glanced behind her warily.

"Well, it sounds as if Mr. Homer is feeling better," John said, sticking his foot in the door before she could close it in his face. "How fortunate for us. Now, if you would be so kind, please tell Mr. Homer that the FBI is here to see him."

Reluctantly, Lilly Evans stepped back and permitted the pair to follow her into the foyer.

"If you'd wait here, I'll just see if he's agreeable."

"Well, we have one question answered without even having to ask it," Genna whispered as the woman disappeared through a doorway.

"What's that?" John leaned close to hear.

"We know where Michael got sufficient money to permit him to travel around as much as he did. He wouldn't have had anything to speak of when he got out of prison, and chances are he wouldn't have had too many opportunities for employment, but collecting on an inheritance would have fit his plans nicely."

"I wonder how Mr. Homer will react when he realizes he financed his brother's activities," John said.

"Maybe it wasn't the first time." Genna's jaw tightened.

"What do you mean?"

Before she could answer, Miss Evans returned and closed the door solidly behind them.

"This way," she gestured, "but you must understand that Mr. Homer is a sick man. He's not supposed to have visitors."

She opened the double doors that led into what had once been an elegant room, one with plaster cherubs in the corners of the ceiling and ornate stained glass in the large side window. Now, the cherubs had begun to crumble and the glass was cracked.

Clarence Homer, elderly and obviously infirm, sat in a wheelchair in front of the fireplace. On his left was a table that held a nearly-empty carafe and a glass of water that was filled almost to the top. He wore a sweater that had probably been white when it was new, over blue and white cotton pajamas, blue slippers, and a distant expression.

"Mr. Homer, I'm John Mancini," John entered the room behind the housekeeper, then stepped aside to introduce Genna, saying, "and this is Agent Snow."

If the old man recognized the name, he gave no indication. He did not offer his hand to either visitor, nor did he invite them to sit. He merely turned his head slightly to face them and asked, "What do you want?"

"We're looking for your brother, Michael. We're hoping that you can help us locate him."

Without hesitation, without a blink, the old man asked, "What's he done now?"

"We don't know that he's done anything, Mr. Homer," Genna replied, wanting him to look at her. It was suddenly very important to her that he remember her.

"Then why would you come here asking where he is?" He glanced past Genna to John, as if dismissing her altogether.

"We know he was released from prison in April, but we don't know where he went from there or where he is now. We were hoping . . ." Genna stepped forward, refusing to be relegated to a minor role.

"I have no idea of where he is now." Clarence Homer's voice was strong and clear. "He certainly isn't here."

"But he was here," Genna said, trying to get, and hold, his attention.

"Yes. He was here. After his release. He really didn't have anyplace else to go." The man directed his response to John.

"How long did he stay?" John lowered himself casually to the arm of the sofa that sat opposite the wheelchair.

"I don't remember. Couple of days, is all."

"What did he do while he was here?"

"What?" Mr. Homer appeared surprised by the question. "Well, I'm not sure. He spent most of his time upstairs."

"What's upstairs?" Genna asked.

"The family bedrooms," Homer responded as if to an impertinent remark.

"Does Michael still have a room upstairs?" Genna and John exchanged a hopeful look.

"I don't know. I haven't been upstairs in six years, since my stroke. You'll have to ask Miss Evans."

"We'll do that, thank you." John nodded. "Mr. Homer, did Michael have any specific purpose in coming here?"

"I already told you. He had no place else to go." Homer sat back in his chair and appeared indignant. "But where else would one go, but home, to his family?"

"Did you give him money, Mr. Homer?" Genna decided the blunt approach was called for.

"Yes, of course I gave him money. The man hadn't worked in eighteen years. Didn't have a dime to his name."

"May I ask how much money you gave him?"

"I gave him what was due him."

"And what was that?" John leaned forward slightly.

"Half of Mother's estate. It belonged to him. I couldn't rightly keep it. When he showed up after all those years and asked for it, I had to give it to him," Homer said somewhat defensively.

"When did your mother pass away, Mr. Homer?"

"Sixteen years ago." Weary all of a sudden, the old man appeared to deflate somewhat. "She never did get over Michael's going away for all that time."

"How much was half of your mother's estate worth?" John asked.

"By the time the lawyers and the bankers and the tax man got finished, we each got roughly seven hundred thousand dollars."

Genna's eyes widened. Michael had more than enough to keep him moving around for years to come.

"Do you know if he opened an account at a local bank, or invested—" Genna was thinking out loud, wondering if there might be a paper trail to lead them to Michael.

"Far as I know, he just kept it." Mr. Homer interrupted her. "I don't think he bothered to deposit it anywhere but in his suitcase."

"Are we talking about cash here?" John's eyes narrowed.

"Of course we're talking about cash. What did you think we were talking about?"

"You gave your brother seven hundred thousand dollars in cash?" Genna's jaw dropped considerably.

"Yes. It was his money, and that's how he wanted it."

Good-bye, paper trail.

"Did he mention where he was going when he left? Maybe mention visiting a friend?"

Clarence Homer snorted. "Michael had no friends. He never did. The only person he ever put much stock in was Mother."

John stood and pulled one of his business cards from his pocket, offering it to their host.

"Thank you for your time, Mr. Homer. We appreciate it. Please give me a call at this number if you hear from your brother, or if you think of something you think we should know."

"Or if he stops back here," Genna added.

"Why would he do that? He got everything he wanted the first time around."

"Oh, I almost forgot," John snapped his fingers, as if just remembering. "You were going to let us see Michael's room."

"You're welcome to poke around all you want, but I doubt there's anything to see. Anything of value, he'd have taken it." He wheeled himself over to the doorway but did not pass through it. "Lilly! Lilly!"

When Lilly Evans appeared, Clarence Homer pointed to Genna and John and said, "They want to take a look upstairs."

"This way." The housekeeper led them into the foyer and up the wide mahogany stairwell.

"Which room is Michael's?" John asked when they reached the second-floor landing.

"Right down here." She walked briskly to the third door on the right and opened it. "Not much to see."

*Not much to see* was an understatement.

The shades on the windows were pulled down, so John switched on the overhead light, which clicked on loudly but provided little illumination. The furniture was old, though good quality maple. The bed was stripped to the mattress and had no pillow. The top of the dresser was totally bare, as were the drawers, and a peek into the closet revealed only empty hangers. No books sat next to the old lamp that stood on the bedside table, and no paintings hung on the walls.

"Are you sure this was Michael's room?" Genna asked the housekeeper.

"This was his, all right." She nodded in reply.

"Where are all his personal effects?" Genna thought aloud, then looked at Miss Evans and asked, "What happened to all his things?"

"Michael never kept much in the way of things."

"Books?"

The housekeeper shrugged. "Didn't read much."

"Did you strip the bed after he left?" John asked.

"No. There was nothing to strip." She shrugged.

"You mean he slept on the bare mattress?"

"Oh, no. He didn't sleep in here." The woman shook her head. "He slept over there. Across the hall."

Puzzled, Genna and John stepped toward the door.

"In his mother's room," Lilly Evans explained, then crossed the hall and pushed open the door.

Following the housekeeper into the room, Genna gasped softly. If Michael's room had been spartan, the bedroom of the senior Mrs. Homer was a nightmare of Victorian excess. Gold damask draped the windows, the canopy bed, the slipper chair that sat next to the hearth. Paintings in jewel colors lined the walls, and lamps with fringed shades stood like sentinels on the dresser. The scents of gardenia and stale air overwhelmed.

"It's all just as she left it. Except of course for the mess over there." The housekeeper frowned and walked to the window seat, which was heaped with clothes. She began to sort through them, separating them into piles. "You'd have thought he'd have outgrown it, wouldn't you?"

"Who'd have outgrown . . . ?" John asked.

"Well, it's not the worst of what he is, I suppose," she muttered as if she hadn't heard.

Genna lifted a garment and held it up. It was a woman's dress, circa maybe 1950, its skirt cut like a wide circle of lavender cotton. "Was this one of Mrs. Homer's dresses?"

"Guess it wasn't his color," Lilly Evans snorted softly.

"Did Michael's mother know that he wore her clothes?" John asked.

"Know it? If you ask me, she encouraged it. Used to dress him up like a girl when he was little, so I've heard." The woman shook her head.

"When he was here back in the spring," John asked thoughtfully, "was he wearing his mother's clothes?"

"If he was, he was doing it behind closed doors. Mostly he wore jeans then, but with that beard, I guess a dress would have been out of place," Miss Evans said dryly.

"Michael has a beard?" Genna asked.

"He did, yes. Not much of one, mind you. But it was a beard, all the same. Odd, too, because he was always so clean-shaven. Guess that's something he picked up while he was . . . away."

The agents scanned the room, looking, but not touching, lest they sully any fingerprints that may be lifted later. For now, it was enough to inspect the contents of the room, all of which appeared to have belonged to Mrs. Homer.

"Genna." John touched her arm.

"What?" She drew her gaze from the dresser, where a black-and-white photograph of a woman had held her attention. There was something about the woman that was vaguely familiar, but Genna couldn't put her finger on it.

"I said, I think we've seen enough here," John repeated.

"Oh. Yes." She nodded, then turned to follow John from the room. At the doorway, she stopped and asked of Miss Evans, "The woman in the photograph there on the dresser, is that Mrs. Homer?"

"Yes." The woman nodded as she closed the door behind her.

Once downstairs, the agents stopped to say their good-byes to Mr. Homer, but found him sound asleep. *Just as well*, Genna thought as they walked to the front door. She wasn't sure how he'd feel about his housekeeper sharing family secrets.

"Thank you again, Miss Evans. You've been very helpful," John said courteously as they reached the front door.

"Please give me or Agent Mancini a call if you hear from Michael." Genna stepped outside into a muggy evening.

"He's done something again, hasn't he?" Lilly Evans jaw set tightly.

"We don't know for certain," John said. "But we really would like an opportunity to speak with him."

Miss Evans shook her head slightly, as if in bewilderment, as she closed the front door.

"Oh, Miss Evans," Genna asked. "Did Mrs. Homer have a third child? A daughter?"

Lilly Evans stared blankly as if not understanding the question.

"Did Michael and Clarence Homer have a sister?" Genna rephrased the question.

"Not as far as I know," the housekeeper shook her head.

"There was no sister named Anna? Are you certain."

"Yes, I'm certain. Anna Homer wasn't their sister," Miss Evans explained patiently. "Anna Homer was their mother."

"How much weirder do you suppose this is going to get?" John asked Genna after they had gotten back into the rental car. "Not only is Michael a pedophile, but he likes to wear his mother's clothes. And sleep in his mother's bed. Who knew?"

Genna held her head in her hands and began to weep.

John gently rubbed the back of her neck with a strong hand, and simply let her cry.

"The son of a bitch didn't know me," she muttered. "He didn't even know me."

"Did you really think he would, after all these years?"

"He didn't even flinch when I said my name. Not a twitch." She raised her head. "His brother ruined my life, ruined my sister's life, ruined the lives of a lot of young women—and may, for that matter, be coming back around to make sure they have no lives at all—and he didn't even recognize my name."

John pulled her to him and cradled her in his arms, feeling the storm rise within her.

"Maybe he chose to ignore it," John said softly. "Maybe he knew who you were but didn't know what to say. What would you have wanted him to say to you?"

Genna wept softly in his arms but offered no reply.

"Or maybe he's just an old man who doesn't remember what happened all those years ago," John soothed her, stroked her hair and her back and her shoulders, and simply let her cry.

When the worst of it had passed, she sat up and said, "If you ever tell anyone about this—that I fell apart like this—I'll deny it."

He dabbed at her wet face with his handkerchief.

"Understood," he nodded.

"We can go now," she gestured to the key that he'd slipped into the ignition but had not turned.

John handed her the white cloth and waited while she finished mopping up her face.

"What?" She peered at him over the top of the handkerchief when she realized that the car was not moving.

"Do you want to go back in and speak with him privately?" he asked.

"And say what? 'By the way, Mr. Homer, since you don't appear to have recalled on your own, I thought that perhaps I should remind you that my father used to preach in your church. Until, that is, your brother attempted to rape me—as he had a goodly number of my camp-mates, including my sister—and I blew the whistle on him. After which he was tried and convicted on a number of offenses and sentenced to twenty years and my father was removed as pastor of your church. Now, how is it, Mr. Homer, that you don't even recognize my name?' " Her anger had grown with each word she uttered, so that by the time she had finished her soliloquy, her hands were fisted and her eyes wide with fury. "Is that what you had in mind, John?"

"That would probably do it," he nodded calmly.

"And what would that accomplish?" she demanded tersely.

"Well, it seems that after all these years, after all that's happened, you have the right to know if that man in there knew what he was doing when he put his brother in charge of a hundred or so little girls." With the fingers of one hand, John pushed the hair back from her face gently. "That's what you need to know, isn't it?"

"Pretty much sums it up."

"Now's your chance." John gestured toward the house. "It may not come again."

Genna looked beyond John to the front door where the outside light had just come on for the evening. Given Mr. Homer's age and health, this could be her last opportunity to ask questions that had festered for years.

"You'll wait here for me?"

"You have to ask that?" John stroked the side of her face, and she knew that he would wait all night for her if necessary.

Genna reached up to touch his face, drew it close to her own. "Thank you," she said simply, then kissed the side of his mouth, as if to draw strength from him.

"Go on, now, before Miss Lilly tucks him in for the night."

"I doubt I'll be long." Genna opened the door and stood on the sidewalk for a long moment, gathering her courage, before slamming the car door and walking purposefully up to the front door.

Miss Evans opened it on the first ring.

"Did you forget something?" the housekeeper asked.

"Actually, yes, I did." Genna smiled and stepped past the woman before she could react. "I just need to ask Mr. Homer one more thing. I won't be a moment. . . ."

Genna's heels tapped lightly on the hardwood floor as she found her way back to Mr. Homer's sanctuary.

"I thought you might be back," he said without looking at the door. "I thought there might be something else you might want to say."

"Did you know about Michael?" Genna asked from the doorway. "Did you know what he was?"

"You're asking me if I knew what an abomination my brother was? If I knowingly sent you and your sister and all those other girls into the hands of a monster?" he said pointedly. "No. No, I did not."

"You never suspected—"

"I knew there was something . . . different . . .

about my brother. I can't deny that. Knew that, for all his intelligence, he couldn't hold a job. That he'd never had friends or played the way other kids did. That even as an adult, he'd never been able to tolerate anyone, except Mother, of course. And occasionally, me. But never, not for a moment, could I have suspected what he was."

"Was the camp your idea?"

"No. It was Michael's. Why not a church camp, he'd suggested, where children could be guided by the Good Shepherd. Where they would learn the way." Clarence Homer's eyes glistened with tears. "It was the first time that he'd shown any interest in much of anything. I thought maybe he'd finally had a calling...."

"Did you know before ... before that summer?"

"No. My God, no."

"When did you learn?"

"When a reporter from the local television rang my doorbell. That's how I found out," he said bitterly. "From a reporter who stuck a microphone in my face and asked me how I felt about my brother being arrested on multiple counts of child rape."

The clock ticked loudly from the mantel, doling out every painful second that passed.

Finally, he said, "I am very sorry for what happened to you and to the others. I've prayed for you—for all of you—every day that's passed. And every day I ask forgiveness for the unspeakable horror that was inflicted on you."

"And for Michael?"

"God forgive me, I've stopped praying for his soul long ago." The man seemed to diminish in size even as she watched. After another long minute, he asked, "Is your father still preaching?"

"He and my mother died several months ago."

"I'm sorry." He looked sincere. "Reverend Snow knew his fire and brimstone."

"That he did."

"And your sister?"

"She's still recovering."

"And you?"

Genna shrugged.

"Are you really with the FBI? Or are those fake badges, procured to gain admittance to my home?" he asked.

"They're real enough."

He nodded faintly. "Seems you did all right for yourself, in spite of it all."

"Appearances aren't everything, Mr. Homer." She took a few steps toward the door, then turned to ask, "Why didn't you acknowledge that you knew who I was, when I was here before?"

"And what do you suppose I might have said?"

"Just what you've said now. That you hadn't known what your brother was. That you were sorry."

"Under the circumstances, it doesn't seem like much, does it?"

She shook her head, no.

"Sometimes words aren't worth a damn, Miss Snow. I figured this might be one of them."

The silence spread to every corner of the room. Genna broke it by saying, "The words that would help most right now are the ones that could help us to find him. Mr. Homer, can you think of anyplace where we might look for Michael? Did he give you any indication of where he might be going, or what his plans were?"

The old man shook his head.

"No. But one morning, I did hear him talking on the telephone, something about picking up a car, I think."

"A car? He bought a car?" He had her total attention. "Was it from a dealer? Or a private party?"

"I think it might have been a dealer. I saw him through the door," Mr. Homer pointed toward the hallway, "with the telephone book spread open across the desk. Looked like it was opened to the back, where the yellow pages are."

"That's terrific, Mr. Homer. That's the first bit of information we've been able to get. Thank you."

"Thank you." He raised a weary hand as if to wave. "It took courage for you to come to see me today."

"And courage for you to let me." Anxious now to share her bit of news with John, Genna paused in the doorway, then walked back across the carpet to where the old man sat, hunched in his wheelchair. When she extended her right hand to him, he looked up at her before taking it.

"All my life, I tried to do right," he told her. "To use the resources the Lord so generously blessed this family with, to do His work. If I could reach into the past and change just one thing about my life, it would be my brother."

"That Michael had not been what he was?"

"That Michael had never been born at all."

# 20

If John had had any doubts as to the wisdom of Genna going back to speak with Clarence Homer—alone—those doubts were swept aside when the front door opened and Genna marched down the walk, her old energy clearly evident in her step.

"Thank you," he whispered softly to the heavens, grateful that whatever had transpired had apparently lightened, not added to, the burden she carried in her soul.

As she drew closer to the car, he leaned over to open the door for her. "I take it that your chat went well."

"Better than well," she told him as she climbed into the car.

"Then he knew you."

"He knew me," her face softened. "It was as you said. He just didn't know what to say to me. Frankly, I think he was embarrassed by the fact that I showed up here, that after all that happened, he had to face me."

"What did he say?"

"Just that he had always known that his brother was different, but he didn't realize just how different. That he hadn't been aware of what Michael had been doing at camp." She leaned back against the cloth seat of the rental car. "And that he was sorry for everything that had happened."

"Do you believe him?"

"Yes. I do," she nodded. "I don't know what he'd have to gain by lying to me now, and there seemed to be a real anguish inside of him. But more important to our case—he remembered something that could prove to be the first break we've gotten since this mess began." She snapped on her seat belt and looked up at him triumphantly. "He believes that Michael may have bought a car before he left town. He heard him talking on the phone, and on the day he left, Michael left on foot."

"Did he tell you where he might have purchased it?"

"No, but since there are only . . ." Genna pulled a stash of yellow paper from the outside pocket of her handbag, "let's see . . . seven car dealers within walking distance of the Homer house, I'd say we have a damned good chance of finding the salesman. I made a quick stop at the desk in Mr. Homer's hallway. His yellow pages are a bit lighter, but under the circumstances, I don't think he'll mind. Now, there's a GM dealer up on Melrose Avenue. The school we went to was on Melrose, and if memory serves, I think that would be about four blocks from here. That's as good a place as any to start."

"Does Mr. Homer know that you ripped pages out of his phone book?"

"We'll let the evidence folks tell him. I think it's time to call the ERT in, to go through the house. Especially Mother Homer's room. I think we need to start lifting prints, hair samples—"

"Done. That was one of several calls I made while you were inside," he told her. "I also called Egan and filled him in. He's going to dispatch field agents to each of the families of the missing women to bring them up-to-date."

"Then I guess it's time to start visiting all of the car dealers in the area to see if in fact Brother Michael made a purchase."

John turned the key in the ignition and the car eased from the curb.

It had only taken three stops before the dealer who'd sold Brother Michael his wheels was located.

"A 1998 Dodge van, yes, ma'am," the middle-aged salesman who introduced himself as Lou Banning told Genna nervously, glancing at the pocket where she'd placed her badge and wondering, no doubt, where her gun was stashed. "Paid cash on the spot."

"What can you tell us about the van?" she asked.

"It was dark blue. Windows on one side panel, windows on the back doors. Only had about thirteen thousand miles on it."

"Were the windows tinted?" John pretended to be checking out the merits of a new SUV.

"Yes, tinted windows." Lou nodded.

"Can you pull the paperwork for us?"

"Paperwork's locked in the office this time of the night, but I can pull up the transaction on the computer, if that would help."

"That would be fine. But maybe," Genna smiled as she followed him to the glass door, "maybe you can get someone to come in and open up that office so that we can take a look at the paperwork."

"I can do that," he nodded.

"Can you describe him for us?" John asked,

choosing to stand rather than sit in one of the hard plastic chairs that were offered. "The fellow who bought the van?"

"Under six feet, slender, full beard, a mustache . . ."

"What color was his hair?"

"Dark brown, touch of gray running through it, but there wasn't much of it. It was really short."

"May I use your phone?" John asked, reaching for it without waiting for a response.

"Do you think you could work with an artist to prepare a sketch for us?" Genna asked. John would be calling Calvin Sharpe. In no time at all, agents from the nearest field office would be all over Lindenwood.

"Sure. But I don't know that we'll need to," he told her, pointing behind her. She turned and followed his finger, to the nearby corner of the room. "Security camera. We started using it last spring, when our vending machines were being broken into. We caught the guy who was doing it, but I don't know that anyone thought to turn off the camera. It probably just ran until the tape ran out."

"When was it installed?" Genna asked, her heart pounding at this unforeseen stroke of luck.

"On Tuesday, April 11, of this year. I remember because it was my forty-fifth birthday. It had seventy-two hours worth of tape on it."

"And Michael Homer was here when?"

"First thing, Thursday morning. That would've been April thirteenth."

"Is the tape still in there?"

"I never did take it down." He shrugged. "Didn't hear nobody else saying they did."

"Get it down now, then, if you would be so kind."
She turned and called to John. "Off the phone,
Mancini. Lou has a little surprise for you . . ."

By ten-thirty, the tape had not only been viewed
several dozen times, but copied as well. Just as the
salesman had suspected, the man he identified as
Michael Homer was clearly evident. Unfortunately,
the camera angle failed to provide a full facial image.
Still, it was the first glimpse they'd had of their prime
suspect, and it was hoped that by sending the tape to
the lab, some isolated still shots might be obtained
that could be sent out to the media.

By midnight, the first of the ERT members had
arrived from the Pittsburgh office and had been
briefed by John and Genna both. It was a little after
one A.M. when John pulled into the parking lot of the
motel on the outskirts of town where rooms had
been reserved for the two agents.

"Some day, eh?" John said when he turned off the
engine.

"You're not kidding." Genna stifled a yawn and
nodded.

"Tired?" he asked.

"A little. I'm more hungry than tired right now,
though. Do you remember when you last ate?"

"Breakfast on the plane."

"Me too. I think it's just catching up with me."

"There's an all-night diner across the parking lot,"
he noted. "Want to give it a try?"

"Are you kidding? I'd walk over hot coals for a
fresh cup of coffee and something really good to eat."

John smiled to himself as he locked the car. The
return of Genna's appetite was a good sign.

He took her hand and they strolled through the

halos of yellow light that spilled from the poles stationed every twenty feet or so across the lot. The two customers seated at the counter turned to look them over as Genna and John entered the quiet diner. A tired-looking young woman in her early twenties led them to a table overlooking the street and handed them menus.

"We serve breakfast twenty-four/seven," she told them.

They studied the menus and made their selections, and sat quietly, each lost in their thoughts, for a few minutes.

"What would you like to hear?" John asked.

"What?"

"They have an old jukebox," he pointed to a wall behind her. "What would you like to hear?"

"Let's see what they have."

They leaned against the rounded glass front of the jukebox and read off titles of songs, most of which were popular a decade or more ago.

"Wow, some of these records are antiques. Look there, 'Blue Moon.' That was a big favorite back in the Stone Age," John told her as he slipped some change into the slot. "And this one. 'You Belong to Me.' " Grinning, he dropped in another quarter. "Not to mention this one. 'Why Do Fools Fall in Love?' My dad had some of these."

"I don't know if I ever heard any of them."

"You have to be kidding." He turned, wide-eyed, to stare at her.

"Nope." She shook her head just as the song began to play.

"Wow," he muttered, pretending to be shocked, "never heard 'Blue Moon.' It's a golden oldie." He made a few more selections before leading her back to their seats, singing with the jukebox along the way.

"I wasn't born until 1973," she reminded him.

"And I was born in '70," he said as they sat back down. "What's that got to do with it? You weren't alive in the forties, either, but I've heard you singing 'The Tennessee Waltz.' "

"Only because it's an old favorite of Patsy's, and she used to sing it all the time." Genna laughed.

The waitress brought their coffee and they ministered to their cups, stirring as they added cream and sugar.

"So. What are you thinking?" John asked, when he felt it was time.

"I'm thinking we are going to catch this bastard." She looked across the table at him with eyes that glowed with a certainty he hadn't seen there before. "I think those videos will go a long way to helping us when they are shown on the news tomorrow morning. We will be hearing from gas station attendants and waitresses and people who work in drugstores and we will track him down before another victim is taken."

"He may not look the same now as he did back in April," John said, wondering when it would occur to her that there was only one potential name left on Michael's list. "He may have shaved off the beard, the hair could be longer. Maybe a different color."

"I know, I know. But . . ." She hesitated.

" 'But . . . ?' "

"But, well, watching that tape . . . there's something about the way he walks. . . ." her voice faded off.

"What is it?" he asked.

"I can't help but feel as if . . . well, as if something seemed familiar. . . ."

"Well, it's possible that something has stayed in your mind that you don't consciously remember. Your paths have crossed before, even though you were only nine years old at the time."

"Maybe that's it. Maybe it's just an old memory." She sipped at her coffee, then moved her body back to permit the waitress to serve them the scrambled eggs and toast they'd ordered.

"How did you feel, seeing him, after all these years?" John tried to sound as nonchalant as possible, though it had been the one issue that had most worried him since the tape had been found.

She put her fork down, considering the question.

"Mostly, angry. I'm still angry for what he did to me. But I'm even more angry about what he's done to these women. They've been twice his victim." She swallowed hard. "Sometimes I wake up at night, thinking that I hear them calling me. Calling for help. Like they're waiting for me to find them . . ." Her voice trailed off for a moment, then she was back, adding firmly, "But on another level, I am infinitely grateful that I am here, where I am, to be the one who will bring him in and put an end to it, once and for all."

"Well, certainly, you'll be part of it, but . . ." John stopped, and studied her face, not liking what he saw there. "Genna, don't even think about it."

"John, you know I'm on his list. You know I'm the one he's after now," she said softly.

"If you think I'm going to let you out of my sight . . ."

"Stop and think," she lowered her voice and

leaned across the table. "You know he's not going to quit until he's crossed every name off that list. Mine is the last one."

"I was wondering when that would occur to you."

"I never lost sight of it. He's far too clever to be easily caught. He's proven that. Twelve victims so far, and we don't have a clue as to where they are or what he's done with them. You and I both know that this will not end until we find him or he finds me. Unless we get a clean lead and locate him over the next few days, we won't find him at all. I've spent most of my life trying to overcome the repercussions of what he did to me. I will not spend the rest of my life looking over my shoulder, wondering where he is, waiting for him to come back. This time, I'm going to be in control, not him."

"Genna, don't you think he'll expect you to do just that? Do you really expect him to come after you now?"

"I think he thinks he's smarter than all of us. I think he'll find a way to get to me, regardless of how much protection there may be around me."

"Gen, the best thing for you to do right now is to go underground with Patsy and Crystal—"

"Oh, my God, someone needs to warn them—" The color drained from her face.

"Someone already has." He reached out for her hand and took it. "I called Patsy while you were in talking with Mr. Homer and suggested that she and Chrissie prepare to leave the lake for a while."

"Leave the lake?" Genna frowned. "Patsy'd never agree to that."

"*Au contraire,* my sweet," he told her. "She's probably packed by now."

"To go where?"

"We agreed that perhaps Brian's house might be a good place to stay."

"No." Genna shook her head. "I will not put Allison and the kids in the middle of this. We'll think of someplace else to send them."

"To send you," John reminded her. "Not just them. You. And me."

"Why you?"

"To make certain that you stay put until this is over."

With the tines of her fork, Genna mashed the remains of her egg. By the look on her face, John knew she was getting ready to bargain.

"Suppose I agree to go off someplace with Pats and Chrissie. How long do we have to stay away?"

"Until the danger has passed."

"And if we don't find him?" She raised an eyebrow. "Do I hide for the rest of my life?"

"I don't think it will take that long."

"But if we don't find him, John, what then?" She got up and slid in next to him on the booth's opposite side. "John, I know that you want to protect me, and I love you for it. Actually, it's occurred to me lately that I love you for a lot of reasons, but that's a conversation for later. There was a time when we talked about making a life together. What kind of a life would that be if I have to begin every day wondering if today would be the day he would find me? If every day, I have to be afraid?"

John struggled for an answer, but wasn't quick enough to come up with one.

"We've lost so much time together, John. We deserve so much more than having to worry every time we step outside. Let's just catch him and have it done with." She put her arm around his neck and whispered, "Let's get this sucker now so that we can get on with our life. What do you say, John?"

"I'm still working on the part where you said you love me." He turned his head slightly to rest it against hers. "How do I know that's not just a ruse to get your way?"

"You know me better than that."

"Yes," he sighed, "I do."

"So?"

"So let's think it through." John accepted the check the waitress handed him in passing and placed it on the table. "We're assuming that Michael's goal was to take revenge on the women who put him behind bars. He has all of them except one. Now, if you were anyone else, it would be a lot easier. But you being who you are, and having the resources that you have at your disposal—i.e., the FBI—it's going to be a lot tougher. He knows we'll be all over you. So what will he do? Will he lie low for a while, waiting for us to get careless? Or will he anticipate that you will set a trap with yourself as the bait, and find a way to get around it, just to prove he can?"

"He'll expect the FBI to use me to draw him out. He won't be able to resist trying to prove that he's smarter than we are. Particularly, smarter than I am."

"So we—"

"We frustrate him a little, to see if we can get him to do something a little rash. Maybe you're right," she leaned against John's shoulder. "Maybe I should disappear for a while. Even a few days could make him antsy. Which will hopefully make him careless."

"Or more dangerous."

"How much more dangerous can he be?" Genna tried to smile.

"Good point," John nodded. "So how do you see this playing out?"

"I see us back at your room making up for lost time."

John spewed coffee back into his cup.

"I mean, ah," he cleared his throat, "this thing with Michael."

"Oh, I'm going to go underground for a while—maybe a week—with Pats and Chrissie, just as you suggested." She stood up and held her hand out to him. He took it, and with the other hand, dropped a twenty-dollar bill on the table. "Then, when he's good and crazy, we'll let it be known somehow where I am. Sooner or later, he'll come after me."

"And we'll be waiting for him," John said as he pushed open the door. "Of course, that's the short version. Subject to refinement. For now, it's enough to know that you're willing to disappear for a while."

"And you're willing to disappear with me?"

"Wither thou goest . . ." he kissed the tip of her nose.

"Well, then, that much is settled." She slipped her arm through his and slowed the pace. "How does that song go?"

"Which song would that be?"

"The one you played on the jukebox? Moon something."

" 'Blue Moon?' " He sung a few lines before slowing the tempo and taking her into his arms, slow dancing there in the parking lot in a halo of halogen from the light overhead.

He dipped his head to hers, and she stretched

upward, eager for the feel of his mouth on hers. His tongue slid between her lips and traced their outline slowly before seeking the warmth within. Holding her tighter, closer, he drew her into his body, his need for her increasing with every beat of his heart.

"Do you still have the envelope that I gave you earlier, the one with the room keys in it?" He disengaged himself long enough to ask.

"Yes." She pulled him back to her.

"Did you happen to notice what the room numbers were?"

"Yes, 236."

"What was the other?" he asked, wondering if one might be closer than the other.

"I think they were both 236." She grinned.

"Well, then," he lifted her from her feet and carried her across the parking lot. "Room 236 it is."

"Put me down," she laughed. "And stop at the car, please. I need the bag I left in the backseat."

"Later," he told her, pausing at the foot of the outside stairway that led up to the motel's second level to set her on her feet, "I'll come out for it later. Got the room key?"

"In my pocket."

"That's all we'll need for now."

They walked hand in hand up the steps, stopping once at the midlevel landing to look up into the night sky, where stars danced and thin fingers of dark clouds streaked across the face of the moon. From below, a trace of juniper rose from the narrow stretch of turf that separated the parking lot from the motel property, where someone had attempted a bit of landscaping.

"It's a beautiful night, isn't it?" she asked as he slid the card into the door to open it.

"The most beautiful night in recent memory," he agreed, after closing the door behind him and opening his arms, wordlessly inviting her to step inside. She did.

Desire washed over her in turbulent waves, demanding more and more of him. She wanted to feel him, to taste him, to know that he wanted the same of her. Mindless, with no thought but to become one with him, nothing but the need of him burning inside her, she let him lead her to a place where aching swirls of sensation skimmed her body and singed her soul. Together they fell onto the king-sized bed, together rolled across it, passion winding around them tightly like a rope that bound them ever closer. His mouth was everywhere, pressing heated kisses into ever more exposed skin as she pulled her shirt over her head and grappled with the buttons of his shirt in a desperate need to feel flesh against flesh. Somehow, her skirt had hiked up to her hips, and even as his lips traced a wet line from her throat to her breasts, somehow she managed to free him from his trousers. Arching her body to meet his, she drew him down with her legs until her reached her center, then offered herself to him wordlessly, and just as wordlessly, he slipped inside. She fisted her hands in his hair as he fed upon her, and gave in to the frantic rhythm of their bodies. Gasping, she called his name, over and over, until the world shattered around her and they both came tumbling down in a flood of pleasure so acute it bordered on pain.

"Oh. My. God." She whispered when she could find her voice.

"You took the words right out of my mouth," he chuckled softly, his head still resting on her chest, "though I'll bet it's even better with all your clothes off."

"Really?" She lifted his head so that she could look into his eyes.

"That's what I've heard. Of course, for some of us, it's been so long, we have to rely on rumor."

"It has been a long time, hasn't it?"

"Longer than I like to think about." John leaned up on one elbow. "The last time we were together, was at your apartment. Right before Woods got really crazy and had me—"

"No," she pressed her fingers to his lips. "I'm done with the past, all of it. I'm tired of cursing Woods for what he did to you, and I'm tired of waking up in the middle of the night, tired of the nightmares. I want it done with. Hell, John, I've spent so much time looking back, I've forgotten how to look ahead. I want to look ahead. I want to have that future we used to talk about. I want to believe in dreams again."

"The dream's the same, Gen. It hasn't changed."

She traced the line of his jaw, content for the moment to bask in the love she saw in his eyes. "I wish I could see ahead to what's in store for us."

"Well, I have a pretty good idea of what's in store for the rest of the night." He rolled over and pulled her on top of him.

"You lead, then," she grinned, settling down on him and feeling him stir inside her, "and I'll follow. For now, that's enough. That's more than enough. . . ."

*    *    *

Genna had just finished showering the next morning when John tapped on the door.

"I brought your bag in from the car," he told her. "It's right outside the bathroom door."

"Thanks," she called back.

Wrapping one towel around her body and another around her hair, Genna opened the door.

"John," she said, "do you think we should call—"

She had stepped out into the room's small vestibule. John stood in front of the television, watching Calvin Sharpe on the first-hour edition of a popular morning show.

"And the FBI thinks that this man is behind the disappearances of the twelve women who have gone missing from as many states over the past several weeks?" the usually perky host was asking.

"Yes. Yes, we do." Sharpe cleared his throat. "We'll be holding a press conference at nine this morning, but we're so sure that someone—possibly many some-ones—have seen him, that we did not want to run the risk of having a potential witness miss seeing this tape because they left early for work. We've sent this video-tape to every network and major news show, and we're asking that it be run over and over until we find him."

"Let's run the tape," the host signaled to the tech-nical staff, then watched silently as the tape of Michael Homer played once, twice, three times, the last in slow motion.

"If anyone thinks they recognize him, what should they do?"

"Call the number that should be running across the bottom of the television screen," Sharpe told her, then paused to ask, "Is it there? They said the num-ber would be there."

"It's there," the host nodded. "But if the number isn't handy, could someone call their closest FBI office or their local police?"

"Absolutely." Sharpe nodded. "As long as we get the information as soon as possible."

"I understand there's been a ten-thousand dollar reward offered. Would that have anything to do with the fact that the FBI suspects that a potential victim is one of its own? Do I understand that Agent . . ." she glanced down at her notes, "Genna Snow—who is, ironically, on the special team assigned to investigate the abductions—is thought to be a potential target by this suspect?"

Sharpe nodded, and began to explain Genna's history with Michael Homer.

"I wish he'd waited a day or so to get into that," John noted. "I'm not sure that now is the time to give out so much information about you."

"Why not? What's the difference?" She picked up the bag he'd brought in for her.

"Well, I would have liked to have had a day or so to get you out of the way." He turned to look at her, and in his dark eyes she could see a trace of fear.

"He's not going to get me, John. Whatever else happens, he will not win this time." She went back into the bathroom and closed the door.

John sat down on the edge of the bed, and tried not to sweat. Having Genna back in his life was a miracle he'd waited a year for. The fear of losing her again, of having her fall into the hands of Michael Homer turned his insides to water.

*Well, then,* he told himself, *whatever it takes, we'll have to find him first. Genna's absolutely right about this. Wherever he is, we'll just have to find him before he finds*

*Genna. One way or another. Because he cannot, he will not, have her. . . .*

"What are you thinking?" Genna asked as she emerged from the bathroom dressed in khaki pants and a short-sleeved red tee, her hair still damp and curling around her face.

"I'm thinking about how much I love you," he told her simply. "And how I would kill him with my bare hands, if I had to, to keep you safe."

"Let's hope it doesn't come to that. I don't like that image," she told him as she put her arms around his neck. "Though I do like the other part. About how much you love me."

"I do," he whispered. "You know I do. I always have."

"I do know." Her hands rested on either side of his face. "I love you, too. I'm so sorry that it took me so long to think things through. I think I just loved you so much, that I couldn't even think of going through the pain of losing you again."

"You won't have to," John kissed the side of her mouth where the ends turned up. "I promise you that."

"Well, then," she smoothed his shirt collar. "I guess it's time to get on with it. What do we do first?"

"First we go to the lake and we pick up Patsy and Chrissie," he told her, "then we fly to Atlantic City Airport, where we will be picked up by Angie's brothers-in-law."

"Carmen's brothers?" Genna's brows knit together. "Why?"

"Because Michael might make it past the FBI, but he'll never make it past the Philly mob."

"You are kidding, right? Tell me you did not call out the DelVecchio boys?"

"Yes, I'm kidding. Of course, I'm kidding." He forced a smile. "Now throw your stuff in your bag. We have a plane to catch."

"Are we really going to Atlantic City?"

"I'm not sure where we're headed. Sharpe is going to meet us at the airport in Erie and we'll talk about it. He wants as few people as possible to know where we're going."

"Your boss is coming out to meet us?" She paused as she gathered her things.

"So I've been told." He walked to the door of the room and waited for her.

"Well, then," Genna turned off the lights and swung her bag over her shoulder, "let's not keep him waiting."

He caught her by the wrist as she walked past him.

"We will find him, Gen," he promised her.

"I know we will." She smiled up at him, then stood on tiptoe to kiss his mouth softly. "Now let's get started. There are twelve frantic families out there waiting to find out where their loved ones are. Let's see if we can find them."

# 21

____

He stood staring at the television incredulously, watching the image of the bearded man walk through the doors of the car dealership.

"Son of a bitch!" He shouted. "SON OF A BITCH!"

Panic began to rise within him as he watched the video. And continued to rise, as he listened to Calvin Sharpe describe the manhunt that was, even at that moment, being put into place.

"All right," he said aloud, forcing himself to take a deep, calming breath. "Mother always said you couldn't think right when your mind was in a churn." And right now, God knew, his mind was churning.

He turned up the volume just a little, and forced himself to sit and listen quietly, lest he miss some important tidbit of information that he might be able to use to his advantage.

". . . organizing a manhunt," the FBI agent on the television was saying.

And then he laughed out loud.

"Oh, that's rich. That's truly rich."

His laughter was short-lived, however, when he heard Genna's name.

". . . being sent to a safe house until Michael Homer has been caught."

A safe house?

He lifted the blinds, affording him a fine view of the whitewashed cottage and the lake beyond. Patsy stood on the front lawn, looking down the road and shielding her eyes from the sun, as if looking for something. Or someone.

No, no, that would be too obvious, they'd never let Genna come back here.

Or would they? He pondered the possibilities. Might they be playing with him? Cat and mouse?

He looked out the window again, just as the big orange tabby sauntered across the grass and rolled over at Patsy's feet, and he grinned.

He just loved it when there was a sign.

"So. The FBI thinks they are the cat and I am the mouse," he tapped his fingers lightly on the window ledge. Perhaps a word or two with Patsy might go a long way to finding out when that cat thinks it might pounce.

He slipped on his sunglasses and unlocked the front door, heading toward the woman who had now walked as far as the mailbox.

"Hi," he called to her.

Patsy looked up, and waved at his approach, as if relieved to see him.

If *she* knew, *he'd* know in no time flat.

This would be all too easy. Like taking candy from a baby, he sighed.

And then his collection would be complete.

Revenge would be so sweet.

# 22

Patsy paced back and forth, wondering where Crystal could have disappeared to. Lately, the young woman had gotten into the habit of walking early in the morning, taking a brisk stroll around to the other side of the lake and back again before breakfast. But usually she'd returned by this time. Patsy poured herself another cup of coffee and sipped at it thoughtfully.

It wasn't enough that Genna had been identified as the next and final target of Michael Homer, that bastard—yes, she had said *bastard* and she meant it!—and that they'd all have to go into hiding for a while. Though of course, if it would save Genna, then it was no sacrifice. No sacrifice at all.

But where was Chrissie?

Patsy went back inside to check to see if there were any messages on the answering machine, though why she thought there might be, she couldn't say. It was just a means of wasting time.

She'd give Crystal five more minutes and then she'd take the car out and drive around the lake to look for her.

Patsy's mind sought a logical explanation. Maybe she stopped to talk to someone.

Crystal didn't know anyone at the lake, she reminded herself.

"Well, maybe she met someone." The words slipped out impatiently.

Patsy checked the clock again. Crystal was now almost thirty minutes late. Trying her best not to jump to conclusions, Patsy took her car keys and went out to start the Buick. It would only take her a few minutes to take a spin around the lake. If there was no sign of Chrissie, she'd call Brian and see what he recommended.

Patsy drove slowly, as one was forced to do on the narrow, winding road. Chrissie didn't know that they'd be leaving that day. She had crept out that morning before Patsy had turned on the television for the morning news. Before Calvin Sharpe himself had called to tell them that Genna and John would be picking up Patsy and Crystal and heading off to some secret location. That the FBI would be everywhere around Bricker's Lake over the next week or so.

Patsy glanced around as she drove.

If the FBI was there, they sure did know how to make themselves scarce.

She stopped at the stop sign at the first crossroads, thinking back to the night before, when she'd gone out onto the deck to call Crystal for dinner. The young woman stood at the end of the dock, stock still, looking up at the road, as if frozen.

Patsy had turned to see what could have spooked the girl so. Kenny Harris was just passing the cottage, and he had paused to greet Nancy, who had just arrived earlier in the afternoon. Nothing unusual there. When Crystal had come into the cottage for dinner, she had appeared distracted, distant, but when Patsy had questioned her, she had merely shrugged and said something about her imagination playing tricks on her.

Patsy drove past Sally's Lakeside, where the restaurant parking lot was empty except for Sally's car and a delivery van. She continued along the road, peering over the steering wheel, then turned around where the road dead-ended and drove on back to her own driveway.

Truly worried now, she parked and got out of the car. The sound of the screen door slamming across the road startled her, and she looked up to see Kenny heading toward her.

*Nothing travels faster than bad news*, she told herself. Kenny must have seen the news this morning, by the look of concern on his face, and wants to talk about it.

*And there's Nancy, poor soul*, Patsy watched her next-door neighbor emerge from her front door. *I surely don't want her worrying about me or Genna, all she has on her mind. Who'd have guessed she was undergoing cancer treatment all this time?*

Not that Nancy had ever mentioned it, Patsy acknowledged, silently admiring the woman's strength. Patsy herself wouldn't have known, had she not stumbled onto the fact just the day before. Nancy'd been scarce these past two weeks, and Patsy had been delighted to see her car there in the drive when Patsy and Crystal returned from a trip into town. Crystal had taken the shopping bags into the house to put the groceries away, and Patsy'd gone to Nancy's back door and knocked, calling through the screen door a time or two, but there'd been no response. She'd knocked again, then called as loudly as she could, but still, there was no answer. Tentatively, Patsy had tried the back door, and finding it unlocked, had gone into the cottage.

"Nancy?" she had called.

When there was no answer and Patsy began to fear that something *not good* might have happened, she went into the living room. Nancy's handbag sat open upon the coffee table, a pack of cigarettes next to a glass ashtray.

"She never goes anywhere without that purse, and God knows she didn't once all summer step outside without those damned cigarettes in her pocket," Patsy muttered, then called again. "Nancy! Are you here?"

Patsy poked her head into the small front bedroom that she knew Nancy used, and was greatly relieved to hear the sound of the shower from the bathroom next door as the water was just being turned off.

"Oh, thank heavens!" Patsy exclaimed to herself, feeling a little silly to have let herself get so worked up over nothing. She'd just go on out the way she came in before Nancy could emerge from the shower and find her there, and none would be the wiser. Surely Nancy'd be startled to find her there, and then she'd for certain feel like a ninny for having let her nerves get the best of her.

But turning back to the door, it was Patsy who was startled.

There, on the bed, was Nancy's pale blond page boy.

"Oh, my!" Patsy said aloud, reaching a hand out to touch the wig.

"Patsy." A voice from behind made her jump.

"Oh, my stars, Nancy!" Flustered, Patsy turned to face the cottage's occupant. "I was so worried about you. I knocked, and I called, knocked and called, and when you didn't answer . . ."

"So. Now you know." Wrapped in a white terry cloth robe, her bald head shiny from the shower, Nancy stood in the doorway, her face a study in stone.

"Yes. And oh, Nancy, I'm so very sorry." Patsy clasped her hands in front of her. "But I wish you had told me."

"Told you?" Nancy raised an eyebrow.

"My sister Connie was a victim of this terrible disease almost ten years ago. I know what chemotherapy can do to a body." Patsy's eyes filled with tears. "Now, if there is anything I can do for you, will you let me know? Anything at all, dear."

"I appreciate that, Patsy," Nancy nodded slowly. "I really do. But if you wouldn't mind . . ."

"Oh, of course, dear. You need your privacy, of course you do. But why don't you just come on over when you're done, and we'll have some iced tea and lemon pound cake."

"Thank you. That sounds very nice. But I'm a little tired tonight. . . ."

"Oh, of course you would be," Patsy sympathized. "Did you have a treatment this week?"

Nancy nodded, and backed out into the living room. Patsy followed.

"Then you need your rest. Now, it's been nice and peaceful up here these past few weeks, so you should be able to relax. I've missed you, by the way, but of course, I understand," Patsy chattered as she headed for the back door. "Now, you just take it easy and feel free to stop on over any time you feel up to it. . . ."

That was before the phone call from John last night, Patsy recalled. All hell seemed to have broken loose since then, if the morning news was to be believed.

Well, she was packed and ready to go whenever Genna and John got there.

But where was Chrissie?

Patsy checked her watch as Nancy and Kenny approached, making small talk about the morning's weather, and wondered just how much she should tell them about their planned hasty departure. Should she tell them anything at all? Would they be in danger if she did not? She wrestled fitfully with her dilemma, but knew that her immediate problem was Crystal. It was time to call Brian. And then, if he thought she should, the state police.

"So, how much longer before we get there?" John asked for the fourth or fifth time.

He was much more comfortable as driver than as passenger, but Genna knew the road from the airport in Erie like she knew the back of her hand, and so it made perfect sense for her to drive. John just didn't like it much.

"About twenty more minutes," she laughed, mildly amused by his discomfiture at having to sit back and let someone else take control.

"How do you think Patsy will feel about going to Maine for a few days?"

"She'll be fine with it. I'm glad Sharpe agreed with my suggestion that we spend a week at the Sangers' camp. I never did get to see it last year, you know.

And besides, I'm looking forward to seeing Ethan and Leah again." She smiled, thinking of how nice it would be to visit with the newly married couple whose lives had been so closely meshed with her own the previous summer. Leah had come to the FBI seeking help in finding her missing sister, and the case had become Genna's. And while, in the end, all that had been recovered of Leah's sister was her remains, bringing closure to that aspect of her life had permitted Leah to find her heart. It was the sort of love story that people wrote books about, Genna mused, and she'd been pleased to have been even a small part of it.

"We're lucky that they offered to make room for us in the inn," John told her. "Not only because they're booked solid this time of the year, but because of the purpose behind our impromptu vacation."

"I explained everything to them very thoroughly. But they both agreed that White Bear Springs was probably the last place anyone would think to look for us. And besides, I'm not planning on being there for all that long. I'm just happy to be getting Pats and Chrissie out of the way."

Genna stopped at a stop sign, and in her face, John read hesitation.

"Where are we?" he asked.

"We are at the corner of Freedom Road and Tolliver," she said quietly.

"And the significance of that is . . . ?" He suspected there was one.

"The camp is about two miles straight ahead," she told him. "For as long as I've had my driver's license, I've made a right turn here, choosing to go miles out of my way rather than to drive past it. It's occurred to me that I don't have to take the long way home anymore."

After waiting for a pickup truck to pass, she accelerated and went straight through the stop sign.

"Chrissie and I went to the camp a few weeks ago," she said, "did I tell you?"

"No. No, you did not. Why did you do that?" He found himself frowning.

"Because Chrissie wanted to. She said that her therapist told her that if you face your fears, they lose their power over you, so she wanted to go up there. She thought maybe she could shake the memories."

"Did she?"

"I doubt it. I know I certainly did not. If anything, the nightmares have gotten worse," she admitted.

"You didn't tell me you were still having nightmares."

"I never stopped. They're just different now."

"Different how?"

"I don't know how to explain it, except to say that somehow, it feels like someone else's nightmare now."

While John was pondering what someone else's nightmare might be like, she pulled to the shoulder of the road and slowly stopped the car.

"It's back there," she told him as she rolled her window all the way down and pointed across the road. "Down that dirt road. It's hard to see it, of course, because it's so overgrown, but there's one lane there. It goes straight for a while and then it dips sharply to the left and drops down at an incline. We didn't stay too long because a storm came up on us, which was just as well. I couldn't wait to get out of there. So much was as it was back then, and yet so much had changed."

John noticed that her hands were beginning to shake. He took them in his own in an attempt to soothe her.

"The cabins almost looked the same, except they're overgrown now. And they had numbers painted on them. When we talked about what happened there, at the trial, we had to refer to the cabins by number. The water was still in the pool but the water was black. I still heard the voices but they were different this time. I still hear them in my sleep."

She closed her eyes tightly, hearing them, as she had every night in her dreams since the day she and Chrissie had visited.

*Please . . . help . . . us . . .*

She shivered, and John leaned over and put his arm around her, then looked out the window. He stared for a long minute, looking skyward. She followed his gaze, and watched the dozen or so birds circle slowly over something that lay in the fields back behind the trees.

"Vultures," she whispered, her eyes shifting back to the opposite side of the road.

"That's what I thought they were," John said. "We used to see them every once in a while, on the back roads to the shore. But I've never seen so many in one place before."

She stared out the window for a very long time, trying not to think what she was thinking.

*Please . . . help . . . us . . .*

"Ohmigod," she threw the door open and ran across the road before John could react. "Ohmigod. Ohmigod, John."

She doubled over, her arms across her midsection. Like a shot, John was right behind her, holding her up.

"Genna . . ."

"Ohmigod," she sobbed, her voice exploding in ragged blasts. "They're there! They're there! Oh, my God, they're there!"

"Who's there?" John sank to the ground along with her, trying to make sense of what she was saying. "Who's where?"

"At the camp," she gasped. "Back at the camp. The women . . . Michael took them to the camp . . ."

Her entire body trembled violently as the sobs ripped from her throat. "My God, I was there! I left them there! Hurry! Hurry . . ."

He grabbed her and pulled her, against her will, back across the road, leaning her against the car while he made first one, then a second, call on his cell phone.

"John, please," she gasped, "we need to go—"

"I've called for help, Gen. Listen to me. I know your instincts tell you to go back there now, but you have to wait. We have to wait, do you understand? If Michael is back there, he's waiting for you. We can't take that chance, babe. We just can't."

"But—"

"No, no," he held her tightly. "It's just going to be a minute more, I promise. Then we'll go back and if anyone is there, we will tend to them. But I'm not letting you go back there without an army of state troopers. We don't know if those women are dead or alive, Gen—"

"They're alive, I heard them," she looked up at him with haunted eyes. "I heard them. They called to me and I heard them and I didn't understand and I left them there. I thought it was the wind . . . I left them there—"

"Shhhh," he cradled her against him, watching over her head as the three state police cruisers came into view. "If they're there, we'll find them."

"You Agent Mancini?" A burly state trooper stopped on the opposite side of the road.

"Yes."

"We're on our way down," the trooper told John, "we'll let you know what we find."

"I'm going, John," Genna told him. "I'm going with him."

"No. You'll go with me." To the trooper, John said, "We'll follow you down. Let's do it."

The terse parade wound slowly along the narrow dirt road, with John, driving now, falling in behind at the end. Genna leaned forward in her seat, her eyes wide and frantic. As the cars came to a stop, still in their straight line, Genna bolted from the car and ran to the cabin area, John and the troopers close on her heels.

At the top of the clearing, Genna stopped, tilting her head to listen. She took several steps toward the first cabin to her right, then stopped.

"In there," she said, turning to the state officers. "Call some ambulances. Quickly. We may be able to save them."

The trooper closest to Genna brushed past her, a look of skepticism on his face, and took the cabin steps two at a time. Pushing open the door to the cabin that bore a large, hastily painted black number five on the outer wall, he stepped in, only to rush back out, his hands over his mouth.

The porch railing sagged as he leaned over it and lost his battle to keep his lunch.

"Get water," he gasped. "And get that ambulance here as fast as you can. I think she's still alive. God help her, I think she might still be alive. . . ."

Of the twelve women that Michael Homer had abducted, half of them had not survived the weeks of horror spent gagged and tied to the old metal camp beds. Of those six who had managed to outlast the unspeakable torture and abuse, the insects and the dehydration, the rats, and the lack of food, two more were near death when they were rescued and another was catatonic.

Three of them, however, had managed to hold on to their lives and their wits, and it was hoped that at least one of these three women could assist the FBI by providing the information that would aid in tracking down their abductor and bringing him to justice. Once, of course, they were able to speak again. Weeks of dehydration had taken its toll on their vocal chords.

It was late afternoon by the time a totally drained Genna slumped back against the car, exhausted and haunted by the possibility that one or more of the dead women might still have been alive when she and Crystal had been at the camp the week before. Might still be alive if she had only followed the voices that had been carried on the wind. The guilt weighed heavily on her soul.

Somewhere, among the throng of law enforcement and emergency medical personnel that had invaded the campground, John guarded the corpses of the women who had died while chained to their beds, then dragged into an open field for the vultures to feast upon. Genna had tried to keep that vigil with him, to be ever the professional. In her time with the FBI, she'd seen corpses mutilated beyond description, beyond recognition. But these were the remains of women who had been children with her, children with whom she had shared an important time in her life, children who had once been brave enough to stand in an open court and tell the truth.

Genna took the deaths of each of them personally, but knew she had to look to the living if the dead were to be vindicated.

Overwhelmed by sorrow, sickened with grief, Genna sat with the living while each awaited her turn for an ambulance, talked to them, praised them for their ability to have outwitted their captor and for having survived such horror. Apologized for not having understood their cries for help. And promised them that, with their help, the man responsible for their nightmare would be punished.

Just as the sun began to lower itself behind the trees, bright lights flashed from somewhere up near the road.

"Great," she muttered. "The media has found us."

Genna located the officer in charge of the scene and pointed out to him that they were no longer alone, suggesting that he have the entire upper end of the field placed off limits, which he agreed to do even if it meant appealing for backup from the National Guard.

Accepting a bottle of water from one of the emergency crew, she twisted the top off viciously, her anger barely contained. It was a hell of a thing, when a woman who had survived abuse as a child became a victim of that same abuser all over again as an adult. A breeze rustled through the trees as she prayed that they would be smart enough to outwit him. She knew she would not have a moment's peace until they found him.

There was a flurry of activity as the first of the body bags was brought up from the field.

"That oughta set the news people into a frenzy," she murmured, wondering just what would end up on that evening's news.

It occurred to her then that she hadn't called Pats to let her know that she and John would be late. She'd be frantic by now.

Reaching into the car window, she grabbed her big leather bag that sat on the backseat. Sifting through it for her phone, she started to dial, when she noticed the message light blinking. Hitting the play button, she heard Patsy's voice.

"Now, I don't want you to be worried, everything's okay now. But your sister gave me a good enough scare today. Something spooked her and as God is my judge I don't know what that something is, but I mean to find out. She up and took off to go back to Kentucky and to the psychiatrist she was seeing down there. Left me a note apologizing for borrowing the money from my wallet for her bus ticket. Well, I called the bus line, and I found out that that bus will be stopping down in Slippery Rock around five-thirty. I guess you know that I'll be down there waiting when that bus comes in. So don't you be worried when you get to the cottage and we're not there. We'll be there, before the night is over, and we'll find out what set Chrissie off. In the meantime, if you'd do me the biggest favor. I couldn't find Kermie before I left, and I know he's going to be out there howling on the back deck before too much longer. He hasn't had his insulin since this morning, and, well, you know what could happen if he goes much more than twelve hours without it. I'd sure hate to lose that old curmudgeon, Gen, and I know that you would, too. So I'm hoping you'll be able to find him and give him his shot when you get here. I figure you and John should probably be here by dark, and if you could please try to round up that tabby, feed him then give him his shot, I'd sure appreciate it. . . ."

Genna could all but picture a worried Patsy standing out on the deck, watching for Kermie even as she left the voice mail. That old cat meant the world to both of them.

In another hour or so, it would be dark, too late to find Kermie or much else up here. She started up over the rise to look for John, and saw that he was deep in conversation with a member of the ERT that had arrived an hour earlier. He'd be a while yet, long enough, surely, for her to run down to the cottage, find Kermie, give him some food and inject him with his insulin. She'd probably be back before John finished his conversation.

The car keys rustled in her pocket. She'd had all she could take for one day. For one lifetime. A few minutes away from it all would be most welcome.

"If Agent Mancini is looking for me, tell him I had to run down to the cottage for something, but I should be back within an hour," she told the young state trooper who stood by the lower end of the road. Searching her wallet, she found one of her business cards, upon which she wrote Patsy's phone number.

"Just in case he's forgotten," she told the trooper, "the number's on the back. But I should be back before he even realizes that I'm gone."

She paused, wondering if it was wise for her to make the trip to the lake alone. It was not, she sighed. Getting out of the car, she searched for a trooper who looked as if he could use a half hour away from the madness. It wasn't hard to find a likely candidate.

"What's your name?" she asked him after he'd cleared her request to accompany her with his superior.

"Don Emerson," he replied.

"Well, Don Emerson, I appreciate your company. We only have a short drive, but it's one I probably shouldn't take alone."

She drove away in the blue Ford they'd rented earlier in the day, with no thoughts but to find Kermie and to escape, for just a little while, from the terrible reality that evil, still and always, was alive and well at Shepherd's Way.

Chatting aimlessly with the young trooper, she eased into the driveway by the darkened house.

"Would you like me to come in with you?" her companion asked.

"If you like," she nodded, "though I'm sure the cottage is locked. I'll only be a few minutes. Unless, of course, I can't find the cat. Then we'll need to do a little searching."

He smiled in the dark and got out of the car when she did.

"I'll just keep a lookout, out here," he told her.

"That's fine," Genna nodded, searching for the cottage key amongst the other keys on the crowded ring. "I shouldn't be long."

Her back covered, Genna disappeared down the driveway, her only thoughts on finding the old orange tabby that meant so much to Patsy and her, and now to Crystal. For everyone's sake, she hoped she wasn't too late.

# 23

He should have been tired, having been on his feet for several hours now, and he should have been starving, having had his last meal on the plane that had flown them to Erie that morning. But John Mancini was at his efficient best when chaos threatened those around him, and the events of the day had more than qualified. He'd stayed in the upper field until the last of the bodies had been removed, and was preparing to follow the last of the ambulances to the hospital, hoping that at least one of the women would be able to give them enough to begin the search for Michael Homer.

His eyes darted around the parking area, searching for Genna. When he could not locate her, he walked back to the car, thinking perhaps he'd find her slumped down in the passenger seat, sound asleep, though he figured it would take more than common fatigue to remove her from the action.

He was more than a little surprised to find that she had left the camp entirely.

"She said she wouldn't be long, but for you to call her at the cottage," a young trooper told him. "She sounded like you would know what she meant. One of the troopers went with her. Oh! And she gave me the number in case you'd forgotten it."

"I have it," John said as the man began to search his pockets.

John dialed the number and listened to it ring and ring. Perhaps she had done whatever it was she'd set out to do, and was on her way back. He called her cell phone, but there was no answer there, either. He paced next to the car, trying to decide if he should be worried or not. He dialed the cottage again with the same result.

"Hey, John," one of the field agents from Pittsburgh came toward him from across the clearing. "I just heard that one of the women at the hospital is insisting on talking now. Sharpe wants you there pronto to get a description of Homer from her. A forensic artist is already on her way. You're to follow Detective Shivers from Wick's Grove."

"I'm on my way," John turned back to his car, then stopped, and called to the young trooper, "How long do you expect to be here?"

"No one's said, but I'm expecting we'll be around all night."

"Will you watch for Agent Snow? Just tell her I went to the hospital to speak with one of the victims, and ask her to call me when she shows up." John got into his car, adding, "I'll probably catch up with her before then, but I'd appreciate you watching out for her."

"I'll do that, sir," the trooper nodded. "But take care up there by the road. I heard there's all kinds of media people up there. All of the networks and CNN and you name it, they're up there."

"Thanks." John waved as he started the car and

rolled up his windows. Stopping to chat with the press wasn't on his agenda.

John called the cottage twice more, and a nagging fear had begun to prick at his senses. He'd decided to have one of the field agents go up to the lake to check on her if no one picked up on the next try.

Someone did.

"This is John Mancini," he said when an unfamiliar voice answered, taking him off-guard. "Who is this, please?"

"This is Patsy's friend Nancy, John. From the cottage next door."

"Oh, Nancy, of course. Patsy and Genna have both spoken about you."

"I was sitting out on my deck, and I heard the phone ring and ring and ring, and I thought, I should probably run over there and answer it if it rings again, since it seems like someone's pretty anxious to get in touch with Patsy. Of course, she's not here, you know."

"No. I didn't know. Do you know where everyone is? Have you seen Genna?"

"Well, Patsy's gone off looking for Crystal," Nancy told him, filling him in on Chrissie's sudden departure as Patsy had related earlier in the day. "And Genna is out on the dock putting the cover on that flat-bottomed boat of Patsy's. Looks like it might rain. Do you want me to run down and get her for you?"

Relieved, John said, "No, but I'd appreciate it if you'd tell her that I called and that I'm on my way to the hospital outside of Wick's Grove."

"Oh, my, I hope you're all right?"

"Oh, fine. But if you'd tell her that I'm meeting an

artist at the hospital, she'll know what I mean. And tell her to meet us there as soon as she can."

"I'll certainly do that, John. Now, I should tell you that Genna was looking a little peaked, and so I suggested that she stop over for a bite. I made a lovely shrimp salad this afternoon thinking I'd have plenty to share with Patsy, but of course she isn't here. So I offered to make up a plate for Genna—she did tell me that shrimp salad is such a favorite of hers—so if she's a teensy bit late, you'll know not to worry, that she's having a quick meal and will be on her way soon enough."

"And what about the state trooper who accompanied her?"

"Oh, he's helping her with the cover. I imagine they should be finished in another few minutes."

"Thanks so much for looking after her."

"Oh, it's my pleasure, believe me, John. Now, I'm looking forward to meeting you soon."

"Likewise." He hesitated for a minute, then said, "Look, Nancy, if you'd do me a favor . . ."

"Of course."

"Go across the road and ask the guard who's staying in the cabin . . ."

"Kenny Harris."

"Yes. Kenny. Ask him if he'd come on over and stay until we can get back there. And tell him that I'll call in backup from the state police for him as soon as we finish this call."

"Oh, my! This sounds serious! Is something wrong?" Nancy's voice dropped to a dramatically low level.

"You'll see it on the evening news anyway." John sighed, then gave Nancy the short version.

"You think he's here? That awful man? Here, at Bricker's Lake?" Nancy sounded shocked at the possibility.

"I don't know where he is, frankly, though if I had to make an educated guess, I'd say he's put some distance between here and wherever it is he's hiding out. But if you'd just keep your eye on her while she's there, I'd be grateful."

"Just don't you worry, John, I'll be watching her," Nancy assured him. "I won't let her out of my sight."

Michael Homer looked down at the woman who lay, bound and gagged, at his feet.

"Not for a second," he said, then began to giggle. "Now that was a fine turn of events, wouldn't you say, Miss Genna? Having the fox put in charge of the henhouse, so to speak?"

He leaned down to look into her face. Her eyes were still closed, her lips still parted just ever so slightly.

He felt for a pulse, hoping he hadn't killed her, worried, because off the top of his head, he couldn't really recall just how much force it had taken to render her unconscious. He'd intended on applying only enough pressure on her windpipe to knock her out for a while, but it was so easy to get a bit carried away with the spirit of things sometimes. But yes, there was a pulse. She just hadn't come to, yet. Unlike that young state trooper. He'd had every intention of putting him out for a long, long time. And he had.

He went into Patsy's bathroom and came out with a washcloth that he'd soaked in cold water. Just in case he needed it to revive her when he got to the holy place. It wouldn't do to have her out cold then. One had to be conscious, didn't one, to be consecrated? How could he fill her with the spirit if she wasn't aware of what was happening?

He was pondering this minor philosophical point as he lifted, then carried her through the cottage over his shoulder, out onto Patsy's deck and down the steps with little effort. He whistled as he strolled down to the dock as if unencumbered, not worried that anyone would see him. The neighbors on the right hadn't been there all month. And Kenny wouldn't be coming over to see what was going on this night or any other night.

Yes, life was sweet when things worked out your way.

With one foot, he kicked the gate open on the side of the boat, and stepped down cautiously. He really didn't much care for boats, though he was grateful for the opportunity Patsy had given him to learn how to run one. He'd watched her operate this baby several times; enough, he hoped, that he could manage to get it from the dock to their destination. Of course, he didn't much care for water, either, if the truth was to be known. Hadn't he watched Patsy land a nasty looking pike right out there in the middle of the lake? He'd shivered at the thought of the damned thing swimming with him.

But tonight, the lake was his friend. His means of fulfilling the last of his tasks. And once Genna had been taken care of, he would be free.

Hadn't Mother told him not to leave loose ends? To finish what you'd started?

It had taken nineteen years, but better late than never.

"I didn't mean for them to die," he said aloud. "I'm sorry. I did not mean for them to die."

A sound from Genna drew his attention.

"No, I will not untie you, and no, I will not take off the gag, if that's what you're asking." He looked down upon her smugly. "We're not really so clever after all, are we, Miss Genna FBI Snow?"

He leaned down and looked into her face. Her eyes were still closed. He looked around for the washcloth, then remembered he'd left it on the kitchen counter. He hesitated, wondering if he should run back up to the cottage to get it, but then remembered that John had promised to send someone over to keep them safe. He decided to skip the washcloth. If she was still out when they reached the beach, he'd use some cool lake water.

Checking that the bag he'd earlier placed in the boat was still there, he fished in his pocket for the boat key he'd taken from the nail by Patsy's backdoor and started up the motor. With great caution, he backed the boat away from the dock, holding his breath, lest he hit one of the pilings. It had looked so easy when Patsy did it.

*There now, not so very difficult,* he congratulated himself as he successfully navigated the boat into the lake and then steered to the right. Giving the throttle a bit of a jiggle, he made slowly for the opposite side of the lake. He wanted to savor every minute in her company—even though she wasn't technically there to share it with him. He glanced back at her still form there on the deck and hoped she'd come to on her own. He hadn't come all this way, done all he'd done, to have her spoil this last, most important event for him. And it was going to be an event, he nodded to himself as he looked ahead, searching in the dark for the landmarks he'd so carefully scouted over the past month.

There, to the left, was the house with the flagpole, and though the flags had been taken down for the night, the lights at the very top were still on. And there, just a few cabins down, was the long dock that had the large fake owl perched upon the first of their pilings. He turned toward shore slightly, knowing that within a minute he'd come to the darkened area that would be the old camp beach. This would be the tricky part, though. There would be no lights there— and he couldn't very well use a flashlight, someone would surely see that and he couldn't take that chance—and he wasn't sure of the water's depth, or how close he could get to the shore. These things he'd had to leave to chance.

He slowed as much as he could, cutting the motor when he heard the bottom of the boat scrape against the sand beneath them. Taking a deep breath, he counted to three and lowered himself over the side of the boat into the shallow water, grimacing as the long fronds of lake flora brushed against his legs.

"Ugh," he muttered his distaste, but proceeded to drag the boat with the rope tied to the bow, careful now not to damage the bottom. After all, he'd need it to escape later.

He still hadn't decided just what to do with Genna when he'd finished purifying her. He certainly couldn't take her to the cabins as he had the others. Maybe he'd just leave her tied up there, in the woods. It was such a remote spot, they wouldn't likely find her for several days.

"It would serve her right," he muttered to himself

as his feet found purchase on the slippery lake bank, "if they didn't find her at all."

Not, of course, that he intended that she die out here. The entire camp should be considered a crime scene, he rationalized, and so the law, if they had any sense at all, should search the entire premises for . . . well, for whatever might be there. In this case, the whatever would be Genna Snow. A thoroughly consecrated and pure Genna Snow.

What was the expression about pure snow? Pure as the driven snow? He giggled at the pun and wished there was someone he could share it with. But alas, he knew he was his own, his only, audience.

He held the rope slack in his hands and looked around the darkened beach for something to tie it to. Finding nothing but the fallen trunk of an old tree, he looped a knot around a section twice and hoped it would hold. There was a bit of a breeze picking up now. With any luck—and he had to admit his luck had been pretty darned good lately—there would be no wind to coax the boat away from the shore before he was finished. Satisfied that he'd secured it as best he could, he waded back into the lake and climbed awkwardly over the side of the boat. Lifting the unconscious woman, he kicked open the gate with one foot, then slid back into the water.

Across the narrow beach, he carried her limp form in his arms, searching for the path he'd earlier marked by tying strips of white cloth to trees along the way. Following his markers deep into the woods, he came to the clearing he'd prepared for the job at hand. He placed Genna on the ground, then leaving her still tied, returned to the boat where he retrieved the bag that held all he would need to complete his mission.

Retracing his steps, he removed the white ties from the trees. Just in case . . .

Genna lay on her side, one ear to the ground, and listened as his footsteps pounded softly through the earth beneath her. She rolled her head gently as best she could, encumbered as she was by her bindings, and sought to collect her wits. By laying quietly in the bottom of Patsy's boat, she'd figured out early on that they were on their way to the beach at Shepherd's Way. By counting the seconds it had taken Michael to carry her from the beach to the place where he'd laid her down, she'd been able to roughly pinpoint their location in the woods. They were about as far from the cabin area—which was crawling with law enforcement agents—as they could be, and still be on campground. With all of the missing women having been accounted for, there would be no reason for a search of these dense woods, particularly at night.

Forcing a few deep breaths to calm her, she tried to formulate a plan to escape, acknowledging that it would be damned hard to get away with her hands tied behind her back, and her ankles tied together. She would need to be rid of at least one or the other—the ankle or wrist ties—to get away from him.

Her senses came on full alert, hearing the first echo of footfalls that rang through the earth below her. The thought that she had escaped him once before, in these very woods, gave her courage.

And it was then that it occurred to her that if he had plans to rape her, he'd have to untie her ankles. Had she not escaped once before by using her legs, her feet, to hurt him, to surprise him? Would he be remembering that detail tonight?

Around her the night sounds of the forest seemed to hush as he came closer. She turned her head just slightly so that she could see him enter the clearing, but her heart all but stopped in her chest as he drew near.

Appearing like some malevolent specter, Michael was dressed in the white robe he'd worn so many years ago. From the bag he carried, he set white candles into the ground around her in the shape of an arc. One by one, he lit the small candles, chanting as he did so.

When the last candle was lit, he lowered himself to the ground, his legs on either side of hers, and began to pray.

Following the unmarked Wick's Grove police car along the dark and narrow country roads, John tried to put his finger on what precisely it was that was nagging at him, pricking, thorn-like, at his weary brain. It had been a very long day, and there would be hours more ahead before it would end. He recognized the fatigue for what it was and knew that something more than merely being tired had set him on edge.

His stomach rumbled, reminding him once again how long it had been since he'd last put something in it. Maybe at some point over the next few hours, he'd be able to steal five minutes to find something besides crackers from the hospital's vending machines and too-dark coffee. Though right now, he conceded, even that didn't sound so bad.

Not as good as homemade shrimp salad, he

sulked momentarily, thinking that he should have asked Nancy to send some back for him with Genna.

It took another thirty seconds for it to hit him, and when it did, he slammed on the brake, stopping in the middle of the darkened road. He sat there, thinking back to the conversation, astounded that it had slipped by him.

"... so I did offer to make up a plate for Genna—she did say that shrimp salad was such a favorite of hers ..."

Genna was allergic to shellfish.

The sudden realization stunned him, all but suffocating him with its certainty.

The car he'd been following had failed to notice that he'd stopped, continuing on ahead as if the driver, like John, was experiencing impaired reactions of his own that night. John made a U-turn on the narrow road and headed back the way he'd come, with his foot all the way down on the gas. He searched his pockets for his phone and hit speed dial, hoping, praying, that he could reach someone, and that it would not be too late when he did.

It took him ten minutes to find his way back to the little cottage that overlooked Bricker's Lake. He wasn't even aware that he left his engine running after pulling into Patsy's driveway and slamming the gears into park.

He found the young state trooper laying in the driveway, a rope wound tightly around his neck. John stopped to check the man's pulse, and was not surprised when he failed to find one.

Racing into the house, he called her name, knowing that she would not be there.

But where?

He ran next door, kicked in the backdoor, turning

on the lights as he went from room to room. On a bedside table was a brown leather handbag, and the wallet inside contained a driver's license in the name of Michael Holmes. A Styrofoam form on the dresser held a blond wig styled with bangs. The style was reminiscent of that in the photograph of Anna Homer, which Genna had lingered over in the front bedroom of Clarence's house.

"Shit!" John yelled to the night as he went out the backdoor and slapped his hands on the railing of the deck that overlooked the expanse of lawn, which flowed down to the lake like a green river.

Where had he taken Genna?

From somewhere out in the night, a cat wailed.

Kermie.

John started tentatively across the grassy area, his eyes searching the dark for the orange tabby.

In the moonlight, the cat appeared like a Halloween caricature, standing on the end of the dock, his back arched, his tail raised straight into the air. As John approached, the cat wailed again, and it was then that John noticed that Patsy's flat-bottomed boat was missing.

"Son of a bitch," John growled, searching in the dark for the kayak.

A canoe rested against the large trunk of an old pine. Though not his first choice for water travel, it would have to do. He hoped he could manage to get it from one side of the lake to the other without tipping over.

"I'll make sure there's some extra Fancy whatever that cat food is called in your bowl in the morning," John told Kermie even as he dragged the canoe to the lake and kicked off his shoes. Climbing awkwardly into the small craft, he tucked his Glock under the seat and leaned the paddle over his lap while he juggled his cell phone.

There was no doubt in John's mind where Michael would be taking Genna. He only hoped that his call to the state police would get them—or him—there on time.

John forced himself to paddle methodically, trying to match his strokes evenly, one side to the other, to keep the canoe on course, hoping that the wind would not turn to his disadvantage. It had been so much easier, paddling with Genna, matching her strokes. The fist beneath his sternum tightened as he thought of her at the mercy of the man whose evil had stolen her childhood. Something she had said to him that afternoon as the surviving women had been bundled onto stretchers came back to him, something about how terrible that these women had been victimized first as children, then as adults, by the same evil force.

John's jaw set firmly and he paddled a little faster, careful not to lose the rhythm he'd painstakingly developed, with one thought in mind: Michael may have destroyed a piece of the child, but he would not destroy the woman.

The clouds cleared from the moon, sending a ribbon of moonlight across the lake as if to light the way. Watching the shore as he passed by, hoping that something would appear familiar as he glided by, John scanned the landscape. And there, off to the left, was an open stretch of beach. Paddling more cautiously, he approached in silence, gliding across the lake, a chilly wind now at his back pushing him toward shore. There, close to the beach, Patsy's flat-bottomed boat rode the faint ripple of lake tide, rising and falling ever so slightly in the shadows of the moon.

John angled the canoe behind the boat, then sat motionless, listening for some sound in the stillness of the late summer night. All he heard was the lapping of the water against the sides of the boat, and the occasional groan of the rope tied to something on shore. Hopping quietly out of the canoe into the warm lake, he dragged the canoe onto the beach and leaned over the side to locate his gun.

"Aaaaahhhhh!" An agonized scream rose over the trees and through them. Somewhere in the woods ahead, someone had been hurt badly.

Firing his gun twice into the air, hoping that someone from the vast law enforcement community gathered at the camp several acres away would hear, John ran to the edge of the woods. He had no flashlight, nothing to guide him except his instincts. Pausing, he strained his ears, hoping for one more such scream to guide him through the dark, but no sound came. He searched for something that could be an opening in the shrubs leading to a path, and finding one, proceeded to follow it, hoping it was the right one.

Seventy-five feet into the woods, he saw what appeared to be a faint glow off to his left. He slowed and made a concerted effort to make as little noise as possible as he passed from the shelter of one tree to the next, until he could see the pale yellow light of the candles in the tiny clearing straight ahead. He crept closer, silently, until he could hear a murmuring, as if an angry prayer was being uttered. A white-shrouded figure covered something on the ground.

His heart in his mouth, John knew with certainty what that figure was.

Lowering his gun, John sought an angle that would not put Genna in danger, but could not find one.

"Ah, hell," he whispered, then hastened into the clearing, and smashed the butt of his gun against the back of the hood.

"Uhhhh!" The figure grunted and fell forward, then arching his back suddenly, threw John backward with a fury.

Using both hands like a club, Michael swung at John, connecting with his head, knocking him off his feet and throwing him backward. John landed on the ground with a thud, and managed to get off one shot as Michael fled into the woods.

John paused long enough to pull the gag off Genna's mouth.

"Go after him!" Genna gasped as he sought his pocketknife to cut her hands free.

"I'm not leaving you here so that he can circle back around and slit your throat," John told her, pulling her to her feet. "Besides, I think I hit him in the back of the leg. I don't know how far he'll be able to go."

He wrapped his arms around her and held on for a very long moment.

"Are you all right?" he whispered in her ear.

"I am now," she told him, leaning into him, letting the intoxicating euphoria of relief engulf her. "Thank you."

"My pleasure," he replied. He rocked her in his arms for one more moment, kissing the side of her face with utmost gratitude as he said a silent prayer of thanksgiving.

She flinched.

"Did he hurt you?"

"Only when he smacked me across the face," she nodded, touching the back of one hand to her cheek. "I think it was his way of telling me he didn't appreciate being kicked in a sensitive area."

"You kicked him . . ."

"It worked the first time, I figured it was worth trying again. Unfortunately, it took me too long to get up with my hands tied behind me." She tilted her head to one side and said, "I hear someone."

"Too loud to be one person," John said dryly. "It must be the reinforcements I called for."

"Mancini!" someone yelled from yards away.

"Here!" he called back.

"How'd you lose him?" asked a member of the task force that had been formed that night, as he stepped into the clearing.

"Well, it was a choice between running blindly into the woods, where in all probability I'd get lost so that he could circle around and finish her off," he nodded toward Genna, "or wounding him enough to slow him down while I untied Agent Snow. I opted for the latter."

"Good choice," the trooper nodded, "any idea which way he was headed?"

"He went off through the woods there to the left, but he could be anywhere. He's obviously spent a lot of time around here these past few weeks, and knows the woods a lot better than any of us, especially in the dark. But if we could get some good flashlights back here, maybe we'll be lucky enough to find a trail of blood and track him that way."

"Well, we were lucky enough to find this." A

young officer wearing the uniform of the Wick's Grove police department stepped into the clearing, Michael's white robe over one arm. "And judging by the hole in the back, I'd say you did in fact hit him."

He held up the back of the robe and turned it inside out, displaying a splatter of red in the flashlight's glow.

"Good," John said dispassionately. "Now let's see if we can figure out where he's gone to lick his wounds."

# 24

It was almost three in the morning by the time Genna and John returned to Patsy's cottage accompanied by two state troopers, two FBI agents, and Patsy's nephew, Brian.

"Anyone know where my Aunt Pats might be?" Brian asked as the dark blue car with state government plates eased into the narrow driveway.

"Somewhere between here and Slippery Rock, last I heard," Genna told him.

"I'm assuming she was driving her car?"

"I'm certain she was. What are you thinking?" Genna asked.

"I'm thinking I might want to put out an APB for her."

"You think she's in danger?"

"I don't know what to think." Brian ran his fingers through his dark brown hair. "There's absolutely no way of knowing where Michael could be, or where he's headed. Or what Patsy might have told Michael—that is, Nancy—about her itinerary."

"My guess is that Patsy and my sister probably stopped at a motel somewhere between here and there, and they're sleeping peacefully, blissfully

unaware that there's been any excitement whatsoever up here." Genna paused on the dirt drive and
turned to him. "But is it possible that Pats could have
called Nancy—Michael—and told her—er, him—not
to be concerned that they weren't home yet, that they
were staying over someplace and told her where?
You betcha."

"I agree. That's totally in character for Pats. She
might have left a message on the answering machine
in there, expecting you to listen to it when you
arrived last night. Michael could have played it—
hell, if Pats called while Michael was in the cabin, he
could have answered the phone and given any one of
a number of reasons why he was in the house. So yes,
there's certainly a good chance that Michael knows
where to find Pats and Crystal, if he's looking for
them."

"Then I think if we can have them located without
having them alarmed, that would be the way to go."

"I agree." Brian walked out onto the road and
spoke softly with the two young state troopers who
had accompanied them from the camp.

Genna stood in the middle of the yard, hugging
herself, looking up into the heavens and giving
thanks, not for the first time that evening. The moon
still hung brightly over the quiet lakeside community, and the stars still danced overhead, twinkling
like glowing gemstones in the night sky. But the
beauty of the evening could not diminish the ordeal
she'd been through, and John suspected it took all of
her professional pride to hold her together at that
moment.

"How 'bout we go inside and get some ice for that
face of yours?" John asked gently. "You're going to

have some shiner come the morning. And then maybe we can grab a bite to eat—I'm ravenous—and you can lay down and get a little rest."

"I doubt I can sleep tonight." She shook her head. "He's out there someplace. He's angry as all hell now, and he won't stop until he finishes what he started."

"Then let's go inside and at least tend to your eye." John took her hand and led her to the front door, which still stood open.

"Crime scene," one of the detectives reminded them.

"Can we just grab some ice from the kitchen?" John grumbled.

"You'll contaminate the scene." The burly trooper crossed his arms over his chest, challenging John to pass him.

"In case you hadn't noticed, Agent Snow's face is swelling like a helium balloon. I think you can give us access to the kitchen. It's right through the door there."

"I'll get you some ice," the trooper told him as he disappeared through the doorway.

"Hey!" John called. "See if you can rustle up a sandwich while you're in there."

"There's an all-night diner out past Wick's Grove," Genna tugged at John's arm. "It'll take us maybe twenty minutes to get there."

"I can last that long," he conceded, and searched in his pockets for his car keys as the trooper came back outside holding a plaid dish towel packed with ice cubes.

He handed it to Genna, who immediately raised it to her face and tilting her head back, eased the cloth onto the area right below her left eye.

"Genna, are you sure you don't need to be checked out?" Brian asked for the fourth time.

She shook her head. "Except for my face, I really wasn't injured. All I really need right now is food and eventually, a little rest. A trip to the emergency room would only delay both. I appreciate your concern, but all I really want is a hot meal. A few aspirin and the ice should take care of the face."

"I'll follow you down to the diner, if you don't mind," one of the Pittsburgh agents said, joining them. "There are some questions that I need to ask Agent Snow."

"And there are some questions that I want to ask Agent Mancini," she said as they started toward John's car. "Like how did you know I was in trouble?"

He told her about Nancy's comment about the shrimp salad.

"If she'd said anything else, I'd never have caught on. But she picked the one thing that you'd never eat."

"Shellfish," Brian muttered. "I remember that you never could eat it. Damn, what are the chances of that?"

"But how did you know where to look for me?" Genna asked.

"Well, when I came down here looking for you, I found the trooper who'd accompanied you down in the driveway. When I found the cottage empty, I ran next door to Nancy's—I mean, Michael's—cabin, but there was no one there, either. But both your car and hers were here. Then I heard Kermie caterwauling to beat the band out on the dock. When I went down to see what was wrong, I saw that the boat was gone. I remembered that the campgrounds came down as far as the lake on this end, so it wasn't too hard to figure out where he'd be taking you."

"Kermie. My hero. That old furball started all this. When I came back to the cottage tonight, I went around to the back. Kermie was there at the door, laying on his side, panting heavily. All I could think of was getting some food into him so that he could get his shot before he started to convulse. I carried him into the kitchen and opened a can of cat food and let him lick some off my fingers—he was already pretty weak. Looking back, I think I left the backdoor wide open; I was so anxious to take care of the cat. After he'd eaten a bit, I gave him his insulin and sat with him for a few minutes on the floor. He seemed to be okay, so I put him down on the living room carpet and went back into the kitchen to toss out the can of cat food—heaven forbid that Patsy should come home and find an empty can on her counter—and that's all I remember. Until the phone rang, and I heard Nancy talking to someone and realized that Nancy wasn't Nancy at all."

"How did he get away with that?" Brian asked. "How did he manage to fool you all, all summer long? Didn't you recognize him?"

"How could I have done that? At camp, as a child, I never really saw his face. And except for the one day of trial when I testified, I only looked at him when the judge told me I had to, to identify him. Other than that, I was too afraid of him. And he looked so very different then. His hair was long and dark, he was much younger, and please remember, I was very young at the time. There was no way I could have recognized him so many years later, especially when he was dressed as a woman. There was no way to see through that—and he made a mighty convincing woman, I might add."

"That's because he had so many years of practice," John muttered.

"That's true. I think he was Sister Anna. As Michael he would rape the girls, as Anna he would tend to them afterward." She shivered. "And while Anna was dark-haired, and Michael wore a blond wig as Nancy, I think it was the photo of his mother in her bedroom that jiggled something in my mind, but I didn't quite put it together."

"That Nancy looked like Mrs. Homer?"

"That Mrs. Homer looked like Sister Anna. I didn't connect Nancy to either of them at the time. That's why I asked Mr. Homer's housekeeper if Michael and Clarence had had a sister named Anna."

"I remember that. She said that Anna was Mrs. Homer's name."

"And it made me wonder if Mrs. Homer had been at the camp taking care of her son's victims. But if that had been the case, she would have been identified and forced to testify at the trial. She could have been prosecuted as an accomplice, had it been proven that she'd known what Michael was doing to the girls."

"But she—Sister Anna—simply disappeared on the day Michael was arrested. The police could never find a trace of her, and Michael refused to give any information about her at all," Brian said. "I remember it drove the district attorney crazy that they couldn't locate this witness and possible accomplice. Anna disappeared because she didn't exist. She was just another of Michael's personas."

"I'm surprised no one put it together, back then," John said.

"Michael really had his act together, John. If you'd been around Nancy, you'd never have suspected that you were in the company of a man. I even remember watching her and Patsy together one day and thinking that she was more feminine than Pats. And I remember seeing Sister Anna around the camp. I'd never have put her and Brother Michael together."

"I wonder if he used the Nancy role to help him abduct some of his victims," John thought aloud. "That could explain how he was able to get close to them without them being alarmed."

"Nancy looked like your average woman in her mid to late fifties. Nothing out of the ordinary," Genna nodded.

"I'm hoping we'll be able to get good, solid statements from our victims. Those who are still lucid, that is." John looked at his watch. He wondered how much the women had been able to tell the other members of the team who had made it down to the hospital. Suddenly, he was anxious to be in on the conversations. "Let's head out to that diner, Gen, then maybe we'll both be revived enough to drive down to the hospital and see if any of our ladies are still talking."

"Let me just check to see where my feline hero is. I don't want to leave him out all night."

Genna started toward the rear of the cabin, then turned back to the road, and looked across it.

Kenny Harris sat in the screened porch that went across the front of the Millers' cabin. Genna stood under the front porch light, raised an arm and waved, calling out to him, "Hi, Kenny."

He waved back, the glow from his cigarette making a thin red arc in the darkened porch.

"Someone should probably go over and tell Kenny about what's going on," she said.

"I'll do it," Brian told her. "I'm glad to see he's still up and keeping an eye on things. I didn't expect him to be."

"Tell him I said thanks," Genna called to Brian as she took the first steps down the driveway.

She stopped in her tracks and turned around slowly, watching Brian's figure disappear into the dark shadows surrounding the Millers' cabin.

"Kenny doesn't smoke," she said slowly. "He has asthma. . . ."

"Oh, shit." John broke into a run, calling Brian's name.

Genna unlocked her car and grabbed the gun from her bag, and following the others across the road, approached the small house. The cigarette's glow was gone, but the faint trace of smoke lingered on the breeze.

"Fan out," one of the agents yelled.

"What's out behind the cabin?" someone else asked.

"Woods," Genna told them grimly. "If he gets to the woods, we're back to square one."

A shot rang out from the back of the property and somewhere nearby, a door slammed.

"John?" Genna called anxiously. "Brian?"

"Here!" Brian answered, backing around the corner.

"Where's John?"

"He must have gone around the other side. I didn't see him."

Stealthily, Genna crept around the side of the cabin where Brian indicated John had gone. She leaned against the old siding, pausing, listening. She heard cicadas and she heard the screech of an owl. She did not hear the silent footsteps behind her until it was too late.

"I'll have the gun now," he hissed into her left ear as he reached around her, grabbing for her wrists.

"You got it," she said, spinning sharply to escape his grasp and firing twice at point-blank range into his chest.

Once would have sufficed.

# 25

——

Genna woke just before dawn, her heart racing, her pulse pounding. It had been almost a week since she had fired the shots that had brought an end to the violence that defined the life of Michael Homer, but the memory of that night still haunted her. She'd never killed at point-blank range before, and though she had no regrets, she found herself questioning, over and over, the fact that it had just felt so damned good to pull the trigger, to have been the one to take him out. She'd finally admitted as much to John the night before.

"I guess it would feel good," he'd told her. "Don't lose sight of the fact that, in his lifetime, Michael Homer destroyed or damaged countless lives. And how many others might there have been, who, like Chrissie, never came forth to testify? I don't think we'll ever know just how many victims there really were. So, what's the problem?"

"The problem is that, I don't know, I guess I think it should have been harder for me to pull the trigger."

"All right, then, give me one good reason why it should have felt *bad*."

"It should never feel good to take a human life."

"In my book, he was a few degrees less than human." John's jaw set tightly. "And I can tell you with all certainty that I would have been more than happy to have delivered the killing shot myself, Gen. I actually thought I had there for a moment, when I broke down the backdoor of the Millers' cabin. If Michael hadn't slipped out the side door when he did, the shot I fired could very well have taken him down. I was very sorry to have missed, though frankly, shooting him was a much kinder end than he deserved. It was a far better death than he permitted any of his victims. And it's a far better world without him in it. For a lot of people."

Genna couldn't argue.

Interviews with the survivors had told a heartbreaking tale of starvation and neglect, terror and torture, chained for days to their beds, the most fortunate of them locked in the cabin with the leaking ceiling that permitted rainwater to cascade in during heavy downpours. By turning their heads a certain way, several of the women had been able to catch the water in their mouths, and it had proved to be their salvation, Michael's rations being painfully insufficient.

Surprisingly, none of the women had been raped.

"I don't think he could," Genna had told John over dinner. "I think he couldn't perform, but he didn't stop trying. I think he thought it would be an indescribable thrill to relive the acts he'd committed years ago with the same victims. He'd even set the stage in exactly the same way, wearing the white robe and setting up the candles. But his prey were no longer children. He couldn't make that the same.

And I think that just fed his frustration and his anger. These were the same people who'd testified against him, the ones he needed to punish, but they were no longer the same, though in his mind, they were still children. I think it confused him and angered him. He wanted them to be the same as they had been, to feed his fantasies in the same way, so that he could be gratified and feel the same high. But I don't think he was physically capable of having sex with an adult woman. And so they were spared, at least, that."

"But he didn't stop the abductions, even when he realized this."

"He couldn't stop. He had to take us all, all of us who had testified against him, in the same order he'd taken us before. And frankly, I don't think he accepted the fact that he couldn't complete the act. I think he thought that it was the victim's fault, but perhaps the next one would be right."

"I wonder what he planned to do with you all, after he finished with you."

"I think he would have taken me to one of the cabins and kept me there, just as he was keeping the others."

"For how long?"

"Till we died. Six of them had already died. It was only a matter of time before the others would die off, one by one. Though some were certainly more resilient than others and might have had a better chance to survive. The women in cabin seven, for example, were amazingly resourceful. There's no doubt in my mind that Lani Gilbert kept several of her cabin mates from going over the edge by keeping them focused for several hours a day with her humming games."

"Very clever of her." John nodded. "Humming a few bars of a song, then stopping so that someone else would have to pick up and hum the next, and so on around the cabin until the song was ended. And then she'd start a new one."

"Shannon Potter said that was the only thing that kept her sane, even though their vocal chords were ragged and barely functioning toward the end. It was the only diversion they had. Other than when Michael's daily visit to bring them food and take them to the outhouse."

"I'm still not certain I understand why he just didn't leave them to die the way the other six did."

"Why, that would have been killing. I don't think he planned on killing anyone. Except for that young state trooper and Kenny Harris, it seems. Killing them was necessary. Killing the *children* would have been a terrible sin."

"And raping children is not a sin?" John asked dryly.

"The Bible doesn't say, *Thou shalt not rape*," she told him. "But it does say *Thou shalt not kill*. I think he saw himself as some sort of instrument of the heavens or something. The entire time he was tying me up, he was muttering Scripture and praying and mumbling something about needing to consecrate the children."

"Which was probably his means of justifying his pedophilia."

"That's as good a guess as any, since we'll never really know what he was thinking," Genna noted. "I guess that's part of what's bothering me. About having killed him, I mean. I think I'd have liked to have known why. What it was that made him what he was. How the same environment that made one son a pillar of the community could turn out another who was so evil."

"Number one son didn't wear his mother's clothes and sleep in his mother's bed," John reminded her.

"There is that," she sighed. "John, I think that when Michael was Anna he was—"

"Exploring his feminine side?"

"Not a joke, John," Genna grimaced. "I think he was *being* his mother. Being nurturing. Maternal."

"Do you think he really thought he *was* her?"

"Maybe. Who knows? But when he needed another persona to get close to me, it was easy enough to pass himself off as a woman. He'd been doing it for years. Of course, Patsy is totally beside herself that she hadn't seen through him. Though I don't know why she would have. She, too, was only in court that one day, with me."

"But Crystal saw it," John reminded her.

"Crystal saw something in *Nancy* that she recognized, though she didn't immediately connect it with Michael. And to tell the truth, there had been something about Nancy that had struck a very distant chord with me, too, that first time I saw her. But it was so vague that I just dismissed it. I had no reason to think that Nancy was anyone other than who she professed to be. But for Chrissie, in her fragile state, well, seeing Nancy was enough to spook her and send her running back to Kentucky," Genna said. "She thought she was having another breakdown when she looked up and saw Nancy walking down the driveway and had a flashback to seeing Michael walk across the clearing in the camp."

"That's what sent her packing?"

"That was it. But fortunately, Patsy was able to catch up with her. Of course, by the time she got the truth out of Chrissie, we'd already figured out that Nancy wasn't . . . well, wasn't *Nancy* at all."

Now, in the early morning hours, Genna wrapped the lightweight blanket around her and tried to make sense of the past week of her life.

"Cold?" Without opening his eyes, John reached out a hand for her and caressed the first body part he touched, which happened to be her leg.

"No. Just restless."

"There's a cure for that," he said drowsily, pulling her down to lay beside him and turning to cradle her in his arms.

John drifted in and out of sleep, never fully asleep, never completely awake, the thought never far from his mind that he'd almost lost her forever this time. For that alone, he wished Michael Homer's soul a Godspeed to eternal fire. And he knew with total certainty that he would never again want to wake up without her next to him. While conceding that, all things considered, that might not be possible, he decided to opt for the next best thing.

"Will you come home with me next weekend?" he asked later that morning as they concluded a very late breakfast. "Sharpe's offer of a few extra days off still stands, you know."

"Well, I was hoping to get up to the cabin to help Patsy close up for the season," she told him.

"If we can put that off till the following week, I'll help too."

"Really?" Genna grinned. Patsy would be delighted.

"Yep. I can winterize with the best of 'em," he said solemnly, and she laughed. "My mother wants to celebrate that you escaped from the bad guy and that good has triumphed over evil."

"What did she really say?" Genna's eyes narrowed suspiciously.

"That it's her sister Connie's birthday and if I value my life I'll be at Uncle Vinnie's restaurant at seven on Saturday with the rest of the family. And if I know what's good for me, I'll bring you along."

"Well, then, I guess we do know what's good for you."

"I guess we do," he grinned, taking her by the hand and leading her back down the short hall to the cozy bed with the rumpled sheets.

The narrow street in front of the Grotto, one of many small Italian restaurants that sat tucked between two row houses in the genial neighborhood that made up South Philadelphia, was packed, bumper to bumper, with cars bearing license plates from six different states. John had had to park his Mercedes in the alley behind his mother's house and walk the five blocks to the restaurant, but he didn't mind, since it gave him a little time to think over, once again, what he was about to do, and the manner in which he'd do it.

John linked his hand with Genna's, and together they strolled leisurely through the streets where John had grown up. There was a comfort in the familiar houses, with their window boxes overflowing with the last of that season's petunias and the concrete urns that sported geraniums gone leggy so late in the summer. A car sped around the corner, its tires squeaking, its muffler bellowing, and John sighed with contentment. There was, for true satisfaction, no place like home.

In honor of his wife's sixty-fifth birthday, John's Uncle Vinnie had painted the front door of his restaurant sky blue—which she'd been after him to do for years though no one knew why—and closed for business for the night, choosing to open the doors only to family. When John and Genna arrived, the party was in full swing, and apparently had been for some time, judging by the number of cousins who had clearly been at the bar a little too long.

"Johnny!" His mother spotted them the minute they walked through the door. As he knew she would. "Genna! Everybody, my Johnny and his Genna are here!"

A cheer went up from the bar. Even the DelVecchio brothers raised a glass in their honor.

"You're heroes, the two of you," Rita Mancini grabbed them both, kissing each of them on both cheeks without missing a syllable. "Catching that pervert . . . Genna, to be as brave as you are! Madre mia, when I heard what was going on out there! I would have been terrified if Aunt Magda hadn't put the eye on that Michael person . . ."

"That must have been what saved me," Genna nodded solemnly, then tried not to register surprise when Rita grabbed her by the hand and called to her aunt, "Did you hear that? She's crediting you with saving her, Aunt Magda! It must have been the eye, she said. Did my Johnny pick the right girl or what, I ask you?"

"Actually, I did pick the right girl," John said, taking Genna's hand and leading her to an empty seat next to his cousin Maria. "I'm hoping she'll let me keep her."

Trying not to blush, Genna looked up into John's dark eyes that suddenly lost all hint of playfulness.

*What in the world,* she was thinking, as he dropped slowly to one knee in front of her, and seemed to search her eyes for the answer to a question he'd yet to ask. The voices in the crowd began to hush, as one by one, cousins and aunts and uncles elbowed each other into silence, and craned their necks to watch, not knowing exactly what John was up to, but certain that they didn't want to miss a minute of it. Somehow, it was understood that the stuff of family legends was about to take place.

"Genna, over the past few years, we've been through so much together. We've shared the very best and the very worst of our lives and of ourselves. These past few weeks have made it very clear to me that we've spent far too much time apart. That I do not want to spend another day without you." He paused and asked, "So I need to know. Do you feel the same way about me?"

The audience faded away, and all she could see was John.

"Yes. I feel the same way," she said softly.

He drew a black velvet box out of his jacket pocket, and opened it. Taking out the gold band with the glittering solitaire and sliding it onto her finger, he asked, "Will you marry me? For better or for worse?"

All she could do, was nod.

"Oh, my God, he gave her a ring," Rita Mancini declared, breaking the silence and clutching her left hand to her heart as she plopped back into her seat.

"Tess! Did you hear that? Nate, are you taking notes? Is my Johnny a poet or not? Did you ever? Vinnie! We need champagne! My Johnny's getting married!"

Music poured from the jukebox, and someone handed Genna a glass of bubbly wine.

"You certainly didn't make it easy for me to say no," she laughed above the festivities, touching John's face and drawing it near for a kiss.

"True. But you can't blame me for stacking the house. It was a chance I didn't want to take," he said, kissing her back. "Though you could always change your mind. I could turn off the jukebox and you could make an announcement—"

"In this crowd? I don't think so." She shook her head. "Looks like I'm stuck with you."

"Looks like you are."

"For better or for worse."

"So far this month we've had a little bit of both."

"I liked the better part best."

"So did I." He felt in his pockets for change, then ducked over to the jukebox, telling her, "Don't move. I'll be right back."

He slipped a few coins into the slot and punched a few buttons, then returned to put his arms around her, and lead her in a slow dance as the music began to play.

"So, your Aunt Magda put the eye on Brother Michael," Genna said, swaying to the sounds of harmony.

"That's what she says."

"Think she might like a job with the Bureau?" Genna asked.

"If they pay in gold bracelets, they might be able to work something out."

"What's this song, anyway?" Genna strained her ears to pick up the words.

" 'You Belong to Me,' " he whispered, pulling her close. "It's an old South Philly favorite. . . ."

"Okay, what's going on here?" Genna stood on the back deck of the cabin, her eyes narrowing with suspicion. Below on the lawn, stood John, Patsy, and Chrissie, obviously conferring on something. "What are the three of you up to?"

"Just planning ahead," John grinned.

"Planning what?"

"The future," he told her, reaching up to the deck to take her hand and lead her down the steps.

"And what exactly do you see, when you look into the future?" she asked as he walked her across the grass to join Chrissie and Pats.

Taking her by the arms, he turned her toward the cottage.

"I see a second floor there," he told her as he settled her into the circle of his arms, her back leaning against his chest, "with a couple of bedrooms and a bath."

"I thought a little balcony across the back might be nice, in the event that whoever was staying there might be able to step out and catch a sunrise or watch the moon come up," Patsy said.

"Hmmmm. Sounds lovely," Genna murmured. "Who might be staying there?"

"You never know," John said. "And Patsy mentioned that she'd been dreaming for years about a screened porch across the back. You know, so that she'd have a place to entertain on rainy days, or to eat on those nights when the bugs are so fierce."

"Entertain?" Genna frowned. "Patsy, you never entertain."

"Then she thought that maybe a slightly larger kitchen might be in order," John continued on as if he hadn't heard.

"So, of course, while she's doing that, she might as well add a few more feet onto the other side and make the bedrooms a little larger," Crystal added. "Maybe even add one more room downstairs."

"What in the world are you talking about?" She twisted in his arms to look at the three beaming faces. "Just who do you think is going to be coming to stay?"

"Well, Patsy figured that Crystal needs her own room. And then there's you and me, but we can share one room. Then there needs to be a guest room, so that there's a place for my mother to stay when she visits—"

"Your mother?" Genna laughed. "When do you think your mother is going to visit all the way out here in the middle of nowhere?"

"Well, I'm figuring that once we have children, we'll want them to spend some time in the summer up here at the lake. And I figure that my mother will want to spend time with them, too, so we thought maybe we should plan on adding one more room, just in case."

"I see," Genna said thoughtfully. "And what do you think Mamma Mancini will think of Bricker's Lake?"

"Oh, I think she'll love it, once she gets over the fact that it doesn't have a boardwalk and no one sells saltwater taffy like they do in Avalon and Ocean City."

"Somehow, I just don't see your mother out there with a fishing pole, tying May flies onto a hook," Genna mused.

"Maybe not at first, but you know, Patsy's pretty tough to get around. You know, when she sets her mind to something . . ."

"Which reminds me, John. Let's get moving here. The day is passing and the fish are lively." Patsy patted him on the back and headed for the lake.

"I almost forgot, I made a little lunch to take with us." Crystal started for the house, but Patsy called her back.

"It's already in the boat, honey." She swung an arm over Chrissie's shoulder and walked with her toward the dock, calling back to John, "Time's wasting, John Mancini."

"Right, Pats," he called to her, then told Genna, "We can talk about the addition later. Patsy tells me there's a big bass out there calling my name. She's going to help me to find it. Want to come along?"

"No, I want to get the rest of my reports on my interviews with Michael's victims e-mailed into the office. I want it all behind me, once and for all. After this weekend, I don't want to have to think about it."

"Now, you know, that's not going to be possible. There's a long road ahead of us, between now and the time that it's all put away for good."

"I know. But once my reports are done, I won't have to dwell on the details." She frowned, adding, "That is, of course, until the next case comes in. . . ."

John bit his bottom lip. Now just wasn't the time to share with Genna the phone call he'd had from Calvin Sharpe the night before. Three young boys had gone missing in a small Texas town. The team of four—Genna, John, Dale, and Adam—had been so highly praised that the Bureau thought they might just send them all down to look into it.

Well, she'd hear about it soon enough, John figured. She just didn't have to hear it today, when she seemed more relaxed than she had for weeks. And she didn't have to hear about it here, where the last bit of summer served up the scent of clematis and the first touch of gold on the maple trees that huddled close to the edge of the lake.

"Last chance," Patsy warned as she started the engine of her flat-bottomed boat and prepared to shove off.

"You heard her." John stole a quick kiss, then turned to the lake. Over his shoulder, he called back to Genna, "Patsy says there's a ham supper down at Stillwell's tonight, so we won't be out on the lake too long."

Genna laughed and waved, watching her city boy take long strides across the lawn and down to the dock, where he effortlessly boarded the boat just as Patsy prepared to pull away.

They wouldn't be more than an hour or two, plenty of time to finish up that last report. She'd save it on a disk, then print it out when she arrived back at the office on Monday. She paused momentarily to sniff at Patsy's yellow roses on her way past a flower bed, and savored the last little bit of summer, feeling infinitely grateful to be where she was.

*Bricker's Lake suits me just fine*, she sighed with pleasure. *And it seems to suit Crystal. Even John appears to be perfectly content here.*

Genna continued her walk back up toward the cottage, trying to envision the changes John had talked about making. Another room would bring the back wall at least as far as that clump of hydrangeas there on the right side of the property. And the screened porch would bring it out even farther. Of course, there was plenty of room between the back of the small house and the lake, more than enough room for the proposed addition and then some.

A second floor would be lovely, a bedroom with a balcony overlooking the lake would be lovelier still.

Genna looked back over her shoulder to the lake, where Patsy was handing over the wheel to Crystal and, no doubt, giving her instructions on steering. Watching from the shore, her eyes misted with the knowledge that that little boat held everything that mattered most in her life, that there on its deck, her past and her present merged with her future.

The reports, she realized suddenly, could wait.

"Hey!" she called, breaking into a trot and heading for the lake. "Wait up . . . !"

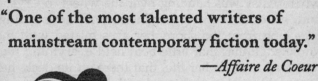